SNAPSHOT

Ruairí McCormac

InFlight Books

For Cormac, Ruairí and Alex

InFlight Books is an imprint of Immel Publishing Ltd,
20 Berkeley Street, London W1X 5AE

© Muiris O'Scanaill 1993

Typeset by Icon Publications Ltd, Kelso, Scotland
Printed and bound in Guernsey, C. I. by Guernsey Press Ltd

ISBN 1 89816230 1

CHAPTER 1

I **read the** letter with a certain amount of disbelief, as though it might be a joke, a trick of the light; then I read it another couple of times, by which stage all the doubts of the previous months had vanished, totally forgotten, as if I'd never even been *near* the breadline, never mind living from hand to mouth for weeks – the selectively short memory of the incurable optimist firing on all eight cylinders. By the end of the third reading, I was sitting there, grinning inanely at the two sheets of cream A4, shuffling them back and forth so that I could alternatively beam at the heading which, in majestic curlicues, read:

P. R. Steele M.U.B., M.R.C.U.S.
Carrickpedder House,
Knockmore-on-Sea,
County Galway.

and the signature, which, though equally stylish, was totally illegible, a couple of inches of ECG tracing.

It wasn't that I'd been feeling down or worried or negative, at least not that I'd been aware of, but I suppose I must have been – the contrast between now, after the letter, and before, was too marked. I read it again and basked in the expectation or a suddenly rosy future, once again the optimist in me refusing to entertain, even briefly, the thought that this letter might be a one off, the solitary swallow that didn't make a summer. No, this letter was the advance party of a whole flock of swallows and summer was just around the corner. I would be run off my feet. Turning clients away. Apologetically but firmly.

3

Almost six months before I had quit my safe, secure, but slightly predictable post as one of eleven junior assistants employed by one of the largest and best-known veterinary partnerships in Ireland. I had been growing increasingly restless with my stolid, fairly prosperous midlands county town and, after two years, it had struck me that I was slowly sinking into almost the same rut of unrufflable respectability which was inhabited contentedly, almost wilfully, by most of its residents. Nothing ever seemed to happen there, but that was fine by them – nobody seemed to want anything to happen anyway. Even the younger ones lacked the tiniest spark of rebellion and were busy learning the ropes of the family drapery or hardware business or whatever; the occasional black sheep did crop up but seemed to vanish as if by magic – whether they were banished by their families or left of their own accord, unable to face the stultifying banality of their futures, I never knew. It was the only sizeable town I ever came across which didn't have its share of colourful characters, not even a decent town drunk.

I had also discovered early on that I wasn't a 'company man' and, as time passed, found it more and more difficult to accept the rigid hierarchy of The Partnership. The senior partner was referred to as "The Pope" but only, as far as I knew, by us juniors, and never within earshot of the other partners. With a fine disdain for accuracy of description or continuity of metaphor, his large redbrick Victorian house half a mile out of town on the Dublin Road was, for some unknown reason, codenamed The White House, but again, only by the secret netherworld of us assistants. Otherwise it was 'Homeleigh' – as per on the gate pillars. When on duty, everyone referred to and addressed everyone else as Mr, Miss or Mrs. This applied to all the vets (12 Mr; 5 Miss; – all juniors; 3 Mrs – all Partners and all married to Mr Partners), the radiographer (Miss, about to become Mrs – with the most junior of the partners, the poultry and the exotic avian specialist), the senior lab technician (Mr), and the practice manageress (Mrs – the Pope's widowed sister-in-law). You can see how it might become slightly claustrophobic. The lower minions went by their first names.

It hadn't been an easy decision – the job had been hard

enough to secure in the first place; John Cunningham and Partners (all eight of them), with their state-of-the-art facilities, their top specialists, their impressive client list, and the broad range of species represented by their patients, afforded young graduates an opportunity to gain skills and experience not readily available anywhere else, at least not all under one roof. Consequently, The Partnership always had the pick of the available assistants and, though I say so myself, employed only the cream; having worked for them (that is, for longer than the initial three-month trial period) was an impressive addition to anyone's CV. But now I wanted out. I wanted to be my own boss for a while, to be just ordinary Frank Samson, not just some pseudo-special *Mister*.

I also needed to find somewhere more interesting to live, to look around the country a bit. Normally that would have entailed my moving from job to job, six months here a year there, and it was while I was trying to figure out some way of short-circuiting that time-consuming and cumbersome process that it occurred to me that the answer would be to avoid full-time jobs altogether and set up a locum service instead, providing cover whenever and wherever it was needed, a kind of Have Stethoscope, Will Travel. I thought about it for a couple of weeks, talked it over with a few close friends, weighed everything up and made my decision; when I had done that, I duly sought an audience with The Pope.

My parents thought I was mad and said so. Repeatedly. My fellow junior assistants couldn't figure me out; they shrugged and wished me luck but not one of them tried to talk me out of it. I suppose they looked on my departure as one less wellingtoned foot jostling about near the lowest rung of the ladder – in the pecking order of The Partnership I was the senior junior; now everyone would shuffle one step along and my replacement would have to join at the rear – junior assistants moved sideways; it was only partners who inched their way vertically. John Cunningham himself was surprised to the point of being almost hurt. On my way in to tell him after morning surgery, I wondered briefly what I would do if he offered me a partnership – not necessarily at once, but in the foreseeable future – but my speculation was academic; he didn't. He hinted at it but without any firm offers, and I didn't ask. I assured him that my two years with The Partnership had been happy and fruitful ones but that I wanted to see different places and meet different people, and that was that. We shook hands, he wished me all the best and, though we were in daily contact while I worked out my month's notice, he never mentioned it again. We hadn't even said goodbye as he was on leave the day I left. However, he had left me an embarrassingly glowing reference (handwritten, in a separate sealed envelope) along with my salary cheque, tax records and all other relevant documentation. A very thorough man.

And that was the last real pay packet I earned. In the half year since, I had had three separate months of work and nine scattered weekends, six of those for an ex-classmate who was engaged to a girl from Nottingham and was busy shuttling back and forth to keep the flames of love and passion fanned. To make matters worse, we had been friends rather than just class mates, so I couldn't really charge him. What the hell. I had nothing else to do anyway.

My bank manager had been reasonably supportive, at least at the outset, but by this stage he was beginning to show signs of nervousness and had taken to muttering darkly about The People From Area Head Office giving him a hard time – he made Area Head Office sound like a cross between Castle Dracula and the Gestapo HQ – but I found myself unable to offer him much in the line of consolation or reassurance. I couldn't continue airily telling him that these new ventures were always a bit slow to take off – I'd been telling him that since the second month and by now it had reached the point where we both agreed that 'slow' was a relative term, subjective and vague, notoriously open to different interpretations by different people, look at the case in point. The letter would cheer him up no end. The blood fiends of the Area Head Office would be placated for another day.

Between scrolled heading and serrated signature, the letter informed me that P. R. Steele would be going to America to attend his son's wedding, would be away for nearly two months, and would like me to take over the running of his practice for the duration. It also told me that his was a one-man practice and that I had been recommended to him by John Cunningham. (So much, I thought to myself, for the power of advertising – I had been placing notices in the professional journals for months now, yet Steele had to hear about me from The Pope.) The snag was that Steele was scheduled to fly out the following Monday, a mere three days away. He apologised for the short notice, explaining that he had arranged for a stand-in months ago but this had suddenly become unstuck when the replacement broke his arm. It was his frantic search for a late stand-in that had prompted him to phone to see if his friend, John Cunningham, mightn't be able to spare one of his many assistants. He hoped I could take over at such short notice. Either way, could I please ring him at once. He sounded even more anxious than I was.

As I pulled the phone towards me I wondered why, if it was that urgent, Steele hadn't phoned me. Then I realised that I was *assuming* The Pope had got my address from one of the journals, all of which carried my telephone number. Obviously not. It looked as if he had just passed on the forwarding address I had left with the girls in the office. Did anybody ever read these things? Or did they just bung them straight on their tables in their waiting rooms? Just as well the service was free. I'd hate to be paying for it.

I got through to Steele and passed him the good news. His sigh of relief was straight from the depths. He explained that he would be leaving Knockmore early Sunday morning, spending the day in Dublin, and flying out on Monday. I promised to be there by lunchtime the next day at the latest so we could have all the afternoon for him to show me around.

Then I phoned The Pope and thanked him for his interest, his confidence and the recommendation. I gave him my telephone number, just in case. Not that I thought The Partnership might ever find itself short-staffed or in need of a locum, I hastened to add, but if any of his friends... I tried not to make it sound like I was recruiting him as a sort of agent, but I don't think I managed very well. However he assured me that he would keep his ears open and pass on anything he could. I was pleased with my call. A word from John

Cunningham would be worth all the ads in all the journals there were.

I suddenly found myself short of time to do all the things I had been planning to tackle at my leisure; they were mostly small things, but there were one or two important projects, the matter of transport being the major one. I had intended, during the work-barren weeks ahead, to have a major job done on my ageing Land Rover, provided I could arrange suitable credit terms with the local mechanic, a gloomy and lugubrious type who had been baulking fairly steadily. However, his refusals of late were getting less and less emphatic and I was beginning to scent success; it seemed a shame to have to take the pressure off now when I was within a couple of hard luck stories off victory.

As usual the girl in his cubby-hole of an office said he wasn't there when I phoned. I told her to tell him that I had decided against having the job done and could I please talk to him just for a moment. She obviously suspected a trick and repeated that he wasn't there.

"Isn't that his voice I can hear in the background?" I couldn't hear anything but the throb of a compressor. "Perhaps you could check again. Maybe he's just come back in."

"Oh...," she said, flustered. "Hold on... I... I... think... eh... eh... maybe he's just come back in!" She rushed the last bit.

I could almost feel his suspicion when he picked up the phone, as if he expected it to squirt water out of the ear-piece. I told him that the job was off for the time being, that I had suddenly found myself employed and that I would be back after that was over, flush, I hinted, with money. In the meantime, would the Land Rover keep going? He pointed out that nothing in life could be guaranteed and went on to highlight this with examples: he might be dead in the morning. I might be dead in the morning. Tracy, the office girl, might be dead in the morning. I bore with the philosophical discourse; it was only when he looked like extending the list of people who might be dead in the morning from the garage staff to members of the general public that I interrupted; once free of the confines of the workplace, he could go on forever.

"Whoa, Mick! Back up! You're talking major disasters now. All I want is a guess, an educated guess: if, by any chance you're wrong and there *isn't* a nuclear war before morning, will the old jalopy keep me going for another couple of months? That's all."

Eventually, and with copious disclaimers of any clairvoyant gifts, he thought that, if I didn't dog it, it might get me around. And that was as good as I was going to get.

The second important item on the agenda had cropped up recently and was in no way connected with work. It could have been described as a matter of the heart, but only insofar as my blood pressure was involved; the nobler sentiments which that phrase generally implies, were conspicuous by their absence. I hardly knew the girl.

Marnie was a fashion photographer, a Dutch fashion photographer; "top", "aspiring", "inspired", "up-and-coming", "much-sought-after", were all qualifiers I had heard prefixing her job description. Tall, blonde as sunny August cornfields, eyes blue as cornflowers, nose, mouth and teeth all in keeping, it seemed to me that she was at the wrong end of the camera. Someone once told me that fashion models should be flat-chested so maybe that was why Marnie didn't make the grade, but she moved with a loose-limbed natural grace which would have gone down a bomb on any catwalk. To me she was a creature of wonder, exotic in her accent, mannerisms, profession, dress, attitudes and I developed a rapid and serious case of the hots for her. Before the job cropped up, I had, as it were, been planning a strategy which, if I played my cards right, should have seen me installed as number one man somewhere towards the following weekend. I had only met her twice, the first time less than a week ago and I was still sussing it out.

She was in Dublin on holiday. There was a music festival on and she was a fan of – and quite an expert on – Irish traditional music. I happened to find myself sitting beside her at a De Danann concert the previous Sunday night. I was on my own – tickets were as rare as hen's teeth but I had been given a complimentary by Frankie Gavin, the fiddle-player and driving force behind the group and a long-time friend of mine. Marnie was part of a group of four – one man and three beautiful girls. She had bought an album in the foyer on the way in and had enlisted my aid in translating the track titles, which were in Irish. She and her friends were delighted when I offered to take them backstage afterwards to meet the group but they couldn't stay for long because of a prior supper date. Marnie, who spent most of her time talking to me, gave me a list of pubs and clubs she intended to visit during the next few evenings, all of which were hosting music sessions and left with the hope that we might meet at one of these. This was delivered with a smile which I later decided had been private and enigmatic. That was when the hots began in earnest.

By Wednesday evening, I had done the rounds of the pubs and, though I had heard some great music, there was no sign of Marnie. I was in the process of throwing my hat at it, deciding that the smile had, after all, been just an ordinary one and that any privacy or enigma which I had attributed to it had been solely in my head, when Frankie rang to say that De Danann were doing a gig in Searson's and why didn't I come along and we could go for a Chinese afterwards. I said that I might and I might not as I was a bit tired and didn't really fancy a late night; Frankie earnestly protested that he didn't either. But these things have a habit of going on and on and I knew Frankie of old – once he got started, there'd be no stopping him. I had more or less decided to give it a miss when I remembered that Marnie had told me that De Danann were her favourite group, so, on spec, I went.

She was already there when I arrived about ten. With the same people. She saw me almost at once (I, of course, immediately decided that she had been watching hungrily for me), waved, and fought her way through the throng to meet me. She laid a hand on my arm and said it was great to see me. The crowd pressed us together and I asked her what she wanted to drink, hoping to prise her away from the group.

"There is room at our table, Frank. Come and sit with us. I have a drink there already. Just for yourself, get one." The foreign accent made my scalp tingle.

She stayed with me while I pushed through to the bar and tried to catch the attention of one of the hassled, sweating barmen. When it looked as though my arm and finger were in danger of setting in a raised position, she squeezed in beside me and said "Excuse me" in a quiet voice at a distracted-looking barman who was scuttling by behind the counter. This brought him up with a jerk. She looked at me. I told her what I wanted and she relayed the order to the curate who, by now, seemed to have broken off communications with the rest of the world bar Marnie. Back at her table, I shared her leatherette seat with her; she insisted. She made introductions but the names got lost among the skirling notes of the music and the noise of the crowd; anyway, my brain, full with the awareness of her nearness, could not have held them.

While everyone was tapping feet or rapping knuckles on the table, in thrall to the infectious rhythms of a selection of reels which slid from one into the next without a pause, I was busy reading the omens, poring, as it were, over the entrails. Unable to fix the man's position within the group when we had met before, I now decided that it wasn't that important: had he been Marnie's boyfriend, then I would have been given her seat and her thigh would now be moving up and down rhythmically against his instead of mine. I also figured that she didn't find my physical nearness unwelcome – she could have shared with one of the girls, leaving her seat to me. The entrails looked very promising indeed, but then, to a born optimist like me, they always did.

It was not to be; at least not that night. Performance over, Frankie and two of the band came to join us for a drink, then decided it was time for the 'Chinese' we had arranged earlier. I asked if anyone (meaning Marnie and only Marnie) was interested in coming along and I think she would have if Helene, who had gone very quiet during the previous hour, hadn't announced that she felt like death. In fairness, though I cursed her silently at the time, she did look pretty awful, and Marnie understandably insisted on staying with her. So the Gang of Four departed.

"Give us a ring," said Marnie as she left, handing me a phone number.

11

"Sure. I'd love to," I replied, and I hoped that the 'us' was used idiomatically and not literally.

That was Wednesday; this was Friday. I had phoned (about twenty times) on Thursday but no one had answered. I thought maybe I had left it too late in the evening and decided not to take the same chance to-day.

Marnie answered and sounded delighted to hear my voice. "Did you ring yesterday evening, Frank? The phone stopped just as I reached it."

"No," I lied for no understandable reason and then, feeling petty, lied again. "I tried several times to get through but there was a strange tone on the line. I thought maybe your phone was on the blink."

"Oh...."

"How's Helene?"

"She is very good now thank you. A twenty four hour bug."

"Good. So... Any plans for this evening?"

"There's a party. Are you going?"

"I haven't heard of any parties. I haven't been invited."

"If I invite you will that be good enough?"

"Great. But can you? Who's party is it?"

"I don't know their name but it's not a formal or a fancy party or anything like that."

She was certainly right about that. The party, when we eventually located the basement flat in Rathmines, was crammed with people who all seemed to be sniffing, snorting or puffing various prohibited substances – not my idea of fun at all. Still, I decided to stick it out for a while: Marnie might soon decide she wanted to leave and I didn't want to be missing when and if that happened. Besides she now had a hostage, my camera.

En route, to her delight, she had found the camera on the shelf beneath the dashboard and, despite my unspoken but obvious disapproval, she had insisted, with some petulance, on taking it to the party with her. She had her way; the hots, by this time, having achieved maximum intensity, I was in no mood to deny her anything, even unto half my kingdom, which was just about what my camera was worth.

So I moved about hither and thither, drifting amongst the smokers and the sniffers, the snorters and the puffers, trying to keep up with Marnie without it seeming like I was slavishly following her, and feeling more and more out of place.

"You want some dope?," a suave effeminate type asked me, proffering a joint in a pudgy, much-beringed hand.

"No thanks," I shook my head, peering over his head for sight of Marnie in the crowd. Every few minutes the flash of a flashgun helped pinpoint her whereabouts.

"What about some coke? I've got some good stuff here. Do you snort?"

"Only when I've got a cold."

"Oh! So that's the way it is? Well lovey, they're shooting up in that room there. Toodle pip!"

I stuck it out for the best part of an hour, but you're either into that or you're not, and I'm not. Marnie, on the other hand, was in her element, and wouldn't hear of leaving. Eventually, I did well to get my camera back. She wanted me and it to stay.

"No Marnie. I've got to be off. I was late last night and I've got an early start in the morning."

"When will you be in town again, Frank?" she asked, inhaling fiercely on the joint she held between thumb and forefinger. "You sure you don't want some of this?"

"I'm sure thanks. I probably won't be back now for at least six weeks. Maybe more. It depends. I'd better leave you the film so you can have it developed."

"I did not finish it. You finish it and maybe you call around with the prints next time you get to Dublin? I like it here and I'm going to try to stay for a few months. Look for a job."

"Okay then. I'm off. Maybe I can give you a call when I get settled in? If you get tired of the bright lights, you could take a trip to the west to recuperate and rebuild your strength for the continued struggle. You're sure now you can get home?" Hope springing eternal.

"Ja." She looked around her at the sea of admiring male faces were turned towards her. "I'm sure."

I was sure too. "Okay," I said. "See you around."

As I turned on to the main Rathmines road, two carloads of grim-faced men turned into the quiet street I was just leaving, their drivers in blue uniforms. I watched in my mirror as they pulled in to the kerb behind the lines of cars of my recent fellow revellers and I shuddered. I couldn't imagine that ten of Dublin's finest were making a house-call to plea for a reduction in the noise level at the festivities. To me, they had Drug Squad written all over them and if I was right, they were in for a field day.

CHAPTER 2

My tyres swished through evidence of what the radio had called "heavy pre-dawn showers in all areas", but by the time I reached Maynooth, the ominous grey blanket loitering overhead had been hustled on by an army of small clouds, the rearguard of which was now swabbing its way eastward, leaving the sky up ahead a hot dry blue. By the time I turned left in Kinnegad, there was steam rising from the fields of lush aftergrass and the long empty road ahead shimmered in mirage.

I reached Knockmore and located Steele's house just in time to join them for lunch; Mrs Steele apologised for its makeshift nature – she was up to her neck in packing. An hour later, I had been installed in my home for the next few months – a classic whitewashed, thick-thatched, climbing-rose-covered cottage in an acre of garden, the lot going under the slightly inappropriate name of "Fernditch". All in all, very much the des. res. As I followed Steele back down the path to the rose-arched gate, I was thinking that Marnie would love it; once she saw it, she would surely want to clock in for the duration.

We had a hectic afternoon. First he showed me around the surgery, kennels, cattery, and the loose boxes for larger in-patients, giving me a quick run-down on the various inmates; next came the office, which was really the bailiwick of Eileen who doubled as nurse, secretary and practice manager and to whom, he informed me, I could turn in almost any crisis. Then we headed out on the afternoon rounds, Steele pointing out as we went, important landmarks, crucial crossroads, alternative routes, shortcuts. I did most of the work. Steele didn't ask me to: I just said, when we got to the first case – a cow with a retained placenta – that, if he liked, I'd do it and he said fine and that was the pattern after that. As the afternoon wore on, he looked less and less worried about leaving his beloved practice in a stranger's hands.

"Well... What do you think?" We were about half way through our list of calls.

"So far, it all seems pretty manageable. All fairly routine," I replied. "Any surprises in store? I once did a locum which had a large salmon farm on its books."

"No. No surprises. There's one client who runs what amounts to a private zoo but he has an exhaustive knowledge of his animals and he rarely needs attention. Just in case, how are you on exotics?"

"So so. I've read the books. But not an awful lot of experience."

"Who has? I suppose that's why they're called exotics. Anyway I've a few books at the surgery and Bob Jennings – the zoo man – has a huge library."

"Hopefully I won't be needed at the zoo. Any other exotics?"

"Not unless you count Catamaran."

"Catamaran? *Catamaran?* You mean... *the* Catamaran?"

"Yes. *The* Catamaran."

"He's *here*?"

"Yes. Down the road at Bally Ard. Gilbert Norris's place. That's where he was born. I delivered him. His dam, Tropical Kayak was the best mare Norris ever had but she's gone now. Sold. Like nearly everything else in the place." There was a distinct note of disapproval in his tone, then he went on: "Norris owns a ninth share of the horse. Catamaran is syndicated nine ways."

"A wise move that. Keeping one share."

"*Keeping*?" he snorted "Not keeping! *Buying!* Catamaran was sold as a foal along with the other foals. Norris bought back in again." I gathered that this was what had generated the disapproval, the buying back in.

"So! I have the great Catamaran as a potential patient! Wow! I didn't know he was here in the west. I never thought about it, mind you, but, if I had, I'd have presumed he'd be somewhere on the Curragh. Ah well... I suppose, when all's said and done, he's just a horse. Just another nag. He must be worth a fortune though. Never beaten, was he?"

"Never. Never even looked like it. As for what he'd be worth... that would be hard to say. He's insured for thirty five million but he's worth a lot more now."

"Oh goody goody." I said sarcastically. "Just what I need: Catamaran with a heart attack or an acute fit of the vapours. How's his state of health?"

"He's fine. He had a cut on his nose a few weeks ago but that's well on its way; it was nothing much. Anyway we'll be seeing him soon. I want to introduce you to Norris. As you can imagine, security is pretty tight, and I want you to call in at least once a week like I do, just to have a look. So I had better smooth your passage with Norris and old Jack in the gate lodge."

We made Bally Ard our last stop. I was introduced to Jack, the gatekeeper and had my features closely scrutinised and, presumably, committed to memory as he opened the massive double gates and swung them to.

The house was a grey stone affair set in pleasant gardens and lawns. The driveway which curved gracefully up from the gate, had, over the years, become a canyon between tall rhododendron hedges which cut off any view of the house itself until we were almost upon it so that it was impossible to see it in its entirety; there was, however, an overall impression of impending dilapidation; Norris, Steele told me, had been widowed some years before and he didn't seem to have the same interest in the place since. I stayed in the car while Steele climbed the steps to the front door and rang the bell. Almost at once, a very odd-looking mongrel appeared from around the side of the house and came bounding over to Steele, tongue lolling in welcome. They were obviously old pals and Steele bent tickling a nondescript brownish ear until the door was opened by Gilbert Norris himself.

They spoke briefly, Norris looked over at the car (obviously Steele had mentioned me), then Steele turned and beckoned to me. I joined them on the doorstep and introductions were made. Norris turned as if to lead us into the house, mentioning something about joining him for an evening drink, but Steele declined.

"Thanks Gilbert. We'd love to but there's no time. I'd better get home and help Marion with the packing. She's been at it all day on her own."

"What a pity. But, if you must, you must."

"We're just going to take a look at Catamaran before we go. I want Frank to see him."

Norris didn't seem any too pleased at having his evening snifter postponed for some sightseeing.

"But... but... why? Why do you want to see him?"

"Just to introduce them. It'll only take a minute."

"But Peter," he protested, "he'll have settled down for the evening by now. It's going to get him all worked up to have strangers around". He turned to me: "The stud season is just over and he's going to get the wrong idea if there's activity in the yard."

Personally I'd have thrown my hat at it at that point but Steele was adamant.

"It's really quite important Gilbert. I want Frank to see that nose wound while I'm here. He has to know what it's like now to be able to judge its progress later... No?"

"But that nose thing was *ages* ago, for God's sake! I'd really prefer not to disturb him, Peter. I mean it."

I was getting embarrassed. Norris was looking at me as if I was some kind of spoilt brat nuisance demanding to see the horse for no good reason, regardless of the trouble involved for one and all. I glanced at Steele to give him an it doesn't matter sign but he wasn't looking at me so I shrugged apologetically, but helplessly, at Norris while Steele pressed on. Of course what was really worrying him was the fact that I might be overawed if I did have to attend the great animal; and it was quite likely that I would be. Catamaran was world famous. During his racing career, he had taken on and hammered all comers from all over the world; winning a record amount of prizemoney, he had galloped through the record books... Yes, I reckoned I would be in awe of him.

"It will only take a minute, Gilbert, and I think the insur-

18

ance people would expect me to hand him over formally."

"I'll get my boots," Norris replied without much grace, and went into the house leaving us standing on the step. On the way to the yard, which was down past the house some few hundred yards along a farm road, Norris returned to his theme: "I really don't think, Peter that this is at all necessary. After all, if Mr... eh mm... "

"Samson."

"If Mr Samson does, by any chance in your absence, have to attend Catamaran, then I'm quite sure that the horse won't be too upset to find that he doesn't have his usual vet in attendance. Sensitive they may be, these thoroughbreds, but this..." He shrugged. He was short and stocky with a shock of white hair and his ruddy weather-beaten features made it difficult to guess his age with any accuracy – fifty-five to sixty-five I guessed. His legs were extremely bowed, indicating a lifetime in the saddle.

"Just the same, Gilbert, I think it's essential that we introduce them. Just so that there are no surprises if they *do* have to see each other. On either side."

"I'd still prefer we didn't upset him," Norris persisted. "He wasn't quite himself yesterday evening."

"Why? What was wrong?" Steele slowed and his tone sharpened.

"Well... he had a bit of a shiver and he didn't eat his meal with the usual relish."

"What? Why on earth didn't you call me?" Steele asked, flabbergasted. Obviously, I reflected, a 'bit of a shiver' in a horse of Catamaran's value was enough to set up a tremor of the order of 6.7 on the Richter Scale in his vet. "My God, Gilbert, you can't be too careful! You know that! The time to get all these chills and flus is at the very start! You ought to have called!"

"Well it was so slight, it didn't seem anything to worry about. I said I'd leave it overnight and this morning he was back to his own self again."

"Well that's the end of *that* discussion. We'll *have* to take a look at him now. I want to check him out." Steele marched on.

"But he's perfectly alright now!" Norris trotted to catch up.

"I just feel that a new face might upset him, stress him a little and bring him down again. With whatever he had. Perhaps Mr..."

"Samson," I said.

"Yes, Samson. Forgive me," he turned to me, "I'm hopeless with names... Perhaps Mr Samson might like to wait outside, at the gate..."

"That won't be necessary and anyway, as I said, I want him to see the wound on the nose." Steele was becoming quite testy.

We stopped at tall double gates of vertical iron bars which came into sharp points at their tops and, while Norris went through the complicated opening process which included a combination padlock as well as two other padlocks, and an electronic device which was released by the insertion of a plastic card into a slot in one of the pillars, I surveyed the yard beyond.

There was a row of loose boxes diagonally across to the left, about twelve in all, all with the top halves of their doors open, hooked to the wall to prevent them slamming closed in a sudden gust and decapitating any of the occupants which might be having a quiet look around. At the sound of the gate swinging inwards on an incongruously squeaky hinge, a head appeared in one of the doors about half-way down the row. Only one head appeared and, as its muzzle had a bright purple patch on it, I deduced that the head belonged to the fabled Catamaran, the purple patch being due to a wound dressing containing gentian violet.

"And how's my big fella this evening? Ay? How's the luvly boy?" Norris began baby-talking to the horse while we were still a good ten yards away. Liquid dark eyes in a rich bay-brown head regarded our approach with supreme indifference, cocked ears rotated like radar dishes as the strong jaw worked rhythmically without cease on what sounded like a crunchy carrot. Then, as we got within arm's length, the head withdrew and vanished into the dark interior of the box.

"Oh!" said Norris. "That's not very polite, now, is it? Who's a naughty boy? C'mon Cat! Let's see what a nice boy you can be. I've brought someone new for you to meet."

There was the sound of a door closing from behind us and we turned. A man of about my own age and build with a head of copper curls, so bright it was almost orange, came ambling across the yard. He walked slowly, buttoning his shirt as he came, his pace unconsciously measured to arrive as the last button was done up.

"Evening, Mr Steele," he said in the soft-sharp nasal accent of Cork.

"Good evening Tom. I'd like you to meet Mr Samson who'll be looking after things for me while I'm away. Tom Kelly, Frank Samson."

We shook hands, muttering wordless 'pleased to meet you' noises.

"We'd like to have a look at Catamaran, Tom. Perhaps you wouldn't mind taking him out for us. It should only take a minute."

"Right you are, Mr Steele. I'll just get his bridle from the tack room."

"And Tom...," Norris called after the retreating figure.

"Yes sir?"

"Bring a rug for him too."

"A rug, Mr Norris?"

"Yes Tom, a rug." Kelly looked puzzled for a moment, then he turned and continued on to the tack-room.

"The evenings are getting a bit chilly, don't you think?" Norris turned to me.

"Well," I shrugged, "perhaps a very little..." In fact, to me, it didn't seem at all cold. The warm sun was still a good two hours above the paling horizon, but I didn't argue; like their human counterparts, horse prima donnas also probably liked to have their petty, precious eccentricities pandered to as a mark of their celebrity status.

The groom returned, bridle in one hand and the rug, the equine equivalent of a string vest, draped over the other. Without a word he passed through the door of the box and a moment later emerged leading Catamaran. We stood back, giving the animal plenty of clearance, waiting for him to settle.

"He's always a bit frisky when we take him out, especially at an unusual hour. He probably thinks there's a mare to be covered. The stud season isn't long over," Norris repeated, "and the memories survive. He'll quieten down after another few weeks."

While Norris was explaining this to me, I was studying the famous horse. I had seen hundreds of pictures of him at one stage, he appeared more often in the press than did the politicians but the three-dimensional, live image was a totally different experience. Through the holes in the light rug which covered him from withers to haunches, I could sense rather than see solid muscle burgeoning beneath taut brown skin. Whinnying in sharp bursts of high spirits, he reared and bucked alternately like a rocking horse, looking around alertly for the mare he expected to be awaiting his attentions in the covering shed. At last, helped by the groom's soothing tones, he got the message and settled down. Only then did we approach him gingerly.

Steele examined his eyes, felt the pulse in the artery lying on the curve of his jaw, peered up his nostrils and palpated the glands lying in the fork of his mandible behind the root of his tongue. Everyone was silent during the examination except Steele who said things like 'Mmmmmm!' and 'Huh!' intermittently.

"And he ate perfectly normally today, Tom?" He glanced at the groom.

"A.1. Mr Steele. He's in great fettle. That nose thing didn't knock a feather out of him; he was never better."

"Well he certainly seems fine. I don't think we need bother taking his temperature." He turned to me. "That's an ordeal, Frank. He hates it. Here, take a look at his nose." I moved closer and inspected the purple-sprayed area on the velvet-black muzzle. "It's almost cleared up now," he continued. "It never was very bad, only a slice of skin missing – about the size of a fifty-pence piece. The subcutaneous tissues weren't damaged at all, luckily enough."

"How did it happen?"

"We don't know really. Probably the tin nailed over the door to stop him from chewing the timber. We don't want him to turn into a crib-biter. It only went a couple of inches down on the inside, but the edge seemed flush with the timber of the door so I can't see how he managed to jag himself on it. But I can't for the life of me think of anything else that could have done it. Anyway, we've replaced the tin with a sheet which goes all the way to the bottom now, so, if that was the problem, it shouldn't be a danger any longer." He stepped back a few paces, viewed the horse overall for a moment, then nodded at the groom. "That's fine thank you, Tom. You can put him back now."

We left soon after, having refused Norris's second offer of a drink.

"Well then... Bon Voyage, Peter. Wish Michael and his new bride every happiness from me." His argumentative mood seemed to have been left behind in the stable yard.

On the way home, Steele asked me if I was a racing man and I replied that no, I couldn't call myself that.

"Hah! I thought not."

"What made you think that?"

"A racing man would have been dumbstruck at being so close to Catamaran."

"Oh I was impressed alright."

"Of course! But not dumbstruck. And it's much better that way." After a moment's reverie, he continued: "I used to be a racing man myself. I still go now and then but I gave up betting..."

He seemed to be awaiting my 'why' in order to kickstart the rest of the story so I complied.

"Why?"

"Can't trust anyone."

"Bookies?"

"No! Not the bookies. The bookies are alright. They're as honest as daylight compared to the jockeys and trainers! I gave it up because one day I happened to overhear a conversation between the trainer and rider of a horse, a supposed dead cert I had just lost a small fortune on. 'How did he go out there?' asks the trainer. 'So-so,' says the jockey. 'I had the beatings of the four that finished ahead of me, no bother, but I'm not so sure about the ones behind.' Could you believe that?"

I had dinner with the Steeles, wished them Bon Voyage and, shortly after nine-thirty, walked the half mile to

'Fernditch' which stood on a quiet road on the outskirts of town. It was owned by Marion Steele's brother who had been travelling in the States for some months; they were to meet up with him at their son's wedding. My brief visit earlier in the day had afforded me the opportunity for only the most cursory of examinations but I had liked what little I had seen. Now I explored it more fully and was really impressed. The kitchen and bathroom were well-equipped and modern but the living quarters were furnished as one would expect of a wealthy confirmed bachelor – lots of old leather and dark wood. The only modern items in the living room were the TV/Video unit and the Hi Fi/CD system, all of which were housed in a single high-tech column occupying one side of the heavy bookcase that covered one wall of the room. It was a huge change from the usual accommodation I was offered, a room in a boarding house or small hotel, or a Spartan flat over the surgery.

An inspection of the kitchen cupboards and fridge revealed that someone, presumably Marion Steele, had thoughtfully laid in essential provisions, and I made myself some coffee.

On page six of the paper I had bought on my walk to the cottage, there was a short article about Black Marias having to be called in to cart away all the people who had been arrested during a raid by Drug Squad detectives on a house in the Rathmines area of Dublin the previous night. They were to have been arraigned in court this morning. I thanked my lucky stars. Though no names were mentioned, I knew it had to be the party I had been at. The cops couldn't have missed it. The pungent fug that hung above that house must have been like the Star in the East.

I turned on the news but it was half over and there was no mention of the haul in the bit I heard. I went to bed and dreamt of being driven away to some unknown destination in a Paddy wagon. I was rattling the bars and screaming that I was innocent. I was the only one protesting; all my fellow occupants were cool as breezes, smiling happily and saying things to me like 'Cool it man' and 'Hang loose babe'. And that went on for hours.

Sunday passed uneventfully. There were a few calls and I

Steel
lacked in... to them without too many wrong turns –
against the ... map made up for in local knowledge what it
informed me th...cy. My quartered Sunday Press, propped
headline "Drug Sq... my lunch table at a local restaurant,
name – inevitably brack...kiss goodbye to Marnie. Under the
among the list of foreigners ...res Many Arrests", I found her
tion orders had been issued. ... he names of her three friends –
... whom immediate deporta-

CHAPTER 3

*T*hough it was ~~~ blow up in my face before evening, Monday began ~~~ell.

When I ~~~ived ~~ the surgery at 8.30 I found a full waiting room ~~~, with Eileen supplying pertinent information on the foibles and quirks of patients and owners, I cleared the lot in little over an hour. Afterwards, as we sipped coffee, she talked me through the morning round of farm visits, giving directions and drawing little sketch maps as required, and I got through the nine calls almost as quickly as P. R. Steele himself would.

On my way back in to the surgery, I found myself passing the high wall of Bally Ard and I slowed down; a glance at my watch showed me I had time on my hands, so I swung in. Waiting for Jack, the elderly gate-keeper, to answer the bell I hoped that Gilbert Norris would not misconstrue my calling so soon after I had last seen Catamaran as over-anxiety on my part or, worse still, an abuse of his privileged position by some sort of celebrity groupie. What the hell. I wanted to check the horse. Steele's orders.

By alternately ringing the bell and blowing my horn, I managed, at last, to attract Jack's attention and he came and peered with myopic suspicion at me for a long time before recognition finally dawned. "Ah yes! The vet! You're the new vet, aren't you?"

"That's right," I nodded. I'd been telling him so all along, in varying degrees of loudness but obviously, he was either a man who liked to make up his own mind about these things or he was hard of hearing.

"What's wrong with the stallion? Himself said nothing about sending for you. He'd have told me on his way out if you were coming. To expect you, like."

"Nobody sent for me," I shouted. Mr Steele asked me to keep an eye on Catamaran, so I thought I'd call as I was passing."

"Oh, I see."

"Mr Norris has gone out, you say?"

"Aye. Near an hour ago."

"Is Tom at the yard?"

"Tom's gone home. To Cork."

"Oh... Well if there's no one...," I began, thinking of the locked yard gate.

"His mother's in the hospital. They broke into her house on Saturday night and frightened the poor creature half to death. Shock, Tom said."

"Who's they?"

"What was that?"

"I said: 'Who broke in?'"

"Hooligans! Thugs! Who d'you think?" He sounded as if he'd have expected me to have known that. "The poor woman lives on her own. I'd like to see them try it here..."

"That's too bad. I hope she wasn't badly hurt."

"Shock, Tom said," he repeated.

"Maybe I can call again later..."

"Young Hynes from the town is looking after things at the yard," he said, inserting a key. "But take your time driving up there. I'll have to phone him that it's the vet that's coming 'cos you're new and he won't know you and if he doesn't know you he won't let you in and then you won't be able to see the horse." A man who believed in spelling things out.

He opened the great gates and waved me through and I saluted him as I passed.

'Young' Hynes, who was a couple of years older than me, was already at the gate when I arrived and we went through the 'who-sent-for-you?-what's-wrong?' routine again.

"It's just a passing visit," I assured him as he opened the gate, a far simpler procedure from the inside; he removed the padlock and turned the handle. "I want to check up on him. Mister Norris thought he was a bit off colour at the week-end. How has he seemed to you this morning?"

27

"Fine, I suppose. But then, I don't know a lot about horses and the last time I saw this one was in March. Tom Kelly goes off to Cheltenham every year, no matter what, and I come in then, but really only for security. There's plenty of help with the horses then because it's the stud season and all the temporaries are here; I just stay here during the night because there's supposed to be someone in the yard all the time. Not, mind you, that anyone has ever come up with any brilliant suggestions as to what I should do if some crowd arrive in the small hours some morning armed to the teeth and intending to do a Shergar on Catamaran..."

He lost my attention there. Even from half the yard away, I could see a change in the horse. His eye lacked the fire which had been immediately obvious on Saturday evening and he didn't retreat into his box as we approached; he regarded me with a calm docility that disturbed me as I stood in front of him, a prudent arm's length away. In the interests of absolute safety, Hynes had pulled up a few steps to the rear. I raised a tentative hand towards the violet muzzle and the horse didn't move; nor did he object when I touched him and began to stroke his face. I peered at the nose wound but there was no sign of a breakdown in the healing process. I checked his eye and it too, seemed fine – not in any way as spirited as it had been, but clear and free from discharge. His nostrils were clean and there was no swelling of the glands under his jaw; his pulse rate was marginally elevated but only marginally. I peered past him, into the relative dark of the box and immediately noticed the full hay net hanging from a ring on the back wall, the sweet grey-green stalks bulging through the mesh.

"Did you give him that hay?" I asked, knowing full well that he hadn't. I couldn't see Hynes entering Catamaran's box, even with the distraction of a full hay net.

"I didn't. The boss did."

"When?"

"I don't know. Before I got here this morning."

"What time was that?"

"Eightish. Give or take."

"He hasn't eaten any of it. It's nearly one now. Five hours. At least five hours."

Catamaran was off his grub again like Norris had reported a few days ago – hardly cause for alarm, but still, Steele had been pretty alarmed. I looked again. It was hard to see the horse's body because of his colour; the dark skin in the dark box showed up as little better than a silhouette. "When do you expect the boss back?"

"He didn't say."

"Do you think we could take him out of the box ourselves?"

"I don't know. Are you any good with horses?"

"So-so. Maybe we can do it in easy stages, one step at a time. Let's see first if he'll let us put the bridle on without us having to open the door."

Hynes looked unsure for a moment, then he shrugged: "You're the doctor." His tone had more than a touch of Pilate asking for the hand basin. "I'll get it from the tack room."

When he came back, he handed me the bridle and stepped pointedly away. I arranged the leathers over my left hand, the bit stretched in the span of my fingers. Catching the horse by the forelock with my right hand, I pressed the bit against his lips and with just moderate resistance, he let it into his mouth and began to chew on it. Slowly I moved the brow band up along his forehead until I could push the poll strap over his ears. I fastened the buckle of the cheek-strap and it was done. "So far, so good," I said over my shoulder. "Now for the dicey part."

"Taking him out," Hynes replied, and he moved even further away to make sure that there was absolutely no doubt that, if anything went wrong, I was on my own.

Wishing I had gone myself to the tackroom to look for something more substantial than the flimsy bridle – like a cavisson – I eased open the door, all the time waiting for the surge of power; but it didn't come, at least not in the strength I was steeling myself for. He came through quickly enough and wheeled me round a couple of times, but soon settled. I held him a while, talking softly and soothingly, tense in case he was only drawing a quiet breath, but the moment when he might have exploded came and went and I knew I had him. I walked him around the yard a few times; he tossed his head, wheeled, pulled, neighed, reared up once or twice and walked crabwise a fair bit, but there was none of the wildness I had seen before and, after four or five rounds, we had settled the matter of who was leading whom. While all this was going on, Hynes was constantly on the move too and, with the skill of a very small referee in a heavyweight boxing ring, he nimbly managed to maintain the maximum distance between himself and the other occupants who might, indeed were *expected* to, erupt in a flurry of violence at any moment without warning. At last I managed to cajole him into holding the horse and stood with him for a moment until he felt confident enough to go solo. Then I stepped back and observed my patient.

He looked fine. On physical signs alone, I couldn't fault him. He was a normal-looking thoroughbred stallion (apart from the purple muzzle), well-muscled, strong, alert and eager. But he wasn't as fiery as he had been on Saturday evening and he had had a shivering attack only a few days previously and he hadn't eaten his hay and he was my responsibility. Also he was worth millions. I decided to give him the full treatment. As much for my sake as for his.

I checked the heartbeat beneath his left elbow, then moved the bell of the stethoscope over his rib-cage on both sides, carefully sounding the great lungs for the slightest wrong sounds, wheezes, squeaks, gurgles or pants. There were none. I listened to the sounds in his abdomen; there was nothing untoward in that department either. That left his temperature, usually the first thing I do, but mindful of Steele's warning of how much this horse hated it, I had left it until last. Cautioning Hynes to hold him tight, I gently slid my hand along the top of his rump. Catamaran wheeled away. I tried again and this time, he confined his protest to some vigorous tail swishing. Slowly I grasped the root of the tail and raised it away from the body. The horse made anxious noises and looked nervous but didn't object beyond that. I reached round the back of his haunches and gingerly probed to locate the anus. He whinnied anxiously as I inserted the thermometer, but he let me do it. I could have asked Hynes to pick up a foreleg which would have reduced the danger of my being kicked but he was too uneasy and was hanging on for dear life with both hands. A minute later I withdrew the thermometer. 100.5. Perfectly normal. The comfort

30

of this was offset by my unease at the fact that I had managed to take his temperature in the first place, another pointer that there was something wrong. A change in temperament is often the first sign to appear when an illness is still in its incubation phase, long before the temperature goes up or other signs appear. And Catamaran's temperament had changed considerably since I had last seen him.

"How's his temperature?" Hynes asked, getting involved.

"Spot on. Normal as can be. I can't find anything wrong with him but he just doesn't seem himself; he could be getting a flu or some such. I presume he's been vaccinated against the usual things?"

"I wouldn't know. Haven't a clue. I suppose so." Hynes shrugged.

"Probably." I stood back again regarding the horse speculatively and I was still uneasy. I decided to go a step further.

"Hold him a moment while I go to the Land Rover; I want to take a blood sample or two to send to the lab."

"A b-blood sample?!" The uneasiness came flooding back into Hynes's eyes. "Needles and things?"

"It's no big deal really. Somehow horses never seem to mind it too much."

I came back with a sterile 20cc syringe and needle, an alcohol swab and several different coloured vials, each containing different anti-coagulants. I also carried my camera. I had no intention of missing the opportunity to photograph the famed Catamaran and I wasn't going to get a better chance. I laid the camera on the ground, well away from the horse, set the vials down beside it and attached the needle to the syringe. Then, having swabbed a few inches of the jugular furrow, I pressed my thumb hard in to stop the flow of blood from the head. Immediately, the vein filled, thick as my middle finger and turgid. I waited for a moment before positively shoving the needle through. Catamaran winced but that was all. Slowly I eased the plunger back until the syringe was full of the red-black warm blood. Then I withdrew the needle and swabbed the pin-prick in the skin.

"Do you mind holding him just another minute?"

"No problem." Hynes was reassured by the horse's cooperation during the blood test.

"I'll just put the blood samples in the bottles and then I want to take a few photos. Do you think Mr Norris would mind?"

"Why should he? It'll do no harm, will it?"

"O.K. I'll take a few of the horse first and then maybe you can take one of me holding him. After all, I'm never going to have another patient like him, am I?"

I filled the different vials from the syringe, letting the blood trickle slowly down along the side of the vial rather than squirting it in. This was to avoid causing rupture of the delicate blood cells. For the same reason, I rolled the bottles gently between my palms rather than shaking them to ensure that the anti-coagulant mixed evenly with the blood. That finished, I fished out the camera.

First I took a close-up of the nose wound for my "case box", a box of photographs of interesting cases which I come across; admittedly, the wound was no great shakes as an interesting case, but the muzzle on which it had occurred was. Then I took a few of his head, one straight on and one of each profile. To complete the set, I moved back to focus on the whole animal, taking him from each side, giving Hynes, each time, a chance to slick back his hair and otherwise generally compose himself rigidly into an attitude of strained casualness.

"Okay. My turn now. How are you on cameras?"

"I know as much about them as a hen knows about a bank holiday."

"Well, I'll just set the focus and shutter speed and if you stand here where I'm standing, all you have to do is look through this window thing here," I tapped the view-finder, "line me and Catamaran up in the centre of the frame and press this button here." I inclined the camera towards him, pointing out the bits. "You can't go wrong."

"I'll have a go." He didn't sound too hopeful but in any event, it made no difference. As I turned the wind-on lever to roll the film on, it jammed half-way.

"Shit!" I cursed. "The film's finished!"

"Oh. Tough luck. Have you got another one?"

"Nope. Ah well... some other time."

I gathered up my belongings, put the camera back in its case and got ready to leave. Just as I was about to tell Hynes he could put the horse back into his box, Catamaran, raising his tail, passed dung.

"I may as well take a knob of that with me too," I said. There was a laboratory of sorts at the surgery, the main equipment being a rather ancient microscope. It would be adequate for my purposes, however; all I wanted was a quick glance to eliminate the possibility of intestinal worms. I wouldn't have expected to find any, as worms are generally a sign of bad husbandry and management. I wouldn't even have considered the possibility had Catamaran's timely bowel movement not taken place when it did. Using a corner of a plastic bag, I picked up a section of the steaming, pungent waste and wrapped it.

"Tell Mr Norris that I'll phone him this evening sometime. And tell him to keep a close eye on the horse."

I waited until Catamaran was safely back in his box and left. At the main gate, I told the old man that the horse was fine and drove on hoping that he was.

CHAPTER 4

I **had soup** and sandwiches at the pub across the road from the office and thought about Catamaran. Back at the surgery, I typed a covering letter for the blood samples – not mentioning the horse's name – and addressed them to the local Regional Veterinary Laboratory. Then I investigated the laboratory equipment. It was pretty basic, but I found enough for my needs – a bottle of saturated zinc sulfate solution and a McMaster slide; with the microscope, I had all I needed to do a worm-egg count.

I broke up the dung and removed some of the larger pieces of matter, including some short stalks of hay and two whole, undigested sunflower seeds; the rest I added to the zinc sulfate solution, swizzling it thoroughly around with the end of a ball-point until it became a suspension of separated solid-matter particles. Then I left this mixture aside to allow any worm-eggs present to float to the surface. I rinsed the McMaster slide, a special type of microscope slide which enabled one to count the number of worm-eggs in a measured quantity of faeces – I hadn't bothered to measure as I didn't expect to find any at all. Filling its grid-ruled chamber from fluid taken from the surface of the zinc sulfate/dung mixture, I placed the slide on the stage of the microscope and, one eye closed, peered down through the tube, gradually adjusting until the blurred circle of light and all it contained came into sharp focus. Nothing. As I expected. Just broken pieces of vegetable matter and tiny shreds of sloughed intestine lining. I moved the slide a little, bringing other areas into view. Nothing there either. More of the same. I moved it again and suddenly, to my utter astonishment, there was the unmistakable dark oval shape of a worm

34

egg. Amongst the jumbled debris of the remnants of grass stalks it stood out, a smooth latent menace trapped in the circle of light. I sat back with a whistle of surprise. Catamaran had bowel worms!

Roundworms parasitise almost all animals, each species of animal having its own species of roundworms. Though they vary in the species which they infest and in the organs they inhabit, there are some factors which are common to nearly all parasitic roundworms; these include their life cycles and the way in which they spread from host to host. Adult roundworms attached to, for example, the lining of the small intestine, lay numerous eggs and these find their way to the outside world in the animal's faeces. (In the case of worms which live in the lungs, the eggs are first coughed up with the copious amounts of phlegm and catarrh which the worms' presence in the airways causes, and then swallowed). Outside the body, they hatch and pass through a number of immature larval stages before becoming infective larvae; it is only when they reach this stage that they can grow to adulthood when eaten by the right animal species, thus completing their life cycle. The larvae are actively mobile and usually crawl away from the dung pat in which they hatch, often congregating at the tips of grass stalks to improve their chances of being picked up. And so they spread from one animal to another. Where animals are confined in fields or paddocks, the chances of infective-stage larvae being swallowed are very much enhanced.

For some reason, newly swallowed larvae don't go directly to the target organ. Most roundworms are parasites of the digestive tract so they find themselves 'at home' as it were, as soon as they are swallowed. Yet, before settling down, the larvae of most species head off on a tour of other body organs causing damage as they go, the severity of the damage depending on the numbers of larvae on the move at the time. In the case of horse-worms, the larvae tend to go to the great arteries of the abdominal cavity. They bury into the walls of these blood vessels causing a dangerous weakening and consequent bulging which, in medical terms, is called an aneurysm. If it ruptures, as it most likely will, sooner or later, the animal bleeds to death – in the case of major arteries, death would follow in a matter of minutes. I saw it happen once, but only once, and that was in a donkey.

Roundworms which live in the digestive tract can cause all degrees of damage depending on how many there are, the age of the animal (the young are much more susceptible), and other factors. The damage can range from none, to slight digestive problems, to greater digestive problems with consequent debilitation and unthriftiness, to a severe disruption of gut function leading to actual starvation, as food can be neither digested nor absorbed. In really severe cases, for example in heavily-infested puppies, worms can be so numerous that they block the bowel completely and, in such cases, some worms may actually be forced into the stomach and vomited up whole.

The presence of such potentially lethal parasites in Catamaran was inexcusable and, apart from the dangers from an aneurysm to himself, the thought of him spreading deadly larvae on to the very paddocks where, come springtime, foals would graze, was horrific.

Shaken by my startling discovery, I set about rerunning the test, this time measuring. I did the count several times to get a good average and, at the end, I knew that Catamaran had an egg count of 1,100 eggs per gramme of faeces, a pretty substantial burden.

Eileen arrived back from her lunch break and I almost asked about the parasite control regime at Bally Ard but decided against it. There was something amiss and, until I could figure out what exactly it was or who was responsible, the less said, the better. The whole thing was incomprehensible.

I was baffled. I couldn't believe that Norris, through ignorance or indifference could have let such a thing happen – he was one of the leading breeders in the country and, in a country renowned for its horses, that was quite an accolade. Then what about Steele? Surely as vet to Bally Ard Stud, parasite control would be one of his major concerns? And Steele was known amongst the profession as a man of the highest ability and integrity. Surely he would have operated a dosing routine using the most effective drugs available. I discounted the possibility of Norris's or Steele's culpability.

Perhaps the dosing was the responsibility of another member of the staff who, through laziness or wariness of Catamaran, only *pretended* to have done it; if that was the case, then that person was not Tom Kelly. Or maybe, at Bally Ard, a mutant strain of *Strongylus vulgaris* had evolved, a strain resistant to modern drugs? This seemed unlikely, though not impossible. Maybe Catamaran himself was the explanation? Maybe he had learned how to hold the dose at the back of his tongue and spit it out when no one was looking – most unlikely; or perhaps it made him sick and he'd vomit the dose before it had time to kill the worms – a bit more plausible but surely someone would have noticed? Horses rarely vomit. Or maybe Bally Ard had bought worm medicine which was defective in some way, like having the active ingredient left out? On balance, I thought that this was the best explanation I had come up with so far. A mistake at the manufacturers. It was also the most satisfactory from my point of view as it exonerated all the parties whom I had to deal with, a mass letting off the hook.

The discovery of the worm eggs had placed me in an invidious position and, as I negotiated the tricky mountain roads, on my afternoon rounds, I tried to work out what I ought to do. It posed an ethical dilemma to which there didn't seem to be a simple solution. The one thing I was *not* going to do was tell Norris that his prize animal had worms. He would be extremely angry – justifiably so. In the furore that was bound to follow, all concerned would be running for cover and looking for scapegoats and the chances were that P. R. Steele, not being present to defend himself, would end up with the short stick. I had no doubt that the large pharmaceutical firms would shaft him without the batting of a corporate eye. Eventually what it all came down to was a question of my own responsibilities: my primary allegiance was to my patient, Catamaran, but I could discharge that duty without much trouble – as soon as I finished my afternoon rounds I'd go to Bally Ard and get a good worm dose into him. But where my secondary duty lay was a toss up. My client, Norris? My employer, Steele? What about all the other horses that had been dosed with defective medicine – if that theory proved to be the correct one? After a brief tussle with my conscience, Steele won. What decided me was nothing more noble than pure self-interest; if I could be seen, in any way, not to have protected his best interests, then other practitioners might be that much less willing to entrust the running of their practices to me. And who could blame them? That made up my mind. There was nothing in any book of ethics which said a man had to commit business suicide. Steele would be the first to know on his return.

It was just after five when I headed back into the transverse folds of the mountainous spine that separated the coastal strip where I had just finished the afternoon rounds, from the plains around Knockmore. At the end of my first full day, I was quietly satisfied that Steele's practice was well organised and easily worked.

At the crests of the hills on the way to the summit, I began to pick up a weak signal on the radio telephone – Eileen trying to get me. I stopped twice to eliminate engine noise, but the great bulk of the mountain which reared gaunt, granite-strewn and sedge-brown between us, prevented any decent reception. When I descended into the shallow valleys I could hear nothing at all but, as I crested each successive ridge, her voice began to come in, plaintive and urgent, disturbing but, as yet, indecipherable. With a growing sense of unease I wondered why she was keeping up a continuous broadcast for me like the radio officer of a stricken vessel sending out a constant stream of Mayday, Mayday signals into the forlorn ether above a desolate and deserted ocean.

The higher I climbed, the stronger the signal became. It was still garbled, but once I thought I caught the word 'Norris' and suddenly my palms were sweating. Surely it couldn't be Catamaran! Not with an aneurysm! Not on my first day! Good Christ, no! I tried to acknowledge her but my transmitter was not as powerful as hers and I knew from her incessant calling that she hadn't registered my efforts. Replacing the handset, I concentrated on driving.

It wasn't until I breasted the last summit that I could hear her plainly. From that point, I could actually see Knockmore-on-Sea in the distance. Spread out on the green plain below me, the sun reflecting from its windows, it looked like a multigemmed pendant on a jeweller's tray, the silvered river its chain.

"Base to Mobile One, Base to Mobile One, are you receiving me? Over."

"I read you base. What's the problem? Over."

"Oh! Thank God! Where are you Frank? Over."

"On my way in. Just on top of the hill. What's the problem? Over."

"Go straight to Bally Ard. It's Catamaran. Mr Norris has been calling every couple of minutes for the last half hour. It sounds really bad. Over."

"What's wrong with Catamaran? Over."

"He wouldn't say over the phone but he's in a state. Over."

"Okay. Call him and tell him I'm on my way. And Eileen? If you can get any more information from him, let me know at once won't you? Over."

"I will. There's the phone now. It'll probably be him again. Over and out."

With thoughts of all kinds of catastrophes filling my head, especially ruptured aneurysms, I twisted my way down to the valley floor, careered through the town and out onto the road to the northwest which led to Bally Ard. Twenty minutes later, when I was still a couple of miles from Norris's place, I called base again.

"Eileen? Do you read me? Eileen? Eileen? Eileen?"

"Yes Frank. Loud and clear. Over."

"Anything?"

"Nothing. He just said to hurry. Over."

"Nearly there. Another couple of minutes. Over."

"Fine. I'll stay on here in the surgery for a while. In case you need anything. Over."

"Thanks. If you haven't heard from me by six-thirty, lock up. But thanks anyway. You're a star. Over and out."

"Good luck. Over and out."

CHAPTER 5

The gates stood wide open so I changed down into second and roared through, tyres spinning, almost knocking down Jack who stood immediately inside waving me urgently on. Broad-leafed rhododendron branches slapped along the sides of the jeep as I hugged the right-hand curve of the driveway, hurtling towards the house. I slid to a halt in a shower of gravel on the semi-circular parking space. Norris, who had obviously heard my approach, trotted bandily over to me and one look at his face was enough to confirm my worst fears. This was no storm in a teacup, no groundless panic by a hypochondriac owner which would disappear magically as soon as the vet arrived. Despair and anguish were etched on his face as if they were there to stay. Mentally preparing myself for a major catastrophe, I opened the door.

"It's Catamaran," he wailed and, before I could ask what was wrong, he blurted out: "He's dead!"

I closed my eyes and screwed my face up as if I was about to be hit. Catamaran dead! The awful reality began to seep into my shocked senses and with it, the worry. Was it an aneurysm? Or had I missed something obvious this morning? Was it my fault? Even partially? If it was an aneurysm, then how could I explain it without getting Steele into trouble? Automatically I was battening down the hatches, going into damage limitation mode.

"When?" I asked. It came out as a squeak.

"He was dead when I found him. I don't know when."

At least ('Oh thank you, God, thank you!') I couldn't be reproached for not being available when I was needed. The horse hadn't died for want of medical attention. And now I

40

wouldn't have to do anything brilliant either. An ignoble reaction, regrettably true. Euphemistically it could be called 'pragmatic'.

"What happened?" I asked with a bit more composure.

"It's a mystery!" Blank-eyed, Norris shook his head. "How could he have got out?! The yard gate is still locked! I've got the only key!"

"Out! You mean he was *out*!" I asked incredulously, the voice a squeak again. "Outside his *box*?!"

"Outside his box. Outside the yard. Out running loose in the fields."

"But... but *how*?!! Who let him out? Somebody must have!"

"I tell you, I can't understand it!" He shook his head again.

"Mr Norris. How exactly did he die? Tell me what happened. Where did you find him?"

"In the old quarry pit. He must have fallen into it. How am I going to tell the other members of the syndicate?"

While Norris was worrying about that, another flood of selfish relief coursed through me. Hallelujah! It was an accident! An Act of God! I became even more composed.

"Perhaps we ought to go and have a look at him," I suggested, but Norris seemed too dazed to reply. "Is it far away?" I waited for him to answer but he remained lost in thought. "Mr Norris?" I prodded.

"What?" He came back to the present.

"This quarry. Is it far from here?"

"No. About half a mile down the farm road." He pointed a distracted hand in the general direction of the yard.

"We'd best take the Land Rover then. Sit in." He walked round to the passenger door like a zombie, climbed up onto the seat and with a great sigh, pulled the door shut. Obviously, he was dreading the forthcoming ordeal.

On the bumpy drive along the rutted track, some more details emerged. He had been out walking the farm, shooting rabbits. He had been walking for half an hour, shot two rabbits in the lower fields, and, on the way back to the house, Patch, his terrier who 'had a great nose', had gone into the thicket which had grown up around the disused limestone pit, and had started to bark furiously, refusing to respond to

Norris's summoning whistles. It was when he had gone into the thicket to get Patch that he had found Catamaran, lying dead at the foot of the old quarry face.

"It was *awful*! Horrible!" He shuddered all over. "I grabbed the dog and ran as quickly as I could to phone for you. Horrible," he repeated and shuddered again.

I didn't have the heart to ask him what he had expected me to do for a dead horse. I put it down to human conditioning; doctors are always called in when there's a sudden death and his reaction to finding an animal corpse had been to call an animal doctor, me.

"Stop here." He touched my elbow. "It's as near as we'll get."

I pulled up by the gate. Across at the other side of some fields, some five hundred yards away, there was a small spinney; I presumed from the fact that it grew against a steep escarpment, that this was where the accident had happened. Some of the quicker growing trees had almost reached the height of the cliff-face which I could just see, grey, bare and scrub-topped behind them.

We trudged across the field in silence, Norris tending to lag back. At the line of the first brushwood, he stopped. "Do you need me in there?"

"No. There's nothing you can do. There's nothing anyone can do."

"Tchah!" he said, mostly to himself, "it's got to be faced. Come on."

"Are you sure? Maybe it would be better…"

"No. No. Come on," and, with new resolution, he brushed past me and led the way.

We pushed through clinging undergrowth, twisting and turning along some invisible path which didn't seem any different to me than any other bush-clogged route he might have chosen. Suddenly, at the edge of a small clearing, he stopped and, averting his head, pointed straight ahead. "There." At the foot of a cliff about fifty feet high, in a pool of muddy water, lay Catamaran.

The first time I saw his chest rise, I thought my eyes were playing tricks on me. Then it happened again and I knew that

42

they weren't. He was *breathing*! An icy hand clutched my heart.

"Jesus!" I breathed. "He's alive! That animal is *alive*! I turned to Norris and glared at him accusingly, covering my own panic at being suddenly thrust back into a position of carrying full responsibility. My mental preparedness to tackle the crisis had ebbed totally as soon as I had learned that Catamaran was dead and now this had sprung upon me with a suddenness that reduced me to the point of shock.

"Wha...?!!!" was all Norris said and he was now standing rigid, his dazed gaze following the slow, shallow rhythm of the stallion's chest as it rose in shuddering jerks and collapsed again.

"Christ!" I muttered savagely and pushed roughly past him.

This put me in a right fix. Having been told that the horse was dead, I hadn't bothered to bring any equipment or medicines with me; everything I might need was locked in the back of my Land Rover a coppice and two wide fields away – ten to fifteen minutes if I ran there and back – and frankly it didn't look from what I could see at a glance, that Catamaran had that much time left.

I dropped to my knees by his head, the only part of him clear of the muddy water. His eye was flickering rapidly, almost too quickly to see, the eye-ball moving up and down in its socket. On the bare ground, the tongue, unnaturally pale, rested limply, covered in grit. His breaths were taken in slowly, reaching a sudden stop so that each one sounded like his last, and then let out again with a faint snort and flapping of the nostril fold. Tenderly I rolled back the black velvet lip. It had lost most of its mobility and the gum beneath was deathly pale. I pressed my index finger down hard on it and held it for a moment; when I took it away, the resulting white round area barely contrasted with the cold paleness of the gum and it took a long time for it to get its faint colour back again. Catamaran was in deep shock, the blood diverted from the peripheral blood vessels to supply maximum oxygen and nutrients to the vital organs which would now be struggling to keep the last spark of life fanned just a little longer. If he was going to be treated, an immediate essential was massive volumes of intravenous fluids, preferably warmed to body heat beforehand.

Fluids and corticosteroids. That was when I noticed the blood in the water, a cloud darker than the brown muddiness of the pool; even as I looked, it was growing and spreading sluggishly; it had the ominous look of catastrophe. I shook my head slowly and sighed.

Gingerly, I reached into the murky water and felt along the uppermost forelimb from elbow to hoof. I found nothing amiss and I reached deeper to repeat the process with the other forelimb. I felt around the elbow, then down the forearm to the knee. Nothing wrong there. I moved my hand down over the knee, down along the slim cannon bone; half way along, my fingers sank into pulped flesh and felt the warm spurt of blood at the same time as they encountered the jagged spike of protruding bone. Compound fracture. The shattered bone, having knifed through the skin was now irrevocably infected and even with the most modern advances in equine orthopaedics, a successful outcome was a remote hope. I noticed another dark cloud behind the first and then a third at the horse's rear. The second cloud marked an almost identical fracture, this time in the left hind leg, but it was the third which proved the real last straw. I waded into the bloody, muddy pool and began a careful exploration. Inside a few seconds, my probing hand met with a jagged end of broken metal protruding from between the horse's buttocks. I eased it out as gently and delicately as I could but it took a long time in coming. It was some four inches long, three wide and about a quarter thick. The blood it must have had on it washed off as I raised it through the water but some flakes of yellow paint still clung to it. The broken edge showed clean grey metal, freshly broken. I guessed it had come from an old dumper that had been abandoned years ago and stood beside me half in the pool – there was a similar broken edge on a flange of its front bucket. But what made that bit of metal so important was the *position* in which it had lodged. It had been embedded to a depth of at least two inches in Catamaran's body and it had entered transversely between his buttocks. That meant that the anatomical structures of that area had been severed across. And they included the root of the penis.

I straightened slowly and turned to face Norris. The sludge on the bottom of the pool sucked weakly at my boots, nearly toppling me, and I reached out a quick hand to steady myself against the haunch of the dying horse. In the dirty water, his blood swirled and coiled into the sluggish eddies of my movements, clouding into indistinguishability; dust to dust, ashes to ashes, blood to mud...

Norris was slumped, dazed against a rock. I waded out of the pool and crossed to him. "There's no chance," I said quietly. "I'm going to have to put him down. He's got two broken legs – both compound fractures – and," I held up the metal flange, "this was stuck in him. It's cut through his penis. Even if he lived he could never breed again. I'm afraid it's useless. I'm sorry."

He looked up at me in horror, frantically shaking his head in wordless protest. I waited for him to say something and, when he didn't, I said: "I'll just go and get something to put him out of his misery. You ought to come with me." As I made to pass him, he caught me by the sleeve.

"Please!" he implored. "Can't you do something?! You can't just kill him like that! Can't you keep him alive for twenty four hours? I'll have the best teams from the universities, from Kentucky, from Newmarket, here by the morning! All you've got to do is to keep him alive until they get here! Please!" His voice was shrill with frantic desperation.

"I'm sorry Mr Norris. Believe me, he's beyond help."

"Think of the loss to the bloodstock lines of the world!"

"I've considered everything. The fact remains that he can't be saved. Now, I'm going to the Land Rover to get something for him and I strongly advise you to come with me."

Norris suddenly gave in, all resistance flowing out of him. He released my sleeve and his hand dropped to his side. "You're right of course," he sighed. "But, if it's got to be done, please do it at once. I can't bear it any longer."

"As soon as I get the stuff from the Land Rover."

"Can't you use the gun?"

"What gun? I don't have a gun."

"My gun. There." I looked. Against a rock, a double-barrelled shotgun was propped; there were two dead rabbits lying beside it. "I left it when I had to carry Patch to the house. He was hysterical."

"That'll do," I said, picking up the gun and breaking it open. Both barrels were loaded. "Would you prefer to leave? I'll join you in a moment."

"No, I think I ought to wait."

"Whatever you say."

I settled myself on the mud-splashed ground a short distance from the horse's head, lying to get the best line on his forehead. Then, taking careful aim on the intersection of imaginary lines drawn between the inner corner of each eye and the opposite ear, I steadied myself, took a deep breath, held it, and took up the pressure on the first trigger. I squeezed once and, immediately after, pulled the second.

Catamaran gave one massive, convulsive shudder and then slowly relaxed. A brief trickle of thick red-black blood ran from the smoking hole in his forehead, pumped by the last beat of his great heart. His eye closed once, then slowly re-opened and rotated upwards to focus onto infinity in the eternal, sightless stare of death.

Silence returned slowly to the clearing. The sound of the shots reverberated for a long time, bouncing from the grey wall of rock to the green wall of vegetation, back and forth until it worked its way up and escaped into the air above. The shrill alarm cries of the birds lessened and died and soon, the only sound in the clearing was the rustle of the leaves at the tops of those trees high enough to catch the freshening evening breeze.

I arose slowly from the ground and, propping the gun back against the rock, crossed to where Norris stood, immobile as Lot's wife. No words came to me as, side by side, we stood, studies in stone, stunned, staring at the worthless carcase of the once-great horse. I waited for him to decide when it was time to go but, after some minutes I touched his arm. "I think we ought to go now," I mumbled. I went and got the gun and the two rabbits. "Ready?" I intruded on his thoughts.

There was a huge sigh before he tore his mesmerised eyes away from the horse corpse. "Yes. I suppose so."

"I've got the gun and the rabbits."

"You can throw the rabbits into the bushes," he said hollowly.

"It's no trouble. As you've brought them this far, I can carry them..."

46

"No. I don't use them. I try to keep the farm free of rabbits. Burrows are dangerous for horse's legs. I had to put a foal down once – a Seliari foal. Throw them away." He turned, shuffling off.

I swung the rabbits a few times and let them go, watching them arc up and into the dense thicket before I followed his dejected figure along the same invisible path. As I pushed along behind him, I reckoned that either he was a brilliant hunter or his policy of keeping the farm rabbit-free was ineffective. Two rabbits in thirty minutes wasn't bad going in any man's language. Half way across the field, Norris broke the silence.

"But how could he have got out?! That's what I can't fathom!"

"Have you asked Hynes?" I asked. Out of the blue, I had a sudden awful thought: Had we closed the box properly after we had finished with Catamaran in the morning? Then I knew that we had, and I relaxed. Norris had lapsed back into silence.

"Eh... Hynes?" he asked at last.

"The groom. Hynes. At least the stand-in groom."

More silence. "No actually, I didn't. I had Jack ring the yard when I got back to tell Hynes to go; so I didn't see Hynes at all."

"Oh I see!" I nodded vigorously for a while by way of keeping the conversation going, but the silence resumed.

Most of the journey back to the house passed in the same silence, but as we approached the last turn before the stable-yard, he turned to me. "Who told you about Hynes?"

"Hynes? Nobody. I met him this morning when I called to the yard." When he fell silent again, I added: "Didn't he tell you I'd called? I did ask him to."

"No. I didn't know you'd been."

"Of course, you didn't see Hynes, did you? How is Kelly's mother, by the way? Any news of her?"

"No. Why did you call?"

"Well... Catamaran is, was, a great responsibility and I suppose I may have been over anxious... because of the nose wound and the fact that you had noticed him shivering. Anyway, I was anxious to make sure that nothing happened to him while he was under my care," I finished with a mirthless snort.

"Did you find anything wrong with him? With Catamaran?"

"Nothing specific. He didn't seem in the best of form, but then, how could I judge his behaviour? Perhaps he was perfectly normal; I'd only seen him on that one occasion, last Saturday, so I wasn't really in a position to judge. And Hynes didn't know much more. It was just that... he didn't have the same fire in him as I'd seen on Saturday, the same spirit. So I got a bit worried. Naturally."

"Naturally."

"But apart from that, he checked out O.K. I was going to call you this evening. I told Hynes to tell you. Do you want to stop to take a look at the yard?" I asked as we were passing the gate.

"No. We'd best press on to the house. I need a drink. Jack never mentioned your visit to me either."

"I didn't leave a message with Jack."

"Still. It's strange nobody thought to tell me."

I was saved from having to answer by our arrival outside the front door.

CHAPTER 6

Norris didn't need a drink, singular; he needed several and he attacked the Jameson Crested Ten as if there was a distinct possibility that by finishing it off, he might be able to bring his beloved horse back to life, to un-shoot him, to un-break his legs, to break his fall. He was on his fifth double while I nursed my second, well watered with Canada Dry. I hadn't even wanted the first. He drained his glass at a gulp and looked like he was heading for the bottle again.

"Do you not think you ought to call the police?" I asked. That stopped him.

"The *police*?" There wasn't a trace of a slur in his voice; either he had a mighty tolerance for alcohol or incredibly poor absorption. "The police?" he repeated.

I spread my hands. "They'll have to be called." Obviously the idea had not occurred to him.

"For what?" His tone was indignant, as if I had accused him of dropping the horse over the cliff himself.

"To find out exactly how Catamaran managed to get out of his box and out of the yard." Surely he couldn't have thought that it was all over bar the crying; there was all kinds of hassle ahead: pathologist's examination and reports, police investigation, insurance company enquiries, painful meetings of the syndicate... He was coming to terms with the tragedy very slowly.

"Do you know, I hadn't even thought that far," he said quietly after a long pause. "I'm afraid my thoughts are totally scrambled at the moment. I don't know what to do. You're right of course. I'll do it right away."

He went off, freshened glass of Jameson in hand, through a high door to the left of the elegant Adams-style fireplace; he left the door ajar and I could hear him beginning his calls. I didn't envy him. I considered what *I* should do. I could just go home, now that my part in the grim drama was over, but I didn't feel I ought to. Nor, to be honest, did I want to. It was all too momentous to just walk away from – I wouldn't be able to concentrate on much else. On the other hand, there didn't seem to be a lot that I could do and all I had managed to think of by the time Norris came back, was to contact the pathologist who acted for Norris's Insurance Company.

"What company was Catamaran insured with?"

"Town and Country. Why?"

"They'll have to know as soon as possible."

"They'll hardly be open now," he said, looking at his watch.

"No, I don't suppose they will. Do you know who their pathologist is?"

"No. I'm afraid I don't. Do you think that he could contact them? If we could contact him, that is."

"Probably. But also, I ought to try to find out who it is to give him fair warning to get here as quickly as he can. The sooner after death that the autopsy is carried out, the better."

"Will an autopsy be necessary? Surely the cause of death is as plain as can be?"

"Granted. But not the reasons why Catamaran should break out and run amok and fall over that ledge."

"Are you suggesting foul play? Ten men wouldn't have been able to throw the horse over that cliff! He'd have killed them!"

"Not if he was doped to the eyeballs."

"But how could they have got in? The whole farm is sealed off like a security prison! And the yard gate is locked with every kind of locking device. I'm the only one who can open it. Apart, that is, from Tom Kelly and he's a hundred and fifty miles away in Cork."

"It wouldn't necessarily have to be a gang of men. A horse could be given something to drive him mad."

"Like what?"

"Well," I shrugged, struggling to come up with a name. "Some kind of hallucinogen... like LSD for instance. I'm not sure."

"LSD?" Norris looked at me as if I was raving. "*LSD*?" he

50

repeated. "Why should anyone give a horse something to drive him mad?"

He had me there. There wasn't a single thing that I could think of, that a crazed horse could be useful for. This one had ended up getting killed. But that could hardly have been the motive either. If someone had wanted to kill the horse, a far simpler – and surer – way would have been to shoot him. His loose box was an easy rifle shot from the yard gate. A fleeting thought of Norris organising a tortuous insurance rip-off was banished by his next words.

"I don't know how I'm going to tell the syndicate members. We're going to lose a fortune! He was insured for thirty-five million, but after the prices his foals fetched at the sales, he was revalued at nearer to fifty. The policy falls due for renewal at the end of this month and we were to up the cover then. Fifteen million gone down the drain! By a couple of weeks!"

As far as I was concerned, if there had been foul play, then Norris had not been involved. Nobody's timing could be *that* bad.

"I think I may be able to find out who the pathologist for Town and Country is. Professor Wall from the Veterinary College would know. If I can find his home number, he ought to be able to tell us."

In fact it turned out to be the professor himself. I ought to have guessed as much. There was no point in being head of Department and letting others get the plum consultancies. I gave him the facts as I knew them and he undertook to inform the Insurance Company. He asked me to ensure that the horse was locked away for the night and arranged to meet me at Bally Ard the following morning at 7.30. He was going to have an early start; Dublin was a good four hour's drive away.

We waited for the police. Norris glanced towards the bottle once or twice, but made no move to pour himself another. He was impatient, drumming his fingers on the cracked leather of his deep armchair. "I think I'll ring Tom," he said suddenly, springing up.

I wandered round the room looking at the pictures of Catamaran which smothered every available surface; mantelpiece, piano, sideboards and tables were covered in them; even a grey storage heater had been pressed into service during its summer redundancy, as a stand for two small silver-framed photographs. On the walls were mainly paintings, drawings and sketches, but there were a few photographs, nearly all of his foalhood, the days before the latter-day Stubbses and Munningses were queuing up to paint him; most of the photographs included a pleasant, plump, middle aged woman, presumably the late Mrs Norris. The whole house was a gallery, a shrine to the great horse. The hall, I had seen on my way through, had been similarly adorned.

Norris had left the door to the study ajar again and I could overhear his conversation with the groom. First he asked about the health of the mother and by the way he kept saying 'Good, good, good', I gathered that he was getting a favourable, if rather long-winded report of the old lady's progress.

"Well that's great news, Tom. Please convey my best wishes to her, and wish her a speedy recovery." He paused. "Tom?" He paused again. "I'm sorry to say that the news from here is not so good. Catamaran had an accident this afternoon. ...... Yes, I'm afraid it was – very bad...... He's dead, Tom." From a whole room away, I could hear the groom's incredulous squeak. "We had to put him down."

As the conversation went on, I crossed the groom off the list as a suspect, in the case of the autopsy showing that foul play had been done. If Kelly was in Cork, then he couldn't have been in the extreme west of Galway two hours previously, and if he *wasn't* in Cork now, it meant that the phonecall was a sham, a set-up between him and Norris, which meant that Norris had to be involved too, and that theory foundered again on the reef of the timing factor. Presumably, if the accident had been arranged, it could just as easily have been arranged in a couple of weeks time, when the rewards would have been that much greater. As Norris came back into the room, I decided I was jumping the gun, letting my imagination run away with me. There was nothing to suggest anything other than an accident and, until the police or the pathologist said otherwise, my flights of fancy were premature. No doubt there was a perfectly logical explanation as to how and why Catamaran got out. I just couldn't see it. I couldn't even guess at it.

52

"Tom is totally shocked," Norris said, coming back in.

"I can imagine. I'm not feeling too hot myself and I hardly knew the animal."

"He loved that horse like a brother. And Catamaran loved him. He wasn't the easiest horse in the world to handle but, in Tom's hands he was like a kitten. Do you know that if Tom was out in the yard doing something, anything, Catamaran wouldn't take his head in? He'd watch him wherever he went and, unless Tom kept talking to him, he'd whinny and neigh until he did. Sometimes, I almost thought that they could understand one another. Poor Tom." Norris looked vacantly out the window, lost in memories. "Poor Catamaran." And he reached again for the bottle.

CHAPTER 7

When the police arrived, Norris was in the study phoning his syndicate colleagues. I heard the car pull up and looked out the window; there were three of them but only one in uniform and he stood by the driver's door. I knocked on the study door – this time, Norris had closed it – and poked my head round.

"The police," I mouthed, pointing over my shoulder.

He covered the mouthpiece with his hand. "I'll be there in a moment. Can you look after them please."

Norris's housekeeper showed them in and announced Inspector Potter who immediately discharged the business of perfunctory introductions. "Detective Sergeant O'Hanlon, Garda Fitzpatrick. And you sir, I take it, are Mr Samson."

"That's right." No handshake. "Mr Norris is on the phone. He shouldn't be much longer."

"Can you tell us what happened?"

I told him as much as I could and he listened, head bowed, nodding from time to time. O'Hanlon wrote a few notes in a wire-backed notebook and interrupted once or twice. Fitzpatrick stood by the door as if he expected me at any moment, to make a sudden break for it.

"Have you looked in the yard?" Potter asked when I finished, looking up for the first time.

"No. I presume Mr Norris thought it better to wait for you."

He nodded his agreement. "Who's with the horse now?"

"Nobody."

This didn't go down well. "Well then, I think we ought to go there at once. He shouldn't have been left unattended." Seeing my frown of puzzlement, he went on: "You see, our job is to investigate the circumstances, to see if there's been any,

54

what shall I say, hanky-panky?" I nodded and he resumed: "So the earlier we get to the scene of an accident, the better the chances that we will be accurate in our reconstruction of the events which led to it. Also, if there has been any funny business – and I'm not saying for a moment, mind you, that there has, but that's what we're here to find out – then the culprit or culprits might be only too delighted with a few moment's peace to cover their tracks. Maybe Mr Norris disturbed them when he went to get his dog. Mick, you come with us," he turned to his men, "and Fitz., you wait for Mr Norris and bring him down in the squad car when he finishes his phonecall. It's out the road there, isn't it?" He turned back to me, pointing vaguely over his shoulder.

"Yes. About half a mile. You'll see my Land Rover," I said to the uniformed man.

"I expect Mr Norris will know where to stop anyway." Potter said.

He'd also have known which road to take, I thought, narked, but said nothing. Pompous, long-winded git.

O'Hanlon got off at the yard 'to walk around outside a bit'. We drove on.

"You know," I said, "the horse was alone for a good hour after the accident happened while Norris was calling me, and it's another hour since I shot him and he's been alone all that time too." We were bumping along the rough track.

"We can but do our best," was the only reply he made.

On our way through the fields, Potter was on full alert, like a good pointer, straining to detect anything strange. He stopped a few times and listened intently, his head cocked to one side to decrease the sound of the breeze which had become a small wind with the onset of late evening; he peered out towards the west where Bally Ard ran into the sea, now gilding lustrously as the sun approached it – I looked too, half expecting to see furtive figures sneaking about in the hedge-rimmed fields, but I saw nothing untoward. Neither, it seemed, did the pointer.

"A fine farm this," he said at last, "as fine as there is in the county. That cliff over there," – he pointed to a high escarpment which ran eastwards at right angles from the coast and some four hundred yards behind the smaller outcrop of rock which had been quarried away to form the fatal pit – "is the northern boundary, and over there to your left you can see the river – that's the southern boundary. It's wide and it's deep and there are no bridges. It's also the *eastern* boundary because it flows over the cliff in a big waterfall, runs south for half a mile or so, and then turns sharp west and straight out to the sea. So Bally Ard is everything between the cliff, the waterfall, the river and the sea. There'll never be a boundary dispute or a case of trespassing animals on this farm." We continued towards the coppice. "And it would be a damn hard place for anyone to get into or out of without using the front gate. The only gate." His lecture on the local geography wasn't as pointless as it had at first seemed. "And the whole farm," he waxed agricultural again, "slopes south to the river which gives it perfect drainage, not to mention constant exposure to the sun." We walked on a while, Potter resuming his alert silence. As we gained the foot of the gentle slope on which the thicket grew, he stopped suddenly. "They say that the grass grows in those fields along by the cliff right up to January; the cliff shelters it from the north wind and the sun reaches it most days."

As soon as we entered the wood however, his silence took on a different quality and I could tell that he was concentrating on the job, not dreaming of fine farms or southern exposures. I went in front, trying to find the vague path which Norris had led me along, but more than once we had to backtrack when faced with a hostile wall of blackthorn or briar. All the while, Potter maintained a concentrated silence, not commenting when I mumbled my apologies for having taken a wrong course, seemingly not even noticing.

The clearing was in deep shade when we finally reached it, the setting sun obscured by the dense foliage; it would, however, be still bright on top – the dying rays gave the cliff-face from tree-height up, a rosy tinge. A few late scavenging gulls from the shore flew off at our approach. With a silent reverence more befitting a human wake, we crossed to where Catamaran lay.

"Look carefully," Potter said to me in a near whisper, "do you see anything different to when you left? Has anything changed – anything at all? Take your time."

"No," I replied, after considering everything I could think of. "It's exactly as it was – as far as I can make out."

"You're sure?"

"As sure as I can be."

"Good." He made a short emphatic nod, more a bob of the head. "Now, tell me again exactly what happened."

I went through the whole story once more, starting at the point when I discovered that the horse was still alive. I described his injuries, my reactions, Norris's reactions, what I did, Norris initial arguments against my intended destruction of Catamaran and the actual shooting. When I showed him the metal flange, he picked it up and asked me if I wouldn't mind, seeing as I had wellingtons on and he hadn't, wading out to the dumper to see if it fitted. It did and he stored it away in a plastic bag. By the time my story came to its end, Potter was on his hunkers kneading the animal's stiffened ear. He looked up at me: "I've been living within ten miles of Bally Ard for years, and I've never seen Catamaran in the flesh before." He transferred his rubbing to the horse's cheek. "And this is a hell of a way to meet the poor bastard. He was some animal, that's for sure." He gave the cheek one last pat, sighed and straightened up.

Facing the cliff, he backed a dozen steps, looking up, his eyes travelling back and fro along the rim of the quarry, slowly, methodically. "It certainly seems that he fell from up there alright. Let's go up and take a look before it gets too dark to see anything."

We pushed straight through the thicket where it grew against the wall of rock, brushing and snagging our way until we came to a scalable slope and, after a short climb, came out onto the rim; like the floor below, it was covered in wild scrub, though it wasn't as dense and it didn't have any tall trees. We made our way cautiously along, every so often peering over the edge to find the spot directly above where Catamaran lay; once we'd found it, we moved away from the treacherous rim and began a slow search. There was ample evidence of the horse's recent passage – broken twigs on the ground, long, coarse, black tail hairs snagged on branches here and there and even a smudged hoof-print in one soft spot. We followed the trail to the beginning of the scrub where it became open field and at that point, lost it. In the next fifteen minutes, we each covered an area of about a hundred square yards to either side of where Catamaran had entered the scrub, walking slowly around, heads bent.

"Found anything?" Potter came up behind me.

"No. Nothing."

"Me neither. I don't think there's any point in going on. It's getting darkish and we're not having much success. Maybe the last of the Mohicans would be able to read all this like a book, but..." He made a helpless gesture. "Anyway, I'd say we've got enough to establish that he went through the bushes at this point and on and over, so we'd better go and see how things are at the yard. You go and get your Land Rover. I'll walk across the fields in case there's anything obvious between here and there. If you meet Mr Norris on the way, tell him to go back to the yard, that I'll meet him there. I should be there before you."

He was. When I drove up to the gate, Norris was just in the process of unlocking it. O'Hanlon was saying: "So the tracks outside suggest that he actually *jumped* the wall. The ground is all gouged up where he landed and there's a couple of hoof-marks heading off roughly in the direction of the quarry. But the wall is about eleven feet high! So I don't know. No horse could jump that high, especially a flat racer." He turned questioningly towards Norris as he spoke.

"If that's what happened, then I think I know how it could have been done. The dungstead. That comes to within a couple of feet of the top of the wall. We usually get a lorry in to clear it away, but this year, I was letting it collect. A friend of mine was thinking of going into mushrooms and he wanted horse manure as compost. There's no other way that he could have got over that wall – not that I can think of anyway."

At the sound of Norris's voice, barking came from a horse-box which was parked by the gate.

"Oh, poor Patch!" Norris exclaimed. "I forgot all about you!" He turned to Potter. "It was the first place I came across on my way to the phone. There's a phone in the yard but I didn't have the keys with me, so I had to go on to the house. I put the dog into that box to stop him from going back down again." He swung the gate open and stood aside to let us through but as I was about to bring up the rear he put a hand on my arm: "Would you mind letting the dog out. But please... hold on to him. I don't want him running back off down to the quarry."

"Sure," I said to their retreating backs as they filed through the open half of the gate.

"Attaboy Patch, good doggy," I eased the door open a tad. A flat snout pushed itself into the crack as I opened a bit wider, enough to admit my hand. "Good dog, Patch. Easy on Patch." I wouldn't normally shove a groping hand into a dark space containing a dog to which I had not been introduced, but I trusted Norris and I assumed he would have told me if Patch was a biter. There was a brief, cold, wet, investigation of my hand, then the snout returned to the crack of the open door. More confidently, I reached down along the back of his neck and hooked my finger under the collar. Then I opened the door enough to let him through. Patch was the animal that had given Steele the big welcome on Saturday, a strange-looking mongrel – flat snout, long legs, a coarse off-white coat with brownish patches which looked as though they'd wash off; he came to an abrupt end in a short fluffy tail. All in all a strange figure of a dog but he didn't seem in the least bit perturbed that he'd never laid a bulging eye on his liberator before and welcomed me like a brother. He stood reasonably quietly, short fluffy tail wagging furiously at one end, short pink tongue lolling happily at the other, seemingly none the worse psychologically for his recent gruesome discovery. I passed some orange baling twine under his collar and led him into the yard.

The space between the gate pillars was occupied, almost for its whole width, by a trough, some fifteen feet across. At one side there was a narrow concrete walkway to allow for pedestrian traffic because, during the stud season, with the constant traffic of horse boxes going in and out, the trough would be filled with strong disinfectant. Now there was only a couple of inches of sludge in the bottom but it was still too deep to walk in. As I led Patch by his makeshift lead across the catwalk, I studied the trough as I had noticed Potter doing. The sludge was unmarked, no hoof-prints; to my mind that proved that

Catamaran had not come out through the gate – he couldn't have jumped it without leaving clear landing marks on the hard road and he couldn't have walked along the narrow concrete walkway. I presumed that Potter had reached the same conclusion as the group had by now gathered in front of the back wall of the yard, the trough obviously dismissed. O'Hanlon was standing on top of the dungstead, a nine-foot high heap of dry horse manure. All I could see of him was the back of his ample trousers as he leaned out over the wall. The others stood silently looking up at him, awaiting his verdict. Floodlights had been switched on to augment the waning daylight.

"The tracks are right beneath here alright," he said straightening up and dousing his powerful flashlight. "That's how he did it." He came crabwise down the manure heap, being careful not to stand in any of the places where the hard crust had been broken through, punctured by the sharp hooves of half a ton of horse.

"It *had* to be that way," said Norris, reaching towards me for the baling twine lead. Patch went on wagging his tongue, unperturbed by all the activity.

"So far, so good." Potter nodded. "Now let's see how he managed to get out of his stable in the first place," and he headed off.

"This way, Inspector," Norris called after him, correcting his course, and we all trooped off across the yard like a package tour on a guided trip round a museum.

There were black mane hairs snagged on a splinter of timber in the top of the door frame and, inside, the bedding straw had been scooted back from the door so that it was piled up in the middle of the box. As the door was still closed, there was only one inference to be drawn – Catamaran had lunged his forelegs onto the half-door and then pushed so hard with his hind legs that he had forced his bulk through an opening which seemed too narrow to accommodate it. Everyone agreed with that. It was the only thing that made sense.

"But why?" asked Norris of nobody in particular. "Why would he do a strange thing like that? Something must have set him off. And to jump that wall! He must have been... crazy or... Do you know of any reason why a horse would suddenly go mad and do the most odd things?" He turned to me.

"Well, apart from rabies or some other form of encephalitis, no; I can't say that I do. Not at the moment anyway." I didn't mention LSD again.

"But there isn't any rabies in Ireland, is there?" Potter asked.

"No. I wasn't suggesting that Catamaran had rabies. I was just generalising."

"Oh..." He turned his attention back to the locked door. Suddenly there was a deep growl from the dog and the hair along his back erected. Ears pricked, he strained at the baling twine, leaning towards the door.

"Sit Patch! Sit!" Norris spoke admonishingly and yanked at the leash. Patch hunkered down briefly but didn't lose his alert expression. In a few seconds, he was up again, growling threateningly and straining towards the door. "Sit! I said sit! What the blazes is wrong with you?" This time the dog paid no heed and began to bark excitedly as he almost pulled Norris to the door where he began to whine and scratch at the timber. Then we all heard what Patch had obviously heard, a faint rustle in the straw coming from inside the box. At this, the dog began to scratch furiously, scraping white gouges in the maroon paintwork. His barks became excited yelps.

"What was that noise?" Potter asked, his head cocked to one side in case it came again. "Shhh!"

O'Hanlon, who was nearest the door and who had the torch, shone it into the box and leaned in to follow its probing beam. "It's a bloody great rat!" he announced a moment later, turning to us, "as big as a rabbit, he is! Jaysus, Inspector but he's the size of a small rabbit!"

Norris swore a sudden oath, then buried his crumpling face in his hand. "Oh no!" he moaned, "no, no, no!" For him it seemed to be the last straw though I didn't quite understand why. He shook his head slowly from side to side in an extremis of private grief and didn't seem to notice when O'Hanlon took the dog's lead from him, swiftly pulled the twine from the collar and lifted Patch in over the half door. A minute of furious scrabbling and barking ended in ten seconds of shrill screams, then silence. O'Hanlon, who had been shouting encouragement

61

during the brief hunt was now offering Patch congratulations over the door. Potter and the uniformed Garda were exchanging knowing words and nods and Norris was running his fingers through his thick white hair, his eyes screwed tightly closed, his mouth a slash of grief and disbelief.

The door was opened and Patch emerged, proud in his victory, his limp trophy and much straw hanging from his mouth. "Drop it, Patch! Drop it!" Norris commanded and when the dog complied, he repeated the oath and kicked the limp brown body along the yard, stooping to catch Patch's collar to prevent him from continuing his sport.

Nobody said anything for a while until at last, Potter broke the silence. "Well I think that that just about covers everything, Mr Norris. It seems to be a straightforward case of really bad luck and I'm very sorry about it. A tragedy. A real tragedy." O'Hanlon and Fitzpatrick nodded their agreement. "We won't need to detain you any longer. I'll prepare a report for the insurance company tomorrow morning and, if you'd be kind enough to arrange for me to have a copy of the pathologist's report, I'd appreciate it." He nodded to his men and they left.

Earlier, Norris had phoned a neighbour who had promised to gather enough help to manhandle Catamaran through the thicket and have him brought by tractor to the yard. Professor Wall had been insistent that he be kept under lock until he arrived next morning. While we waited in the house for the help to arrive, I asked Norris about the significance of the rat in the loose box.

"Didn't you know?" he replied. "It's a well-known fact that Catamaran had a phobia about rats."

"No, actually, I didn't know," I said, feeling as if in some way it was an admission of professional incompetence.

"Oh yes; he hated them! Feared them! It started when he was just a foal, just after we weaned him. One day, he put his head into his feed bucket and there was a rat in it. The rat clung onto his nose and climbed up along his face and between his ears and down along his back. I was in the yard when I heard his screams and I actually saw the rat on his face, like a brown, furry, moving growth, scurrying up along his nose. He nearly came through the door on that occasion too; we barely held him until Peter Steele got here. He had to keep him sedated for three days. Catamaran never put his nose into a bucket after that; we had to get a wide bakers' tray for him. That's why we assume that the rat was in the feed bucket. He stopped, remembering, then shook his head and went on. "Actually, we could have lost the Derby all because of a rat. A certain well-known gentleman, actually a notorious racecourse bum, who shall remain nameless, was caught within a few feet of Catamaran's box an hour before the race, just before we tacked him up. Someone had told Tom that I wanted to see him, which wasn't true at all. Luckily, Tom happened to meet me right outside the stabling area and when he found out that I *hadn't* called him, we rushed back in and just caught this 'gentleman' outside Cat's box. Tom searched him and in his pocket there was a box with a rat in it. He claimed that the rat was a pet, and there's no law which says you can't have a rat as a pet. He claimed he was looking for the head lad of the stable which was running the second favourite, which, by the way, was the eventual runner-up. The rat-man had arrived at Epsom with this head lad, another piece of nasty work who, I'm glad to say, is no longer employed in this business. Of course, there's no law against two people travelling together either but later, it transpired that they had backed the second favourite with all they could lay their grubby little hands on to win at good odds. As it turned out they ended up losing a tidy sum, but, if Catamaran had seen the rat that day, there is no doubt about it, he'd never have run in the race. No doubt at all. You saw what happened this afternoon. Poor Cat! What an awful way to go."

There was the sound of an approaching tractor and, having first checked with the answering service and established that there were no more calls, I offered to stay and supervise the removal of the remains so that Norris could get on with the business of informing the rest of the syndicate members.

An hour later the job was finished. The broken body of the great horse had been locked away in a large shed which in its young days had been a coach house, the help had been served hot soup, sandwiches and whiskey and had left. Norris came with me to the Land Rover. "Thank you for all you've done. I'd never have managed without you."

I made some suitably disclaiming reply and climbed in. In the bushes, in the dark, something stirred. "That's probably another bloody rat!" Norris growled savagely. "I wouldn't mind, but I spend a fortune trying to keep the place rat-free. Patch!" he called. "Patch! Here boy!"

I left them at it. On the way home the thought struck me that Norris had to have the worst vermin control programme in the world. Despite his expense and efforts, his horse had bowel worms, his fields had rabbits and his yard had rats.

As I let myself into the cottage, a faraway church launched midnight's chimes out onto the warm, still night. I lay on the bed and heard the same church strike one, two and three. In a bucket in the bathroom, my shirt, jeans and socks, muddy and bloody, steeped in cold water, leeching out the organic reminders of the ordeal. Before going to bed, I had washed and rewashed my hands as fastidiously as Lady Macbeth, but they still felt stained. I don't know why. None of it had been my fault.

I can't recall sleeping but I must have; I don't remember any far off clock chimes after three.

CHAPTER 8

I **arrived at** Bally Ard shortly before 7.20. The sun was hours up, the morning already promising a warm day. As I rolled to a stop outside the house, I felt as though I had hardly left at all.

There was one of the larger BMWs parked by the steps, its metallic fawn body gleaming in the morning sun which, robbed of its blinding glare, was reflected as a whitish-yellow disc in the smoked glass of the windscreen. I trotted up the five limestone steps but before I could ring, the door opened and Norris came to meet me. He looked wrecked.

"I see I'm late," I said, indicating the BMW.

"What? No. No, you're not. The professor hasn't arrived yet. That's Dr Field's car, our local G.P. I'm afraid I had to call him over this morning. I didn't sleep a wink all night. I've got the most frightful headache and I need something stronger than aspirin because I've got a feeling today is going to be hectic."

We entered the sitting room and a tall, carefully groomed man in his early forties rose from a chair beside a small table on which stood a steaming cup. Norris performed the introductions and poured me a welcome coffee from the glass pot which stood on a warming plate on the sideboard.

"An awful business this," the doctor commented, when we had all settled down into deep chairs.

"Awful," I agreed, setting my cup back on its saucer.

"Thank God I don't often come across injuries as bad as Gilbert has described but, when I do, I sometimes envy you vets your facility of euthanasia. In many cases it would be a blessed relief."

I wondered if he was giving me a gentle dig about the fact that I had put down the horse so decisively. More than once

65

during the night, I had had the horrifying thought that the insurance people might try to worm their way out of paying on the grounds that euthanasia could only be justified when all else had failed. In Catamaran's case nothing else had been tried so nothing could have been said to have failed. I couldn't even begin to contemplate the implications of that from my point of view.

"But," he went on, giving me a self-deprecating smile, "if you want the opinion of a mere medic, I think you did absolutely the right thing. It must have been a difficult decision. I'd hate to have been faced with it."

Norris chimed in: "I agree. You were absolutely right and I apologise for trying to talk you out of it. But you'll have to forgive me – I wasn't myself at the time. I'm sure you can appreciate that."

"Under the circumstances, you bore up remarkably well," I said magnanimously.

Professor Wall arrived at 7.30 on the dot. His punctuality had been a by-word at college and, during my year of Pathology he had never been a minute early or late entering the lecture theatre, the laboratory or the post mortem room. Still, even for him, it was a feat, driving across country and arriving precisely on time.

He was a tall man with a slight stoop. His luxuriant eyebrows looked more like moustaches which had gone up in the world and they overhung his lively blue eyes like hairy awnings. Despite his obsession with time, he was a very relaxed man, a man to whom we, as students, could relate easily. The strange thing was that he imposed punctuality on himself only and it didn't bother him in the least when others arrived late or left early.

"Ah, Samson! Good to see you again," he said advancing across the room and gripping my hand.

"It's good to see you, Professor, though I would have preferred it to be under different circumstances."

"Yes indeed. Ah yes indeed." He frowned a philosophical frown, nodding in agreement. Then he turned towards Dr Field. I let Norris make the introductions; it was his house.

I related the whole story as we sipped coffee and the only

time he interrupted was when I mentioned the rat, and all he said then was: "Oh *dear*, how unfortunate!" When I finished, he drained his cup and stood up. "Right then, we'd best go and get this over with. Do you have a post mortem apron?"

"No, I'm afraid not."

"Practitioners never have. Never mind. I've brought one for you." He turned to Norris. "Can you show us where the horse is?"

"Of course. It's just down round the corner. A three minute walk. But I hope you don't need me there. I don't think I'd be able for it."

"That won't be necessary. We'll manage thank you." Dr.Field coughed politely. "Would it be in order for me to attend? I'm quite fascinated by it all."

"You'll have to ask Mr Samson about that. It's his case. I've certainly got no objections."

I told Dr Field he was welcome and went with the professor to his car to help with the equipment. Out of earshot of the others, he studied me shrewdly for a moment. "I'd say that right now, you're suffering all kinds of self-doubt?" I gave a vague shrug. "Well you needn't. Have you ever had to put down a valuable animal before?"

"No."

"Then let me assure you that most people who have that unpleasant duty to perform feel the same afterwards – pretty damned shaken. From what you tell me, there was no other course open to you. It was a very lonely decision to have had to take. Very lonely."

Norris led us across the yard towards the locked double doors of the coach house. I carried the professor's case. At the car, he had put on a white lab coat and a white rubber apron and, as Norris unlocked the door, he clipped a dictaphone into his breast pocket and attached a small microphone to the lapel. The horse was already beginning to smell. Norris snapped a switch inside the door and the shed flickered into view in the cold grey-pink light of neon fluorescent tubes. We waited respectfully while he took a long, last, sad look at the great animal and then, wordlessly, left.

The pathologist walked around the body on the floor as he

pulled on his long rubber gloves. After one complete circuit, he looked up at me. "You did the right thing, Samson. No question about it." Then he bent and snapped open his case. "Right," he said, straightening, "we can begin. Perhaps we can have the door closed?" Dr Field moved from where he was leaning against the wall and pulled it shut.

Professor Wall had already switched on his recorder and given it the date and time as a test. He played that back and, when it checked out, went on in a monotone. "Findings of autopsy at Bally Ard Stud, Co. Galway, on the body of thoroughbred stallion, Catamaran, the property of Mr Gilbert Norris of the same address, and others. Autopsy carried out by Stephen Wall and Francis Samson, Veterinary Surgeons. Superficial examination revealed the following lesions: healing skin wound on muzzle approximately one inch high and half an inch wide. The epidermis is missing but repair is taking place normally. Change that to 'has been', has been taking place normally," he corrected. "This wound is roughly rectangular and is situated mainly to the left of the mid-line; it extends into the medial distal commissure of the left nostril. There exists a report of this wound on the file, submitted by Peter Steele, Veterinary Surgeon, date to be checked. Next. New paragraph. Two conjoined wounds in mid-forehead. These are roughly circular, each having a diameter of just under an inch. Skin, frontal bone, frontal sinus and cranial cavity with its contents penetrated. Wounds straddle mid-line." He broke off, covering the microphone with his hand, said "Good shooting, Mr Samson," then continued: "These the cause of death, resulting from the horse being shot with a shotgun by Mr Samson. New paragraph. Compound fracture, right fore involving metacarpus at the level of the buttons of the splint bones. Severe trauma to soft tissues in the area of the fracture. Next. New paragraph. Compound fracture of left hind involving metatarsus at the junction of its proximal and middle thirds. Severe soft tissue damage in the area of the fracture. Right. Next. New paragraph. Transverse, stab-like wound in sub-pubic region about five inches antero-ventral to the pubic symphysis. Probing reveals the wound to be some two to three inches deep and somewhat more long – about three and a half inches.

Structures in the area severed transversely, including penis and associated muscles. Bruising at lips of wound and haemorrhage in its depth. Yellow flakes of paint recovered from wound. Mr Samson reports piece of metal found actually in wound and removed by him. Next paragraph. Cuts and bruises of a relatively, underline 'relatively', minor nature on right side of body all consistent with subject having fallen on that side. No such superficial trauma on left side, compound fracture of hind leg being the only wound on that side."

At this point, he switched off the recorder and took a scalpel from the case. Twenty minutes later, the horse had been neatly skinned and lay, glistening white and red, beneath the humming glow of the strip-lights. Switching the recorder back on, he resumed his monologue. "Subcutaneous lesions. Extensive bruising all along right side, from facial area to rump. Bruising varies in severity, most severe over bony prominences, jaw, shoulder and elbow joints, rib-cage and point of hip. All consistent with subject having fallen on that side. That is, the right side. Left side unaffected."

The pathologist now took a break, doing calisthenics to relieve his back, grimacing as, hands on hips, he stretched and swayed and rolled one shoulder after the other. He smiled ruefully at Dr Field. "I suppose, Doctor, that you don't happen to have any magic potion to alleviate Ageing Back Syndrome on you at the moment?"

"Unfortunately, not at the moment, Professor." Field smiled back.

"In that case, we may as well continue. The back isn't going to get any better. Mr Samson, can you please pass me the saw and that big knife."

The examination of the abdominal cavity was thorough but failed to show up any gross pathological lesions. I was thankful to see that there were no signs of aneurysms and the only thing that went on the dictaphone was a roll call of the abdominal organs with the same comment after each: "Normal position, relations, colour, size and texture." I hadn't mentioned the worm burden and I wasn't going to. It was of purely academic interest now anyway and there was no way that it could have contributed to Catamaran's death. Field peered over the professor's shoulder, obviously engrossed. At one stage he broke in excitedly.

"There's no gall bladder! Look! No gall bladder!"

Professor Wall and I exchanged superior smiles. "Horses don't have gall bladders."

"Oh..." Field sounded disappointed. "I was always told that all animals, humans included, had the same bits and pieces, only varying in size and shape..."

"That's broadly true but there are differences. For instance the animals that we deal with, your farm and domestic animals, don't have collar bones. We have five digits at the end of each limb, the horse just one and two tiny splint bones; the ox, sheep and pig have two; dogs and cats have four and vestigial thumbs and big toes, the dew claws... Cattle have a bone in their hearts. A pig has a bone in the tip of its snout. A dog has a bone in his penis. Cattle, sheep and goats have four very specialised compartments in their highly efficient stomachs, compared to which the simple bags we, in common with cats, dogs, rats, pigs, horses, have been blessed with are a very basic design..." He suspended the lecture in comparative anatomy to ask me for a bottle for the small cube he had just cut from the liver; when he had plopped it in, I placed the capped bottle back with the other samples he had already taken.

Next he tackled the thoracic cavity, sawing through the ribs at their sternal ends; as each one was cut through, he freed it from its neighbour and twisted it up to dislocate it from its junction with the vertebral column. When the last rib fell to his saw, he switched on his recorder again and reported all normal in the thorax. He concluded by giving a resume, beginning in short sentences from which all superfluous words were excised; it only needed the regular interposing of the word 'Stop' to make it sound as though he was composing a telegram.

"End of autopsy. Brain examination not possible as subject shot so cranial contents destroyed. Following samples taken: blood, urine, saliva, stomach contents, intestinal contents, liver and kidney sections. Toxicology and pharmacology only. No recent history any significant illness so histology, bacteriology and virology not necessary. All gross lesions consistent with history. Panicked by rat in box, bolted and fell over quarry-edge,

70

unseen because of bushes. Injuries necessitated euthanasia, carried out by Francis Samson. That's about it Joan. Wait until we get the written reports from Mister Samson and the local police and type it up. Subject to clear lab tests, I record a case of death by misadventure." He switched off the recorder.

While I stored the carefully labelled sample bottles away in the case, Professor Wall stripped off his gloves, apron and white rubber boots and deposited them in a heavy plastic bag which he sealed as soon as I gave him the apron that he had lent me. Then we left the shed, switching out the light and pushing the door to behind us, shutting away the pathetic bits of the once great horse from the world of living things.

As we walked round the corner into view of the side windows of the house, Norris spotted us and came through the French doors. His anxious expression was obvious as he crossed the lawn to meet us, picking his way between flower-beds swollen with late summer colours, his feet brushing a track through the dew-blued grass which was still shaded from the bright sun by the bulk of the house. You've finished?" he asked, taking Professor Wall by the elbow and steering him on to the lawn.

"Yes, we have," the pathologist replied.

"I've had Mrs Flahive cook breakfast for us. I'm sure you could do with something to eat after your early start. This way gentlemen," he added, turning to include the doctor and me. Dr Field declined, pleading an overdue morning clinic and, wishing us a good morning, continued on round the front of the house to his car. I, being both hungry and interested in seeing the case through to its end, followed Norris and the professor. I had a morning clinic too, but I squared it with my conscience by reasoning that Professor Wall might have further need of my services – if indeed he ever had had at all.

Norris led us through the sitting room and into his study which was more a private sitting room than a study, though that was what he called it. It had two armchairs and a two-seater sofa grouped around the fireplace, a smaller version of the elaborate affair in the sitting room. The only pieces of furniture which might have qualified it for the name 'study' were a filing cabinet in the corner by the window and a drop-leaf writing desk of exquisite inlaid walnut; its leaf was down and supported the telephone from which he had made his phonecalls the night before. Most of the pigeon-holes were empty. As with the sitting room, this room was also liberally scattered with pictures of Catamaran. He indicated one of the armchairs to the professor and took the other himself. I sat in the middle of the sofa, fore-arms on thighs, leaning attentively forward.

"Well?" Norris asked.

"Well," echoed the professor, "it seems to be a straightfor-ward case of accidental death."

"*Seems* to be! Have you found evidence of foul play?"

"No! Nothing like that! It's just that we can't give a final verdict until we run some tests on the samples we've taken. That's all."

"I see. What tests?"

"Tests for drugs. There are some drugs which could drive an animal mad and, because of the amount of money involved, we must cover all possible angles. The insurance company would demand it."

"Of course. I understand. One doesn't think of these things somehow."

"It's almost certainly a formality. There wouldn't have been any sense to it. If someone wanted to cause Catamaran's death, they'd hardly have picked that method; they'd have no reason to hope that he'd run where he did – it can't have been much more than a one per cent chance that events turned out as they did. And if they weren't trying to kill him, their only purpose would have to have been to drive him temporarily mad, which doesn't make any sense either. It seems pretty certain that it all happened in the way the police have re-constructed it, starting with the rat."

"I suppose so." Norris lapsed into a short meditative silence, then suddenly pulled himself together. "Forgive me. I'm sure you both want to wash and freshen up. We'll eat then." He stood up and so did we. Stooping, I picked up the case. Norris looked distastefully at it. "Are the samples in that?"

"Yes."

"Would you mind leaving it here. I'm afraid that I'd find its presence in the breakfast room very... upsetting. It will be safe here, I assure you. The door can be locked if you wish."

"Of course. Thoughtless of us. I'm sorry." Professor Wall nodded at me. I left the case by the sofa and we went out, Norris pointedly locking the door after us and pocketing the key.

Breakfast was a lavish one, though Norris merely picked at his. Conversation was mainly about racing which left me a bit out, and, shortly after we finished eating, I made my excuses and left.

On my way to town I turned on the radio and just caught the news item about Catamaran. "Catamaran, one of the most famous racehorses of the century, was destroyed yesterday evening following an accident at Bally Ard Stud in County Galway. Following an unbeaten racing career during which he won all the major classics and a record amount of prize money, he was retired to stud at Bally Ard, his own birthplace. Full details of the accident have not yet been released but it is understood that the horse had suffered two broken legs. A Garda spokesman refused to comment beyond saying that the police were not pursuing any specific line of enquiry at the moment, but were keeping an open mind pending the results of an autopsy to be carried out later this morning." There followed a telephone interview with the chairman of the IBBA, the Irish Bloodstock Breeders' Association, a brief interview during which he professed himself to be 'shocked, devastated, desolated and numbed' by the news, and stated that 'this cataclysmic tragedy is *immeasurably* more catastrophic than the untimely and unresolved mystery of the disappearance of Shergar'. His shock, devastation, desolation, and numbness had obviously not made him speechless and, in the end, the interviewer had to cut him short. The news item finished: "The documentary, 'King of the Sport of Kings' which deals with the career of Catamaran and was first televised last March, will be broadcast again this evening on RTE 2 at ten fifteen, and tonight's edition of 'What's the News?' will be shown at a future date."

Catamaran was to be given the full treatment, to be mourned by the nation like the true hero that he was. Somehow it made me feel uneasy all over again. I was the man who had shot the nation's darling. I'd be infamous.

As I drove towards the clinic through the streets of Knockmore, I noticed several heads turning to look at me and when I glanced in my mirror, the heads were still turned, following my progress. I was already infamous by the looks of things – at least locally.

CHAPTER 9

Driving into the yard behind the surgery brought me back to the world of normality with a jerk, the mental equivalent of stepping off the escalator. In the previous eighteen hours, I had become so involved with events at Bally Ard that my mind had slipped into another dimension, a different gear. I stood by the jeep for a moment, re-orientating myself, then headed for the back door.

Eileen's calm had prevented chaos; she had organised everything, and only those with sick animals had stayed. The rest, the routine jobs, vaccinations, wormings etc. had all been told to come back at another time. As I put on my lab coat, I gave her all the information I had in the barest detail, against a background from the next room of snarls and whines, growls and barks, and an infrequent nervous miaow. Animals kept overlong in the artificial confines of a waiting room, don't much like it – the three-year-old magazines mean nothing to them.

"Better get going, I suppose," I said, heading for the white-tiled consultation room. "Roll them in."

For the next hour I dealt with the usual cases of dogs with skin disorders, ear cankers and impacted anal glands. The only cat had been brought in because it had been constipated for three days; when it arrived on the table however, a total cure seemed to have been effected and I wondered, somewhat unscientifically, if forty-five minutes among a howling pack of strange dogs hadn't – to put it delicately – had a laxative effect on it. Clinic should have been over earlier but each person wanted to know about Catamaran and, by the time the last one came through, I had developed an encapsulated version of the events which seemed to satisfy everybody. It was the same on my morning farm rounds – everyone wanted to know about Catamaran.

By lunchtime, the reporters had arrived. Norris wanted nothing to do with them, so they decided to hunt me down. Three of them found me having lunch in the pub across from the surgery and, though I got a free lunch out of them, they got precious little from me to add to the skimpy typed handout they had been given at Bally Ard.

They hadn't even got to *see* Norris let alone interview him; he had left the typed sheets with Jack at the gate-lodge who, once they had identified themselves as reporters, had handed out a sheet to each and become conveniently deaf again, unable even to hear their questions, never mind answer them. Orders were orders.

"The sly old devil!" one of them said with a wry grin calculated to get me to join in the joke and thus on their side. "He heard me when I asked if we could get in. 'No way!' he said and when I asked him if there was an entrance fee, like say twenty quid, he said, quick as a wink: 'Keep your money! You can't come in and that's that!'" They all chuckled at the memory, showing what nice fellows they were.

But, despite their blatant niceness, I couldn't do anything to help. I couldn't manufacture an excuse to visit Bally Ard in the afternoon, even if I had the time – which I didn't – and even if I did have a reason to go back, I wasn't going to take them along as guests. I assured them that the front gate was the only way in, unless they wanted to swim a deep, fast-moving river, absail down a sheer cliff face, or invade the place from the sea. To pay for the lunch, I described the quarry. Big deal. Then I excused myself and somehow they didn't seem quite as friendly or as nice as they had earlier on. I had the distinct impression that, if I happened to meet them again the next day, I'd be buying my own lunch.

Because of the late start to the day, I finished late, not getting back to Fernditch until after eight. I soaked in a hot bath until my skin wrinkled and read all that the evening papers had on Catamaran. Padding around barefoot, still damp beneath my bathrobe, I considered frying an omelette but managed to push through a vote against it without too much argument from the economy-obsessed side of my conscience. I didn't feel like it and besides, I reasoned that the hectic events of the previous day entitled me to pamper myself a bit. So I opted for the extravagance of an unscheduled, non-weekend, excursion to the local takeaway for something unwholesome (but filling), for consumption in front of the TV. As I came out of the cottage, it looked as if even this simple ambition was about to be dashed, and I cursed sotto voce. In the dusk, the figure of a woman was fumbling for the gate latch. Hearing the door close, she looked up and gave up her gate-opening efforts.

"Mr Samson?" she enquired. Nice voice. I tried to guess what her problem might be. Late. So an emergency. Farm call? Probably not – she would have used the phone. Probably she had a dog in the car – a small bitch trying to give birth to a single large pup. That was it. I placed a bet with myself.

"Yes," I admitted, with more than a touch of the martyr in my tone. The street light outside the gate had not yet come on and, in the dusk, with the remains of the day's light coming from behind her it wasn't at first easy to see her features. Now that I was closer, I noted the absence of a worried expression; I adjusted my bet – maybe a bitch not actually in *labour* as such – just off her food. Yeh. That was it.

"Yes?" I said again, reaching the gate.

"I'm Claire O'Sullivan," she extended a hand over the gate.

"Oh... Hi," I replied, taking the hand, wondering if the name was supposed to mean something to me. I lifted the latch, opened the gate and emerged onto the path. She turned to face me, bringing the evening light full on to her face and I knew at once that I hadn't met her before – I would have remembered, for she was quite breathtakingly beautiful.

"So," I said busily, "What can I do for you?"

"I'm a reporter with The Daily Instructor," she began.

"Oh!" (So much for her anorexic bitch and my Holmesian logic.)

"I'm sorry for bothering you at this hour..."

"No problem." I was relieved that it wasn't work.

"...but I couldn't get here before now. I'm just a substitute

77

really. Our racing correspondent *was* on his way this morning, but he was in a crash somewhere the far side of Ballinasloe and he's in hospital there now with a broken leg."

"That's tough."

"Yes. Tough. So," she continued, trying not to sound pleased at her lucky break, "I had a phonecall at the Westland Row Wives' Association Coffee Morning, which I was covering because one of the Westland Row Wives is a Cabinet Minister's sister, and the editor ordered me west. And here I am. I suppose you've had it up to here with reporters since morning?" she queried, gently rabbit-chopping the bridge of her delicate nose.

"I've seen a few," I conceded. "Three of them clubbed together in a pub today to buy me a bowl of soup and a sandwich."

"Tch! The extravagance! Only those with limitless expense accounts could afford it." She laughed and the laugh fitted her exactly – clear, fresh, a tinkly, pleasing sound. "So, for that I presume you had to Tell them All and sign a pact in your own blood never to talk to a reporter from any other paper?" She smiled. "Never ever ever."

I snorted. "Hardly. When I left, I thought they were going to ask me for the lunch back. Gilbert Norris has prepared a kind of press release, a printed handout…"

"And you didn't think you could go beyond that."

"Not in my position. No."

"Well," she said, "am I allowed to ask what was in the press release? Because I haven't seen it. I went out to Bally Ard as soon as I got here but the place was locked up tight as a drum."

I hesitated. I hadn't read Norris's flyer myself but I could hardly refuse to give her any information on the basis of that; I'd have to give her a synopsis of the facts, fleshing out the bones from the radio reports and the evening papers. She misunderstood my hesitation.

"Oh I'm sorry! You're obviously going out for the evening. Perhaps if you're not going to be too late… I could call…"

"No. No. I'm just going out for a bite to eat. If you like, you can come along and we can talk and eat at the same time. Kill a small flock of birds with the one stone."

"Actually I've already eaten thanks, but I would like to tag along if I wouldn't be in the way? You don't have a date or anything?"

"No. No date or anything – whatever that 'anything' might mean."

She laughed – another tinkly one. "Oh – business, family, a night out with the boys, anything, I suppose, which doesn't fit comfortably under the heading 'date'."

"No. Strictly a solo performance. Nosh for one. I didn't feel like cooking and anyway I'm a lousy cook. I always give myself indigestion and once I nearly committed unintentional suicide with a tuna fish pie."

As we drove long in the Land Rover, I had to do some quick thinking. I had left the house with my heart set on some sort of take-away masterpiece of junk food cuisine – the lot smothered in salt and ketchup, but now that suddenly seemed a terribly unsophisticated ambition and I sorted quickly through my limited knowledge of local geography until I thought of a likely place I had noticed on my rounds. It looked better than it was and its prices were based on its looks.

She sat toying with an indifferent prawn cocktail while I worked my way through the set dinner, fifteen quid, service charge not included; very early on in the proceedings, (between the grapefruit segments and the French onion soup, if I remember correctly), I concluded my report on Catamaran's last moments.

There wasn't an awful lot to tell when you got right down to it. I gave her as much as I knew myself which, judging from the spellbound look in her calm, grey eyes she found fascinating. I didn't tart up the facts or exaggerate my role in the drama, which was most unlike me – given a beautiful woman for an audience, and I left out all references to the suspicious mental exercises I had indulged in immediately after I had put down the horse. Nor did I mention a word of my own reactions during the whole affair; I was still trying to come to grips with them myself. It seemed that, within my own self, within my own psyche which, up until now, I had always thought was a reasonable psyche as psyches go, there lurked another me, a craven me, a me which panicked when faced with the big one and felt secret relief when it found out that there was nothing that could be done.

Not, mind you, that I thought I *ought* to have told her any of this but I was beginning to notice, as time wore on, how important it was becoming that this beautiful woman with the warm grey eyes which looked so steadily back into mine should develop an interest in *my* feelings in the matter, how it had all affected *me*.

"Wow," she breathed, entranced. I thought that this was it. I assumed that she was wowing me, my courage, my tribulations, my doughty intrepidness. I was wrong. She wasn't. "Wow!" she repeated. "A rat! All that caused by a rat!"

"Eh... eh..." I stumbled in confusion, switching wavelengths. "That's right. Incredible isn't it? My Kingdom for a rat aye?" I explained at great length about Catamaran's phobia and told her Norris's story about the attempted sabotage just before the Derby. "But you'd better not print that. Libel laws you know," I advised gravely, showing, I hoped, how knowledgeable I was in all matters, even journalism. Jesus, I thought suddenly, I'm going goofy!

She nodded in equally grave agreement and her face broke into a delighted laugh which sent tiny crows feet crinkling out from her eyes when, dropping my voice conspiratorially, I advised her instead to locate a dead rat (preferably of much the same dimensions as a small rabbit), photograph it, and print it in the paper as "The Rat!"

"Just that! 'The Rat'. The most famous rat in all history!" I began to warm to my theme, to get into my stride. "And can you imagine the lure of a dead rat photograph on the front page! The public fascination!" I flexed my arms tightly, bringing the hands up under my chin – fingers extended forward, wrinkled my nose, stuck my front teeth out over my lower lip, and snapped my head back. And it was while I was rigid in that undignified position with my eyes closed as tight as a dead rat's, that the waiter approached and enquired if I was Mr Samson, the vet.

"Yes," I replied uncoiling myself and unnecessarily clearing my throat, trying to make an immediate transition from arrant twit to dignified professional.

"Telephone for you sir. You can take it at reception."

I knew it would be work because I had given the answering service my number, and it was – the bane of the vet's life – a calving case.

"Emergency, I'm afraid," I told Claire, getting back to the table and draining my coffee. Inside I was dejected.

"What's the emergency?"

"Cow calving." I made writing motions in the air to the waiter.

Suddenly I was desolated. I realised with a shock that I didn't want to say goodbye to this woman that I had met just ninety minutes before, that the thought of it gave me a sense of utter loss. Confused at the intensity of my emotion, I gave her a resigned smile. "Well I'd like to have offered you a post-prandial drink but I'm afraid calving cases claim precedence over everything."

She shrugged and made what to me was definitely a disappointed little grimace. "Duty calls," she shrugged.

"As you say. Come on. We'd better get you back to your hotel."

We were almost there, having driven most of the way in near silence, when she turned to me. "If you don't think that I'd be in the way, I'd love to go on the call with you. I've never seen a birth."

I just grinned at her. It would have been premature to tell her that she had just saved me from a pit of black depression. Before replying, afraid she might change her mind, I did a U-turn and headed back out for the open country. "It's no problem," I said, trying not to sound too thrilled. "No problem at all."

CHAPTER 10

*T*hick, **golden** corn-straw carpeted the floor of the cow-byre and the soft yellow light of an oil lamp showed a quiet old Shorthorn standing peacefully and untroubled, tethered to a ring in the whitewashed wall. She'd been through it all before and was calm and composed, awaiting the moment when the calf would mysteriously appear and she, hearing its snuffling and sharp cry, would lick it dry, stimulating it to take its first shaky breaths. I glanced at Claire as I soaped my hand and arm, and saw the look of fascination on her face; she was obviously mesmerised and I hoped that it wasn't going to be one of the messier ones. They can put people off.

The cow was roomy and the calf lively, and, when I grasped the fetlock of the little foot which lay just out of sight in the vagina, it was jerked back with a violence which caused the mother to look back to see what was going on. I touched the calf's muzzle and he obviously objected to this also because he began to rotate his head to escape my exploring fingers. But that was all that there was, one forelimb and the head. The other forelimb had got left behind and was now probably bent backwards along the underside of the little body. Gently pushing the calf back into the uterus, I created enough room between its body and the floor of the cow's pelvis to admit my hand and succeeded in grasping the wayward limb between the elbow and the next joint down, the knee. At this stage, the powerful contractions of the cow's uterus and abdominal muscles were forcing the calf back at me again and I had to withdraw my hand just as I managed to flex the shoulder and elbow joints. I repelled the calf once more, groped for the leg, this time getting my fingers hooked behind the bent knee. After

82

that it was just a matter of pulling forward and upward a little and inching my hand down along the leg, repeating the manoeuvre until the fetlock and hoof came within reach. Then, covering the sharp points of the little hooves with my hand to protect the stretched wall of the uterus, I bent fetlock, knee, elbow and shoulder and drew the folded leg forward to join its fellow in the birth canal. Gentle traction did the rest and, less than ten minutes after I had begun, the calf flopped onto the golden straw, steam rising from its wet coat.

"Bull calf," the farmer pronounced, dropping the hind leg and moving to the cow's head to untie her.

For the first time Claire moved. Walking slowly, her gaze never leaving it, she approached the calf and hunkered down beside it. The farmer saw her and delayed untying the cow. Some cows don't take kindly to strangers being close to their offspring but someone whose only experience of cows was probably from passing cars wouldn't have known that and, while I was working, he, in his quiet way, had obviously summed up the situation unerringly. Anyway, the look of wonder she had been wearing since entering the shed would have given the game away to anyone. Gently she stroked the wet, snorting head.

It was I who spoke first on the journey back to Knockmore; since leaving the farm, Claire hadn't said a word. "So! What did you think of your first calving case then?" I asked casually, knowing the answer already.

"It was unbelievable! Marvellous!" Once she started talking she went on and the general idea that came through was that she thought that I was a great life-giver of some sort, somewhere, though not much, this side of deity. In fact the actual case had been as straightforward as they came, needing only one of the simpler obstetrical interferences, but I didn't disillusion her – honest I may be, but that much honest is stupid; if she wanted to think of me as one of the lesser gods, then that was perfectly alright by me.

Driving along the dark roads we discussed calving cases in some detail. Claire's fascination with the whole subject was endless and of course, I was in my element. In both senses of the word. After I had explained the interferences for correcting all the problematic presentations I could think of we got on to the really difficult ones.

"What happens Frank if the calf is simply too big to fit through the pelvis?" she asked, eyes wide with horror.

"Dead or alive?" Casual tone, changing down to squeeze speedily past an ancient truck.

"How do you mean?"

"The foetus. Dead or alive?"

"It makes a difference?"

"Sure. If it's dead, you cut it up inside using a wire saw and take it out in bits..."

"Eee-yuck! What about the poor cow?!"

"No problem. Stick in a drop of epidural and then there's a collection of metal pipes we use to protect her insides. It's called an embryotome. Of course if the calf is *alive* then we do a Caesarean section. Same as in people."

"Yeah!? A Caesarean? No kidding? I was born by Caesarean."

"There you go! Didn't do you one bit of harm did it?"

"I suppose not." She laughed. "It nearly killed my mother though. Infection."

"That's always a danger. But somehow cows seem to be able to handle it. If you saw some of the places I've had to operate in, you'd wonder how *I* came out alive, never mind the cow and calf! Muck from wall to wall, flies all over, dust thick in the air. It's Murphy's law in reverse. And it's the only time Murphy's law works in reverse where calving cases are concerned. Otherwise it goes true to form. With a vengeance!"

"Why's that?"

"Well... they always seem to happen at the most inopportune times, as if the blooming cow was just waiting for a man to start relaxing..." I think that subconsciously, I had been building towards a chat up opening. I should have gone on, (meaningfully), about how, when I was just hoping to spend the evening with the most beautiful woman... blah, blah, blah, etc, etc, etc,... but I backed off at the last minute. As openings went it was perfect – smooth, subtle, uncontrived (or seemingly so), and sufficiently vague to be side-stepped neatly ("That's life") or gently encouraged ("It's not *that* late yet, is it?"). Still I backed away. Though I had only met her that evening and she would be gone in the morning, I felt convinced, for whatever reason, that we'd meet again, and I didn't want her to carry away with her the memory of a smooth-talking, flash Harry. I suppose, though I wouldn't have believed it at the time, that I was already in love with her.

"It must play hell with your social life, all these untimely calving cases," she said. "Do you have a regular girlfriend?"

"No," I said, taken aback by the sudden direct question. "Do you have a regular boyfriend?"

She glanced quickly at me. "Why do you ask?" There was a small enigmatic smile on her lips.

"Because you asked me." I smiled back at her.

"Well, I'm a reporter, remember? So my question was professional."

"Well, I'm a man, remember? So my question was personal," I countered, half in jest, whole in earnest. I grinned at her again, disarmingly, to show that she could take it as a joke if she liked.

"I see that you believe in being frank, Frank," she said, still smiling but dodging the question by continuing the cross-talk routine.

"I believe in being clear, Claire," I replied, using the counter-pun to disguise my insistence. I glanced at her again, shooting my eyebrows up in a winning way, taking the seriousness out of it. "But you haven't answered my question."

She laughed, a delighted, delightful gurgle. "No."

"Is that a 'No,' you haven't answered my question, or a 'No,' you haven't a regular boyfriend?"

"It's a 'No' to both." She laughed again, relishing the game. "Two no's; a double negative."

"Which makes it a positive, right?"

"This is the exception."

We had reached the hotel at this point and I turned into the car park.

"Perhaps we could have that drink now?" I suggested, loath just to drive away.

"That'd be nice. I'd some more questions to ask you too. If you don't mind."

"Oh? Fire away. But I thought you said that you'd got

enough. Are we coming to the 'no comment' stuff at last?"

When I switched off the engine, the strains of 'The Hokey Cokey' came thumping through the night air from a row of open windows towards the back of the hotel.

"Sounds of revelry from within," Claire said. "I wonder what's going on."

It turned out to be a dinner dance being held for the benefit and entertainment of a party of French travel agents which was staying at the hotel and, after we had sat for ten minutes in the deserted bar, we decided to gatecrash. During the next couple of hours we boogied and we jived, waltzed and fox-trotted and took part in the Paul Jones' and Congas which are the essence of such functions. There were a few 'Excuse me' dances and I never managed to stay with Claire for more than the first few bars before getting a polite Gallic tap on the shoulder and seeing her being whisked off. But, I noticed with some satisfaction as I cast about for someone else to relieve of his partner, the one who tapped me never lasted more than a few steps either, and, every time I caught sight of her amongst the whirling, gliding merry-makers, she had a different partner. The other thing I noticed was that each time we came briefly in sight of each other, Claire beamed a great smile at me and I began to wonder if she wasn't keeping a lookout for me as assiduously as I was for her.

We even won two spot prizes. It wasn't hard, as the French visitors were hampered by a language difficulty exacerbated by the tubby band-leader's broad West of Ireland accent, and a total ignorance of the jargon of 'in' spot prize buzz-phrases. Thus, when the leader announced with a gappy, devilish smile that the first prize would go to 'The firsht gintleman up here wit a pair o' lady's tights in his hands', the French travel agents looked around them, not knowing what was going on, while I picked up Claire and carried her to the stage to claim our prize, a bottle of whiskey and a box of chocolates. Twenty minutes later, I added a bottle of aftershave lotion and a jar of bathsalts for being the first to respond to his call for a 'spare set o' teeth'. To a seasoned attender of dinner dances in Ireland, that means 'a comb', but to the French, the whole thing must have seemed like some ancient Celtic ritual, a display put on for their entertainment, and they responded with wild applause and much back-slapping, all the while trying to figure out why I had been given yet another gaily-wrapped package for brandishing a *comb* at the man. Which all goes to show the value of local knowledge. Obviously, the band-leader realised that he'd have to internationalise the whole thing to prevent us from making a clean sweep of the goodies on offer because the next spot prize was offered to 'the firsht wan up here wit a franc.'

"Come on!" Claire tugged at my arm. "You're a Frank!"

"Hold on there! Whoa! I think this one is meant to be confined to the visitors. Give them a fair crack at the booty. Anyhow," I said as she sat down beside me again, "we've already cheated, haven't we?"

"You mean because I'm not wearing tights?" she whispered with a conspiratorial wink.

"Yes," I nodded. It was only when I had picked her up to run to the stage that I noticed that the golden silkiness of her long shapely legs owed nothing to man-made fibres.

"Who's to know?" She smiled. "Except the two of us."

We left the ballroom after the third round of Hokey Cokey, having had enough of putting our right leg in, our right leg out, doing the Hokey Cokey, and shaking it all about. As we went out the door into the foyer, where the tired staff waited, hoping we were the vanguard of a general exodus, the tubby band-leader, obviously a member of the Irish branch of the Malaprop family, was announcing with great pride: "In honour of our French guests, the orchestra will now play, `Viva Espana'".

She walked with me to the jeep. Neither of us spoke. I was trying to think of some way to prolong our being together. I don't know what she was thinking.

"Hey!" I said inspired, "you haven't asked me those other questions you mentioned!" Mentally I clapped myself on the back for having come up with a solid reason which could not be construed as anything more than that. I couldn't figure out why I was fighting so shy of chatting her up but I presumed that that was what nearly every man who ever met her did and I desperately wanted to appear different. I couldn't remember a feeling like it since my early teens, but it was real and there was no denying it and it made me feel quite strange.

"Nor have I. Is it too late, do you think?"

"Not for me, it isn't. How about you?"

"Oh, I'm fine! Not a bit tired."

"Okay then. Would you like to go back into the hotel and ask or would you like to stand here and ask or would you like to ramble about the town a bit and ask?"

"A midnight stroll sounds just the job to me."

Under the orange glow of the sodium lights in the deserted streets, she looked green; green but still beautiful. "You've gone all green!" I mocked her gently, once again deciding to forego the comment about being still very beautiful. I was beginning to get annoyed with my strange reticence in dishing out compliments.

"You look kind of seasick yourself," she smiled.

We walked on towards the sea. Her questions didn't amount to much; in fact, they had nothing at all to do with the story she had come to cover. She explained that she was a features writer, not a reporter as such and she had had the idea, during the calving case that she would like to do a feature on a vet's life.

"Kind of 'A day in the life...'?"

"That sort of thing. What do you think? Would you be on?"

All I could think at that moment was that that meant she would have to spend time with me. With a slightly scary start, I realised that I had known all along, almost from the beginning, without any doubt at all, that we would spend more than just one brief evening together. "When would you like to do it?" I asked eagerly, the mask of reserve slipping for the first time.

"Well I'll have to get the go-ahead from the editor first, but he usually lets me have my head pretty much. Not that he prints everything I come up with, mind you. It's often a case of running one of my pieces if there's a space to be filled on the paper. I'm under no illusions that I'm a Woodward and Bernstein all rolled into one! But you wouldn't mind if I hung around with you for a couple of days? *If* he gives it the okay, that is?"

"Not at all!" I replied with feigned indifference, barely managing to avoid remarking that, as far as I was concerned, the editor's blessing meant little or nothing. "Not at all".

We had descended a narrow street onto the harbour and we stopped, looking down on the boats tied alongside, rocking gently on the still, full tide. At the end of the harbour the road turned a corner; after this, there were no more street lights and the town was lost to our view. Ahead, the way twisted and climbed, a pale ribbon in the light of the slice of moon which hung over the mouth of the bay and sent a track of silver along the dark water towards us, a gleaming path which shimmered and disintegrated slowly on the tiny swell which slurped lazily among the rocks below.

We walked slowly, almost in silence. Claire's comments were confined mainly to expressions of wonder at the peace and beauty of night in the country. She marvelled at everything – the moon, the stars, the quiet, the bay; it all seemed so new to her that I began to wonder if she ever left the city at all. While she was poetic about the manifestations of nature as displayed in Knockmore, she was scathing about their appearance from the point of view of urban man – I remember the moon over Dublin being described as looking like a piece of lemon lying in the bottom of last night's gin and tonic glass, while the stars in the city sky came off even worse, being likened to 'flecks of dandruff on the cassock of a very old priest'. Rough stuff.

My contributions consisted mainly of agreeing noises – the night *was* beautiful, the moon-streaked bay *was* magical, the sky *was* alive with stars, but I hardly noticed any of it. Unlike Claire, I was used to them and I was too besotted to take much notice of anything but the lovely creature beside me. Also I couldn't match the metaphors. If put to it, I would have described the rural Heavens as 'very nice', the urban, as 'not very nice'. Such command of the language is apt to induce prudent silences.

The road climbed steadily and soon we could see out beyond the mouth of the bay, out over the headlands, out to the immensity of the ocean – flat, calm and peaceful, it stretched silvery-grey in the moonlight to north, south and west. Suddenly Claire shivered and hugged herself.

"It's getting a bit chilly," she said.

"Perhaps we ought to be getting back."

"Anyway you've had a hell of a twenty four hours."

It was then that I realised that I had forgotten totally about Catamaran. If I had been told six hours ago that I would soon be beavering along as if nothing had happened I wouldn't have believed it. But now I had to face it. Like it or not, Claire had mesmerised me, ousted all other things from my mind.

"Oh, I'm fine," I smiled tenderly, "but you're right; it *is* getting chilly. Time for us to make a move." I removed my jacket and draped it over her shoulders, refusing to listen to her protests, insisting that I was too warm anyway, robbing it of any gallantry. "Honestly, Claire! You'll be doing me a favour by carrying it back for me. It's quite heavy and I'm not all that strong you know. Carrying jackets tires me easily!"

She laughed and snuggled with great exaggeration into the warm garment. "You're sure?"

"Absolutely. Scout's honour," I replied, aware of the chilly goose-flesh which was already shrinking the skin of my arms.

When we got back to the hotel, the dinner dance had ended and the place was in almost total darkness. Claire handed me the jacket. "Well, Frank; thank you for a most enjoyable evening."

I've probably heard those words hundreds of times and yet this time, they sounded unique, as if I had never had them said to me before and as though she had never said them before either.

"It was my pleasure," I responded, trying to sound unique too and ending up sounding hackneyed.

"So... Goodnight," and she tilted her face towards me.

"Goodnight Claire." For one magical instant my lips brushed hers. "Let me know when you hear from the editor, won't you?"

"Yes." She spoke softly, still standing close to me, well within kissing distance. "I'm really looking forward to it."

"So am I, Claire. So am I." I kissed her again, briefly, like the first time and she squeezed my arm, whispered goodnight again and turned towards the hotel. I watched her go, the grace of a ballerina in her movement.

"Hey, Claire!" I called after her, in a loud whisper. She turned. "What about your spot prizes? The chocolates and the bath salts?"

"You keep them for me. We can share them when I come again." She half-turned away, then turned back. "The chocolates anyway." With a happy laugh and a wave, she went through the door into the dimly-lit foyer of the sleeping hotel.

At 3.15 am, my panicking employer telephoned from the States. He had just heard about Catamaran and, understandably, had been jolted to the marrow of his bones. The trouble, it transpired, was that the news bulletin which had informed him of the tragedy had given no details other than that Catamaran had been put down and, not unnaturally, he had begun to wonder if he hadn't left his practise in the hands of a complete incompetent or, worse still, the animal equivalent of a homicidal maniac. It took me ten minutes to persuade him that it had all been a tragic mishap and nothing more. After another ten minutes of questions he seemed reassured.

"Apart from that, everything is just fine," I went on, rather unwisely – it seemed to reduce the incident to the importance of a minor traffic accident in which a tail light has been broken.

A snorted transatlantic 'Hmmmph!' was all that that observation was awarded.

Giving me a phone number at which I could reach him "if anything else like that happens," he said goodbye.

Wondering what exactly he had in mind or if indeed anything else like that *could* happen, I hung up, and, pummelling my pillow into shape, settled down to sleep what was left of the night.

CHAPTER 11

Over the next couple of weeks life returned to normal. Catamaran had vanished from the press after the first few days and, a short while later, even I had begun to forget about the whole business. His passing had not even been the nine day wonder that one of the more cynical journalists had predicted. "Life goes on just the same, my friend," he had said sagely, but I hadn't believed him.

The results of the blood tests came back from the laboratory on Friday morning's post and I glanced at them out of academic interest. All the values were well within the normal ranges and I locked the computerised printout away in a drawer of the desk. The developed prints of the film I had sent off on the same post arrived on Monday and I browsed through them after morning clinic. Most of the prints were of Marnie's druggy party and I shuddered at the memory of my close shave. The shots of Catamaran had come out well and that made me even sorrier that I hadn't managed to get one of me holding him.

Claire took up much of my thoughts. I refused to believe in love at first sight but how else could I explain the way I felt about her? And all after four short hours of being with her – four short heady hours. There were times when I thought she was all a dream, an hallucination brought on by wishful thinking; then, she'd phone and I'd believe again. She phoned two nights after she went back to Dublin to tell me that the editor had sanctioned her idea but that it wouldn't be for another three or four weeks. I tried to keep the disappointment out of my voice. She phoned almost every second night after that, ostensibly to check some fact for the article she was blocking out, but the professional aspect of the calls began to occupy less and less of the time and soon, with the safety of a hundred and eighty miles between us, we began to flirt.

"I bet," Claire said, "that you've wolfed our chocolates already. Attacked by starvation at three in the morning or something."

"Claire!" I replied, shocked. "Do you think I'm a savage?!" I noted the 'our'. Not 'the' chocolates – 'our'. It made me feel comfortable. Snug.

"Or on one of the evenings when you didn't feel like cooking?"

"No way. Those chocolates are sacred!"

"I'd say that they've vanished already and that you'll replace them just before I arrive," she continued, laughing.

"Oh how can you bear to *say* such things?"

"Well, just remember! We've to share them together."

"Could I forget! But speaking of sharing things together, whatever about the chocs, there's no way that the bath salts will be interfered with until you get here."

Her answering laugh was of a different quality, gentle, personal, for me alone, the kind of half-suppressed girl's laugh you sometimes hear coming through the dark privacy of a cinema or from a quiet room in a house where there's a party going on. At least, that was what I made of it. There again, it might just have been the usual wishful thinking on my part, followed by the customary frisson which led to the standard crop of goose-bumps – all in the mind.

During that fortnight, we met on two occasions also, once in Dublin, at Claire's flat and, a few days later in Galway. She had come to cover a lunchtime concert being given at the university by a local blues singer who was making a big impression and was being hailed as the new Billie Halliday. Neither meeting was particularly auspicious, both lacking the freedom from the danger of commitment which our telephone conversations gave us.

I was in Dublin to placate my bank manager who had sent me a nasty letter reminding me that my Term Loan Account had not been credited with the agreed monthly payments since March, and that my Current Account, despite the fact that I had no overdraft facilities, was over a thousand pounds in the red. I had written to him on receipt of his previous letters but this one had been couched in more unambiguous terms. It 'suggested' that I call in person, at my earliest possible convenience – Bankspeak for: 'Get your financially challenged ass in here, NOW!' So, having arranged for the neighbouring practice to cover for me for the day, I had set off. Not looking forward to it at all.

By five o'clock, I had finished all my business and went in search of the address which Claire had given me on the phone the night before. Just as her company had blotted out the bad memories of Catamaran's death on the first occasion we had met, so the mounting anticipation of happiness I felt as I neared her flat banished the thoughts of my recent awkward interview with the bank manager. But the euphoria suffered a sudden setback when, on locating the house, I found a shining black Porsche crouched outside the gate. The car belonged to Paul Markham, a guy I had known vaguely at college and had met on several occasions since – always in the company of beautiful women. Handsome as a cigarette ad., rich as Croesus, he was witty, charming, athletic, widely-read and even more widely-travelled, and he was the man who's car I would least like to have seen parked outside the flat of the woman I was now almost sure I was in love with. That is, given the choice. I had even felt a twinge of unease the evening we had walked out along the bay-shore in Knockmore when his name had cropped up among the list of people whom we both knew in and around Dublin.

Glowering at the Porsche, I went through the gate, up the short path and pressed the bell which had C. O'Sullivan beside it in a little plastic-covered wallet.

"Hello? Who is it?" Claire's voice sang out almost at once through the metal speaker by the row of bell-buttons. Even the crackly, tinny reproduction couldn't disguise the sweetness of her voice.

"Hi! It's me. Frank."

"*Frank!*" the box squawked with evident pleasure. "Come

in! Come in!"

"I will! I will!" I said with matching enthusiasm and pushed through the door as soon as it opened with a buzz and a thunk.

Her flat was on the second floor and she met me on the landing with a beam of welcome and pleasure. I hadn't forgotten how beautiful she was but the memory had blurred into an overall effect. Now, as she kissed me on the cheek, the wonder of it engulfed me again, bewitching me afresh. "Paul is here," she said unbewitching me pretty smartly as she arm-linked me up the remaining steps.

"Paul?" I asked innocently.

"Paul Markham. I think you know him, don't you? He knows you anyway." She stopped and looked at me sideways. "Have you eaten our chocolates?" she asked quietly, secretively. There it was again – 'our'.

"No! After all those threats, would I dare?" I grinned at her.

"And the bath-salts...?" she asked, dropping her voice to a near whisper.

"Untouched by human hand, as per agreement." I dropped my voice too and returned her intimate smile.

"It takes two to have an agreement," she admonished me enigmatically and led me, none the wiser, into the flat.

Paul Markham sat in a high-backed wicker arm-chair looking as fabulous as ever. "Hello there, Frank," he said in his rich masculine bass, unleashing a smile which ought by law, to have had a dip-switch fitted for the protection of oncoming traffic after dark.

"Hello Paul! Good to see you!" I replied returning the opening salvo in what was already a full scale battle.

Claire, seemingly unaware that hostilities had been entered into, herself being the prize, went and made coffee for me while Paul and I made polite conversation. Sparring.

"How about you, Paul?" Claire asked, poking her head round the screen which hid the kitchenette from the sitting room. "Another?"

"Yes please, Claire," he replied, looking into the mug he held in a long-fingered, lean, tanned hand. "This is nearly finished."

"Okay. Two sugars, isn't it?"

"No." He laughed. "Just half a spoon, please. Got to watch the old figure you know, ha, ha, ha."

"Half spoon, OK. Frank, you take two and a smidgin, right?"

"Right, Claire. *My* what a *good* memory you've got!"

One-nil to Samson. In the absence of team-mates, I mentally kissed myself on the back of the neck.

"Paul has been helping me with an article I'm preparing for the weekend supplement," she explained, carrying in two steaming mugs.

"Oh? What's the article about?" I was quite willing to help too.

"Spengler."

"Eh?..." I said involuntarily, groping frantically in my mind to see if there was any little single cell which might have registered what a spengler was.

"You know? Oswald Spengler, the German philosopher..."

"Oh, of *course!*" I said, feeling suddenly that I was playing an away match without any supporters. I could feel my eyes taking on a glazed look, and, whereas Claire went on without noticing my discomfort, its significance wasn't lost on my rival. He sipped thoughtfully.

Claire rambled on: "There's been so much talk lately about his theory on the cyclical patterns in the rise and fall of cultures and civilisations that I thought I ought to do a piece on it and I was all for the theory until Paul pointed out a few basic cracks in it. I can't quite make up my mind whether they make the whole structure of his tenets untenable or not. It's certainly food for thought. Throws the whole thing wide open really. Interesting. Moot."

"Oh!" I said. "Ah!" I wondered if I was sure 'moot' meant what I thought it meant. Claire had told me over her shoulder as we danced a conga, that she had a degree in philosophy and English literature and I remembered hoping at the time that these weren't her only interests or we were off to a very bad start.

A silence developed which was beginning to look as if it might last to the weekend. They were both looking at me so I asked: "And just what are your arguments against Spengler,

Paul?" I didn't have enough sense to disavow all knowledge of, or interest in, Spengler and let them at it.

He began in the beautifully modulated tones of one who knows he's in the driving seat. "There's a certain irrefutable logic in his hypothesis, I admit, but when one examines it in detail, especially as he has expressed it in 'Der Untergang des Abendlandes', one is, I think, bound to concede that there are a few basic flaws which, to my mind at least, leave the whole argument moot." *Another* moot! "Look at it this way. I presume you wouldn't take issue with Spinoza would you, Frank?"

"No. No, of course not!" I replied, aghast at the idea that I would even dream of doing so, whoever Spinoza might be.

"Then if you accept *Spinoza's* philosophy, and here I draw your attention specifically to the points made in his 'Ethics', I don't see how you can *avoid* questioning the Spenglerian conclusions."

I pulled meditatively at the lower lip, nodded vaguely a few times and let my eyes focus on the middle distance in the manner of one not wholly convinced but thinking about it. I was acutely aware of yet another silence which had developed, a silence designed to let me have *my* say.

"I had no idea that you'd taken philosophy at college, Paul. I could have sworn you did geology," I said. Playing for time. I walked into it.

"That's right, Frank. Geology was my subject. Philosophy is just a hobby, but a most fascinating one. One likes to read, to understand, to think for oneself, and, once in a while," he smiled sickeningly, soupily at Claire, "to play the iconoclast."

Jaysus! an own goal. Markham 6 – Samson 1. Disaster!

Luckily for me, Claire butted in at this stage, seizing on some point or other and, for the next five minutes the air was criss-crossed by streams of jargon as they argued the various points, unravelling them strand by strand. I sat there, rigid as a pauper at Sotheby's, lest any movement might be misconstrued as a signal that I wished to add my contribution. Words like 'syllogism' and 'empiricism' and phrases such as 'fundamentalist totalitarianism', 'theistic obscuranticism' and 'socio-economic political naivete' whirled about me and, though I had often discussed such subjects in a pub where nobody else had a clue what they meant either, there was no way that I wanted to get involved here.

Claire glanced my way once or twice; obviously her sense of duty as a hostess was telling her that I ought to be included in the conversation and the danger of her doing so was increasing by the second. But when it came, it didn't come from Claire and it didn't come from a sense of duty; it came from Paul Markham and it came from a sense of *coup de grace*.

"What do *you* think, Frank? You've been sitting quietly there taking it all in and keeping your counsel." He fixed me with a smile like a mongoose's and reckoned I was probably coming up with novel slants on the theory, waiting to pounce and explode their arguments with 'infinite sagacity'. He was giving the arguments which he knew I didn't have, the big build-up so that the sense of let-down would be even greater when my total ignorance of the subject became apparent. He ended up: "So, Frank, you be judge. Give us your ruling in the case of State v Oswald Spengler. Guilty or not guilty? True or false? Right or wrong?" There was a gleam in his eye as he went through the long-winded rigmarole. To him, it was the roll of the drums as the guillotine was being winched up. To me, it was a space for fast thinking, accelerated even more by necessity. It was also a good lesson: if you intend giving someone the chop, do it. And keep the frills until later.

"Sorry Paul?" I said vaguely, "Did you say something?"

"I said: 'What do you think?'."

"What do I think about what?"

"What we've been talking about, Claire and I, for the past five minutes!" His exasperation was controlled but, to me, quite obvious.

"I'm sorry. You must forgive me. I'm afraid I wasn't listening. I've got a very serious situation on hand at the moment and I'm preoccupied with that. It could have extremely grave implications for the bloodstock business. Though I probably oughtn't to be spreading alarmism until I know for sure." I knew that that would get Spengler out of the way; when we had been making smalltalk earlier, Paul had boasted, without it seeming like boasting of course, of his brood mares and his yearlings and his horses in training.

"That sounds awful! What is it?" I had him – even at that early stage. It was now a matter of reeling him in.

"It is awful. If it is it. A potential disaster for the Irish Horse. As I said, I shouldn't say any more. After all it may not be it at all! And I don't want to cause a national panic!"

"What are we talking here, Frank?" Paul asked, getting all friendly and man to man. "Maybe I ought to know, and I can keep things to myself. Fore-warned is forearmed, you know."

"Neatly put, that, Paul. Look... I won't be sure until tomorrow, until I get the results of the tests they're doing even now. All the other tests have been inconclusive, – electrophoretic chromatography, reverse-binding fluorescent photomicrography, auto-immuno assay biometrical titration, Strontium 90 scanning tracings, micro-pico reactive gel-diffusion platings..." I ticked off on my fingers a list of likely-sounding buzz-words, not one of which, as far as I knew, meant anything, only stopping when I ran out of fingers. As the list rolled on, Paul Markham nodded sagely as if they were exactly the tests he would have expected me to do. "But as I said, they were all inconclusive, so I had to bring samples to town today for the definitive tests. That's why I had to come up to town."

"I thought you had to come up to see your... on business," Claire said, correcting herself, not wanting to mention bank managers in front of Croesus.

"I just said that, Claire. I didn't want the press getting wind of it." Claire looked hurt for a moment and then asked, sensibly: "Why didn't you do the test you're doing now first off, if it's the only completely reliable test to show up this disease, whatever it is?"

"Because it's so difficult to do! I was up at four this morning doing micro-surgery! Biopsies from the cerebral medulla, the anterior pituitary, the adrenal medulla, the mitral valve, the stem of the pancreas, Larsen's Peduncle"... I reeled off another list, all fictitious but they sounded great – "Waterman's Ligament, Garcia's Follicle, Heinnemann's Fundus ...." There were a few more which I can't recall but they were going down so well that I almost chanced 'Handel's Messiah.' All of a sudden I was having a whale of a time.

"Look Frank, what is it exactly that you suspect? You can tell me. Us. We can keep a secret. I'm sure I speak for Claire too."

"I thought, Frank, that you would have known that about me already," she said, hurt in her eyes and her voice – perhaps more disappointment than hurt.

"Well... confidentially... it looks like.... Eumitis. I earnestly hope that I'm wrong but... Do you remember, Paul, about four years ago, they had an outbreak of it in Kentucky? Horses dropping dead all over the place?"

"I seem to remember reading about it. But I hadn't moved into the U.S. market at that stage and I don't remember all that much about it. Remind me."

"Lucky for them, they had the peracute form and they managed to control the outbreak by slaughtering all the in-contact animals and burning down the stables. But, here, if it *is* Eumitis, it's the less acute form and the horses take up to a month to die and it spreads everywhere!"

"Of course! Now I remember! What was the name of that stud farm that it started on?" He clicked fingers rapidly, frowning hard.

"I don't know."

"Frank. Will you tip me off if the tests turn out to be positive?"

"Sure. Why not? Tell you what - if you don't hear from me, you can take it that the tests were negative, okay?"

"No news is good news."

"Well put."

We spent another few minutes discussing Eumitis and I invented a whole battery of horrifying symptoms and appalling mortality rates. Then Paul left. He had to prepare paperwork for a deal he had to do in Sweden in a few days, the takeover of a papermill. No less.

When Claire came back from seeing him to the top of the stairs, she said: "There's a great story in that Eumitis thing, but I think you ought to have trusted me enough to know I wouldn't have published if you asked me not to. I thought we understood each other better."

I looked at her, wondering how I was going to handle this

one; telling her I'd made it all up was no problem – telling her *why* was another matter. I cleared my throat. "Claire. I made it up – the whole thing. There's no story. There's no Eumitis."

"You mean there's no danger to the horses?" She looked at me, perplexed.

"There's not even any such thing as Eumitis. Well, there is, in a way. But it's not a disease. It's a silly phrase to cover the multitude of nonsense jobs we get asked about on farms. A farmer calls you for a genuinely sick animal and, when you've treated that, as often as not, he'll say: 'While you're here you might as well have a look at' ... this, that or the other supposedly unwell animal. We call those Eumitis calls because they always begin with 'You might as...!'" I grinned and shrugged.

She stood, still looking at me with a puzzled expression and I was just beginning to wonder how to explain the reason for the whole charade when I saw understanding flare suddenly in her eyes. I nodded to indicate that she had it right and a slow smile began at the corners of her mouth and ended up as a laugh of delight.

"No outbreak in Kentucky?"

"No outbreak in Kentucky."

"So how come Paul remembered it well?"

"I don't know," I shrugged innocently. "You tell me."

She laughed again and reached up and kissed me. "Game, set and match," she murmured in a low, contented voice and kissed me again.

It was a different game but the result was the same.

We met some friends of hers for dinner and after, I headed back for Knockmore. When I took Claire back to her flat, I declined her offer of a nightcap, a move which, of itself, ought to have made me unique amongst men in her eyes.

CHAPTER 12

I **saw her** standing talking to a knot of students and I went up and tapped her on the shoulder. "Sorry I'm late. Another calving case. Just as I was closing the door behind me."

She laughed as she tilted her face to be kissed. "Murphy's Law again. Well, I can't say you didn't warn me."

"It never fails."

She said goodbye to the students and we walked across the green, sun-brightened quadrangle.

"So," I asked. "How was the concert?"

"Fantastic. Who'd ever believe that the west of Ireland could produce such a blues singer?"

We passed under the archway and turned left towards the car park, Claire getting admiring looks which she didn't seem to notice.

Out along the slow river, out past the end of the city, we walked in the warm sunshine. Swans turned expectantly towards the bank at our approach, turning away again in regal disapproval when we had no bread crusts or apple cores to scatter on the dark sliding water, making the transition from hopeful beggars to disdainful aristocrats effortlessly. Further out, coxed eights zipped smoothly upriver, incising the fluid surface with their scalpel-bows, oars suturing the river closed behind them with tiny transient whirlpools.

Claire had gone uncharacteristically quiet; she had hardly said a word since coming on to the river-bank and, as I had decided not to press the issue, I had stopped talking too. The only sound was the lazy gurgle of the stream as it washed by the cut limestone bank, heading steadily for the rushing weir which marked the beginning of its last turbulent stretch before it broke free from the confines of the land into the broad expanse of Galway Bay.

"The shortest river in Ireland," I said quietly, looking out at the oarsmen.

"Mmmmm?"

"Ireland's shortest river. The Corrib." I nodded. "The lake is just up there, around that corner, all hundred square miles of it, and the bay is just a mile or two downstream."

We stopped to look out on the shining flow at a point where steps led down into the water. I took Claire's elbow and steered her down and we sat on the last dry step. Claire took off her shoes and wiggled her toes in the river while, beside her, I sat, balanced slightly precariously, one buttock out in space, flicking small pebbles off my thumbnail and watching them plopping into the sluggish current. There was obviously something bothering her but I didn't ask. She'd tell me in her own time if it was something that concerned me. I couldn't see her face as the curtain of her auburn hair hung between us, so I had no idea of her expression; she sat there hidden behind her hair and watched her toes making tiny splashes. For the next few minutes, she wriggled and I flicked and that was all that happened. Splash, splash went her toes and plop, plop went the pebbles. I stared out over the river wondering what it was that had made her so quiet. Some twenty yards out was a chain of islands, none of them larger than a small boat. Dark channels separated them, overhung by the scrub with which the islands were covered; in the air corridors between them, clouds of insects hovered and darted about in short eye-defying hops, their numbers never seeming to decrease despite the depredations of marauding swallows from above and the ambushes of sleek, unseen trout from below. I ran out of little pebbles and patience at the same time.

"What's the matter, Claire?" I asked gently. "Something's got you worried."

Abruptly the toes ceased their wriggling but she didn't reply for a while. When she did, it was in a small voice and she didn't turn to look at me.

"Nothing... really. Nothing's the matter. Everything is just fine."

"It's just that you're very quiet." When she didn't respond to that, I added: "Thinking deep thoughts?"

"Something like that." There was another silence.

"Perhaps I can help?" I nudged. "Provided of course, it's not another problem to do with Whojee Shpinkler, the acclaimed German whatsit."

That broke the spell of gloom a bit. She laughed, shook her hair back and looked at me. "No, Frank. Nothing as trivial as that. And it's Spengler, not Shpinkler. Or Sprinkler either. Oswald Spengler."

"Ah yes, to you it may be plain Spengler but to me, fluent as I am in the dialect of lower Bavaria, it's Shpinkler. Shhhhpinnnn-kler. I assure you. You may quote me if you wish."

"You may be right," she said, laughing again. "But SHpinkler, Spengler, does it really matter? And that," she said getting serious again, "in a way, is what I was thinking about."

I had a fair idea what she was getting at but the heavy discussion was a little way off still so I filled in with more of the same nonsense. "If that is what it's all about, then I'd best come clean. I am not fluent in the dialect of lower Saxony... Never have been in fact. I lied."

"Bavaria, you said."

"Or Bavaria either for that matter, so, stick with Spengler."

"To hell with Spengler!"

"Amen to that," I said with feeling.

"I was thinking more about me. And you," she added a bit tentatively.

"So was I."

"Really? What were you thinking?"

"You first. You're the one who's been concentrating while I was preoccupied with the flicking of pebbles from the thumb."

"But you just said that you were thinking too!" Claire protested.

"Ah! But you were noticeably thinking. So go on. Out with the thoughts. Let's have everything out in the open."

She went silent again, her lovely brow furrowed, composing her thoughts, getting her opening sentences in order. The true journalist.

"Frank," she began at last, "you're a very special person..."
At these words, my heart plummeted; it sounded exactly like
the beginning of the classic brush-off speech, the one that
ended in Victorian novels... "but it can never be for I am
pledged to another..." on receipt of which, Frank went off and
discovered the source of the Nile or opened a trading post on
the Amazon, married a native woman, and died from a mixture
of malaria, curare, snakebite, and the produce of local stills
without ever discovering that he was the long-lost son of the
Duke of Chipping Norton...

"Agreed," I said jokingly, insurance against heartbreak.

"And I'm afraid... that I'm getting more involved with you
than I ought to because I've only known you for such a short
time..."

"What?!" I exclaimed in disbelief, my heart zooming up
from my boots again and soaring unchecked past its normal
position. I couldn't think what to say; I could hardly think at
all. In a daze I heard her go on.

"Even the way I can *say* these things to you, without embarrassment... well, with relatively *minor* embarrassment... shows
how special you are. I can't even begin to think of myself being
able to talk this freely with any other man I know. Since I was
sixteen, I don't think I've ever ended up alone with a man for
an evening without having to spend the whole time trying to
dodge passes, pretending not to notice the unsubtle double
entendres, the half-hinted suggestions, the barely-disguised
leers.. You get sick of it! Really sick and tired! I'm not a prude,
but there's a time for everything; and that isn't ten seconds
after we end up being alone! At least, not for me, it's not.
You're different, Frank. Jesus! I even asked you in for a nightcap the other evening and you said no!"

"I'm not different, you know, Claire," I said softly. "I'm
pretty much the same as the rest of us men. I can't explain it to
you. I can't even explain it to myself! And I've been working
on it since I met you. You're the most beautiful woman I've
ever had a... relationship with – in fact, you're probably the
most beautiful woman I've ever met! I mean that," I said in
answer to her look of mocking disbelief. "But there's something about you, some...... some kind of trust or openness that

makes you the most fascinating woman I've ever met too. It's a kind of inner serenity and calmness... Ah, what's the use? I can't explain it. I have a longing to know that side of you more than the physical side. Or at least as much," I added with a smile. " God that sounds so corny! Does it make any sense to you at all?"

"Yes. I told you you were special."

"Special? I must be mad!" I growled lasciviously and laughed. "So, where do we go from here?"

"That's the problem."

"Why is it a problem? Unless you find me physically repulsive or something and can't see any future..."

"No, it's nothing like that, I assure you. Quite the opposite in fact. It's just me. You see, once I knew a man like you. He was simple and nice and kind and gentle and I suppose I loved him. He was also married, though I didn't know that, and he also had another couple of ladies to keep him company when I wasn't around. I've fought very shy of allowing myself to get emotionally tied up with anyone since, and that, I suppose, is what my silence is all about. I feel, Frank, that with you, it might happen all over again."

"What? Find out that I'm married?" I grinned at her.

"No! Not that! I mean that I'd get more emotionally involved with you and then have to cast loose with all the pain and hurt all over again. For whatever reason."

I thought for a while. She was right. There were no guarantees. Going by the way I felt at that particular minute, I didn't think I'd ever want her to leave, but one had to be sensible. "But, Claire, you can't go through life choking off any relationship which looks like getting serious. That way all you've got left are your one night stands with the good time boys and the sugar daddies. As for our particular relationship, we'd be crazy at this stage to make plans, or promises which, for any number of unforeseeable reasons we might not want to be bound by in the future. As you said, we've known each other for such a short time which means that we've each got a whole lot to learn about the other. Maybe I'll find out that you're not as perfect as you seem and I'm quite sure that I've got lots of faults which I've just about managed to hide from you so far. You're right. We ought to go slowly, at your pace. But I certainly would hate to say goodbye now on the grounds that it *mightn't* work."

She considered this a bit, nodding. "That sounds like good solid thinking to me." She smiled, and there was a hint of relief in the smile, then she leaned slowly towards me and we kissed with infinite tenderness, only our mouths touching. We sat for a while more watching the river and talking. Then it was time for her to catch her train. As we walked arm in arm back towards town, I admitted to her that I had already made a start in trying to even the field in the area of common interests.

"Oh?" she asked. "How?"

"Well, the other night, after the Spengler debacle, when I got home, I found a book on 20th century poetry. And I browsed through it."

"Did you like it?"

"Do I have to be honest?"

"You didn't!" She laughed. "One woman's meat is another man's poison."

"To be honest, I couldn't make a whole lot of sense out of it. In fact, the two most abiding memories I have are that Ezra Pound probably wasn't the full shilling and, if T. S. Eliot had been christened S. T. Eliot instead, his name would have been 'toilets' spelled backwards. Some highbrow, huh?"

All the way back, Claire giggled and chuckled at what she assured me had to be the most original comments ever made in reference to such august figures in the pantheon of modern verse. Or words to that effect.

When we reached the Land Rover, I rooted in the box beneath the passenger seat and fished out the prints of Catamaran. There were eight in all and, to avoid possible explanations, I had separated them earlier from the photographs of the heavy party. These I had left in their original Sureprint wallet, intending to post them on to Marnie, if ever I got her address, though she probably wouldn't want to be reminded.

"Photographs? Of what?" Claire asked, opening the used envelope which I'd put them in.

"Catamaran. The last photographs taken of him. They were taken the same day that he died. That very morning. They

107

probably aren't of any use to you at this stage as he seems not to be news anymore. It's a pity I didn't have them when you were doing the article but they're not long back from the developers."

Claire was leafing through the prints. "These are great, Frank! Maybe I can do another article on Catamaran based on them – I'm sure the editor would go for it. You've really caught the power in the horse. Look at those muscles rippling under the shiny skin! What do they feed these animals on to develop them like that?"

"There are special formulations all worked out with the same care, or more, than they lavish on the manufacture of baby foods. And, of course, many breeders have their own little secret ingredients which they add in."

"Yeah?"

"Sure. A glass of port, a slice of lemon, a spoon of this, a cup of that, you name it. There are as many secret ingredients as there are owners. Catamaran was on sunflower seeds."

"Norris told you his secret ingredient?"

"No way!" I laughed. "These matters are covered by the Official Secrets Act! I found sunflower seeds in a dung sample I took from Catamaran that morning, the same time that I took the pictures. So you think you might be able to use them then?"

"Very likely. Which ones can I have?"

"Whichever ones you want."

"I suppose that I ought to let the boss decide on that. But maybe he'll want enlargements or copies or something. How would it be if I took the negatives and left the prints with you?"

"That's fine by me, probably a good idea in fact."

The negatives were in the original wallet which now contained only the party pictures. I lifted the passenger seat and, half-obscuring the well beneath, returned the prints of Catamaran to the wallet and removed the cellophane envelope of negatives. Holding them up against the bright sky, I went through the celluloid strips and separated the two which contained the Catamaran negatives. Conveniently, all eight negatives were on two strips, four on each. Claire found an envelope in her bag, removed its letter and placed the strips of negatives carefully inside. I put the remaining negatives back into the wallet and closed down the seat.

"It's a pity that you didn't have one of yourself and Catamaran. That would have made a nice centrepiece for a story."

"I meant to but the damned film ran out. I thought there were a few more to go."

I drove her to the station where she just managed to catch the train. We ran along the platform towards the last open door. There were so many things I wanted to say to her but there was no time.

"Any chance you could make it down at the weekend?" I asked her as she turned to me when we reached the door.

"I think that that might be arranged," she smiled. "I'll look forward to it."

The whistle blew and the train gave a little lurch. I kissed her quickly and she hopped aboard. Then she was gone; out of sight, out over the sea-bridge which was only a few hundred yards along the line. I trudged back to the Land Rover, missing her intensely already. Ten minutes later I was out on the west road heading for Knockmore and a late start to the afternoon calls.

Claire phoned the next night. She wouldn't be able to come for the weekend after all. She had to go across to England.

"There's a friend of Mother's dying in Leamington Spa and I'm going to go across with her. She wants the company."

"That's tough. I'm sorry."

"She's only in her fifties. Cancer of the liver. So, I'm afraid I won't be able to make it this weekend."

"There'll be other weekends."

"There will indeed," she replied after a very slight pause.

I almost told her that I loved her then but we had an agreement. No rushing things. Let matters develop at their own pace. At her pace really. For my part, I was as sure as I was ever going to be.

As it transpired, the weekend was hectic anyway; one emergency after another with scarcely time to eat in between, and, a little after nine on Sunday night I fell into bed exhausted, and was asleep in seconds.

CHAPTER 13

*T*he last of the late evening half-light was dissolving into darkness as I brought the jeep to a halt outside the cottage late on Monday evening. Mondays are usually hectic and this one had been a lulu. Yawning cavernously, I opened the garden gate; the squeak of the hinges startled a sleeping bird and with a great clatter of wings, it shot out of the apple tree and flapped off over the cottage, squawking its raucous protest. In the dark porch, I fumbled the key into the lock by touch and passed on into the deeper dark of the house. I heeled the door closed behind me and reached for the light switch.

In an instant, my drowsiness shattered. Between the action of raising my hand towards the switch and actually touching it, the skin shuddered tight along my back raising my nape-hairs stiffly; in the impenetrable blackness I sensed rather than heard movement near me – positive, menacing movement. I flicked on the switch.

There was hardly time for me to raise a reflex defensive arm before the masked figure rushing at me knocked me backwards. I came to rest in a sitting position, my hands beneath me. As my assailant wrenched open the door and headed for the night, I overcame my shock enough to have a go. I threw myself at him, rugby fashion, managing to wrap my arms around one leg at mid-shin. I heard a frightened curse as he tried to haul me along the rough path and I was just concentrating on making a grab at his other leg when I became aware of a rush of footsteps behind me. Glancing over my shoulder, I saw, silhouetted against the bright rectangle of the open door, a menacing figure towering over me. In his hands, high above his head, he held a golf-club which at that moment, began to whistle down in a lethal arc.

Instinctively, I released my grip on the leg and tried to get my arms into a protective position; I didn't quite manage it and, though the deadly force was somewhat absorbed by my left fore-arm, the club-head detonated against my temple, scattering my senses in a kaleidoscopic explosion of nauseating pain.

I rolled limply off the path onto the herbaceous border. In my semi-conscious state, I overheard voices from what seemed a great distance: "Jesus! You've killed him!" the first one said in horror. "Run, damn you! Run!" the second one urged, panic-stricken. Then there was the squeak of the gate, feet running on the pavement, the sound of car doors being wrenched open and slammed shut.

Grimly determined, I forced myself into a half-stance and stumbled to the gate, with great difficulty making my mind concentrate on getting the car number, or at least a description of it. However, it didn't come past the gate – it roared off up the side road.

"Damn and blast!" I said disgustedly, and leaned weakly against the wrought ironwork, bent over, dry-retching. My head was a shifting mass of throbbing pain and each attempt at throwing up made it worse. After a while it passed, but I remained doubled over, gulping in huge draughts of cool air and collecting my senses. Then, very gingerly, I straightened and shuffled unsteadily for the door.

In the split second between switching on the light and being attacked, I had just about noticed that the room was a sham-bles, but I was shocked all over again when I saw how total the devastation really was. The once comfortable apartment was now a wreck.

The tall elegant bookshelves had been violently emptied, the books thrown about the room – some had pages torn out, oth-ers had had their covers pulled off and lay scattered around, naked and vulnerable as oysters on the half shell; they lay on the floor, on the slashed sofa and armchairs and, soot-covered, in the grate.

Mingled with the books were the LPs. They had been sys-tematically removed from their sleeves which now lay in a heap beneath the record cabinet; oddly, I noted, the inner sleeves had also been removed.

The state-of-the-art sound system was face down on a pile of LP sleeves; on top of it, the video recorder, all smoked glass, digital display panels and slide control knobs, canted at a crazy angle, while above the whole mess, seemingly defying gravity, the TV perched askew on its shelf. More than half of it stuck out in space; from its outer bottom stud the cardboard backing panel hung, exposing its internal organs. I replaced it and pushed the set back to safety.

The rest of the furniture had suffered a similar fate. An inlaid bureau was lying on its back, ravaged, its drawers torn out and left lying among their one-time contents; a large *papier mache* globe had been smashed open, presumably by the fire iron which stuck out of it like a spoon from a boiled egg.

In the corner by the fireplace there was a tall slim cabinet which housed a collection of birds' eggs; the eggs had been dumped on the floor but had been spared any breakages that I could see, presumably by their lightness. The boxes in which they had nestled lay nearby, the green baize lining torn from the underlying wood, and, though the cabinet was still upright, the baize had been torn away from its shelves and back.

I went into the bedroom to phone the police and found that it had received the same treatment – bed, pillow, mattress, clothes, suitcase, cupboards and drawers had been thoroughly searched inside and out and the stuffing of the mattress plus the insulating material from a couple of anoraks lay on the floor in drifts of grey slush. I had a box-file of personal papers on the side table and it too had been closely scrutinised, though not thrown about.

Jesus! I thought. What a fucking mess!

They had got in through the bathroom window. It was broken and the plastic curtains with the tropical fish on them billowed gently in the breeze.

I dabbed a cold compress on the rapidly rising lump on my head and continued my inspection. The spare bedroom seemed to have had a more cursory examination than had my room, but the kitchen had received the grand treatment; dresser, cupboards, cooker and fridge had all been pulled away from the wall and searched – even the freezer section of the fridge had been emptied and the floor covering had been torn up at the corners and edges. I righted a chair and set the kettle for coffee. When in doubt, make coffee.

As I sat and sipped and nursed my bump, I began to think, but even that hurt and I didn't trust my sore head to retain my thoughts. So I wrote them down, randomly, higgledy-piggledy as they came to me:

(1) *Why? (Motive?).*
  (a) Vandals? Prbly no because:
    – eggs not broken?!
    – LPs ditto?!
    – not young man (late vocation? slow developer?)
    – tweed trousers and brogues (stolen?);
    – high class vandal?
  (b) Assault? No.
    – Only hit me to escape;
    – Could have given me fierce hammering;
    – I've no known enemies.
  (c) Robbery? No.
    – TV, CD, etc. still here.
  (d) Personal grudge? Against me? Not very likely.
    – No known enemies;
    – Isn't my property that's ruined;
    – If true, must know me well because big grudge;
    – If know me well, know it's not my property.
  (e) Prsnl grudge against owner? Quite possible.
    – I know nothing about him, not even his name;
    – He's been away three months as they would know;
    – So why now? Why the delay?
  (f) Psychopaths? Hardly.
    – Two psychos??!!!
  (g). Searching for something? Most likely.
    – Of mine? No. Got no valuables.
    – Owner's? Probably. Seems well off.
    – Looking in books, LPs etc. So… small, flat,…

At this point Potter and the same two colleagues arrived. "God Almighty!" he said, peering over my shoulder as I opened the door. I stood aside to admit them. "Holy God

Almighty! Would you look at this for a mess!" Potter continued, surveying the wreckage.

As we went from room to room, I explained what had happened. When we got to the bathroom with its broken window, O'Hanlon produced a small case and went to work on the sill, dusting it for fingerprints. The Inspector and I wandered back to the living room, me continuing with my story. Every few sentences, he'd interrupt with a question or a comment and when I came to the part about the car being parked in the side-road, he held up his hand to stop me and turned to the uniformed man. "Nip round there, Fitzy, and see what you can see – and bring in that golf club when you're coming back." Fitzy left. "And don't forget not to touch the handle of the club," Potter called after him. "He's a good lad, Fitzy, but sometimes these youngsters get excited." He called again, louder. "Or the head, Fitzy!" He turned back to me: "Your man would have taken it out of the golf-bag by the head." I nodded.

"I put a few thoughts down on paper while I was waiting for you," I said, handing him the sheet. He read through it with an occasional 'Mmmm' or 'Uh-huh' and handed it back to me.

"Nice reasoning, Mr Samson. I'd say you're probably right. Are you certain that you don't have anything of value?"

"I should be so lucky!" I snorted. "I'm certain."

He wandered off looking here and there in a way that I suspected wasn't as aimless as it seemed. I continued with my coffee.

"No wills, deeds, share certificates, nothing of that nature?" He regarded me from under bunched brows. "You're sure?"

"Certain," I replied.

"But what about the owner? Would he have?"

"Mr Maloney?"

"Mrs Steele's brother; I don't remember his name."

"It's Maloney. James Maloney. It's possible that he could have, I suppose, but he's been in the States since the end of March and it's failing me to figure out what would suddenly give somebody an unholy desire to go looking for something hidden by him, months after he could possibly have hidden it. I don't think he'd have hidden anything here anyway. He's a most neat man, fastidious, you could almost say. Anything of value would have been locked away in the bank."

Fitzy came back. In one hand, he carried the golf club (by the neck) and, in the other, a pale yellow latex glove. He carried it as if it had been used in some foul operation, at arm's length, his thumb and forefinger barely holding it by the wrist. "I found this just outside the gate sir," he intoned importantly and dropped it on the table with the gravity befitting 'Exhibit A'.

"Only one?"

"Only one, sir; there was nothing on the other road that I could see, and I went up about three hundred yards."

"Did you check both sides of the road?"

"Of course, sir!" Fitzy said, hurt.

"Good man yourself, Fitzy. Nip in there now and see how the fingerprinting is getting along. I'll want that club dusted as soon as the bathroom is ready – though I think we'll be unlucky by the look of that glove." Fitzy headed off. "Correct me if I'm wrong," Potter continued in a tone which didn't allow for that possibility, "but isn't this a surgical glove?" He poked at it with his pen, then picked it up.

"It looks like it," I said. "May I have a look?" He handed it to me. "Indeed you're not wrong, Inspector. It is a surgical glove – best brand."

"It's not one of your own, by any chance?"

"No. Wrong brand, wrong size."

"What size do you use?"

"Eight. This one is six and a half, too small for me – even though the material stretches." I held up a hand for him to compare sizes. "It's a new one too."

"How can you tell?"

"I can smell the talc. They've got powder in them to make it easier to get them on – kind of dry lubrication. You can still smell it; in fact," I rubbed a few fingertips together, "you can still feel it."

"And the glove is good quality?"

"The best. It would allow almost perfect sensation in the fingertips – just what I'd use for brain surgery. Though I fail to see what this pair needed complete sensation in their fingertips for! The nearest they came to brain surgery was with yon mashie niblick."

115

"Three iron," Potter said automatically, obviously a golfer. "Do vets do brain surgery?"

"No. Not as a rule. I was merely illustrating a point."

"Oh. The glove complicates matters a bit," he said vaguely.

"How so?"

"Well, it gives an air of professionalism to an otherwise very amateur botch-up of a job. Very, very amateur."

"What makes you say it was amateurish?"

"Practically everything about it. Take for instance the mode of entry, the bathroom window – smashed! I had a look at the lock there on the front door and any self-respecting burglar would have had it open quicker than you would using your key; certainly any burglar pro enough to use hot-shot surgical gloves. On the other hand, I suppose we must consider the fact that the bathroom window is the *only* one not visible from the road and they must have broken in at least an hour ago to have done this much damage and, at that stage, it would still have been bright. Maybe the reason they didn't use the front door was that they were afraid they might be seen by passers by. But I still think they were amateurs. Look around you! That's no way to search a place! And I would have expected a pro to be able to handle a job like this single-handed. But most of all, a pro, or in this case, pros, would have been well gone before you entered the house; they don't go in for rough stuff as a rule – thugs, yes, pro burglars, no."

"Perhaps I surprised them. Took them unawares, as it were."

"You didn't. As I said, except for the bathroom, all the rooms have windows onto the path. If they'd been working and didn't hear you coming, you'd have seen lights, wouldn't you? Torches or whatever? That is, unless they were working in the bathroom, which is unlikely, as there's nothing in there to search. So the way you must figure it is: they hear your jeep pull up – or see it – and douse their lights immediately; but that's it! Beyond that brilliant strategy, they can't think what to do and just stand, rooted to the spot until your entry *forces* some action on them. They must have had at least a couple of minutes between the time they heard you coming and the time you turned on the light, and they couldn't even get out the way they'd come in! Some pros!" His scorn was obvious.

O'Hanlon had been working away at the handle of the three iron. He straightened up. "Nothing," he said, disgusted; "and nothing in the bathroom either."

"As I said, not with the gloves." Potter didn't seem too disappointed. "We'll just take another look around to see if there's anything we might've missed. Perhaps you could do the same and see if you notice anything missing."

I finished before them and with just as little results. I made coffee for us all while I waited for them to finish; one by one, they came to the kitchen lured by the smell.

"Anything?" I asked, needlessly.

"Nothing," Potter replied. "You?"

"No." I shook my head – gingerly, in deference to my left temple.

"Well then, that's that, isn't it? There's not a lot more we can do here tonight. I think, Fitzy, you better stay here the night, in case they decide to finish off the job. I'll send McMahon down to keep you company. Now, what about you, Mr Samson? There isn't a bed fit to sleep in and you won't find a hotel room at this time of night at this time of year. I think you ought to come home with me."

"Lord no! I wouldn't *dream* of it!"

"I'll give the missus a buzz right this minute and tell her," he went on as if I hadn't even spoken. "You need that bump looked at anyway, and she's a nurse. The spare room is always ready, so it's no problem."

Five minutes later, he was driving me in my own Land Rover to his house. As I got out in the driveway of the neat bungalow, I could smell bacon and eggs and, as we entered the hallway, I could hear them sizzling; I suddenly realised that I hadn't eaten all day and offered no more than a polite, token show of resistance when Mrs Potter said they were for me. My headache subsided even more as I sat in the warm kitchen demolishing the food as genteelly as I could. Afterwards, we sat talking into the small hours.

They were an interesting and friendly pair and soon we were on first name terms, like we'd been buddies forever. Right cosy it was. During a lull in the conversation, my attention was caught by a glass case full of medals, trophies, cups and the other trappings of successful competition.

"Have the children won all those?"

"No actually," Peter replied, glad I had asked, "that was Joan and me. We won them."

"Oh yeah?" I asked, surprised. "For what?"

"Ballroom dancing. We used to do a lot of it. We were runners-up in the All Ireland Finals twice and semi-finalists six years in a row. We never actually won it; unfortunately, our Paso Doble let us down each year. It was always our weakest." And he whistled a few bars in a catchy rhythm which I assumed was the dreaded Paso Doble.

"Well at least it gives the lie for once and for all to the alleged flat-footedness of the force," I said.

"I don't know about that," Potter replied, raising one leg and studying a foot which was abnormally small for a man of his size. "I'm probably the exception that proves the rule. I take size seven. I think the smallest size they had in the depot when I joined was ten! In those days we all had to be over the six foot mark. Some of them had boots like young violin cases. I was the odd man out. Do you know what the sergeant used to call me?"

"No."

"Guess," he urged, turning to smile over at his wife who was already grinning at the memory.

"Twinkletoes?" I hazarded.

"Uh-huh." He shook his head. "The old rogue used to call me 'The Peter Potter of Tiny Feet'. It used to drive me *wild* especially as I was the youngest recruit in the place."

We laughed happily at the thirty year old pun. Soon after, he showed me to the spare room and wished me goodnight. Despite the excitement of the evening and the pain in my head, I fell asleep almost instantly and, for the first night in a long time, Claire didn't turn up to fill my dreams. Nothing did.

CHAPTER 14

Next morning, it looked as though my luck was in. I nursed a relatively mild headache through a quick, undemanding clinic and afterwards set out with the shortest list of farm visits I had had since arriving in Knockmore. However, a few minutes after noon, the easy day got a kick in the ribs. Eileen came over the radio-telephone with an urgent call for Bally Ard. Deja vu.

"What's the problem?" I asked uneasily. "Over."

"Mr Norris's hunter," she replied uneasily. "Bad colic. Over."

"O.K. I'm on my way. Over and out." I swung the Land Rover around and headed for Bally Ard. Uneasily.

Colic in horses is a strange thing. It can be caused by any number of factors ranging from wind pains and mild indigestion at one end of the scale to ruptured stomach, twisted gut, torsion, volvulus, intussusception and other horrendous conditions at the other. The problem is how to tell them apart.

Often the symptoms aren't a lot of help. Horses are not, by a long shot, the stoics of the animal kingdom and are not known for their silent suffering, so a horse with a build up of wind can act the same as one in the early stages of one of the fatal colics. X-ray machines powerful enough to penetrate the bulk of a horse's body are not usually part of the equipment of a GP and laboratory tests take time. Exploratory laparotomy (in layman's terms, opening up to have a look inside) is a long process and difficult when one is working on one's own, and is not usually carried out. Sometimes, rectal examination can help and sometimes there may be some specific symptoms associated with a specific cause of colic. However, the point is that even if one *does* manage to diagnose the exact cause of a serious colic, there's not an awful lot one can do about it. Most of these conditions require immediate surgery and major abdominal operations carried out single-handed, under field conditions, are more heroic than practical. In an ideal world, they'd be referred to a team of specialists, but this would take too long to organise and, in most cases, cost more than the animal was worth. A sad fact, but surgery is rarely a practical option.

With the way my luck had been running lately, I was convinced that the colic would be one of the deadlier ones and I began to have a waking nightmare of putting down Norris's horses at the rate of a couple a month until I cleaned him out. Then I remembered: he only had the hunter left – he had sold the others to raise the cash to buy into the syndicate. So today, I could in fact, wipe him out. Jesus H.

I swept through the majestic gates of Bally Ard, passed by the house and drove straight to the yard. There was no point in stopping at the house as I knew that Norris, being an experienced owner, would be with the horse, keeping it walking, walking, all the time walking, to stop it from lying, rolling and threshing about; the equine reaction to abdominal pain can easily lead to injuries of the limbs, head or back.

Norris, when he saw me, waved a hand and led the handsome chestnut gelding across to the gate. My attention was riveted on the horse, which, to my relief, seemed to be acting quite normally. There were none of the usual signs of colic, no foot stamping, tail swishing, bending the back, wanting to lie down etc. But he had sweated up badly and his coat was wet.

Exchanging brief words with Norris, I got to work. I checked the horse's pulse, the colour of the mucous membranes of his eye, listened to his abdominal sounds, took his heart rate, respiration rate and temperature, all of which, to my great relief and mild surprise, were normal.

"Amazing," I said to myself more than to Norris. "Was he bad?"

"He was, actually. I was quite worried at the time I rang for you. As you can see, he sweated up a lot."

"I see that." I nodded.

"Then about ten minutes ago, he passed a lot of wind and

that seemed to give him instant relief. I was going to cancel the call, but then I thought it best to let it stand and have him checked out anyway."

"Quite right. Well," I said, looking at the horse again, "whatever it was seems to have gone. Hopefully anyway. I presume that he's been dosed for worms? They can cause colic you know."

"Of course he's been dosed!" Norris sounded vaguely insulted. "We dose here regular as clockwork! Got to. Studfarm. Endanger the foals. Not to mention the brood mares!" He gave me the lecture I'd have given him if he had said no. "Can't have contaminated paddocks. Wouldn't do."

"Just checking every angle," I said placatingly. I didn't tell him that the dung sample I had taken from Catamaran had been positive. Best leave it to Steele to sort that one out when he got back. Still, it was no hardship to check a little further. Sneakily, like. "I'll just take a sample to check that your dosing programme is effective; it's no harm to check it out every now and then."

"It better be effective! It costs enough, that new stuff."

I gave the horse an antispasmodic injection just in case the pain came back, took the dung sample and prepared to leave. Norris however, would have none of it.

"No, no! You must come in for a drink and talk with me for a while! I absolutely insist! We've hardly spoken since... that awful day and I wanted to thank you for being so splendid and for staying with... Catamaran to the end."

"Well...." I began disclaimingly.

"Please?" Norris interrupted. "Just for a few minutes?"

"O.K. then. Perhaps a cup of coffee might not be a bad idea after all."

"Splendid! Capital! Marvellous!" Superlatives tumbled from him as he took a lift with me back from the stables.

He led me up the steps and into the house, then headed straight for a door at the back of the hall, calling for the housekeeper as he went. I barely had time to notice that the pictures of Catamaran had all been removed and replaced with various prints. 'The king is dead. Long live the prints,' I punned to myself irreverently as I followed Norris.

121

"Mrs Flahive!" he called. "Mrs Flahive!"

"Yes, Mr Norris?" Her voice came from behind us; she had emerged from one of the reception rooms off the hall. In her hand she carried a yellow duster.

"Ah! There you are! We'd like some coffee please, at your convenience."

"Very well, sir. I shall bring it to the study presently."

"Not the study, Mrs Flahive. With your permission we shall join you in the kitchen." He turned to me: "It's much more homely – especially for two hard-working men in their working clothes."

"Of course," I agreed, wondering if I had unknowingly got my clothes very dirty during the morning. I hadn't thought so.

Mrs Flahive was looking at her employer in disbelief. Eventually, she found her voice. "In the *kitchen*, Mr Norris?" I thought for a moment that she was going to protest but she didn't. "Very well sir," she said in a disapproving tone and led us through the door which Norris held open for her and then for me.

We sat at a small table in a little room off the kitchen. At one time, it might have been a larder or scullery or housemaid's pantry or one of those now-obsolete rooms, but it seemed to have become Mrs Flahive's own preserve and her displeasure, as she spread a red gingham cloth on the table was positively proprietorial. Norris didn't seem to notice. He was waffling on about my sterling presence in his darkest hour. "Don't know what I'd have done without you my boy! I just do not know."

I tried, once or twice, to protest his lavish and wholly exaggerated praise, but soon gave up; Norris wasn't hearing anything I said. So I simpered self-deprecatingly three or four times and left it at that. The arrival of the coffee put a stop to his gallop, but only briefly. Halfway through his coffee, he suddenly looked at his watch. "My goodness! Is it that already?! I've got to make a phone call. Will you excuse me for a moment?"

Before I could answer, he was gone. His behaviour had been too strange to ignore so I more or less had to mention it to Mrs Flahive.

122

"Mr Norris seems a little overwrought," I commented. "But I suppose that what he's been through would be enough to make anybody overwrought. I only hope that my presence here hasn't upset him – you know, by association or whatever."

"Oh, don't think that, Mr Samson! He's been... like that for the past few days now. At first, after it happened, he was fine. I didn't think he'd get over it, he was that fond of the horse. But he was great, really great. It's only in the last couple of days that it's begun to bother him. He's seemed anxious. Delayed shock, I think it is myself. This morning he had me take down the pictures of Catamaran from the hall as if he couldn't bear to look at them any longer." She shook her head sadly. "He didn't even want to be reminded by empty spaces, it seems, because when he was going back out to the yard after phoning for you, he noticed the bare walls and he and I spent twenty minutes filching pictures from other rooms to fill the gaps. More coffee?"

"No thank you." I looked at my watch. "I really ought to be getting back on the road. Do you think Mr Norris will be back soon? I'd rather not leave without saying goodbye."

"I doubt he'll be much longer. He's left a half cup of coffee and I think he'd have taken it with him if he expected to be away for long. He's very fond of coffee, especially at this hour."

"I'll wait until half past," I said. Four more minutes – a respectful and a respectable time. He had already been gone about ten minutes. By mutual unspoken agreement, the subject of Gilbert Norris was dropped and a silence ensued. We had exhausted our one topic of common interest. Now, the silence in the old kitchen was broken only by the ticking of a pendulum clock which slowly and remorselessly whiled away the years from the vantage point of a hook above the range. It was more than an hour slow. Looking around the kitchen, I noticed that there were beautiful feathers everywhere – in vases, jugs, empty wine bottles, behind pictures, the calendar, and even on top of the tardy clock. Like other houses have cut flowers, this house had feathers. They ranged in size from large quill-like wing primaries and tail feathers to tiny downy ones, and in colour, from the most vivid primaries to the subtlest pastels.

"Are they real?" I asked, vaguely indicating the displays.

"I'm sorry, Mr Samson," Mrs Flahive interrupted some thought. "Are what real?"

"All those feathers!"

"Oh yes indeed, sir! They're real alright."

"What an amazing collection! I feel as though we're surrounded, ha ha ha, by a horde of renegade Apaches!"

Either she missed my subtle witticism or decided that it didn't warrant an answering smile. "They are all feathers from different members of the parrot family. Psittacines, I believe the technical word is?"

"I'm sure you're perfectly correct. Psittacines sounds about right. But where did you come by them?"

"Mr Vernon brings them to me."

"I'm sorry, I don't know him."

"He's a friend of Mr Norris's and he's got one of the largest collections of psittacines in the country. If not in Europe! All free flying."

"Free flying? Do you mean *loose*? Out in the open?"

"Yes. Mr Vernon lives in what he describes as a wooded oasis in the middle of miles and miles of bog, so there's nowhere for the birds to fly to."

"But don't they attract every sparrow-hawk for miles around too?"

"You'd have to ask my son, Eddie, about that. He works with Mr Vernon during his school holidays. I think that Mr Vernon also keeps a large flock of doves to... distract the hawks."

Norris returned just as the conversation was getting interesting and I made a mental note to try to arrange a visit to the wooded 'oasis' in the bogs. He didn't seem to have calmed down any nor had he begun to act more rationally. "Ah, *there* you are!" he said as if he'd just stumbled on my secret hiding place. "Mrs Flahive been looking after you, I trust? Good, good, good. Well, I've detained you long enough and I'm sure you've more to do than sit and listen to a silly old man, so I shan't keep you any longer. Next time, we must make sure we're not interrupted." He remained standing by the door, and I, who can take a hint as well as the next man, stood up.

"Well actually I am quite busy," I lied to lessen the feeling of being chucked out. "Thank you for the coffee, Mrs Flahive.

Good day."

At the hall door, Norris thanked me again for coming so quickly and shook my hand. Obviously, this was as far as he intended to come.

"Wouldn't you like me to have a last look at the hunter before I leave?"

"I'm sure he's fine. You did a good job."

"Still, I think I'll look in on him. I'd feel better."

"Very wise thing to do," he agreed gravely. "Very wise."

"Well... eh... fine then. If there's anything amiss, I'll come back and let you know."

"Yes, splendid. Well, mustn't keep you. Thank you again. Goodbye."

"Goodbye and don't hesitate to call if the pain comes back."

I drove round to the yard and looked in on the hunter; as my shadow fell on the floor of his box, he turned and looked back at me, the picture of health, chewing his sweet hay.

Shrugging, I decided never to look a gift hunter in the mouth, sat into the jeep and drove off.

That evening, I started making Fernditch habitable again. Eileen, her sister and the sister's boyfriend came to help and after a couple of hours, it was as right as it was going to be without actually replacing some of the furniture. I drove into town and bought us pizzas and after, drove my volunteers home.

On my way back, I stopped off at the surgery to check the hunter's dung sample and, though I did the test three times, there was no sign whatsoever of worm eggs. Not one. Bang went my accommodating theory of the worming medicine being defective. But there had to be some explanation and, while trying to figure out what it might be was good mental exercise, it only led me back on to the merry-go-round: how come the precious Catamaran had a fairly heavy worm burden while his stablemate had none? Had Catamaran been dosed at all? Had somebody shirked because he was so hard to handle? Had he managed to spit out the dose? Et cetera, et (ad nauseam) cetera.

One thing was sure: Norris realised the importance of

proper routine dosing and he was under the illusion that his stallion had been dosed. I wouldn't have liked to be in the wellies of whoever had the responsibility for that job, when and if it came to light that the horse had had worms. I gave up and went to bed.

Late the following night there was a breakthrough of sorts. At least I found out what the burglars had been searching for.

About ten-thirty I decided to tackle some of my long over-due correspondence and, a couple of hours later, there was a gratifying pile of envelopes addressed and ready for posting in the morning – the only chore left was to send off a roll of film which I had finished the previous week. I fetched my camera bag and peeled open the velcro-sealed pouch where I keep my used rolls. It was empty.

I knew at once that the reel had to have been stolen. I was sure of it. I *always* put exposed rolls there (in fact I could distinctly remember putting this one in), and there was no way that it could have fallen out; that velcro flap didn't open easily – you had to damn near *tear* it apart. With this discovery, things suddenly began to fall into place, to make some sense. At last. On a hunch, I checked the camera. The exposure counter window showed 'E'. Empty. The new film I had loaded had been stolen too! I opened the camera, double-checking. Empty. This opened a whole new line of thought.

It didn't need any great brainwork to conclude that what the intruders had been searching for in record sleeves, between the pages of books, and under the lining of shelves, was a photograph or photographs that I had taken, and that, having drawn a blank at the cottage, they had moved on to the next most likely place, the camera bag and camera itself. Or maybe it was the other way round – perhaps they had stolen the undeveloped films first. Either way it didn't matter. They had now been through all the photographs I had taken in the past couple of months and I couldn't imagine that what they wanted pre-dated that - surely they'd never have taken the film from the *camera* unless what they wanted was pretty recent?

I glanced at my watch. The new day was almost an hour old – too late to call Potter. Anyway, he couldn't do much until morning. It would keep. I stood up stiffly, yawned, stretched, and turned out the table lamp. Then I did my last round, checking windows and doors, a habit I had developed since the break in.

While I was washing my teeth and getting ready for bed, I tried to think of all the photographs I had taken recently but could only manage a few. I was far too tired – I'd sleep on it, tackle it afresh in the morning. At least, I thought, climbing into bed and switching off the light, there was one good thing about it – now that they had (or had seen) all the prints I had taken in the previous months and, presumably either found them harmless, or destroyed the ones they didn't like, I should be safe. Assuming they were reasonable, rational beings, they would now call off the hunt and I would be troubled no longer. It was a comforting feeling to go to sleep on. However, moments later, just as I slid over the threshold of sleep, I wondered what kind of reasonable, rational beings would steal films and leave a valuable camera, lenses, etc. They might as well have sent me a notice telling me what they were looking for...

But it was too late for further thought. The door to consciousness closed behind me with a gentle click.

CHAPTER 15

In my dream there was a phone ringing. I let it ring for a while before picking it up. "Hello?" I asked in my dream. Claire asked: "Is that Frank Samson, the greatest lover the world has ever known?" In my dream I replied, "Yes. This is he," in all seriousness. It never would have crossed my mind to doubt it; I suppose that that's what dreams are for. The only problem was that during this potentially riveting dream conversation, there was another phone ringing somewhere in the background and it went on and on with such insidious persistence that the dream became bothered, shimmered briefly then evaporated, leaving me groping confusedly for the bedside phone. I wouldn't have minded only I was going really well – getting places. I fumbled the receiver, dropped it on the floor and hauled it in again on its cord.

"Hullo?" I said thickly, coughed and tried again. "Hello?" I tried to make it seductive, like the voice of the greatest lover the world has ever known.

There was an unsure pause. "Is that the vet?" This wasn't Claire's voice! What was… what…

"Yes, yes. This is the vet, yes. Speaking. Yes. The vet." I was coming awake by degrees now, though still largely on automatic pilot. The other person had fallen silent, or maybe asleep. "Are you in trouble?" I asked, helping the conversation along. I was now almost fully awake.

"Well… yes. I'm sorry for calling at this hour, but I've got a young heifer calving…" A cultured voice. Gentleman farmer.

"How young?"

"She's only twenty months…"

"Is she any size?" I asked hopefully.

"No. She's a small one. I didn't even know she was in calf until a while ago. She must have broken in to the bull-field, and the bull is a Charollais..."

"Oh Christ!" I muttered. It was almost certainly going to be a long and troublesome delivery. "How long has she been calving?"

"Couple of hours now."

"Has she broken her waters?"

"Over an hour ago."

"Anything coming?"

"No. No sign. I didn't handle her though. I'd prefer to leave that to the man who knows what he's up to. She's straining a lot."

"Okay." I sighed heavily. "I'm on my way then. What's the name?"

"John Kiernan."

"Of?"

"Oak Hill Farm."

"Can you give me the directions, please?"

"Do you know the 'Cave Inn' on the Galway road?"

I made a mental note of his instructions. "Fine then, I've got that. I'll be there in about twenty minutes. You better have some boiling water ready – she sounds like she might need a Caesarean."

"I know. I'll have the water ready."

With a sigh of resignation I rolled out of bed, dressed in the clothes I had shed a few hours previously and headed for the bathroom. I splashed cold water on my face and winced, made a comb of my wet fingers and headed out into the mild night. On my way through town, I stopped off at the surgery to get a sterile surgical pack from the cabinet, hoping that I'd be returning it in the morning, its autoclave sealing tape unbroken. I wrote 'J. Kiernan, Oak Hill Farm. Heifer calving, 2.30am' on the call book, switched out the light and pulled the door after me. I tried the radio on the way out the road but could get nothing but the squeaks, squeals and whistles that always seem to possess car radios in the small hours. Soon the 'Cave Inn' showed up in the headlights, and I indicated to the emptiness behind me that I was going left. His directions proved accurate and in a short time I rolled to a stop before impressive iron gates, my tyres crunching in the loose gravel of the semi-circular area between them and the public road.

I left the engine running and the lights on and sat for a moment expecting someone to come and open up. My lights-beams, passing through the bars, shone on nothing beyond. There were no ghostly buildings within their range and there was no sign of lights further out again beyond them in the blackness. While I waited, I studied the gates.

They were set in the centre of high walls of cut limestone which curved gracefully out to the roadside. Directly inside them, there was a cattle grid and they were prevented from opening inwards by its raised edge, against which they rested. A large stone prevented them from opening out, and there was a length of chain wrapped round them where they met, which prevented them from opening in or out. It seemed silly to me that the gates should be shut at all as the cattle grid looked perfectly sound and capable of doing the job for which it was designed – keeping stock from passing through the gate in either direction. Perhaps, I mused disinterestedly, they were shut to keep people out? Then why were they not locked? Maybe they had been, but had been unlocked for me. But if that was the case, wouldn't the person who had unlocked them have gone the whole hog and actually *opened* them? I yawned cavernously and blew my horn once – just an announcement that I had arrived, not an imperious summons. I waited some more. By now, the airspace illuminated by my headlights was becoming congested with moths and other nocturnal fliers, all performing energetic aerial ballets, and I decided that no one was coming, blast them, so I climbed out to do the job myself.

I unwound the chain, draping it over a crossbar, and turned my attention to shifting the stone. It was too heavy to lift so I rolled it away from the gate. As the side which had faced the gate came suddenly into the glare of the headlights, I was brought up short when I saw the stem of ivy which clung to it. Despite being broken at both ends, it was fresh and full of sap, and its single three-pointed leaf stood stiff, shining and bright green. Obviously, it had been broken from the parent plant in the very recent past – a matter of hours at the most – and an uneasy feeling that something was very wrong began to well up warningly inside me. I started to straighten reflexly, quickly, just in time to see grotesque shadows leaping onto the limestone walls; over the knocking of the diesel engine, I could hear the crunch of footsteps rushing towards me.

I spun to face them but, being blinded by the Land Rover lights, all I could do was raise an arm to protect my head from the blow which I could sense coming. I raised the wrong arm. There was a dull thud as a club of sorts struck me on the right cheekbone and then I was being borne to the ground under the combined weight of my attackers. Feverish arms wrapped around me, pinning mine to my side; someone grabbed a fistful of hair at the back of my head and twisted it to steady my frantic struggling; a knee pressed down on my ear, further immobilising me and a pad, reeking of chloroform searched for and found my mouth and nose. I immediately stopped fighting because I had enough presence of mind to remember that chloroform is toxic to the heart and liver and a sudden gulping breath of almost pure chloroform would be specially dangerous to a heart already under severe stress. So I breathed as slowly as possible in the circumstances, in, out, in, out, in...

My last thought as consciousness ebbed away was that the stone had been placed at the gate with the express purpose of getting me out of the Land Rover and bending. Then I went under.

CHAPTER 16

*V*ery slowly, I floated up through the swirling black depths of unconsciousness. Crawling and clawing my way upwards, I broke surface into a pitch dark pitching world of pain. I tried to move my head, but the agony which burst in it drove me back down towards the abyss again. Next time I surfaced, I didn't dare move – I just lay there wallowing sluggishly on the surface of the ocean of oblivion, rising and falling with the swell and ebb of pain, being washed over by waves of nausea. At this stage, all I felt was a primitive satisfaction at being alive.

Gradually, some brain function returned. The first thing I worked out was that the calving case had been bogus, the next, that its purpose had been to set me up for a chance to capture me, and the next after that it had succeeded. I began to explore with my senses, not daring to move.

Smell: dank, unused, mouldy, unclean.

Touch: rough, hard, mattresslike, all under my back – an old bed; iron bed-end through the soles of my shoes.

Taste: bile, blood, chloroform.

Hearing: painful breathing, pumping heart.

Seeing: nothing. I was being kept in total darkness. Either that, a sudden horrifying spark of precocious logic mocked me, or I had lost my sight! I could be blind! This possibility worried me obsessively while I checked out my injuries.

Gingerly, I moved my legs; both worked, causing more discomfort to my head than to themselves. My arms told the same story; only the thumb and forefinger of my left hand had any trouble in moving and I remembered how they had been twisted back under me in the struggle at the gate. It seemed that my head, which was throbbing as though a giant piston were kneading my brain, was the most severely damaged part of me, and I reckoned that this was in large measure of chemical origin – the chloroform – and would quite quickly ease. Already it felt better than it had when I had first awoken. Just so long as I wasn't blind! Please God, let it not be that! I shuddered.

Reason began to return. It was now pretty obvious that the films from the camera bag *hadn't* been the right ones and that thought snookered me for a few moments. Then I remembered! They had *not* seen all the photographs I had taken during the last month, as I had thought in my earlier mental exercises – I had forgotten the ones I had taken to show Claire that day in Galway. Suddenly it all began to make sense. Apart from the few shots of Catamaran and Hynes at the end, that roll had been all Marnie's dodgy handiwork; a potential minefield! All that candid camera stuff at a party where drugs of all types were being passed around like canapés! She must have caught someone doing something they shouldn't have been doing (she could hardly have missed!) and now the chickens were coming home to roost. With me in the role of chicken farmer. The telltale prints now lurked in the box beneath the seat of the Land Rover and even in my fugged mental state, I had enough sense to realise that it was entirely possible that my continued existence might hinge on the fact that I was the only person who knew where they were. Silently and painfully, but with great feeling, I cursed Marnie for capturing mass lawlessness on *my* camera and then leaving me stuck with the baby.

It was at this point that a more practical problem presented itself. I became vaguely aware of faraway noise and listened intently, staying my breathing to do so. The noise became clearer, now recognisable as the opening of a door somewhere, followed by the unmistakable and loudening tread of approaching footsteps. Nervously, I composed myself to lie doggo – I had no intention of facing the next part of my ordeal until I had formulated some plan, or at least got my story straight. There was the sound of a padlock being opened, a bolt being drawn back, the door of the room opening, and I was uncomfortably aware of a presence.

"Are you awake?" a man's voice called softly, the voice of John Kiernan.

There was silence while he waited. I lay unmoving on the bed. Suddenly a light came on and the sudden brilliance, even through my closed lids, caused me to jerk my head away in reflex recoil. My fear that I had given the game away was outweighed by the elation of knowing that I wasn't blind. He must have decided that the twitch was a normal reflex reaction for one coming out of an anaesthetic, because he repeated the question just as softly: "Are you awake?"

I felt him approach the bed and I almost flinched when he touched my forehead, presumably to see if I was still alive. When I heard him retreating towards the door, I stole a quick glance – a very stupid thing to do. For one thing, I ought to have known that the light would dazzle me and I would see nothing; for another, he might have been looking back over his shoulder at me as he went, and I'd have blown it for nothing. But I got away with it.

The light went out; so did he, and after he had redone the lock, I heard his steps receding again. I listened until absolute silence settled back, then I listened some more. Finally, convinced that I was neither being observed nor sneaked up on, I sat up painfully and swung my legs onto the floor. I waited for my head to stop throbbing and then set out on an inch by inch journey towards the door, outstretched arms sweeping the space in front, eyes closed tight for their protection. Reaching the door, I groped on either side at about eye-level and quickly located the switch with my left hand. I clicked it down and, once more, the room was blindingly lit. When my eyes had adjusted, I took stock of my surroundings.

The only way out was the door. There were no windows or ventilator shafts and the door didn't look very hopeful. Gently, I tapped it; it had an uncomfortably solid ring to it. At eye-level there was the knob of a Yale lock and I wasn't surprised when turning it didn't yield results. On the same level, roughly in the centre, a crude peep-hole had been freshly cut but when I put my eye to it, I blocked out the light and I couldn't see anything on the other side; I tried standing back from it, but that didn't work either. I licked the top of a finger and stuck it through, hoping to feel the chill of a breeze or a draught but without result. All that that manoeuvre told me was that the door was almost as thick as my index finger was long. I turned my attention to the room.

The naked lightbulb hanging from the damp-stained ceiling lit the meagre furnishings in unforgiving starkness. There was the bed, a narrow, iron-framed thing with a thin, striped mattress, I rolled it back to check the bed irons, but the base was one solid rectangle of angle-iron with wire diamonds stretched tightly across it; it was also rusted fast into position. That was probably the best possibility of a lever/weapon gone and I disappointedly let the mattress roll back. I turned hopefully to the other bits of furniture.

'Bits' was the best word to describe what was left. Against the wall facing the foot of the bed, was a small, flimsy table, barely big enough for a breakfast tray, and beside it, a rickety-looking wooden chair. Either of these would serve as a weapon at a pinch, in its entirety or dismantled – I reckoned I could take them apart with my hands if I needed to – but at this stage, it was best to see how the land lay before beginning to dismember the place. Above the table, fixed to the wall on two brackets, there was a narrow shelf; covered in faded pink oilcloth, it held two little red votive lights in honour of the picture of the Sacred Heart which hung above it. The glass had a long diagonal crack, and the print beneath was brown-stained for an inch or so on either side of the crack. The glass might be another weapon if the going got really rough; the votive lights hadn't been lit for years by the look of them. There was no fireplace and, apart from the door, there were no other breaks in the wall; lots in the plaster, but none in the wall.

Since instant escape was out, I was forced to deal with the problem of what to tell my captors at our no doubt imminent interview. I couldn't very well deny that the photographs existed – Marnie must actually have been seen taking them, otherwise none of this would have happened. I switched off the light and retired to the bed to think.

There were several possibilities, but telling them where the prints were was not one of them; it was odds on that I wouldn't last five minutes after they got their hands on them.

So what was I going to tell them? It was a long time since the party so it was pretty unlikely that I would still have the film lying about undeveloped. Anyway, they'd just ask for the undeveloped roll; it wouldn't matter to them either way – developed or not would be all the same. But I couldn't give them the undeveloped roll, could I? Some smart plan.

Maybe I could say I had sent them to Marnie? She would surely be safe in Holland. Or would she? Someone was certain to have her Dutch address – she had been a very popular lady, had Marnie. The trouble with that story was that it wouldn't take them long to find her and to find out that she *hadn't* received any prints from me. If they didn't believe her, then Marnie presumably would end up like me, a prisoner, until somebody, somewhere actually came up with the goods. I rejected this plan, not only on the vaguely chivalrous grounds of protecting Marnie but also because it wouldn't win me any worthwhile time. Also, it might even have been Marnie who fingered me! She, or one of the Gang of Four were the only ones (as far as I knew) who knew that it had been *my* camera. Only one of them could have tied me in to the picture at all. No, it would not be wise to mention Marnie; even if my abductors hadn't spoken to her, it wouldn't take them long to do so; thus, for a short gain timewise, I would have shown myself to be an uncooperative liar who would need the closest watching at all times. Some clever plan, that.

My next idea wasn't very bright either. I could claim to have sent the reel for development and to be awaiting its return. It was sound inasmuch as it would suggest that I had never actually *seen* the prints and could not, therefore, be a threat, but it fell flat because they would only have to check with the lab, claiming to be me, to find out that I had not, in fact, any films awaiting processing, and had not had for weeks. Back to square one. Another washout.

That looked like being the shakings of the bag, that it would have to be a choice between them, when I suddenly had another idea. What if I were to claim that the camera had been loaded incorrectly, the film not caught on to the take-up spool and therefore not wound on when the lever was worked? It was, admittedly, pretty far-fetched, but it was possible. It had happened to me once, years ago. If I could only manage to get this bluff accepted, I'd be home and dried; no film meant no threat. I'd be in the clear. A highly convenient story all in all, but one which I might possibly push past them with a certain amount of luck. The one thing which might make them believe me was the fact that they couldn't know that I already knew that photographs were what they were looking for and they just might think that I couldn't come up with such a plausible story on the spur of the moment. It was a gamble, but it was worth a try.

I was refining it when I heard him approach again, and I decided to face him at this point – I wasn't going to be more ready. I swallowed hard and painfully as I heard the steps stop outside the door. Then it opened and the light came on.

CHAPTER 17

I sat bolt upright, as if the light had just awoken me. "What...
what... Where am I?" I mumbled semi-coherently, slewing my
head around in all directions. So far, so good. I had considered
trying to pretend that I thought I was the victim of a traffic
accident and that he was a kindly householder, and so drive
home the message that I was totally ignorant of what was going
on, but one look at him decided me that I'd have to forego that
bit of atmosphere setting. Kindly householders do not come to
see how the objects of their kindliness are getting along,
dressed in black balaclavas with nylon mesh sewn over the
mouth-hole, black anoraks and reflective lens sun-glasses. And
they usually carry grapes or bananas or mugs of Ovaltine, not
wicked-looking revolvers.

"Who are you?" I stared fixedly at him in awed fascination.
He said nothing and didn't move; he continued to regard me
through the mirrored lens of his glasses. I find those glasses
freaky at any time and now, on him, they almost totally
unnerved me. He was about fifty, I judged, more from his
hands than anything else because they were all I could see of
him. He was quite well-built, a couple of inches under six feet,
and broad shouldered. His trousers were tweed, his shoes
brogues. I was willing to bet that those were the same trousers
that I had wrapped my arms around the night the cottage was
broken into.

"Who are you?" I asked again. "What's all this about?"
He coughed nervously and shuffled his feet. I had the distinct impression that he was as uneasy as I was, and it puzzled
me. Vaguely I felt that it could only be good for me. He still
maintained his awkward silence.

"Is this political or something?" I threw in a red herring for what it was worth. Physically I was shaking but my mind kept clear.

"You...," he croaked and coughed again to clear the frog. "You will be held here... until we... complete our business with you. If you... if you cooperate, you will be released unharmed, but if you don't, it will end up... nasty." It was John Kiernan. Definitely.

"What do you want from me? You can have anything I have! I don't have any valuables!" I waited for him to tell me and, when he didn't, I said petulantly: "Tell me! How can I cooperate when I don't know what you're after?! What is it that you want?"

Instead of replying, he put a hand into the pocket of his anorak, pulled out a shiny set of handcuffs and threw them onto the bed beside me.

"Put them on. You don't need a key – they snap shut."

Reluctantly, I did as I was told, reckoning it as a move in the wrong direction. Apart from the physical restriction of having my hands bound together by a foot of chain, there was the psychological blow of having followed orders. With the click of the second cuff, my early developing confidence took a nose dive. His, on the other hand, rose by a similar measure.

"You've got something we want," he said, walking to the chair and pulling it out into the middle of the room. "Sit here."

"What is it?" I asked, moving to the chair. Another submission. Bad. "You can have anything I've got! I've told you that already! What is it?"

"You've got photographs." Assembling a frown of bewilderment, I launched into the grand performance.

"*Photographs*!" I squawked as if I wasn't sure I'd heard him correctly. "You mean *ordinary* photographs? That *I've* taken?"

"That's correct."

I considered this. "Are you sure you've got the right person?"

"We're sure."

"Well..." I said, at a loss for words and shrugging instead of a far more expressive spread of the hands, "take them! Take them all. I don't know what good they are to you, and I don't particularly want to know, but you're welcome to them." I felt

I was doing brilliantly.

"These would have been taken within the last couple of months."

"Well that doesn't leave many! I've been too busy lately to take many photographs." Then (surprise, surprise) a thought struck me. "Was *that* what you were looking for at the cottage? It *was* you, I presume? At the cottage?"

"Yes. We were looking for those particular photographs."

"I figured it wasn't burglary because nothing was missing, but... did you not find the photos? They were in the bedroom, plain to be seen!"

"Yes, we saw them, but they weren't the ones we want."

"In that case, you *must* have the wrong man. There *aren't* any more!... Oh, sorry! Sorry. I tell a lie. There's an undeveloped roll in my camera bag. And a film in the camera itself. That must be the answer. The camera and bag are in the back of my Land Rover."

"No. We've already checked those and they're not the right ones either."

"You've already checked them?" I said, feigning puzzlement. "You mean you've had them *developed*?"

"Yes." He nodded.

"Jesus! How long have I been here? What day is it?"

"We had them... removed a while ago, and developed, and they are not the ones we want."

"When?" I asked in amazement. "When did you have them removed?"

"That is of no consequence."

"Wow!" I shook my head in more amazement, setting the stage for the upcoming bluff.

"So... Where are they?" He tried to sound menacing.

"I'm afraid there aren't any more. I told you. That's it!"

"Oh, but there are, you know. There's at least one other roll." He sounded pretty sure of himself. This was going to take some doing.

"I tell you, there isn't!" I insisted. "You've seen the ones at the cottage and you've had the ones from the camera-bag ...right?" I waited for his answer... "Right?" I repeated, insisting. He nodded. "Well, that's it then. There aren't any more." I stopped suddenly. Bluff time had arrived. "Oh ho! I think I know where we're getting our lines crossed!... That must be it!"

"What must be it? What are you talking about?"

"Do you know anything about cameras?"

"Enough."

"Then you'll understand – maybe it's even happened to you."

"What?" His nervousness seemed to be easing; now he began to show ordinary emotions, like impatience. "What may have happened to me?"

"Threading the new film wrongly... not winding it correctly onto the take-up spool?... You know what I'm talking about?"

"Go on. I know." He began to pace, head bent. I waited for him to stop before continuing, but he waved me on absent-mindedly, "Go on go on go on. I'm listening."

"There's really not a lot to go on about. That's what happened."

"When?"

"Oh... four maybe five weeks ago; I couldn't be sure." I gulped quietly.

"What were you photographing at the time? During the time you *say* the camera was incorrectly loaded?"

"That would be a tall order! Who can remember that far back?" I said, trying to ignore his phrase 'you say'. Obviously he hadn't swallowed the story, hook, line and sinker. My heart was pounding, palms sweating.

"Try." It was more a warning than an encouragement, said in a growl.

"I don't know if I can." I had already decided that this would provide me with a reasonable opportunity to introduce a whole shoal of red herrings. The more subjects I could invent, the more likely they'd be to believe me incapable of remembering anything incriminating, and the greater would be my chances of going free.

In the next few minutes I invented a whole plethora of subjects; among them, I mentioned the only two subjects *actually* on the roll – the party and the horse – but only en passant. After I had finished, he continued to walk the floor, head down, concentrating quietly, evaluating my story. I grew more and more uneasy as the silent pacing continued.

When the blow came, I half expected it. It caught me on the side of the head and wouldn't have hurt an awful lot except that it was right on the spot where I had been planked with the golf club. "That," he growled menacingly, his mirror-hidden eyes only inches from mine, "is a damned lie!"

"What?" I tried to move my head back, all the time staring in fascination at my twin reflections where his eyes ought to be. "What's a lie?"

"That story of yours about loading the camera wrongly! There's no point in trying it again. I *know* it's a fabrication, from beginning to end, so don't try to make a fool of me again! Do you understand?" When I didn't reply, he roared: "*Do you understand?*"

"Yes, yes... I understand," I shouted, tucking my head in to my shoulder against his raised fist.

"That is just fine then!" He lowered his arm and gradually straightened up. He was breathing heavily, from the exertion or anxiety. I stared at him, wondering where the collapse of my story left me. There was a tiny alarm bell ringing somewhere at the back of my brain but I had to ignore it. Self preservation was now my main concern and being caught out had probably jeopardised that to some degree. "So," he resumed, chest heaving, towering over me. "Where is it?"

"It's at the processors." I said in a small voice, swallowing hard.

"It's at the processors." It wasn't a question; he only repeated it, mimicking me. "When did you send it?"

"Not long ago. A few days. I'm not quite sure. The end of last week."

"Why the delay?"

"I was in no hurry." I shrugged. "Sometimes I have a film for weeks or even months before I send it away – especially if there's nothing important on it, nothing I'm anxious to get back in a hurry." Another alarm bell sounded, equally distant, equally unidentified, equally ignored.

"Which processing laboratory do you use?"

"'Sureprint.' In Cork. Blackrock." I thought of lying, but

142

then I figured that they would already have known that – all the prints at the cottage were in their Sureprint wallets; perhaps he had just asked the question as a test, to see if I would answer truthfully. So I did. But that left me with the problem that he would now check with Sureprint and, when he found out that no such film had been received by them, I'd be back where I started. I could always insist that I *had* sent it and blame its non-arrival on the post, but I thought that that would be asking a little too much, a little too convenient. "But not this roll," I added, inspired by desperation.

"What?" He stopped short, head jerking towards me, on guard.

"I didn't send these to Sureprint." "Why not?" He looked cagey, like one who was preparing not to believe a word of it.

"There's nothing wrong with Sureprint, mind you – they're probably the best in the country, but at this time of the year, the tourist season, they get stretched beyond what they can handle comfortably and they get very slow. Or so I've found in past years anyway."

"I thought you said you were in no hurry..."

"Well... I'm not. But I figured that, if they're overworked, they could just as easily lose the film or mix it up with someone else's or make a bags of the actual developing and printing..."

He snorted and then said in a resigned voice, humouring me: "So what lab *did* you send the film to?"

"That's just it, you see... I can't remember." I could see that that went down like the Titanic and I went on: "It was one of those labs you see advertised in the Sunday paper colour supplements – very cheap, guarantees, free film, free albums, etc. There are lots of them. Every Sunday."

"Where was the one you sent the film to?"

"Dublin."

"What *part* of Dublin?" he went on with tired patience.

"I don't remember that either."

"How did you pay? Cheque?"

"No. Postal order." I wasn't going to fall for that one. Cheques have stubs with the payees' names written on them.

"Did you get the Postal Order in the local Post Office? In Knockmore?"

143

"No. Galway. At the GPO in Eglington St."

That stopped him for a bit. I presume he knew I was lying but he could do nothing much about it either way. He tried. "I don't believe you!" he said in a challenging tone.

"It's true!" I insisted with the guilelessness of the good soldier Schweik.

He looked at me long and hard but obviously failed to think of any way to catch me out. "What address did you give?"

"I *told* you! I don't *remember*!"

"Not for the lab! For you! Where were they to send the prints?"

"I gave them my address here. In Knockmore."

"Here! Here?" he said after three or four seconds. "Where's 'here'? How do you know where 'here' is? For all you know, you might be in Timbuktu!"

But his effort to shake me didn't work. He had been too slow in picking me up. It would have been instantaneous. And he knew it. He didn't continue that line. "What address? The surgery or the cottage?"

"The cottage. Fernditch."

Again, he lapsed into silence, probably reviewing his options. From where I stood, they didn't seem to be many. He could threaten me or beat me up again, but I'd only stick to my story. He could question and probe until we were both blue in the face, but my story was too simple to shake – there were only four or five basic facts and no embellishments. Harming me in any permanent way was not a realistic option (yet), because I'd have to be kept on hand until they located the incriminating pictures and disposed of them. But *after* that...

"Okay then," he said unhappily, "we'll keep an eye on your post, and I hope for your sake, that they turn up soon."

"Oh, they'll turn up alright, but when? That's the problem. I've often waited weeks for prints to come back. I'm sure you have too?"

"We'll give it a day or two..." He began to walk again, and I realised that the interview wasn't over yet. I had a fair idea what was coming next. "Tell me," he said in deceptively conversational tones, "how come you made up such a fancy story first?"

"How d'you mean?" I asked, knowing full well how he meant.

"The film not being properly loaded. You only found out a minute before that we were looking for photographs and yet you came up with that remarkably pat tale. Even if you hadn't been under pressure, you'd have had quite a time concocting that one."

I shrugged. "It just came to me. I thought it would be a good way of getting out of this mess, which by the way, I still don't understand. Once I heard you mention photographs, it seemed like a good plan. To prove to you that I don't know what the hell is going on. And I don't want to know either!"

"That would be wisest." He stood in front of me staring at me. I tried to outstare him but at last dropped my gaze. "You wouldn't, by any chance, have got the prints back already, seen their significance – if you hadn't noticed it already when you were taking them – and be considering a little judicious and profitable blackmail on the side?"

"Jesus, no!" This was a completely unforeseen and frightening turn of events. "I swear to you! I don't have an idea what's on that reel that worries anybody! *I* didn't take any shots that could give the slightest offence to anyone!" This was the nearest I came to dropping Marnie in it – emphasising the 'I'. At the same time I was vaguely puzzled that he should have said that I was the one who had taken the photographs. Surely they knew it was a woman...

"Because, if that's your game," he went on as if I hadn't spoken, "it might be a good idea to make your proposal now. We're all men of the world after all. I can listen to a proposition as well as the next man..."

"There *is* no proposal! Goddamn it are you deaf?! There is no proposal! I've no idea what you're looking for! How often must I tell you that?"

"So, you just thought up that story on the spur of the moment, eh?" His skepticism pushed out at me through every word.

"Yes! I've told you."

"Amazing."

"It's amazing how being in this kind of fix concentrates the mind."

145

"A regular Hans Christian Andersen we've got here," he said to himself in a theatrical aside, and then turned to me: "I'm going now, but I'll be back soon. In the meantime, you can shout your head off if you want, but it won't get you anywhere. There are four solid doors between you and the outside world, and this," he said, pulling open the door of the room, "is the most solid of the lot." He rapped the stout timber with his knuckles. "As you can see, it's been fitted with a dead bolt and padlock, so that's secure. What else?... Oh yes. Before I come in again, I'll knock, and you go and lie on the bed. I'll be able to keep an eye on you through this peephole here... look.."

"I've seen it already."

"Right. I'm off. I'll check your post and I'll bring you back something to eat." He went out and locked the door, letting the heavy padlock fall back against the wood with a significant thud.

I listened to his footsteps receding along the passage outside; then there was the sound of another door closing and being locked. After that, a very faint footfall, which I couldn't even be sure I heard, and then, nothing. I strained to hear the other two doors, the slam of a car door, the noise of an engine, anything; but there were no further sounds. He was dead right – there wouldn't be any point in shouting for help. I went and lay on the bed.

CHAPTER 18

I **lay on** the thin mattress, staring at the stained ceiling, and tried to make a list of plusses and minuses. The minus list was, alas, dead easy:

— nobody, including me, knew where I was;

— nobody, *except* me, knew about the photos — I had thought it too late to phone Potter (a fine time to develop a sensitive streak!);

— my captor was armed, while my arms were cuffed at the wrists;

— the stout door, with its padlock *and* dead bolt, was escape-proof...

There were, undoubtedly, many more minuses but, as each one I added nudged me closer to despair, I forced myself to stop; I concentrated instead on a search for some silver linings. It was a struggle but I managed a few:

— I had written Kiernan's name on the book and, when I didn't show in the morning and Kiernan (if he existed) could throw no light on the 'calving case,' the search would be on at once;

— same thing if Kiernan was bogus — Eileen would know;

— I had a variety of improvised weapons which, though no match for his gun, could nevertheless do the job if I could catch him unawares; even handcuffed, I could brain him with a table-leg. (However, he might notice at once if there was a leg missing from the table and, without the element of surprise, I was a goner... I scrubbed that one from the plus list.)

— the man himself seemed far from confident, as if all this was as new to him as it was to me;

— time was on my side (I reckoned on about a week) — they

147

might *doubt* my story but they'd have to give it time;

– collecting my post daily would be very dangerous for them, specially if the police were looking for me.

I began to feel quite buoyed; once again, the entrails were looking pretty good. Yessir. I'd be out of here in no time. There'd be a nationwide search. Potter and his cohorts would soon be surrounding the place. No need to worry. Right? Yeah right. Sure. No sweat. Just hang in there.

An hour later, an eerie age without any external sounds whatever, my optimism had slipped back towards reality. There might not even *be* a search for chrissake! How did I know how cleverly they might have stage-managed my disappearance? My fertile and graphic imagination promptly weighed in with all sorts of unhelpful suggestions:

Suppose they had left the Land Rover on one of the cliff-top roads, doors unlocked and light-switch on, wouldn't people think I had fallen or jumped? 'Young man...' 'believe he owed the bank *thousands*...' 'something about a girl...' 'I know he *seemed* happy but, you know what my husband always says, they're the ones to watch...' Or suppose they had pushed it off the end of a pier with the windows open, wouldn't the obvious conclusion be that I'd lost my way, driven off the pier, tried to escape through the window, and drowned? It would be no surprise when my body didn't turn up. 'New to the area...' 'wrong turn...' 'maybe a few drinks too many...' 'to forget...' '*thousands* I heard...' 'if they don't find him today, then I'm afraid...' 'washed out to sea...' 'treacherous area...' 'undercurrents you know...' I shivered. I'd have to forget rescue, put it out of my mind for all practical purposes. I was on my own and I'd have to rely solely on myself if I was going to get out of here. So far, nothing suggested itself, but it was early days; I didn't know enough. For the moment, all I could do was observe everything he did, remember everything he said, note any changes in his behaviour, and hope that, from amongst that lot, something would emerge which I might turn to my advantage. I'd have to keep a very clear head, that was for sure.

I closed my eyes and recalled our recent interview. Gently massaging my injured thumb and forefinger, I tried to pin down what had caused the vague alarm bells to ring in my

148

head. I went over the whole thing, step by step, as near verbatim as I could, but got nowhere – the harder I concentrated, the further away I seemed to be. Eventually I began to wonder if I hadn't been imagining it all.

When I heard him coming back, I dashed to the door and switched out the light. Groping my way back to the bed, I wondered why I had wanted the light off but couldn't think of any reason apart from the fact that nobody likes to feel they're being peeped at through a small spy-hole. I lay and waited, and heard him stop outside.

"Are you on the bed?" The voice, muffled through balaclava and a few inches of wood, was barely intelligible.

I knew what he'd said but couldn't think why I should make it easy for him. "What was that?" I asked. "Did you say something?"

"Are you on the bed?" He called. Louder.

"I am."

"Put on the light." Still loud – if he had dropped his voice back to normal, I was going to ask him 'What?' again.

"You can put it on yourself when you come in. I'm trying to get some sleep."

"Put it on now. You'll have lots of time for sleeping."

"What?"

"Put the light on! Switch on the light!" Exasperated, he raised his voice again.

There didn't seem to be much point in resistance for its own sake, or in annoying him just for the hell of it, so, mumbling oaths, I tumbled off the bed and slowly crossed to the door, reminding myself to squint when the light came on.

"Now go back and lie on the bed," he ordered, and waited until I had done so. I watched the mirrored lens watching me through the peephole all the time he was fiddling with the lock. Then he opened the door and came in.

In his right hand, he had the gun; under his left arm he carried a cardboard box from which the smell of roast chicken and chips emanated. He heeled the door closed, then stopped, puzzled – he had obviously just realised, for the first time, that, once he was in the room, the door would be held closed only by the Yale lock, which, even handcuffed, I could easily reach. He stood perplexed for a minute, stymied, perhaps annoyed, by this unforeseen hitch. Then he came up with an answer and nodded to himself.

"Get under the bed," he said with a wave of the gun.

"*What*?" I asked, perplexed. "Why?"

"Just until I get the food set out. I don't want you making a rush for the door…"

"Christ, haven't you got a bloody *gun* pointing at me? Why would I do a crazy thing like that?!"

"Go on! In under! I don't want to take a chance on having to use this. Things are bad enough as they are."

"Sure enough, I couldn't be in much deeper water, could I?"

"I wasn't talking about you," he said.

It was an odd comment and I stored it away for later consideration as I rolled in under the bed – a retrogressive step, compliance, submission, obedience.

My head stuck out from under the side of the bed and I watched as he set out the food, a whole roast chicken in its takeaway tinfoil tray, a bag of chips, an apple, a banana, a plastic cup of yoghurt and a carton of milk. Despite everything I was quite hungry.

"You'll have to open the milk for me," I said.

"Why?"

"I can't use my left hand much; it got hurt at the gate. It's a two-hand job, opening milk cartons."

"Okay." He finished laying out my breakfast, picked up the carton of milk and looked down at me; he made to put the gun in his pocket, then changed his mind and placed it on the shelf instead, moving one of the votive lights to the end to make room for it. He kept an extra wary eye on me for the ten seconds it took to open the carton, then he retrieved the gun and retreated to the door.

"You can come out now. The key for the cuffs is on the table. When you open them, throw the key here to me."

I hadn't been handcuffed for long but it was good to be free, and I did some stretching exercises before sitting down. I could sense his tension while I was free and moving, and he relaxed only slightly when I sat. There wasn't much hope that he could be taken unawares; he was as alert as a cat with a mouse in its sights.

"They weren't in your post," he said after a minute, almost accusingly.

"Oh!" I cursed myself silently for not having thought to ask. "I was afraid to ask. In case they were." I swallowed nervously: "What's going to happen... eh... when they do come? To me, that is. What's going to become of me?"

He didn't give me an answer though I was obviously waiting for one. I waited a bit more, unmoving, then laid down the chicken-leg I was holding, sat back in the fragile chair and turned towards him.

"Well?"

"That'll be a bridge to cross when we come to it," he replied lamely and with some discomfort. "The main thing is to get the prints."

"Speak for yourself! For me, the main thing is what's the bottom line." I was quite heartened by his obvious discomfort when I pressed the issue and rated it as a minor victory for me in our developing psychological skirmish; he had he gun, he was in command, and yet there he was, acceding to my demand for an answer. He should have told me to shut up. I decided I should push him whenever I could, to see just how far I could go, what I could get away with. "Well?" I repeated, pressing home my advantage.

Again the discomfort and indecision. "Look... The prints will most likely show that there is nothing... of a... compromising nature in them, or at least that you couldn't appreciate the significance of it if there is... in which case you'll be released at once, unharmed. Believe it or not, there's not a violent bone in the body of any of us."

I let that one pass without comment, but turned back, with a pointed snort of derision, to my breakfast. Let him work out the stupidity of that remark for himself.

"I got some Sunday supplements," he announced and fished into the box in which he had brought the food. This required some fast thinking. I hadn't anticipated being faced with specifics.

151

"I don't remember which paper it was in. It was an old one – it must have been, I found it at the cottage and the owner has been away for months. If it's any help, there was an article on the Galapagos Islands on the same page, with, if I remember correctly, some great pictures of seals and iguanas and things." I painted in a supportive backdrop.

"Well these are all recent, all from the last few weeks." He went through the four or five magazines calling out the dates and the names of their parent newspapers. "But we'll go through them anyway. They probably advertise week in, week out and maybe the name will come to you."

"Sure," I said, and raised the waxed-paper milk carton to my lips.

After I had wiped my hands, taking my insolent time about it, on a sheet of newspaper which he – having first checked it carefully for ads for developing labs – passed to me, I reached one hand towards him. He came forward the few steps to hand it to me – another tiny victory, I thought.

"Look through them. Carefully. Take your time. We've got all the time in the world." Languidly I did so, slowly turning page after page. All the time he watched me closely, and once or twice I paused speculatively just to show that I *was* trying. There were names like 'Snappysnap' and 'Phastphoto' and 'Printopronto' and 'Kwikpic' – all glib without being clever, all completely forgettable. "I'm sorry," I shrugged after a decent interval, "it could really be any of these... any of the Dublin based ones anyway." He continued looking at me as if he didn't believe me, and, self-consciously, I added: "None of them rings a bell. I'm sorry."

"Okay," he said at last, "put the cuffs back on and get under the bed again... It looks as though we shall just have to wait to see what comes in tomorrow's post."

"And if they don't come tomorrow?... What then?" I asked, clicking the first manacle into position.

"We wait another while, I suppose. But," he added quickly, "that doesn't mean to say that we're willing to go on waiting ad infinitum."

"Aren't you concerned that the whole country will be looking for me by now?"

He gave a nervous little laugh. "You can forget that one. Put it out of your head. This morning I phoned your surgery and told the girl that you'd had to go to Dublin last night on a personal matter, and on the way back, your Land Rover had left the road and that you were in hospital, under observation for a few days. I told her I was your uncle and that you had asked me to phone her."

"And?...." I demanded, when he seemed like stopping.

"And nothing. That's it. She sent her best regards; she said that you weren't to worry about the calls as she'd arrange for the neighbouring practice to service them. She said you were only to think about getting better and she didn't even ask what hospital you were in. So don't start listening for the bugles of the seventh cavalry coming down the passage, my brave boyo me lad."

"You seem to have thought of everything, don't you?" I said with a sneer. Inside I was relieved that the story they had dreamed up would not cover anything in the nature of a *permanent* disappearance. Little things like that could make a big difference in the end.

"No actually," he said thoughtfully. "If we had, you wouldn't be here now, would you?"

Another odd remark. "How do I know?"

"Less guff out of you!" he said suddenly, adopting a rough tone. "I thought I told you to get back in under the bed. Go on! Do it!"

As I lay on my back looking out from under the side of the bed, I noticed with interest, that when he cleaned away the leftovers of my meal, he held the cardboard box to the edge of the table and scooped everything into it; but, most interesting of all, while he carried out this two-handed operation, he placed the gun, without any hesitation whatsoever, on the shelf.

"Stay where you are until I leave the room," he ordered, looking down on me from his five feet ten. "I'll be back this evening. I'll leave the magazines – even if they don't refresh your memory, they'll help while away the time. There's no point in making this harder than it is. For anybody. Don't you agree?" He paused a moment. "I'm sure you'd find us equally

153

amenable to... eh... comfortable, shall we say, arrangements?... if you suddenly remembered anything... helpful in regard to those photographs. If you see what I mean?"

"I'm sorry," I rolled my head backwards and forwards along the floor, "I can't help. I don't know what photographs you're looking for and I certainly have no wish to find out. None whatsoever." He looked at me surmisingly until the silence became embarrassing. To cover my unease, which I was afraid he might read as guilt, I joked lamely: "But if you want to know whether I prefer the stick treatment or the carrot, then, my vote is for the carrot."

Abruptly, he turned on his heel and went out. About five minutes later, as I sat on the bed reading about: "Pools Winner! 'It will NOT change my life!' says Bert Witherspoon, Bootle, 97 year old bachelor, winner of £3,628,000," I was surprised to hear his footsteps returning and I looked over at the peephole. His lens-covered eye appeared at it, and the door opened just enough to admit an arm holding a plastic bucket, then closed again. From the other side of the door which was having its padlock replaced, his muffled voice came: "That's as much as we can do by way of a loo; I'm sorry." Then he went away and I picked up another glossy and read: "'I've always loved Bert Witherspoon', declares barmaid, Mimi (23), 'but I've been too shy to tell him!'"

CHAPTER 19

During that day, which seemed to drag on forever, I re-read the magazines many times. Otherwise, I dozed fitfully or thought. I spent a long time trying to come up with even an embryonic escape plan, but the longer it eluded me, the more depressed I became, and the more depressed I became, the less clearly I thought and the more unlikely it became that I'd come up with a plan, etc. etc. – a regular vicious circle that I was lucky enough to recognise before it plunged me too deeply into despair.

There were times too when I almost managed to capture the half-thoughts which had caused faint alarm bells to ring in my head during my recent interrogation. Maybe 'alarm' was the wrong word – they didn't, I felt, warn of any danger to me; they were more like my brain objecting to little inconsistencies in logic, but whether in mine or his I could not tell. They swam tantalisingly out of reach in the dark pools of my subconscious, fleetingly breaking surface only when I was thinking of something else, then maddeningly sinking down again as soon as I tried to focus on them, always just eluding me. The harder I reached, the deeper they sank, so I stopped trying and concentrated instead on the practicalities of escape.

By evening, I had got no further than working out that my only chance was to get him when the gun was on the shelf; at all other times, it was pointed at me. However, as yet, I could see no way of working it so that I'd be near him when he laid the gun there; no doubt, I would be languishing under the bed at the same time. Either I'd have to think of a totally different approach or come up with some way of *not* being under the bed at that precise, critical time.

That evening, what seemed at first to be a very negative develoment, turned out to be a blessing in disguise and provided me with my chance.

When he came, we went through the peephole/under the bed routine as we had in the morning. He laid out the food, opened the carton of milk – placing the gun on the shelf as he did so – and told me to come out. It was a repetition of the morning's procedure, except that he was very quiet. It was I who initiated whatever desultory conversations there were, and he who killed them off monosyllabically as soon as they began. By the time I had slowly worked my way through supper, I had given up trying to figure out what was bothering him; I couldn't even decide whether it was good or bad for me.

"Have you finished?" he asked, long after it should have been obvious that I had.

"Yes." I answered warily.

"Then put on the cuffs again." He watched until I had snapped on the first and then said: "Hold it there!"

I looked up at him, leaving the other cuff swinging from my left wrist at the end of its chain.

"Go and sit on the bed." The gun was directed at me in a hand which I could see was shaking. There was something big coming up. I did as I was told, reluctantly.

"Go on. Up to the top," he directed. Even more uneasy now, I shuffled along until I had the pillow under my left thigh. All the time, I watched him warily.

"Right. Now, pass the chain around the bar," he indicated the bed-head with a nod of his head, "then put the cuff on the other wrist."

"What!?" I demanded. "What for?"

"Because, basically, we think you may be up to something. That story of yours this morning was just a wee bit too good to be true. So, for the night, we don't want to take any chances, and my colleagues and I have decided that this is the safest way to guarantee your inactivity."

"*Fuck* you and *fuck* your colleagues!" I blazed in fury. "What am I supposed to do? Eh? What can I get up to in this Godforsaken dungeon? Hey? Tell me that! Go on! Tell me! What?!" I glared at him in impotent rage.

"Look! I'm sorry about this, but I must insist! There's too much at stake. If there was any other way of guaranteeing your... harmlessness, then I would gladly eh... em... adopt it. I told you already – we are not violent people, none of us!"

"*Boll*-ocks!", I snarled with blistering scorn, turning my head away.

"So come on now. Do as I say." When I didn't immediately comply, he continued: "I can quite easily arrange another chloroform session, you know, but this way saves everybody a lot of trouble, not least you."

I had to accept the reasoning of that and, with as much bad grace as I could muster, I anchored myself to the iron top of the bed.

"Right. Now I've said I'm sorry and I meant it. That's why I left it as late as possible to bring you your evening meal – it's now...," he checked his watch, "nine-forty-seven and I'll be back before eight in the morning, so really, it's not that long. Maybe I'll have the post with me by that time."

I stared obstinately at the ceiling, refusing to look at him or to acknowledge him at all, but I knew that he was standing half way between the bed and the door, the gun now held down by his side, no longer needed. I had ceased to be a threat.

"How about the light?" he asked. "On or off?" When I didn't reply, he said: "Very well then. I'll turn it off. Good night." He went to the door, opened it, and just before pulling it to, he flicked off the switch. The room was suddenly very dark and very lonely.

"Leave it on." I said.

"Right then." He switched it on again, waited a few seconds and repeated his 'Goodnight'.

I continued to stare at the ceiling in sullen, mute rebellion. What the hell did he want? Some kind of *approval*?

It had all happened so quickly that he had gone by the time I got to thinking straight again. There was no sense in my being so completely restrained. One hand chained to the bed would have served their purpose every bit as well and still allowed me a minimum of movement, a very important minimum. I shouted as loudly as I could, hoping he might have delayed briefly in the house but, if he had, he didn't hear me or, if he did, he didn't heed me. Furious with myself for not having had the presence of mind to take advantage of his sincere-sounding protestation that he wished there was some less drastic way to guarantee my immobility, I composed myself to make the best of a very uncomfortable bad lot. Within minutes, I began to itch in the most inaccessible places. I tried to sleep.

That was a real no-hoper. Apart from the excruciating restriction of my arms and the erratic flights of my thoughts, the backs of my eyeballs felt as if they were being massaged roughly by two large thumbs. This was because the naked globe of the light-bulb hung directly above my face; at last, I had to roll off the bed and drag it across to the door until I could reach my leg up and switch off the light with my foot. I tried to sleep again.

The nearest I managed during the next few hours was some sporadic dozing. As soon as I nodded off, my automatic efforts to adjust my unnatural position would jerk me awake again, and I began to occupy myself less with thoughts of eventual escape and more with trying to work out how to avoid another night in such discomfort. Sometime in the small hours, the two aspirations crossed paths and fused, and the embryo of a plan slowly took form in my head. I examined it in detail as I lay in total darkness and silence.

What it all came down to in the end was whether or not he was genuine in his regret at having to confine me so completely and if his professed desire to find an alternative method of restraint was real. If it was, I only had to think of another way and convince him to accept it. I had to provide him with a substantial-looking lock, but one for which I would have a secret key.

And already, I could see the vague outlines of it in the dark.

CHAPTER 20

When he came in the morning, my wrists were raw and wealed. He didn't notice at first; he checked through the peep-hole, opened the lock and, with a forced, cheery 'Good morning' – which I didn't bother to reply to – immediately went to the table and set out my breakfast, placing the gun on the shelf as he opened the milk carton. It wasn't until he approached the bed that he saw the reddened flesh of my wrists. It pulled him up sharp. That was what it was meant to do – so far so good. It just remained now to see if he had been serious when he said he wished there was some other way to guarantee my immobility besides chaining me to the bed; if he hadn't, then the plan was a washout before it even got going and I had put myself to a lot of pain and grief for nothing.

And it had been painful. Before starting, I had hauled the bed over to the door again and, by fishing about with my foot, found the switch and turned the light back on. That done, I shunted the bed back to its position by the wall. I didn't want him to know that I had been able to move. Then reluctantly, but afraid to postpone it, I gritted my teeth and began the process of self-mutilation; grimacing with pain, I twisted and ground my wrists against their sharp bracelets until they were both ablaze with a stinging raw soreness. In my anxiety, and without any means of knowing time, I had started much too early and, after inflicting as much damage as I could bear, I had to lie for ages in agonised frustration, eagerly awaiting his footsteps.

"Jesus!" His breath hissed in and the hand that was reaching with the key stopped in mid-stretch. He looked at me, turning his head so quickly that he almost dislodged the sun-glasses. I stared back at him with silent reproach. "Jesus," he repeated, "I'm sorry." When I still said nothing he said: "I'm really sorry."

"Yeah yeah," I said scornfully. "Big deal. If you're so fucking sorry, then get these cuffs off and give me a break."

"Of course," he answered solicitously and hurried to comply. "I'm sorry," he repeated. "Really I am."

"So you said," I replied testily, sitting up and gently rubbing my chafed wrists. He retired to the door, leaving the key on the bed, and stood there with the gun on me as before. Again he offered his apologies and told me that breakfast was laid out. "Take your time. Whenever you're ready."

I stood and stretched and reviewed the results of this latest skirmish, the first of the day. His remorse seemed genuine – he had even felt guilty! – and he had, without realising it, carried out my curt order to remove the cuffs. Removing them had been his intention anyway, but I reckoned that he would, if he had been more self-assured, have made some comment about who gave the orders around here. But he hadn't, and I added that to the lengthening list of plusses.

I decided to push my luck further, see how it went. I walked, swinging my arms, restoring circulation. The day before, he had forbidden movement except for the short walk from under the bed to the table and back again. Now, though he was taut with wariness and gripped the gun fiercely, his guilt feelings wouldn't let him object. Another plus. Good. I pushed again, mental fingers crossed.

"I presume that this establishment doesn't run to First Aid kits for the benefit of its inmates?" I stopped in front of him, though more than a safe arm's length away, and addressed him with heavy sarcasm. "A bit of wound dressing? A bandage or two?" Getting him used to me stopping close in front of him was going to be crucial. Next time I would stand a little bit closer, and then a little closer still... The gun was at the ready all the time, an extension of his arm, and almost as nervous as he was – God, I hoped it wouldn't go off on its own!

"Eh... Ehmmm... I'll see what I can do. Sit down and eat your meal and... I'll see... what I can do."

I sat. The meal was laid out, an apple, two bread rolls

(already buttered so I wouldn't need to use a knife), slices of cheese and the all-important carton of milk.

While I ate, he went off without saying a word. This was new behaviour, and I wondered if I hadn't been wrong in deciding so precipitously that he was a creature of habit. I had come to that conclusion because, when he had arrived with my first meal and found himself facing the conundrum of how to prevent me from making a bolt for the door, which was unlockable from the inside, the only thing he could think of was to order me under the bed. In his position, I would have put the box on the floor and let my captive do the rest himself – I wouldn't have left the door at all – but he was obviously unable to go against established practices: a/ he carried food; b/ food always went on tables – *never* on floors; c/ there, by the wall, was a table. To effect b/, a/ had to go on c/. So, regrettably, unwisely, but quite unavoidably, the door would have to be left unguarded. I prayed that I had not misread him. My plan relied on him being what I thought he was, a man fixed in his ways, not a great improviser.

He returned some twenty minutes later. Before entering, he knocked and called out: "Get under the bed!"

I didn't object. I was glad to see another pattern being adhered to. If things went well, in no time at all, I should be able to predict his moves, and then start little patterns of my own which he would quickly get used to. And be totally shocked when I suddenly deviated from our established accepted routine. Or so the plan went. He waited until I was under the bed, then entered carrying a green plastic case with a red cross in a white circle on its lid. He didn't venture far from the door and threw the case onto the bed. Unlike food, *it* didn't have to go on a table. "O.K. You can come out now."

I found a tube of soothing dressing and applied it liberally. There were also some bandages; I bandaged my left wrist without any trouble but asked him for help with my right. He declined, with apologies, so I made do as well as I could. In fact, being almost ambidextrous, I could have done a near perfect job, but I deliberately made extra heavy weather of the operation to make him think that my left hand was still badly injured. I couldn't take the chance on him deciding that I'd be able to open my own milk carton in future.

Afterwards we talked for a while. This time I didn't forget to ask if the prints had come in the post. They hadn't, surprise, surprise, and that ended *that* particular conversation.

"How do you do it anyway?" I asked. "Hang about the gate of the cottage and ask the postman if he's got anything for me?"

He answered with a snort which translated as: 'Don't be daft!'

"Break in after he's been and gone?"

Another snort.

"It's got to be one or the other. Aren't you afraid someone'll see you climbing in and out of the window some morning?"

"What do you mean, climbing in and out the window? We've got the house key from the bunch in your Land Rover! We check at night."

"Oh! I never thought of that." For some reason, I became suddenly depressed – I'd missed that fairly obvious conclusion; not that I had given it any thought – it's just that I have never liked asking stupid questions and in this case it was particularly annoying. It might even be dangerous – it could conceivably be the cause of letting him re-establish control, or at least his *feeling* of being in control. Which, I reflected glumly, amounted to much the same thing.

In a while he ordered me back under the bed, placed the gun on the shelf, and scooped the remains of my breakfast into the cardboard box. Then, promising to be back in the evening, he went off. I didn't bring up the topic of chaining me to the bed and nor did he. I didn't mention it because I didn't want to increase the chances that he might discuss it with his colleagues. They might come up with an escape-proof method of restraining me which would be *really* escape-proof! Maybe he was intending to discuss the matter with them anyway but there was no point in my reminding him of it.

I hadn't slept a normal sleep since the telephone summoned me to the bogus calving case almost thirty-six hours before, and now, despite the excitement of the plan taking shape, and the throbbing pain in my wrists, I stretched on the bed and fell into a deep, exhausted, dreamless sleep. I seem to recall waking briefly once or twice but that was all; otherwise I slept right through, my eventual awakening coinciding with my captor's return.

"Under the bed!" He rapped the door with what sounded like the gun butt.

When I had complied, he came in, set the food out, leaving his gun (as usual) on the shelf while he opened the milk carton; retrieving it, he retreated to his customary position by the door. By this stage the routine had become so firmly established that I rolled out from beneath the bed without his telling me to. Without a word, he threw the key onto the bed. I opened the cuffs and dropped them on the bed, the key still in the lock. So far, neither of us had said anything. This suited me as I was rehearsing in my head the next vital stage of the plan. He watched in silence as I windmilled my arms, his wariness at peak, almost coiled. I approached the table with undisguised distaste. I wasn't in the least bit hungry; I had done nothing all day but sleep, so I had wasted no energy and besides, the air in the room had become distinctly stale; it made me feel queasy, as if I had been on a mighty bender the night before. Listlessly I ate a banana, staring at the wall and forming my opening sentence. He didn't interrupt. I reached for the milk and raised the carton to my lips, but, without drinking any, I lowered it again and turned quickly to him.

"I've come to a decision." I announced firmly.

"Oh? What about?" He stirred, surprised by my sudden vehemence.

"I've decided – and I mean it! – that you can shoot me or chloroform me or whatever... but you're not chaining me to that bed tonight. And that's final." I ended it quietly but with unmistakable conviction, and, not taking my eyes off him, took a deep slug from the milk carton.

"Actually... I've been meaning to talk to you about that.." He sounded uncomfortable, like he was going to say something unpopular.

"What about it?..." I looked at him belligerently.

"I've talked it over with the others, and we agree that it would be needlessly painful to... do the same thing..."

"So?"

"Well... they don't want you roaming about free at night... we don't, and we decided that the best... eh... compromise would be to lock only *one* hand..."

"No!" I interrupted violently. "To hell with that! It's not my wrists! After all, they're bandaged now. Protected. It's my legs, or my *hips* to be more precise."

"Your *hips*?" I could almost see his frown behind the mask.

"Yes! My hips! I broke my pelvis four years ago in a car accident and I've got arthritis in my hips. I'm supposed to walk at least three miles every day. At *least* three, preferably more. If I don't, I get horrible pains." I let that sink in, thanking my guardian angel that I had thought the plan through, anticipated their compromise, and prepared a reasonably plausible fly for their ointment. "Even when I do get my walking done, I often have to get up during the night and walk some more. I tell you! I won't stand it! Not unless you can get me some injectable cortisone to reduce the inflammation!" I paused again to let him think it out. "I can't see what the hell you're so afraid of anyway! What do you think I can get up to? *Please* leave me loose!" I added with a fervent prayer that he wouldn't.

"I *can't!*" he protested. "Believe me, if it was only me, I would!"

"Well then, for Christ's sake, ask your accomplices if you can't use some other arrangement, like, for instance, the GI Truss..." That was it, the bait. I tried to let it slip off the tongue as if it had just occurred to me, a mutually satisfactory answer to a mutually vexing problem.

"The *what*?" He nibbled at it, interested; or maybe just curious.

"The GI Truss," I said, as if he should know and then, when he didn't answer, I hesitated. "You know? The GI Truss?..."

"No." He shook his head. "What's The GI Truss?"

"You don't know the GI *Truss*! It's a simple way of restraining prisoners. Of war, I presume, because I suppose it's called after the way the American GI's tied up their prisoners. At least I *presume* that that's how it got it's name; why else would it be called that? They used to handcuff the prisoners as usual, but pass the chain of the cuffs down *inside* the belt at the front

164

and thread the belt so that it buckled at the *back*. Simple."

He didn't say anything and I went on, storming him so that he couldn't examine it too closely. "That restricted the movement of the arms to a circle of about six inches around the navel, so the prisoners were no danger to their guards and their chances of escape were almost nil as they couldn't reach, never mind *manipulate* anything outside that small area. And, when you think of it, they'd find it hard to manipulate anything *inside* that area either because, if they were standing close enough to touch it, they wouldn't be able to see it, would they?"

I left off again to see how it was going down. He said nothing. He looked like a man who was weighing it up. I ploughed ahead. "Obviously, where there was a crowd of prisoners, a whole bunch of them, one could free the other's belt so there was a kind of heavy-duty staple-gun affair to staple the belts closed at the back and that was it. I believe that the biggest advantage was that it allowed men to have a pee without them having to call the guards..."

"How come you know so much about all this?" he interrupted. Good question, but luckily one which, again, I had anticipated.

"War comics," I said as if it ought to have been obvious. "The same as every other kid of my generation. We were almost reared on sixty-four-page war comics. We used to use the GI Truss ourselves when we played war. Not with cuffs and staple-guns and the like of course, just the principle. But you can see," I continued, not leaving well enough alone, "how important it would be for prisoners to be able to have a pee when they wanted, especially somewhere like the Russian front where it was so *cold*. Prisoners couldn't wet themselves..."

"The Americans weren't on the Russian Front."

"Well, wherever. Just goes to show," I added lamely, "what happens when you learn your history from sixty-four-page war comics. Anyway, I presume that the other armies soon copied it." I let him consider it for a while before pressing on again. "So, what about the GI Truss? Aye? Please talk to them anyhow. I've told you, I'm not going to be chained, not without a hell of a struggle! You don't need a staple-gun," I cajoled, "there's nobody to release my belt at the back." I watched him, wondering if I ought to press him further, fearing that I might already have gone too far. He hesitated a moment longer, obviously on the brink of a decision.

"O.K. We'll do it your way, then. There's no need to check with the others. If it was good enough for the U.S. army, I suppose it'll be good enough for them."

I looked my thanks at him, not trusting my voice to hide my relief and excitement. I had swung it. It had worked like a dream.

"Well," he said, with relieved munificence, "you know better than I do what to do, so... do it." His relief at having circumnavigated the thorny problem of my determined resistance, was plain.

I stood and unbuckled the heavy brass buckle of my wide leather belt; then, pulling it free of the loops, I held it up, showing it to him in the manner of a magician asking a member of the audience to see for themselves that it was just an ordinary belt. I threaded it through the loops again, this time starting at the back and continuing forward by my right side until the loose end reached the back again. There I buckled it, leaving it as loose as I dared. While I was doing all this, I kept turning so that he could watch what my hands were doing – which he did with an interest bordering on suspicion. I kept up a running commentary, a patter which I had practised, the sole purpose of which was to interfere with any thinking he might be attempting on the subject of flaws in the GI Truss.

"Now, as you can see, there's no way that I can possibly inch the belt round to the front to a position where I can reach the buckle; the buckle is too big to pass through the loops – right? And," I continued when he didn't reply, no doubt reserving judgement until the end, "equally, there's no way that I can pull the buckle round by just hauling it through the loops and tearing through them as I go, is there?" By ending each sentence with a question, I hoped to make it harder for him to concentrate, to ignore my unasked-for soliloquy, and so disrupt any thought sequences which might be going on in his suspicious head. "Denim is much too strong for that, wouldn't you agree? Eh?..."

"Go on, go on. Get on with it!" I won from him, impatiently.

166

"Right so. Now it's just the handcuffs. Do you want to do that part now? I mean, are you leaving now?"

"In a minute. You might as well do it now."

"O.K." I picked up the cuffs, pulled the smooth leather of the belt away from my belly and fed one cuff down inside so that the chain hung on the belt, a cuff on either side. With a helpless grimace, I snapped them on.

"Now. That's it. The GI Truss. Voila! Check for yourself." I walked towards him and he let me come. I tried not to let my elation show; when I had been restrained by the wrists only, he hadn't even let me walk about the room unless there was some reason for it, like going to or from the table. Now, at a stroke, I had achieved the freedom of movement essential to my plan. Some stroke. Some bluff.

When I was three steps away from him, I turned and reversed the rest of the way, the least threatening way I could think of in which to approach him. With satisfaction I noted that he showed very little alarm at my nearing him now; the gun remained pointing at me but no more menacingly than when I was sitting on the bed or at the table and much less so than when I was walking from one to the other with my wrists joined but my arms free. I flinched a little when he reached out and caught the buckle, tugging it experimentally, trying to pass it through the adjacent loops at either side of it. It wouldn't go.

"See?" I said in an I-told-you-so voice, "it won't go, will it? And, in case you're worried, I won't be able to reach round there either because, even if I was strong enough to tear the chain of the cuffs through the loops of my jeans, my hands are locked together and I'd have to reach them both round at the same time, right?"

"Uh huh... So?"

"Well, for God's sake, how do you expect anybody to be able to reach his *right* arm all the way round his *left* side to the small of his back? Or vice versa? Unless you suspect me of being a contortionist or some kind of Houdini or something!" That had been an unexpected bonus in the war of psychological point-scoring; he had unwittingly allowed himself to appear slightly silly in front of me. It may have been nothing much, but every little helped and it cheered me no end. He spun me

167

round by the shoulder and checked the pinioning of my arms. Obligingly I tugged outward to show how little scope there was.

"Satisfied? Am I or am I not harmless? Of course, I *could* knee you in the goolies," he folded suddenly, reflexly, defensively, squeezing his thighs together and I laughed, "but what could I do then? Even if I managed to knock you out, I can't reach up to the door knob, can I?" I snorted: "Those GI's knew their stuff, didn't they?"

He gave a last tug at the belt, turned me round again and repeated it at the back, then gently pushed me towards the bed.

"O.K. That seems to do the job nicely." His tone lacked absolute conviction but, on the other hand most of the suspicion had left it. The initial euphoria I had felt at having secured my aims had become tempered with the worry of the next thirty-six hours. During that time, if he thought hard about it, would he not spot the one obvious flaw in the GI Truss? I felt that it was so clearly visible! Hopefully he had so much on his mind already that, having accepted it, he probably wouldn't give the matter an awful lot more thought. But, what about his accomplices? Would one of them not spot it when he thought about it in cold light, free from the confusion of my disruptive and diversionary monologue. I had steamrolled my gaoler, but what about them? Would he even discuss it with them? Wouldn't they have more important things to talk about? I decided that, if he hadn't spotted the flaw by morning, then I was as good as free. In the morning he'd find me tied as securely as he had left me and he would accept it all as hunky dory.

"Right. In under the bed!"

"What!"

"I want to clear away the food. I'm going."

"Jesus! What's the *point* in the fucking GI Truss if you think I can still make a run for the door! Don't you see? I can't reach the knob of the lock unless I turn it with my teeth!"

He thought about that for a minute.

"Anyway, I'd need to use my arms to shunt myself under," I reasoned. "I'll lie *on* the goddam bed, if that makes you feel better." And I did so, again taking an initiative which robbed him ever so slightly of another tiny slice of his psychological advantage. He looked at me, feeling as if he ought to make a point of having his wishes complied with, but, seeing no practical advantages to it, let it be. While he scooped away the practically untouched food, he automatically laid the gun on the shelf beneath the picture of the Sacred Heart. Then, box under one arm and gun in the hand of the other, he went to the door.

"Light on or off?" he asked, giving further evidence of his amazing lapsing into habit.

"Leave it on. I can always turn it off later when I want to. With my nose."

"Right then. I'll be off. It's ...20.26, nearly half past eight," he said, rubbing the sleeve of his left arm along the front of his anorak to expose his watch, "I'll be back in the morning before eight."

"In one way, I hope you have the prints then, and, in another, I dread it."

"Not tomorrow anyway," he said. "It's Saturday."

"Is it?!" I asked, as if I didn't know. "My, how time flies when you're enjoying yourself," I said drily. It was no harm to send him off thinking I was so confused that I didn't know what day of the week it was.

He went out. Again I lay in perfect silence to listen for some tell-tale identifiable noise, and again, all sound ended with the closing thunk of the second door. I let out my breath.

I don't think I'd have been able to sleep even if I was tired, which I wasn't. My escape plan was going precisely as I had hoped and, having managed to bring phase one to fruition, I now had to rehearse in the same detail, the equally important phase two. I had already made a start, when I had approached him to let him check out the security of the GI Truss.

In spite of the tension, I smiled broadly to myself – no wonder he had never heard of The GI Truss! *No one* had ever heard of the GI Truss! I had only just thought it up myself the night before! For all I knew, or cared, the soldiers of the Axis armies might have worn *braces*, not belts. I had come up with the name because, had I proposed it baldly as an idea *I* had come up with, he would, no doubt, have examined it far more closely and with greater suspicion; he might even have rejected it solely on the grounds that there must be a catch in it somewhere, even if he couldn't quite see what the catch was. Giving it the imprimatur of the Joint Chiefs of Staff of the Pentagon had just seemed like smart packaging. Fancy wrapping paper.

The next day would have to be spent getting him used to how helpless I was, how negligible a threat I had been rendered by the GI Truss, and how safe it was to allow me to walk around the room. Provided that he hadn't wised up by morning or become suspicious all over again, it shouldn't prove a great hurdle to overcome. Tied as I was, I was harmless. That was obvious.

I shuffled about for hours. The restriction of my arms was maddening, though it was a definite improvement on the previous night's confinement. My thoughts alternated between wild hopes and black despair; I thought of Claire but it proved more worrying than comforting, leaving me prey to a greater sense of loss than I already felt. Towards morning, I slept a little.

CHAPTER 21

*F*rom the moment he peeped through the spyhole next morning, he was a target, an audience for a command performance – with me (hopefully) doing the commanding.

I was dozing when the outside door opened but I heard it as plainly as if I had been straining my ears all night, waiting for it, which, in a sense, I probably had. By the time his eye appeared at the peephole, I had arranged myself so that my restrained hands were obvious to his first glance. I lay on my left side, facing the door, feigning sleep. I stirred only when the bolt pulled noisily back.

"Good morning," he said, heeling the door shut and crossing to the little table with the inevitable box of food. I didn't reply, being supposedly too busy with the process of waking. I noted with relief that the gun went on the shelf as before while he opened the milk carton. It always did, yet I always waited in trepidation in case it mightn't. He didn't mention getting under the bed. He would have if he had rumbled the flaw in the GI Truss, during the night. I was almost there.

"How's the hand?"

"Still sore. Stiffish but improving a little."

"And the wrists?"

"They'll survive. At least the hips are okay."

When he unlocked the cuffs, I stretched for a long time before going to the table. At the door, he didn't look particularly happy about it but didn't forbid it either; he was watchful and tense and kept the gun pointed at me no matter where I moved. That was good; the last thing I wanted was for him to get so blasé that he'd leave the gun in his pocket, though it wouldn't have been the end of the world either. I had worked out so many contingency plans during the night that my head began to reel and I gave up in the end, but there was one headed: 'What To Do If Gun In Pocket.'

After I had picked fitfully at the food, I stood and began to pace. Again, he became extra alert while I was moving about and there was no position in the room from which I could look at him without seeing the small black circle of the barrel of the gun trained on me as though I were a magnet.

"I can't eat!" I exclaimed. "The air in here is lousy!" And I went on with my pacing. It was true, the air *was* lousy.

"I think you had better sit down." It was an order, not a suggestion.

"*No*! I want to move!" I windmilled my arms again, defiantly, demonstratively.

"If you don't sit down, you'll have to put on the cuffs again!" he warned.

"Here!" I extended my wrists towards him. "Put them on if you like, but I'm not sitting down or lying down either – on or under the fucking bed! I'm fed up of sitting and lying! I want to *walk*!"

"Have it your own way then.... Put them on."

"Coward!" I said witheringly and picked the handcuffs up off the bed. Without being told to, I locked myself in the 'GI Truss' again and he immediately relaxed.

I kept him there for over an hour, and all the time, I paced up and down, passing him countless times, getting him used to my nearness and my helplessness, using every opportunity to demonstrate the limited range of my fettered hands. I bent double to scratch my nose, sidled up to the end of the bed to ease an itching thigh and hip and backed into the corner of the table to bring relief to a supposedly pruritic bum. And all the time, I kept up a steady flow of conversation designed to keep him from leaving. I wondered aloud if perhaps I hadn't inadvertently given the processing laboratory the name of the small hotel I used as a base while I was in Dublin between jobs.

"You see, when you're like me, doing locums all the time as a full time thing, you have to have some sort of base and they give me the commercial rate and hold my post for me... There has to be somewhere that people who want me can contact me..." Neither of us had a pen or pencil so I had to repeat the address of the hotel several times for him to memorise it.

Then I got on to Claire. Could I send her a letter which, of course, he could censor? Could I make a cassette recording to send to her, in the event of... a nasty end?

As I talked, I walked up and down, up and down, ceaselessly. On several occasions I stopped in front of him, facing him from no more than a few feet away in order to make some point more emphatically. The first time I did this, the gun jerked up warningly, a move which I, in my shammed agitation, pretended not to notice, but with each successive stop, his reaction became less and less marked until, in the end, he gave up reacting altogether. At last, muttering the address of the hotel repeatedly to himself, he left. While he was clearing away the food, he made me lie on the bed; this disappointed me slightly as I thought he had come to accept that I was *totally* harmless. Still, I reflected as I lay watching him, everything was more or less on course, and he placed the gun on the shelf unthinkingly – as always.

The evening session was much the same except that I began to move in on him almost as soon as he came in. I joined him at the table as he was actually laying out the food, and though his hand snaked at once towards the gun on the shelf, I arrested it before it got there with a derisive snort and a demonstrative tug on the belt-confined handcuffs.

"My! Aren't we nervous!" I mocked as I closed the last few steps and forced my eyes down to the food which was half laid out. "What have you got? I'd eat a farmer's arse through a blackthorn hedge this minute! I'm starving." It was a plausible excuse for joining him so quickly at the table – "I ate nothing this morning," I added in case he didn't realise exactly *why* I was starving. Nothing could have been further from the truth. Actually I was feeling quite nauseous, a feeling due in equal parts to the foulness of the air in the room and a rapidly mounting inner tension and excitement. Having said I was starving, I had to go through the motions, and once I had been unlocked and had done my stretching exercises, I had to fall on the foul repast with every evidence of extreme gusto. It was as much as I could do not to throw up. Afterwards, I managed to hold him again, though for a shorter time than in the morning. As before, I walked while I was talking, manacled in the GI Truss.

I continued to demonstrate my helplessness, stopping every so often to scratch against whatever angular projection was near, rubbing up and down like a cow at a gatepost. At one time I backed up to him and asked him to scratch between my shoulder-blades, directing him, ("Down a little, left a bit, just there... Aaaaaaaaaaaaah! That's great!"). He obliged without question. I had planned this particular move earlier as a kind of insurance policy. As a vet, I knew the significance of grooming in animal populations; it indicated a bond, a kinship or co-tribalism, shared welfare, almost a mutual defence pact and I hoped, perhaps somewhat optimistically, that if it did come down to violence in the end, this 'grooming relationship' might just make it that tiny bit more difficult for him to turn on his 'groomee'. The fact that it was often the *inferior* animal who did the grooming had its own significance, especially in the context of the psychological battle I had been waging, and, while he was dutifully scratching my back, I was busily moving myself up another notch or two in the pecking order of my prison.

"Listen," I said when he began to look as though he might be thinking of leaving, "Tomorrow's Sunday, right?"

"That's right. Sunday. I'll be a bit late. I've got to go to church."

"Oh!" I replied, refraining from the mirthless scoff that *that* deserved. "Well, what I was thinking," I went on, "is, the prints can't come tomorrow so I'll be stuck here for another day, maybe a few days if they don't come early in the week, so... Is there any chance you could bring me something to read? You wouldn't believe how boring it gets..."

"Of course!" he said. "We ought to have thought of that sooner. What would you like?"

I shrugged. "The Sunday papers... Magazines... A few novels... Anything that'll help pass the time. Really," I shrugged again, "I don't mind. I'll read anything! Except of course the Telephone Directory! Ha, ha!" I ended with another (lame) attempt at matiness.

"Fine. I'll see what I can do."

174

"Thanks. And a toothbrush and some toothpaste. My teeth feel like they've got fur all over them. Another few days without washing them, and they'll rot in my head."

"Okay," he replied, and made moves to clear away the debris of my supper. I immediately got as far away from him as I could and kept up a steady patter of small talk. Reassured by my obvious disinterest in what he was doing, knowing from my incessant chatter exactly where I was in the room, secure in the knowledge that I was safely bound in the GI Truss, he didn't mention lying on the bed. Or perhaps he was just too polite to interrupt me while I was speaking. Either way, I had succeeded in gaining that little extra all-important freedom – his permission to remain standing while the gun was on the shelf.

As he made for the door, I reminded him again about the reading material and toothbrush, and he went off carrying with him the box of food remains and the distinct impression that I was reconciling myself to an extended stay. That was the impression he was meant to get. I wasn't.

I waited for about the hour I had already decided on and it wasn't easy. I didn't really think he was going to come back for anything, but if he had he'd have caught me in the middle of my preparations and that would have put an end to my carefully-staged build-up, and two days of plotting and scheming would have been reduced to a shambles. At last, with a final silent prayer, I began.

I knew the routine by heart and it worked like a dream. In theory. Now it was for real.

I eased my shoes off by catching the heel of each with the toe of the other. Next, I opened the top button of my jeans and pulled down the zip; that left only the belt holding them up and a few undignified wriggles later, I had managed to coax the belt down over my hips. This had involved a fine balance between pushing gently on the chain at the front and rubbing my back up along the end of the bed; after it all, I stood, barelegged, my jeans hanging by their belt from the chain between my wrists. That was phase one successfully completed.

Phase two involved the modification of the GI Truss. The first step was to remove the belt. Sitting on the bed, my jeans heaped on my lap, I undid the buckle and pulled the belt free of the loops, a move which left me with the jeans and the belt separated and my handcuffed hands free. I laid the jeans to one side. Now I went to work with my teeth on the adhesive tape on my left wrist, and when I had bitten one end loose, I pulled it with my right hand, teasing it gently until I had a four or five inch strip free; this I bit off. I needed the tape to bind the spike of the belt to the buckle; left loose, it might snag into one of the holes later on, which would be disastrous.

When I had finished this, I pulled the bed away from the wall. The next requirement was a length of the grey and white two-strand cable which I had noticed tacked along the top of the skirting board. I pulled it loose from the skirting, popping the staples out easily as I went. I could easily have bitten through it but I couldn't tell if it was carrying current, so I turned the bed on its side and, using the sharp angle iron of the base as a toothless saw, rubbed the cable on it until I had cut a length of about six feet. As I only needed one of the two strands, I separated them; the surplus strand I rolled into a ball and left by the wall before setting the bed back to rights again.

I spent a few minutes biting a hole in the leather at the very end of the belt, gouging at it with my canines until I had worn away a small rough puncture. Using my teeth again, I stripped the plastic covering from either end of my strand of cable exposing about an inch of gleaming copper wire. Then I fed one end through the hole in the belt-end and pulled the cable through until its half-way mark; at this stage, I wound the bared wire ends of the cable together a couple of turns. I now effectively had a belt about seven feet long – four feet of leather and three of doubled plastic-coated wire. Now came the tricky part.

With the jeans lying in a heap on my lap, I threaded the "wire end" of the seven foot long belt through the first of the six waist loops, the right back, and then on in the sequence which I had repeated ad nauseam to myself: right side, right front, through handcuffed hands, left front, left side, left back, over buckle with taped-down spike, again through right back, right side, right front. The whole ensemble to be tightened when the jeans were back on by pulling the wire drawstring which would lie within easy reach of my once again restricted hands. So far, so good.

176

I put my legs into the jeans but before pulling them up beyond my shins, I used my hands to replace my shoes. Then I pulled them up, zipped up the fly, closed the top button and, by drawing gently on the wire end I slowly tightened the "real" belt, feeling it passing through the loops with minimum resistance. Lastly, I unwound the twisted ends of the wire and, by pulling on one end, pulled it free. That was it. That was what he was going to see. My hands were chained, the belt went through the chain, and was (presumably) buckled at the back. All in order. Just like yesterday morning. And afternoon.

All in order. Except the belt *wasn't buckled*. It just *looked* that way. With a frisson of excitement, I clasped my hands together, tensed my body, drew a deep breath and swung my arms out and upwards in a swift smooth arc. The belt snaked through the loops without any resistance and came free with a vicious slap. I repeated the procedure twice more and each time it worked perfectly. Only one minor snag occurred; it was not possible to tuck my shirt in at the back when I was pulling up the jeans and though that was probably not a disaster, I felt better when I worked out how to eliminate it. On my last dress rehearsal, while the jeans and the belt were lying separate on the bed, I stepped forward through my joined hands, brought my arms up behind me, tucked my shirt-tail into the waistband of my underpants, and stepped back through my arms again.

Feeling quite the perfectionist, I completed the other steps and settled down, nervously, to await the arrival of my captor. I felt like the human equivalent of a tautly coiled spring.

CHAPTER 22

In spite of my vigilance and anxiety, he almost caught me off my guard. I had been trying to relax, like a boxer before a major bout, and I must have dozed off momentarily; he couldn't have been more than two or three steps away from the door when I became aware of his footfalls. Instantly I was awake, my nerves almost sticking out through me with feverish, throat-tightening excitement. I hoped that none of it was visible to the mirrored lens that appeared at the peephole as I tried to give the impression of just waking from a long night's sleep. I was lying facing the door, stretched out so that my hands were plainly visible; he couldn't fail to notice that the chain was still down inside the belt.

When he came in I blinked at him. "Oh! It's you," I said, disappointment in my sleepy tone.

"Yes." He stopped and said in a tone like he was smiling beneath the balaclava: "Why? Were you expecting guests?"

"I was dreaming." I shook my head, stifling a yawn." Christ, I'm all cramped! Can you open the cuffs? I need to stretch!"

"As soon as the food is laid out." He seemed to be in an almost sunny mood and I wondered if perhaps his problems hadn't begun to sort themselves out and if so, how that might affect me. Not that it mattered as I had no intention of hanging about to find out. Then again maybe his good form was solely due to this morning's visit to church. Maybe God had told him that he was doing the right thing, encouraged him to keep it up, that he was doing His work on earth. Maybe he was one of those nuts... "I've brought you something to read." He glanced quickly down to check my hands as I had, by now, stood up. Just as I had yesterday morning.

"Oh, great! What?" This was it. This was for real.

"Selection of the Sundays,... Time Magazine,... Newsweek,... Private Eye,... eh,... National Geographic... and a couple of novels," he read out, making a stack of them on the table.

"That's great! They'll pass the time nicely! Let me see!" I said eagerly, and I moved with feverish casualness towards the table. His mirror-hidden eyes flicked towards me, then down again to my belt-restrained hands, then around to the gun on the shelf. Finding all in order, he went on unpacking the food.

Standing almost beside him now, my nerves at screaming point, I dipped towards the table and picked up the book on top, 'Bonecrack,' by Dick Francis.

"I've read this," I said, "but no matter, I'll enjoy it the second time round, I'm sure." Next in the pile was the National Geographic.

I was, by now, almost trembling with anxiety and excitement. It would have to be now or never – the food was almost laid out. Any second, he'd be taking the gun off the shelf again and telling me to remove the cuffs. At that stage, he couldn't fail to spot my deception.

"National Geographic!" I exclaimed in delight, "one of my favourites!" I inched in towards the table again as though to replace the novel and pick up the magazine. I laid the paperback on the table and turned towards my left – towards the pile of books. Then, with a silent prayer, I yanked my hands out and up in one smooth, continuous movement, at the same time swivelling on the ball of my left foot. With a sharp crack, the belt slapped out through the loops, and my freed, clasped hands continued up in their vicious arc to explode against the point of his jaw, clacking his teeth together with a noise like a door slamming in a high wind.

I don't think he knew what hit him. His head jerked up with a snap and he teetered backwards, toppling over the end of the bed and ending up sprawled in an ungainly heap on the floor. Before he had even slid to a halt, I had grabbed the gun off the shelf.

I must have almost knocked him out because, when I got to him, his head was shaking and his eyes were blinking rapidly,

almost fluttering. The hated sun-glasses had skittered off somewhere out of sight.

He opened grey eyes which drooped a few times drunkenly
out of focus but soon zoomed in on the gun a short distance
from them; then they moved warily past that and on up to my
face.

I wanted to neutralize him as much as possible as a threat
and the only thing I could think of was hardly original.

"Get in under the bed!" I ordered. "Lie on your back, head
and shoulders only out." He went slowly, all the time regarding
me balefully through the holes in the balaclava.

"Right now! Very slowly, pass me out the key of the cuffs."
Watching me warily, he made rummaging movements under
the bed; then his right hand came out with the key and held it
up to me.

"Drop it on the floor," I ordered, "and put your hand back
in under."

I sat on the floor at his head and, never once letting the gun
waver, slowly opened and removed the manacles. Free at last, I
stood up. My first thought was to leave him until I could send
Potter for him – once I shot the bolt outside, he was a prisoner
– and I was heading for the door when it struck me that, if his
accomplices turned up in the interim, they could free him and
then they could all vanish. On second thoughts, I'd better lock
the padlock, maybe the others didn't have a key for it. Anyway,
maybe I'd need a key to get through the second door, or the
third, or however many doors there were, how did I know. Or
for his car.

"Pass me out the keys. The same way. Slowly and carefully." While he rummaged, I had another disturbing thought.
What if the others were actually here already? In the house!
Never mind arriving in the interim? There mightn't *be* an interim! "Where are your companions?"

"What companions?" he asked gruffly.

"The ones who were with you when you kidnapped me."

"They're around," he replied but not very convincingly.

"We'll see," I said drily. "Anyway, I'm getting out of here,
so you can be my hostage, if, as you say, they *are* around.
Which I doubt."

The keys dropped on the floor and I scooped them away with my foot before picking them up. Keeping the gun trained on him, I went to the door and quietly opened it. My cell was at the end of a long corridor. Still watching my prisoner, I stepped out for a moment. The difference in the air was unbelievable and I stood, inhaling great, grateful lungfuls of it and taking stock. There was a wooden stairs at the end. At the top of these was an open door through which I could see a bright sun-bathed room – a kitchen, I surmised, from the formica wall cupboards which were the only things I could see from where I stood. It took a lot of effort to turn away from that bright exit up into the world of normality and face back into my stinking, airless cell again, but I couldn't just leave. I really might need a hostage.

"Right so. This is it!" I said brusquely. "Take off the mask."
He shook his head.
"I said: 'Take off the mask'!"
He shook his head again, watching me warily.
"Look... Just take off the bloody mask," I said with strained patience. "I'm not going to shoot you for it... but I'm not putting up with any of this bullshit either."
He shook his head again, refusing to move.
"O.K." I said, "have it your way then. If you won't, then I will!"

I bent to pull the balaclava off but, as I laid my hand on it, the bed shot violently sideways at me, the iron of the base caught me an agonizing, crunching blow on the bridge of the nose and sent me staggering backwards. In a half-sitting position, I slammed into the corner of the room and slid down to finish in an anguished heap on the floor. Though the pain was incredible, I knew I didn't even have time to wipe away the blood that was streaming down my cheeks, much less to sit still for a moment to catch my breath. I fought the instinct to keep my eyes tightly closed and, through the blur of tears and blood, I could see that he was wasting no time in scrambling out from under the bed. He reached a crouching position about the same instant that I was coming to rest in the corner. At that moment we were both desperate men. Whoever got out and locked the door was the winner; the one left inside was a goner.

Perhaps he would have made it if he had gone straight for the door, but he didn't. I saw him hesitate and then take a step towards me. Maybe he thought I was out of it, that he could take the gun from me and so avoid the stalemate of me being locked in the cellar but armed to the teeth. Who would put an eye to the peep-hole then? On reflection, his action was probably the correct one. He advanced a cautious step more.

"Stop!" I shouted. "Stop! Or I'll shoot!" I had hung onto the gun, hung on to it for dear life. I watched his hesitating, blurred image as I fought to keep my eyes open. I didn't know if he was complying with my order, getting ready to spring at me or going to head for the door.

"The safety catch is off!" I warned, though I didn't even know if the gun *had* such a thing; if it didn't, then the bluff didn't matter anyway. Facing him resolutely, left hand against the wall behind me, I began to inch my way upright, my right hand keeping the gun in his direction; though it was probably wobbling like a half-set blancmange, he was almost too close to miss. I was nearly fully upright when he made his move and everything happened in a split second. He dived for the door, I pulled the trigger, the gun cracked waspishly, and I pushed myself away from the wall, launching full length in a desperate dive at the already closing door. The shot hit one of the votive lights on the shelf beneath the picture – if he had come at me, it would have caught him in the chest – and before the shards had hit the floor, I had managed to curl my fingers round the bottom corner of the door just as it was about to slam snugly into its jamb. I howled as waves of agony shot up my left arm; outside, he grunted with strain as he threw all his weight behind his desperate effort to pull the door closed. But the presence of my mangled fingers made it impossible. He'd have to pull hard enough to amputate them; I couldn't withdraw them now even if I'd wanted to. I inched my body along the floor and finally got my knees braced against the wall. Then, sweating with pain and effort, I began to pull against him. Gradually I felt the pain in my trapped fingers easing very slightly but I couldn't figure out if it was a result of the pressure on the door easing off or a loss of sensation in my mangled hand. Either way, it was a welcome respite and it allowed me to pull more steadily. I tried to screw the barrel of the gun into the narrow crack between door and jamb but it wouldn't quite fit; my idea was to use it as a lever or at least a substitute for my fingers. I pulled again when I thought I felt a slight slackening of the pressure, gathering all my sapped strength into one, huge effort. Suddenly the barrel slotted in. I let him pull the door to again, clamping it, and withdrew my pulped digits.

A moment before, this had been the height of my ambitions, but now it struck me that I was once more in a position of strength. I pulled downwards on the butt of the gun until the barrel was pointing up at where I judged him to be. Obviously, he hadn't noticed the gun and, with much grunting and straining, was going on with his now futile tugging.

"Hey!" I shouted, and there was a temporary lull in the grunts from the corridor. "Look down!" I gave him time to do so. "The gun! Do you see the gun?" I gave him a few seconds to realise his position. "I'm going to count to three and then I'll start shooting!"

"Jesus Christ!" I heard him squeal as if he'd just discovered that the door-handle was red hot.

"One!" I shouted warningly. "I mean it!" I waited, coiled for the sudden release of pressure. Nothing happened; there was more frantic panting from the other side. "Two!" I called menacingly and got ready to yank open the door and run like I had never run before. I was uncomfortably aware of the fact that the kitchen door could act as an equally effective barrier if he got through first and managed to lock it after him.

Suddenly the pressure was gone; I jerked open the door and heard him thundering along the stone passage, making all speed for the stairs. Flat out, I took off after him, holding my jeans up with my injured left hand, the loose end of the belt slapping against my knees. "Stop!" I shouted. "I'll shoot you!" I warned. I had no intention of shooting him – I was far younger and faster and I had no doubt that I could outrun him – but I wanted to stampede him so that he couldn't think straight. Only a couple of paces behind him, I shouted "Stop!" again, and pulled the trigger, aiming towards the ceiling.

"Jesus!" he squeaked, seemed about to stop, then accelerated, panting, and took the wooden steps in a couple of bounds, rocketing into the kitchen. As he passed through the door, I shot again at the ceiling to make sure he didn't turn to slam the door, but even if he had, I had already gained so much on him that I probably would have made it through anyway.

I almost had him in the kitchen. I reached out my injured left hand for his shoulder as we raced past a table, but sensing it, he jerked at a wooden chair, knocking it directly in my path and bringing me down in a tangle of legs. He vanished through a door opposite and, as I picked myself up, I heard the thud of a heavy door being slammed and the rapidly fading crunch of running feet on gravel.

I sprinted through the door; the feeling that I was in control had vanished with my ignominious tumble and I was having serious regrets that I hadn't shot him in the legs or shoulders or somewhere non-vital. Since I had 'captured' him, only a few minutes had passed, and already, on two occasions he had managed to outwit me soundly. He was obviously no slouch when it came to quick thinking; he also, I thought wryly, had a way with furniture – first the bed, then the chair...

I came to the hall door. There were tall narrow glass panels on either side covered by net curtains and I was just in time to see him slam down the boot of a red Ford Cortina and turn, heading through a gap in a hydrangea hedge which was the border of the wide gravel forecourt in front of the house. My heart lurched sickeningly when I saw the long gun he carried; I couldn't make out if it was a rifle or a shotgun because he was far away and my eyes were still not seeing clearly, but it was of academic interest anyway, as I was now well and truly outgunned. I revised my opinion yet again, regretting at this stage that I hadn't shot him regardless, anywhere – head, heart, liver, spleen, anywhere.

Obviously, hot pursuit was no longer a viable option. I stood, hidden behind the net curtain, watching for further sight of him, but he didn't show at either end of the twenty-odd yards of hedge; nor did he cross the lawn beyond it, towards the boundary wall which was marked by a spaced stand of tall conifers between which sparkled the calm blue waters of a narrow bay. I assumed that he had taken up position behind the screening hedge and was waiting for me to show. I continued my watch for another minute or so, painfully and awkwardly replacing my belt as I waited, nervously placing the gun on the window ledge as I did so.

It was no time for weighing options; while I knew where he was, I had to try to work out an escape plan. *Another* fucking escape plan, I thought in disgust, as I took a last peek through the curtain. Pausing briefly to check the phone on the hall table, which was dead, I took the stairs two at a time and did a quick round of the upstairs rooms. There were no other houses in sight but I thought I recognised the countryside. I reckoned I was five or six miles from Knockmore on a little-used coast road.

From one of the back windows, I got the first bit of good news I had had in a long time. Some way up along a gravel road which snaked up along a rhododendron-covered hill, was a garage, and, backed into it, its bonnet barely nudging out of the gloom into the morning sunshine, was my Land Rover! It was like the face of an old friend and I decided to make for it at once and call for help on the radio telephone.

I rushed back to the front room overlooking the hedge. He was still there but he looked as if he was about to make a move; I had to get going at once. I raced for the kitchen and located, in a small pantry off it, a back door. It didn't look as if it had been opened for a long time and made such a loud scraping noise when I pulled it open that I thought he *had* to hear it. I jerked it closed behind me and dashed across the narrow back yard into the rhododendrons. Heart pounding, I waited to see if he would arrive at the double but he didn't and, after a couple of minutes I decided that he hadn't heard the door after all and therefore wouldn't know that I wasn't still in the house. I set off stealthily uphill.

After what seemed like ages of alternately creeping through the undergrowth and stopping to listen, I arrived opposite the garage and took stock. To the left, the road ran downhill for sixty odd yards, between the bushes for most of its way, then along the side of the house before turning ninety degrees around the corner to continue, presumably as the forecourt, along in front. To the right, it was visible for a shorter distance;

it curved out of sight after a mere ten yards or so, amongst the rhododendrons which grew thickly on both sides. I watched for another minute for sight of him but there was none so I made a dash across into the gloom of the garage doorway and crouched there long enough for him to approach if he had seen my dash.

Once I was sure that I hadn't been seen, I hunkered down by the wheel on the driver's side and felt up under the wing for the magnetic box with the spare key which is always there. When I detached it, I dislodged a pile of dried mud which accumulated in a little pyramid underneath and I took care to disperse this before straightening up, opening the door, climbing in, and locking the door again behind me.

The radio telephone didn't work, presumably because I was in the garage and, with that life-line so unexpectedly denied me, I climbed dejectedly over the seats into the deeper dark of the back to sit amongst my medicines and equipment and try to work out a cure for my present predicament and to take stock of my position.

Physically I was a mess. My nose felt broken, my eyes were starting to puff up and the fingers which had been caught in the door were purple and stiff, but still movable. Psychologically I was probably in an even worse state – I think the blow of finding that the radio telephone was useless had knocked the stuffing out of me. Now I felt trapped in the Land Rover, claustrophobic and cooped up, skulking in the dark like some cowardly cockroach. Briefly I considered climbing out again and trying to capture him but I was outgunned, I didn't know the grounds and, if his accomplices were to arrive, then I'd be outnumbered too. One of my worst ideas, on any subject ever.

Next I considered trying to escape on foot. The problem with that was that I wasn't sure where I was, how far away the nearest telephone might be and what kind of countryside lay round about; this was important as I would have to avoid the road like the plague – with my luck, I'd probably end up being offered a lift by my captors. And accepting. Scrub that one too.

I pondered a bit more. It seemed unlikely that my erstwhile gaoler could afford to hang about for much longer – the longer he went without sight of me, the more he'd have to assume that I had already escaped; therefore he would soon have to start expecting a regiment of police to descend upon him. He could not afford to be caught on the premises. He knew that I would not be able to identify him positively, never having seen his face, so it would be by far the most prudent approach for him to cut and run, get as much distance as possible between himself and the house. Always, of course, assuming that he didn't actually *own* the house in the first place. Then he was caught anyway. But I didn't think that he did. He certainly didn't *live* there; it had that unmistakable abandoned, deserted feel to it.

The pressure was on him and it would be increasing rapidly. I decided to sit it out, for at least a couple of hours.

Sitting there I had the sudden sobering thought that I wasn't such a hot-shot planner after all. I had made a bee-line for the radio telephone which, even if it had been able to transmit at full power, would have been useless anyway. It was Sunday morning. Eileen wouldn't be at the office and the receiver would be unattended, not even switched on. Some planner! As if I needed any other negative thoughts.

My seat on the metal side boxes left a lot to be desired; there were rivets and screws sticking up all over – they weren't built to be sat on. As I was facing a couple of hours of waiting, I decided to make it as comfortable as I could. I folded a brown dust-coat into a rough cushion and half rose to put it under me. And that was when I saw his shadow sliding along the road in front of the garage.

Instantly, I froze, my skin shrinking with a chill dread. Had he heard any noise? Had he seen the Land Rover move? Could he see the bonnet from where he was? Hardly daring to breathe, I watched in fascinated horror as the shadow slid along further, lengthening all the time, crawling closer.

I made a snap decision that he hadn't seen or heard anything – he'd surely have stopped if he had. I was trapped in a half-standing crouch, my right hand gripping the back of the driver's seat, holding me up; the gun was on the floor in the corner behind me. I had to get seated at once, had to get my hand off the seat and back into the dark; but above all, I had to get the gun. Taking my weight on my left hand, I lowered myself onto the side box with the gentleness of eiderdown settling, and, not daring to take my eyes off the bright entrance, I groped for and retrieved the gun. From my sitting position, I could no longer see the shadow or mark its progress.

The first I knew of his arrival in the garage was when the handle of the driver's door rattled suddenly, the noise making me start convulsively. He moved quickly once he found the door locked, crossing in front of the jeep, stooping briefly to peer under it, then trying the passenger door. Finding it locked also, he probably assumed that the jeep hadn't been disturbed since he had parked it – after all, as far as he knew, he had the only key. I could see his grey eyes looking casually in, but he wasn't expecting to see anything; I could tell. He didn't wait for his eyes to accommodate to the gloom and he didn't try to overcome the reflection from the dusty glass by cupping a hand to the window. So he didn't see me, and he didn't see the gun which was pointed at the middle of his balaclava, and he didn't see the whiteness of the knuckle which was squeezing the trigger.

If he had, I'd have shot him.

CHAPTER 23

When at last he moved on up the road, I got ready to go. I had changed my mind pretty quickly and now I was against sitting it out in the Land Rover. *Totally* against it. I had come too close to being trapped. I couldn't see my nerves letting me keep still for the next few hours. Besides, *how* would I know when the coast was clear? It was probably as safe now as it would ever be – at least now, I knew his general whereabouts.

The problem was how to start the Land Rover quickly and quietly. Diesel engines are not noted for their soft purring or their instant one-touch starting and this would very likely be slower and noisier than usual because of several days inactivity. To make matters worse, the battery had been fairly low lately. Ideally, I'd have pushed her out of the garage, let her freewheel down the hill, starting her on the roll, but this was made impossible by a low concrete threshold across the doorway, a mere four feet in front of the wheels. Even in the whole of my health, I'd have been stymied by that. I thought for a moment and came up with a plan which, though very risky, was worth trying, at least once.

Crouching low to minimise my shadow, I sneaked into the road to check – he wasn't in sight. Back in the garage, I released the handbrake, jiggled the gear-shift into neutral, and pushed until the front wheels rested against the threshold. The next part depended on the dodgy battery. I checked the road once more – still no sight of him – then, with the awful feeling that I was putting myself into a position from which there would be no chance to escape, I climbed into the driver's seat and put the key into the ignition. I left the door open to give me a better chance of hearing a telltale soft foot-fall on the

189

gravel, and sat there, pre-heating the engine, ears straining. I forced myself to wait until the engine had to have had sufficient heating before trying the starter; it couldn't have been more than a minute but it felt like a lifetime – particularly as the more forward position of the jeep had brought the front seats, and me, into the full glare of the morning sun. My heart was pounding as I turned the key.

The result was an inauspicious sick whirring. To me, it sounded like blast-off at Cape Canaveral but I knew that there was no way that it was going to get the engine started. I had decided to allow ten seconds for the engine to catch but, by the count of six, it was obvious that it wouldn't, so I put the back-up plan into action.

Shoving the gear-shift into first, and letting the clutch out, I turned the key again. The starter sounded even weaker this time, but the Land Rover lurched forward, laboriously hauling its front wheels up over the threshold. I locked the steering wheel to the right, hoping that she would begin to roll down the hill at once, but she didn't; she hung there stubbornly, strad-dling the cement ramp, her rear wheels tight against it. With a feverish glance up to my left, I turned the key again, and again the starter turned, but this time so weakly that I thought it couldn't last. It almost didn't; it stalled on the turn that brought the rear wheels just to the top. I pressed in the clutch, knocked the gear into neutral and felt indescribable relief course through me as the Land Rover began to roll, slowly at first, but soon picking up momentum.

Suddenly I was running smoothly, coasting freely down between the high, green rhododendron walls. I kept one eye on the road ahead and one on the rearview mirror, and, before I had gone twenty yards, I saw him round the corner, running flat out. I decided to wait no longer. Pressing down the clutch, I put the gear into third, rolled another few yards and let the clutch out. The wheels locked and slid through the dry surface gravel, only catching when they met the drag of the harder underlying material; the engine locked for one horrifying second, then it caught, turned, and suddenly coughed into wheezing life. I nursed it for the moment it took to develop a healthy roar, then accelerated away as far as the corner of the house. Here, I had to slow almost to a stop to negotiate the ninety-degree turn onto the forecourt; I took a last quick look in the mirror. He was no longer running, and for a moment I thought he had given up the chase, that is, until I saw a neat round hole appear in the corner of the back window and the left half-panel of the windscreen shatter and disintegrate. He was shooting at me! Christ almighty! In my haste to be off, I nearly stalled the engine.

As I came up to the red Cortina parked at the front, it struck me that I would be home and dried if I could put it out of action. I stood on the brake but skidded on a few feet too far, coming to rest ahead of it. As coolly as I could manage in the circumstances, I put my head and shoulders through the window, turned back, gun-arm extended and aimed carefully at the front tyre. Needless to say, I missed – I had never shot a handgun before, I was in an awkward, twisting position, the Land Rover was vibrating, my hand was shaking and my eyes were being drawn, in spite of me, to the corner of the house round which I knew he was about to appear at any second. I should have known. What did I expect? Yet I was dismayed and incredulous when I saw the spurt of gravel which my shot kicked up some four inches from the wheel. Any thoughts I might have had of a second attempt vanished when he suddenly appeared around the corner. I let out the clutch and sped off around the turn in the drive. If he tried another shot, he missed.

As soon as I reached the road, I knew where I was. The area was to the west of Knockmore, about eight miles out. The road was a bad one with many stretches under repair, a fact which I reckoned was in my favour, as the Land Rover ought to be able to take the bad road conditions in better stride than his Ford. Within the first mile, he appeared in my mirror; by the end of the second, he filled it.

I zig-zagged along crazily, weaving from side to side in an effort to keep in front – once past me, he could race ahead and set up an ambush; I had to concentrate on staying ahead. It soon became obvious that this could not be the position for long; he had nearly managed to steam by on a few occasions already, despite my efforts to throw him off. I had tried braking suddenly when he was close behind, hoping that he would impale himself on my tow-hitch but, as I already knew to my cost, his reflexes were very good; so, it turned out, were his brakes, and I gave up that plan after a couple of efforts. In fact, it was a dangerous ploy on my part, because it slowed me up and, with his superior acceleration, he almost got by twice. Then he began to use his head. On gravelled stretches under repair, he would drop back out of sight in my dust cloud, then come hurtling suddenly out of the swirling dust, hoping to get by me before I saw him. Again, he nearly succeeded on a couple of occasions. Just as I was beginning to think that it was inevitable that he pass me, I had an idea, a slim one, but a hope. And the perfect place to try it was coming up fast.

Nose to tail, we raced along, swerving and jinking, he thrusting, me parrying. The first road-sign said: "MAJOR ROAD WORKS AHEAD, 400YDS. REDUCE SPEED NOW!" I passed it flat out and he was right with me, as if I had him on tow. The next sign said: DANGER! SURFACING WORK IN PROGRESS! MAX. SPEED – 20 M.P.H." We passed it doing about sixty.

Almost at once the tarred road ended and we were on rough gravel. His visibility was reduced immediately by my dust and I was afraid that he'd try his dropping back trick again. Now, we were almost there. We took the bends at wild speed, he began to close in on me. Coming in to the last one, he was really close. I pushed up the speed even more and and the Land Rover listed alarmingly as she gamely held her track rounding it. I checked quickly in my mirror to confirm that he was still with me and then, in mid-bend, at the point of maximum tendency to skid, I reached out to the dashboard and flicked on the headlight switch.

The effect was instant. Reflexly, when he saw the red tail-lights appear suddenly a matter of feet in front of him, he jammed on his brakes, and, before he could work out that they were *not* brake-lights he was in a skid. At that speed and on that surface, he had very little chance to control it.

I saw his slide beginning, then I was around the corner and he was lost to my view; and he didn't re-appear between there and Knockmore. I watched my mirror all the way.

192

CHAPTER 24

I **headed straight** for the police barracks. Traffic was practically non-existent, most of the cars in town being drawn up on either side of the road outside the tall, imposing church. It was obvious, from the crowd loitering and chatting outside, that Mass was being read within. As I navigated the narrow channel between the parked cars, a reflex outburst of chest-tapping rippled through the chattering crowd and I could hear faintly, the tinkle of the consecration bell.

I pulled up outside the police station and went straight in. The duty officer looked up from his Sunday tabloid and seeing my brutalized face, sat up quickly, shocked.

"What happened to you?" he asked, eyes widening.

"Where's Inspector Potter?" I rejoined.

"You're Mr Samson, right?"

"Yes. Where is he? At home?"

"No. He's out looking for you. We've all been out looking for you for the past few days. Hang on a tick. I'd better tell him you're here. I'll just send out the word – the radio is in the back."

"Tell him to check on the Braggan road – three or four miles out, where they're doing it up – there may be a car gone off the road there. A red Cortina. It'll be the man who was holding me for the past few days. It only happened a matter of minutes ago so maybe the car is still there."

He was back in a couple of moments. "The boss said to tell you he's delighted you're safe. He'll be in in about twenty minutes and he asked you to wait here for him."

"Sure. No problem. You told him about the car?"

"I did," he nodded. "You may as well wait in here." He

193

opened a flap in the counter. "The bathroom's through that door, first on your right. I'll put the kettle on."

I got a shock when I looked in the mirror. Now that I could see my whole face, and not just isolated islands of battered features, like in the mirror of the jeep at sixty miles an hour, the effect was devastating. I seemed to have aged by about ten years. Rough stubble covered my jaw and chin, my hair was filthy and straggling, and, between grimy stubble and wild hair, my face looked back at itself, dirty, sweat-streaked, and blotched with crusts of caked blood. I was an absolute mess and I felt just as bad as I looked.

I filled the basin and, with the aid of wads of toilet paper soaked in warm water, gently dabbed away the superficial blood and grime. When I had finished, I was still a mess. The skin had cracked in a straight line across the bridge of my nose and through the split, soft flesh pushed like a pouting, purple lip. Both eyes were receding into mounds of soft, rapidly-darkening tissue. I looked like the Lone Ranger with his hat off.

Back in the duty room, I drank strong tea and felt better. I gave the duty officer a synopsis. "I won't go into details, if you don't mind," I said, "because I'll have to do it all over again when the others get here. The one telling can do it all. How did you know I was missing anyway? I mean missing and needing looking for?"

"The lassie in your surgery – Eileen?"

"Yes, Eileen."

"Did you know she used to go out with a sergeant we had here one time a year or two back?"

"No. I didn't know that," I confessed, wondering what that had to do with anything.

"Well she did. But nothing came of it."

"So it would seem." I waited for him to go on but he seemed to have gone into a kind of wistful reverie. Perhaps he fancied Eileen himself or maybe he was dreaming of sergeant's stripes. When I thought that he had had enough nostalgia, I butted in: "You said Eileen raised the alarm about my disappearance? But how did Eileen know I had gone missing and needed to be searched for? That's what I'd like to know."

"Well she phoned the barracks the morning you didn't show

194

up for work, because someone had phoned to say you'd had an accident way over the other side of the country near Dublin the previous night and that you were in hospital for observation, but there was a night call written in the book in the surgery for two-thirty in your writing, so she got suspicious, especially after the break-in at the cottage the few days previously. The man that called said he was your uncle, but when we traced your home address, we found from the gardai there that you didn't *have* an uncle. So the boss had us check all the accident reports for that night all over the country and not one involved a Land Rover. So we put two and two together... and we've been searching since."

"Do my parents know I was missing?"

"No. Not as far as I know. I think they were intending to tell them this evening, though."

There was a commotion in the hall and Potter came in.

"Christ, man!" he said, aghast. "What happened to you? Did your head go through the windscreen?"

"No, that was a bullet."

"A bullet! You mean they shot at you, actually tried to *kill* you!?"

"That's right."

"Holy God Almighty man! Another fraction of an inch and you could have lost both eyes, or even got it in the brain!"

"Not this," I indicated the pulped nose. "The *windscreen* was broken by the bullet. This... well... this was... because I was hit by a bed. On the ah... nose."

"A bed! You were hit on the nose... by a bed?! Maybe you'd better tell us about it from the beginning. Is there any tea left in that pot, Burke?"

"I'll make some more, Inspector. This is cold by now."

"Do then." He turned to me. "Now... I can't wait to hear about the bed, but can you tell me anything definite first, like who kept you or where... or even why they kept you?..."

"Only where I was kept for sure. And what they wanted."

"Where is a damned good start. Where?"

I told him, or at least described the place which he identified at once. He interrupted me to issue an order for a squad-car to go there immediately. "Just seal off the house, lads... and the grounds. Have a quick look inside but don't touch anything, O.K.? Off with you then. Burke, you get on the blower to the surrounding stations and tell them to get some roadblocks up for...?" He turned to me, eyebrows raised.

"A red Cortina – not the latest model, the one with the sloping boot – being driven by a man of about five-nine or ten, well spoken, I'd guess in his fifties, but I can't be sure. He wore a mask all the time. He'll have a rifle with him and maybe a grey balaclava. I'm sorry I didn't get the number of the car... I never even thought of it! Everything just happened so fast... I couldn't think straight. Oh! And he'll have a digital watch," I added, remembering his exact times. "And he's probably a Protestant."

"Huh!?" Potter looked at me, obviously wondering how that was going to help identify him at a road block. "A Protestant? You think that's important?"

"No. I don't even know why I said it. I'm not sure what he is."

"Maybe it is important. Under what circumstances did he say he was a Protestant?"

"He didn't." I was beginning to regret starting speculation on such complete trivia as the religious persuasions of the various characters involved but I always had the impression that one should tell the police everything no matter how unimportant it might seem to the uninitiated layman. "Last night he told me would be late this morning because he had to go to church. A Catholic would have said 'go to Mass'. No?"

He shrugged and repeated the two phrases a few times to try them out, then made a face and shrugged again, this time dismissively.

I felt pretty stupid. Waffling on about the semantics of different religions when I had missed the most basic thing of all, the number of the car. "I'm sorry I can't be of more help."

"You're doing fine!" Potter reassured me. "It'll come back bit by bit. Don't worry. We'll get him. You did damn well to get away at all! So whenever you're ready..." He pushed the microphone of a tape recorder across the table towards me.

During the next hour, I recounted the whole story over and over. I went and fetched the Sureprint wallet from under the seat of the Land Rover and, when Potter had made space on his chaotic desk, spread the prints out in four rows of seven. The eight prints of Catamaran we put back into the wallet.

Potter sent the negatives off to the official police photographer to have copies made and we sat and drank a fresh brew while we went over the photographs again and again.

"I'm having two sets of prints made, one for us here and one for the Drug Squad in Dublin. The originals, you ought to keep, Frank, and have another look at them now and again – just in case something strikes you, even though you didn't actually take them."

Conversation became general as we waited for the photographer to finish his work. He was a local freelancer who was on a retainer and he wasn't a bit pleased at having his Sunday morning interrupted; the whole episode resurrected the question of an increase in his retainer, a topic which, Potter told me, surfaced often.

The general consensus was that I was a 'very lucky man' to have made my escape – 'very lucky indeed.' Inwardly, I snorted at the idea of someone who had been burglarized, brutalized, kidnapped, beaten, incarcerated in an airless cellar, hunted, shot at, attacked with various items of furniture and had his nose broken (probably), being referred to as 'very lucky indeed,' but I forewent any comment. I knew what they meant. I had had it all explained to me a long time ago by a philosophical old farmer whose one and only cow had, without warning, kicked me in the belly and sent me sprawling, full length onto a mound of soft manure. As I picked myself painfully up, he pointed to an adjacent clump of nettles and told me I was 'lucky'. Angrily I demanded to know what the hell was so 'lucky' about it. I'll always remember his reply. "Well now, son," he said, after thinking for a minute, "look at it this way: I've only had two teeth in all my head for the last thirty years or more – just two," he curled back his lips on one side to expose two, long, wicked-looking, multi-coloured stumps, "and every morning and night for those thirty years, I thank God that they're opposite one another. Things can always be worse, me boy."

Reckoning that I wasn't fit for work, I phoned around and

eventually managed to find someone to take over for a few days. I needed a break but I couldn't neglect the practice either.

An hour later, the photographs arrived back. Potter put one set in his files, gave another to me and sent the third to Dublin by courier. He insisted I avail myself of his hospitality again and I didn't argue; on the way to his house, we stopped by Fernditch to pick up some personal things and a change of clothes. His men were already at work on the quiet road, knocking on doors, asking about strangers or suspiciously parked cars which might have been seen near the cottage around the time the postman made his rounds, red Cortinas, middle-aged men of about five ten, ... anything at all unusual or odd,... anything out of the ordinary at all?...

Joan Potter made me as welcome as she had the night of the burglary and, after I had soaked in a hot bath, fed me like a king.

Afterwards, I phoned Claire; she was back from the funeral.

"Frank! I've been trying to reach you for the last couple of days!"

"I've been busy. How was your trip?"

"Oh! Don't talk to me about the trip! It was harrowing! An ordeal! She died about two hours after we got there. Which proved, everyone said, that she'd been hanging on until Ma got to see her one last time and of course Ma, God love her innocence, now feels that Mabel would still be alive if she hadn't gone near her... Some logic, huh?" She paused for breath, and then went on, a bit tentatively: "I was thinking I might make a trip to Knockmore tomorrow... I could do with getting away for a few days... Would that be alright with you?"

"That would be perfect with me. Actually I've got a few days off myself."

"How come?"

I told her. At first she didn't believe me, but when I did manage to convince her, she became really concerned; despite the various aches, pains and bruises, when I hung up, I felt that God was distinctly in his Heaven and all was definitely right with the world.

I stayed at Potter's for the afternoon. He kept coming and

198

going. He'd arrive in, ask me a few questions, check a detail or two and then race out again. On his visits he also brought little snippets of news: the revolver was untraceable, American make, over twenty years old and in poor working order.

"It worked for me alright, every time I fired it."

"We might have better luck in tracing the bullets. They're new and a brand not commonly available. Dublin tells me that they are only sold in ten or twelve shops throughout the whole country but we can't get on to that until tomorrow. Hopefully, by that time, we won't need to. The only clear prints on the gun are yours; we raised a few smudges but they could be anybody's. Can you remember anything else your man might have touched in the room?"

"Nothing more than I've told you already. The padlock and bolt of the door, the food cartons and containers and of course, the books and magazines. I presume he must have touched them when he was putting them into the box and taking them out." I tried to concentrate, to throw my mind back. "That's all I can think of right now – apart from the sun-glasses and the loo bucket, and I'd say he only touched the wire handle of that. Unless he touched the bottom of it when he was emptying it?"

"We've dusted that all over and we got a few reasonable prints. They may show up on the computer but I'll have to send them to H.Q. for that. I'm thinking of sending the food containers, the cardboard box and the books to Galway for dusting. O'Hanlon isn't bad, but they've got a real expert and all the latest equipment in there.

"By the way, the house belongs to a Herr Manfred Pfeiffer, a German businessman. He comes over once a year for the Mayfly fishing on the Corrib. He doesn't have anyone locally looking after it. His wife and family come over a week before him and get it ready and they usually stay on for a few weeks after he goes back."

He went off again but returned inside an hour. This time, it was the car he wanted to know about. Could I remember if it had any bumps or dents? Any scratches? Any badges or emblems? Was it clean or dirty? A tow hitch? Spotlights? Radio aerial and if so, front or back, right side or left? The more details he asked about the car, the worse I felt. I was unable to give him a definite answer to any of his questions. I continued to feel awful about not having had the presence of mind to take the number; if only I had done that, the whole thing would have been over by now. Potter had been very understanding and argued fiercely with me when I was being self-critical. Hadn't I managed to free myself and escape? Hadn't I nearly succeeded in capturing my captor and doing the police's work for them? Had I not come up with the most likely explanation for my abduction? With all the help I had given them, the police ought to have no trouble in wrapping the case up in double quick time! Still, I thought I saw a look on his face as though he was wondering how a brain that could stay cool enough to come up with the GI Truss and make it work, could have been so scattered that it would miss something as *basic* as taking a car number.

"And you can't remember even a single letter or number from the reg?"

"No. I'm sorry but I can't. Not one."

"Was the number plate itself white or yellow?"

"Just an ordinary number plate I suppose. It didn't make any impression on me at all, I'm afraid. For all I know, the car might not have had *any* plates on it. I'm sorry. I really screwed up on that one!"

"Not to worry. I told you; you did fine. Did you notice if the car might ever have been out of the country? Did it have an 'IRL' sticker on the back?"

"I don't honestly know. I was in a bit of a panic at the time. He had just shot out my windscreen, dammitall!"

"Relax, Frank! Relax. I'm not saying that you're not helping! You've done great so far. I just want to see if anything might have come back to you now that you've had time to draw your breath. That's all."

"I'm sorry."

"Well, you needn't be. You've got nothing to be sorry about. I don't suppose you could go closer to the car's colour than 'red'?"

"It was the same colour as tomato soup," I said after a moment's consideration. "It wasn't pink and it wasn't scarlet, if that's what you mean."

"Good. That's a help. The road blocks haven't had any luck so far. I'll keep them in place for another few hours and then I'll move them about two miles back..."

"Why?"

"He may have hidden his car off the road somewhere and be keeping a roadblock under observation. If he sees it leaving, he'll probably think that we've given up, believing that we've missed him. Then, he'll move, anxious to get the hell out of the area, and we'll snag him a couple of miles down the road."

"Aren't you the devious ones?" I said in admiration. Potter smiled.

"In the meantime, we're checking all the red Cortinas we know of in the area and you wouldn't believe how many of those there are! That's why I wanted something to narrow the field down a bit. Not, I hasten to add, that I expect it to be a local car. Knockmore is a bit short on drug barons. We're also checking the newsagents to see if anyone can remember selling the items he brought you this morning but we've only got the papers to go on because the novels aren't new. So there's not a lot of hope there, I'm afraid. You know what newsagents are like during the few hours that they open on Sunday morning! Thronged! As for the groceries, there was nothing special, hardly anything that would cause a check-out girl to recall who bought them."

He went off again and when he returned in the evening, all he had to announce was that, so far, they had drawn a blank. No progress had been made. I began to feel lousy about the car number all over again, only this time, worse.

Despite the Potters' protestations, I insisted on going back to the cottage for the night. For one thing, I wanted to be on my own and, for another, I wanted to be ensconced there when Claire arrived. What eventually won the Inspector over to my side was the fact that I might be an attractive bait for a trap, an inducement to the gang to have another go. So, with cops hidden all round the place, I went to bed and slept like I'd had an anaesthetic.

CHAPTER 25

I **pottered about** the house all morning doing unnecessary chores – I arranged the books according to their subject matter, put the LPs in alphabetical order and, with the aid of the many reference works I had at my disposal, managed to re-match most of the eggs with their name-tags on the display trays. Several times I almost caught the half-thought which had been making flash appearances ever since my first interview with my captor but had, so far, maddeningly eluded me. It was like seeing something in very poor light; by looking at a point near it you could detect its presence, vaguely and without resolution or definition, but when you looked straight at it, it vanished. There was a name for that, I thought: (something) vision or your (something) spot. I was putting the back issues of Time magazine into chronological sequence when Claire pulled up outside.

Her sprightly step faltered and the smile fell from her face when I opened the door. Wide-eyed, she stared at me, as if I was a perfect stranger and a mean-looking one at that.

"Christ, Frank! You're ruined! I had no idea it was *this* bad!"

"Nothing that can't be cured by the kiss of a certain special woman." I smiled and walked out into the light to meet her. She kissed me as fiercely as her respect for my battered features would allow, then stepped back and surveyed me.

"Either you ought to change your witchdoctor or I'm not the certain special woman prescribed. You still look awful."

"That's because it needs continuous therapy from the certain special woman. Like a drip."

"Who are you calling a drip, hey? You'd better watch it or

you've had your one and only dose of medicine." She gave me a gentle poke in the ribs, immediately apologising concernedly.

"Don't worry. All the damage is visible. The rest of the body, I assure you, works perfectly."

"Really?" She smiled a strange little smile. "Glad to hear it."

"Yes... well. Anyway, Claire, you're a sight for sore eyes and here I speak from first-hand experience." I had been rehearsing the 'sight for sore eyes' crack since morning but it fell flat.

During the next hour I told her the whole story as we went through the photographs and then came the questions – an endless stream of them.

"Listen," I interrupted at one point, "why don't we go for a drive somewhere and we can talk about this on the way. It's a shame to sit indoors on such a lovely afternoon."

We drove in Claire's Escort through the mountains and on down to the coast. Eventually Claire ran out of questions and conversation turned to her work, what was happening in Dublin, general stuff like that.

We parked on a grassy bank and walked down towards a long, deserted beach. Claire threaded her arm through mine.

"So," I said. "Your trip to England was pretty harrowing?"

"Don't *remind* me..."

"Oh. Sorry. That bad huh?"

"That bad. Still, I did manage to sneak into Stratford one evening and get to the theatre."

"What play did you see?"

"Henry the Fourth, Part Two."

"Did you not make it in time for Part One?"

She started to laugh, then stopped and glanced quickly at me, not sure if I was joking or not. I looked back blankly and decided I'd have to stop this foolery, stop confusing the woman.

"Just kidding!" I held up a hand of peace. "Just kidding. Part Two right. Now all you need are parts three, four and five, The Return of Henry the Fourth, The *Revenge* of Henry the Fourth, and you'll have the set."

"What about Henry the Fourth Strikes Back?"

"Indeed. And Henry the Fourth Rides Again? We forgot that one. The best of the lot."

The kidding stopped as we climbed a particularly dodgy dry stone wall and side-stepped down a steep sand dune onto the beach. We walked across the dry, crackling seaweed line down onto the cleaner sand and linked arms again.

"I haven't seen Paul Markham since," she said in a gently teasing voice.

"Who he?" I asked in wide-eyed innocence.

"Spengler he. That who he."

"Oh!... You mean Markham-Spengler! The one and only, world-famous, Hiberno-Teutonic, double-barrelled, industrialist-philosopher!..."

She laughed and after a pause: "You know... he used to pop in for coffee a couple of times a week."

"Perhaps you make lousy coffee?"

"I do. But it never stopped him before."

"Before...? Before what?"

"Before the evening you almost wiped out the entire equine population of the whole country single-handedly with galloping eumitis."

"A highly fatal condition that proved to be. For some... D'you think he fancied your ass?"

"You're such a poet, Frank. I wish I had a pen to write that down."

"Don't worry. I'll remember it. Well? Do you?"

"Mmmm... I think he liked me. Yes."

I noted the past tense but didn't say anything. "Well then it's obvious what happened. Faced with my *joie de vivre*, my *je ne sais quoi*, my *sang froid* and *savoir faire* not to mention my *mal-de-mer*, *fait accompli*, *au revoir*, *bon voyage*, *fleur-de-lys*, *boeuf aux champignons* and *appellation controlle*, he decided that it was no contest and quit the field."

"I think your conclusion is correct but I also think your reasons are way off."

"Why?"

"I think he got the message from me," she replied simply.

"Oh..." That put a sudden end to the banter and we walked on in silence for a while.

"Do you notice anything different about me?" Claire asked.

"Eh... eh... " I examined her as she smiled expectantly at

me. "You've changed your hair?" I hazarded.

"No!"

"I give up. What?"

"About my attitude."

"Attitude to what?"

"My demeanour!"

"No. I can't say I do. It's the eyes you know... they're all swollen and not working to full capacity. You'll have to give me a hint. Animal, mineral or vegetable?"

"Forget it. Forget the guessing. Do I seem to you like a woman who has come to a decision and is happy about it or do I remind you more of a woman who is still dithering, letting the ghosts of the past haunt her?"

We stopped and I turned to face her. "Give us a hint?" I smiled.

"*Another* hint?"

"Make it obvious... like the last one." She slid her hand up to the back of my neck and gently pulled my mouth down to hers.

We walked on again in contented silence. The sea, without a breath of air to ruffle it, lay in the bay like molten pewter. Offshore, on small rocks, cormorants squatted motionless, necks folded back, wings hung out to each side like suppliants. Out along the western horizon a bank of white clouds had marshalled, but without any wind to move them they just hung there, a lace hem on the blue mantle of the sky.

On a small grassy patch above a cove we sat and rested and in a little while, when the time was right for both of us, we made love.

I lay, contented and fulfilled, lazily watching the tiny specks of seagulls wheeling effortlessly on the thermals way way above us. Beside me, Claire dozed, her head resting on my chest. Half asleep, I rolled a few strands of her hair between my thumb and fingers.

Suddenly and with startling clarity, the elusive thought was there, right in front of me, as clear as a lighthouse beam.

"Bloody hell!" I sat up with a jerk that dumped her head onto the grass. "I'm a fool!"

"What?" she asked, blinking in the sudden sun. "What's

wrong?" She began to look about her to see what had disturbed me so much.

"It's the *horse!*"

"Where?" She twisted her body around looking for the horse.

I was staring straight out to sea, focussed unseeingly on the long ridge of distant clouds which seemed to rise out of the heat haze like the snow-capped peaks of Atlantis. My head was swarming. The flood of possibilities and explanations which the sudden realisation had released into my brain was numbing. Though the knowledge was hardly twenty seconds old, all sorts of little facts had already begun to stick together like iron filings to a magnet, and I knew it was right. "I'm a bloody idiot, Claire. A blind imbecile, do you know that? A gomm." She was still regarding me with a puzzled frown.

"Why do you say that?"

"The photographs they were after were the ones I took of the *horse!* Not the goddam party! They had nothing to do with it! Not a bit! How *stupid* can you get! It's Catamaran!"

"How do you know?"

"Remember I told you that I first tried to bluff my way out of it by telling my captor that the film hadn't been wound onto the take-up spool properly?"

"Yes." She nodded.

"Well the only way you can tell for sure if that happens is if the winder keeps going on and on long after the film ought to have ended. For example, if you're taking your fortieth photograph on a reel which is only supposed to give you thirty-six, then obviously, the film has not been attached to the take-up spool and in fact, hasn't moved at all. But the reverse is also true. The only way you can know for certain that the film *has* been correctly loaded and has been winding on as it should, is when you come to the end and it refuses to wind on any further. *And he knew!* He knew for sure that the film had come to an end! I know that he knew. He was so *definite* about it. Come to think of it, he was never more assertive during all the time I was there, than he was at the moment he told me he knew I was lying about the film. So he knew that it had come to an end, and that happened when I was photographing Catamaran,

just as Hynes was going to take one of *me* with the horse." I
tailed off, trying to see where that irrefutable fact led me.

"You think Hynes is involved?" Claire asked after giving me
time to see if I had finished.

"No. If there was any reason why I *shouldn't* have pho-
tographed the horse, he would have tried to prevent me from
doing so at the time. I even *asked* him if it was alright for me to
do so, if Norris would mind, and he told me to go ahead. It's
much more likely that the film's existence was unknown until a
short time ago. That is, to anyone besides Hynes and me. I
wonder who else he told."

"And when."

"And when is right. That's important. When." Other
thoughts began to come to me, suspicions which didn't make
sense. As yet. "There's only one way to find out. Let's find
Hynes and ask him. I know where he lives. I had to see his
mother's Cocker Spaniel the other day."

On our way to Hynes's, we went by the cottage so that I
could pick up the photographs which I had hidden back under
the bread bin. I didn't think the burglars would be back but I
was probably getting slightly paranoid. No bloody wonder, I
thought.

In the car I examined the photos of the horse but could find
nothing glaringly obvious in them, nothing to excite anyone. I
passed them to Claire and headed for Hynes's.

I swung the Escort into the short street of neat bungalows
just in time to see Pat Hynes emerging from the gate on to the
tree-lined path and turning towards the town centre.

"There he is." I pointed at the retreating figure a hundred
yards along and pulled over.

"Why are you stopping?"

"Suppose we're wrong."

"About the horse?"

"No. About Hynes. About him not being involved."

"I see what you mean."

We sat in silence until Hynes turned a corner out of sight
onto the main road to the town.

"He doesn't look bothered to me," Claire said after he had
passed out of our sight. There was another, shorter silence.

"What are you going to do, Frank?"

"We may as well talk to him. He can hardly pull a gun on us in the main street, can he? And we should be able to tell if he's involved as soon as I mention the photographs of Catamaran. Then we can go for Potter if he acts strangely."

Why not go for Potter now?"

"As soon as we talk to Hynes. You worried?" I asked, letting out the clutch.

"Not really. More excited than worried."

He was walking at a brisk pace and had gone a surprisingly long way. I let the car coast silently up behind him and braked as we drew abreast. A tourist asking the way, he probably thought. I folded myself down in the seat, trying to get my head low enough to be able to see further up than the breast pocket of his summer shirt.

"Howya, Pat?" I called across Claire, my chin almost resting on the lower rim of the steering-wheel. He bent down to see who I was, looked for a moment in puzzlement and then beamed in recognition.

"Ah, it's yourself! The hard man! I didn't know you for a minute there with the shiners. They're two beauties! I heard you were kidnapped and bet up but got away in the heel of the hunt. Fair play to you. What did they want off you?"

"I never rightly found out, Pat. I... left before we got to that part."

He laughed and winked at me with a sharp ducking of his head. "Fair play to you!" he repeated. "It's the talk of the town. The place hasn't had such excitement since Alcock and Brown landed out the road! Catamaran a few weeks ago and now you getting kidnapped."

"Where are you headed?"

"Town."

"So are we. Hop in." I reached back towards the door behind Claire and painfully pulled up the lock button.

"Did you get a new car?"

"No," I laughed. "It's not mine, unfortunately. It belongs to Claire here." I introduced them, Claire swinging round in her seat to nod, smile and offer her hand.

"I heard the Land Rover was riddled with bullets."

"You heard wrong. It was riddled with just one bullet. In the back window and out the front. If she'd been a left hand drive, I was jiggered for sure. Jiggered."

"Still. You were lucky."

"I sure was."

"By the way, how did those snaps turn out? The ones of Catamaran and me holdin' him? I often meant to ask you only I didn't see you."

He had caught me on the hop. There was I trying to think of a way to bring up the photographs in a casual, offhand manner, and suddenly, it had come up on its own. I stiffened, glanced at him in the rear-view mirror – which only showed one innocent eye – and said as easily as I could: "They haven't come back yet, Pat."

"You might let me have one or two when they do. The ones with me in them. Not, like, that I want snaps of myself or anything... but, the way it turned out. That very evening! I couldn't believe it!"

"It was pretty grim, alright. I'm sorry I didn't get one of me holding Catamaran too."

"That was a pity." I saw him nodding to himself in the mirror. "The way it turned out like and all."

"As soon as they come back, I'll let you have a look at them and you can tell me which ones you want."

"Thanks. I'd like that – just one as a keepsake. You can let me off at the next corner, please."

"We're going right in to town," I protested. I had bargained on much more time, a chance to probe gently enough so that he wouldn't realise that my questions had any significance. I had to find out who he had told about the photographs. And when.

"No thanks. Here's fine. I have to call for the girlfriend – actually, the fiancée now. We got engaged a couple of weeks back."

"Congratulations."

"Time to make an honest woman of her," he laughed in embarrassment. One hard man to another.

"Actually, Pat, I was going to call around to see you anyway about those photographs," I started as he got out.

"Oh? Why?" He turned and bent down, looking in the open door.

"Well," I improvised, "the press seems to have heard that I'd taken photos of Catamaran the day he died and they've been bothering me since. I just wondered how they heard. I didn't tell them."

"Neither did I. No reporters came to talk to me at all." He sounded aggrieved, peeved. "I mentioned it to Jackie – that's my girlfriend but... I'm sure she didn't talk to any reporters. She'd have told me. Maybe she mentioned it to someone else... I'll ask her. Is it important?"

"Not really. I just wondered. And you didn't tell anybody else?"

"No. Nobody else. Only Mr Norris. And he *certainly* didn't tell the press. I heard he refused point blank to talk to them at all! Anyway, by the time I told him, all the reporters were well and truly gone. Sure it was only last Sunday, a week yesterday, that I met him buying the papers. I'll ask Jackie and let you know – alright?"

"Fine Pat. Do that. As I said it's no big deal. See you around."

"Yeah. See you."

CHAPTER 26

"**W**e've got one of the gang for you," I said.

Potter looked searchingly at us, made to speak, thought better of it and gestured us into his tiny office. Calling for coffee, he closed the door.

"Who's that?" He looked from me to Claire and back to me, not sure that we weren't pulling his leg.

"Norris."

"*Norris!? Gilbert Norris?*" Now he was convinced we were joking. "What has Gilbert Norris got to do with drugs?"

"Nothing. As far as I know. They weren't interested in drugs! They were looking for the shots I took of Catamaran the day he died, though don't ask me why." I went through the steps which had led me to that conclusion, and, as he listened, his face grew more and more grave; he obviously didn't like the idea of one of the county's leading citizens being implicated, but he couldn't fault the logic.

"You've already spoken with Hynes, you say?"

"Yes."

"How come he didn't mention the photographs to Norris sooner?"

"Because *Sunday* was the first time that he saw him. And, if you remember, my troubles began the very next evening – with the break in."

"What about the day Hynes was on duty at Bally Ard? The day the horse died? Didn't they meet then?"

"He didn't see him that day. Norris himself told me that he had Jack phone the yard to tell Hynes that he could go."

"Jesus!" Potter said in a fed up voice, and went silent for a few seconds. He shook his head. "Any ideas about why those shots might be important?"

"No." I took the eight prints from my pocket and handed them to him. He didn't have copies of the Catamaran prints.

"Let's have a look then," he said, spreading them out. While we looked over the prints, the coffee arrived and Potter told Burke to get the photographer over double quick as he needed copies. "And tell him that we don't have the negatives so he's to bring whatever he needs."

In silence we scrutinised the pictures. I couldn't see anything incriminating in them.

"How would a drugged horse look?" Claire asked.

"Depends on what drug you're talking about. Do you mean sedated?"

"Whatever." She shrugged. "I don't know. Any drug, I suppose, but mainly a sedative or a depressant because you said that Catamaran was much more subdued when you saw him on Monday than he'd been on Saturday."

"Maybe he'd be carrying his head low, possibly his lower lip might be hanging a bit loosely or he might be drooling or his eyelids might be drooping or his membrana nictitans..."

"His *what*?" asked Potter.

"His third eyelid. It's under the other two – on the eyeball, if you like – and it comes across the eye from the inside corner. It might be halfway across if he'd been doped. But it doesn't show in any of these. Also his... private parts," I said with a rare attack of decorum, "would most likely be visible, which it isn't. But none of these signs is a must. It would depend on what drug, at what dosage rate, how long it had been administered, any number of factors; and I can't see anything to suggest that that horse is doped."

"The pathologist found no dope," Potter pointed out.

"True. But there are millions of drugs and he probably would only have checked for the more obvious ones. Also, I presume that some are untraceable. According to Agatha Christie anyway, and she should know." We went back to silently studying the prints.

"You know," I said at last, "it could *still* have been an accident. In fact it probably was. The reason I say that is that the timing is so bad. Catamaran's insurance was to have been

212

upped, nearly doubled, at the end of this month, so, if there *was* foul play, surely Norris could have waited until then. I know he only gets one ninth of the insurance money, but one ninth of fifty million is a hell of a lot better than one ninth of thirty-five."

"If it *was* an accident, why would Norris be so frantically trying to get his hands on the photographs?" Potter asked.

"Look at it this way. Suppose that Norris was doing a bit of do-it-yourself work on the horse, even something as innocent as shoeing or paring his feet, and decided to give him a sedative to make the job easier all round. And suppose that the drug had the *opposite* effect – that can happen, you know – and the horse went wild instead, and from then on, it all happened as we thought it did. I doubt the Insurance people would pay up in the case of someone causing an animal's death by having a go themselves. If that *was* the case, Norris might be afraid that the photographs would show evidence of his meddling, with the consequent loss of the insurance pay-out, and that would be sufficient reason for him to try to get them out of circulation. The other two in the gang might have been members of the syndicate too, whom he consulted and who also stood to lose a great deal of money."

"Somehow I don't see syndicate members driving red Cortinas. Rolls Royces would be more like it," Potter said.

"Perhaps he hired local thugs," I persisted, knowing full well that the one who had acted as my gaoler was no thug for hire, local or otherwise.

"Then what about the rat?" Potter objected. "We now have *two* reasons why the horse went berserk! The rat and the sedative."

"Sounds like the title of a fairytale," Claire mumbled. "The Rat and The Sedative."

"Improvisation. To cover the real reason that the horse went mad. So that you wouldn't, if you'll excuse the pun, smell a rat?"

"Alright, Frank." Potter was adopting an attitude of pained patience. "Let's assume that you're right, that it was that way. How long would you say the 'accident' had happened before you got there?"

"An hour maximum. The horse couldn't have lived much

longer than an hour with the wounds he had."

"If I gave you an hour, starting from now, would you be able to catch me a rat? A live rat? Specially on a place that's supposed to be ratless, and specially if you didn't know you had an hour, if you were expecting to have the vet arrive at any moment and knew you had to be there to meet him? I don't think that you'd even waste your time trying. Assuming that it took you the first fifteen minutes to even *think* of the idea in the first place!"

"No. You're right. And anyway, Norris was on to Eileen every five minutes during that hour. And he couldn't have arranged with one of his accomplices – later accomplices – to do the rat catching, because if it was an accident, then he wouldn't have *had* accomplices to turn to, would he?"

"It all looks mighty suspicious, but we're a bit short on hard evidence. It's circumstantial, most of it, and, on this one, we can't barge in feet first. Maybe Hynes's girlfriend did tell some-one else who told someone else, etcetera. Maybe half the town knows you took those shots! We'll sniff around a bit."

"But half the town had no connection whatever with Catamaran, had nothing to win or lose by his death, had no reason for giving him drugs..."

"I know. But, as you said yourself, you could almost call Norris a loser too. If this had been a couple of months later... Anyway, we'll ask around, follow it up as discreetly as possible. If it is Norris, we'll get him in the end."

"It's him alright. I know it," I said.

"We'll see," Potter said non-committedly. "Keep in touch. And listen... both of you. Not a word about this to anyone. Okay?" He fixed us with a stern look until we nodded.

We didn't speak until we were in the car and driving. I was teasing the problem out in the mind but I failed to make any headway worth talking about. This time, Claire drove.

"Your policeman friend seems to have some difficulty in accepting Norris as the villain of the piece," Claire observed, doing a slalom between two dogs and a bike.

"I can't say that I blame him really. Norris is a fairly big-wig locally and we hardly gave him watertight proof of his involvement, did we? We weren't even able to say what he's supposed to have done wrong! If Potter were to gallop off and put the arm on him now, he'd have so many writs slapped on him that his head would be spinning. As he said, it must be handled with 'great delicacy'. Only trouble is: if Potter, while being 'greatly delicate' lets Norris get a whiff of the fact that the finger has been pointed in his direction, he'll have his tracks covered before the cops even get to talk to him!"

"Yes, but they can hardly rubber-hose him, I suppose. To some extent, Potter's hands *are* tied."

I didn't reply for a moment. An idea was materializing in my head, a tempting idea, which, the more I thought about it, the more appealing it became. "Maybe Potter's hands are tied," I said at last, "but mine aren't."

She took her eyes off the road for a second to shoot me a surprised glance. "What do you mean by that?"

"I mean that it might not be the worst move in the world for me to call to say hello to Norris. Look at it this way," I hurried on to stall her protest. "It would stir up matters and perhaps something might float to the surface. Also I could throw him a red herring by telling him we suspected that the photos the kidnappers were looking for were the ones of the party, and make life a hell of a lot safer for me."

"Big deal! Supposing he just takes the opportunity of grabbing you and sticking you back in durance vile?"

"No chance, because you, my intrepid reporter, will be sitting in the car in the driveway and I'll tell him that Potter is expecting me and knows where I am."

"You've got it all worked out, haven't you?" I could tell by her tone that she was totally against the idea.

"Sure I have – and it's all thanks to you," I said, soft-soaping winningly.

"To *me*?! How do you figure that?"

"Well, after that excruciatingly exquisite and ecstatically exciting experience in the cove this afternoon, my mind, indeed my whole being, became suffused, a finely tuned precision instrument capable of great feats..."

"Frank!" she warned, "stop spoofing!"

"I'm not spoofing, Claire. Honest! Is it or is it not a fact that, a matter of moments after we made love this afternoon, I was inspired to come up with the solution to the problem of what the kidnappers actually wanted? I tell you, you inspired me!"

"That was *coincidence*." She insisted, laughing.

"No it wasn't!" I teased gently. "It was *inspiration*!"

Claire said something that sounded like 'Pshaw'.

"Any regrets about this afternoon?" I asked in a gentler tone, reaching my hand across to cover hers.

"None." Her whole expression softened as she answered quietly. She glanced unsurely at me. "How about you? Any regrets?"

"Of course not. Well, ... maybe just one teeny-weeny regret."

"Oh? And what, may one ask, might that be?"

"I'm sorry that I got the inspiration about Catamaran."

"Why?"

"Well, if I *hadn't* become inspired... we could've stayed on... *and done it all over again!*"

"Frank! You've got a one-track mind!" She elbowed me playfully in the ribs.

"I know. Model railways." I reached over and flicked on her indicator. "This is where we turn for Bally Ard."

"You really think it's wise?" she asked dubiously, but she turned all the same.

"I can't think of a better way to get the ball rolling."

"Do you not think that you've already done your bit? Why not let the wheels of justice grind to their inevitable ends?"

"Because by that time, I may have been ground to *my* inevitable end. I've been close enough to it," I said bleakly. Claire noticed, I think. Anyway she dropped the subject, concentrating on the road until we arrived at the imposing gates of Bally Ard. Now they stood open, mute testament to the fact that the priceless animal they had once guarded no longer resided within.

"Drive on up to the house and stay in the car. I'm going to ask him if I can use the phone because I'm late for an appointment with Potter. That ought to guarantee my safe return. What time is it, by the way?"

"Almost a quarter to six."

"I'll say the appointment was for half-five."

Norris himself answered the door. There was a brief flash of uneasy surprise in his eyes which was replaced instantly by his customary urbane expression, a process, no doubt helped by the friendly beam I had managed to impose on my reluctant features.

"Hello Mr Norris!" I said with a jauntiness I didn't feel. "Sorry to drop in on you like this, but I need to use a phone pretty urgently and I thought, as I was passing, perhaps..."

"Of course! Of course! You're more than welcome! Come in!" he said effusively, which I thought was a pretty good recovery. "You know where it is, I think?"

"Yes, I remember. Through here, isn't it?"

"Yes that's right. In the study."

"Thank you." I left the door open so that he'd be sure to miss none of my 'conversation' and pushed the buttons for Fernditch, the only number I knew for certain would be unattended.

I let it ring five times and began my monologue: "Hello? Hello? May I speak with Inspector Potter please?... Samson. Frank Samson... Thank you." I hummed a snatch of 'My Lagan Love' into the receiver as I waited. I didn't think that, from the other room, he'd be able to hear the Fernditch phone still ringing but there was no point in taking a chance so I hummed as noisily as was reasonable in a relative stranger's house. "She... eeee hath my hea...a...a...a...a...art in thrall," I went, then broke off suddenly. "Oh!, I see," I said after listening for a moment, "well then, it doesn't matter because I'm late too – I had some car trouble – but if he does come in before I get there, tell him I'll be there about six-thirty. I'm phoning from Bally Ard and I've got to go back to the house to collect some stuff so, I think six-thirtyish. O.K.?... Right... Thank you... Goodbye."

"Did you get through?" Norris asked solicitously when I joined him in the next room. Nice touch. As if he hadn't listened to it all.

"Yes thank you," I replied equally innocently. "Actually, it turns out that the panic wasn't so big after all – I was to meet

217

Inspector Potter at the station at five-thirty, but he's late too, so there's no harm done."

"Well if you don't have to be there until 6.30 now, can you stay for a drink? Bring in the young lady." I hadn't mentioned 6.30 to him.

"No thank you, Mr Norris; it's very kind of you, but we'd best get along. I've got some paperwork to do before I meet Potter."

"Some other time perhaps."

"That would be nice." I felt it was time to introduce the red herring; I also felt it was quite odd that he had made no comment about my battered face – significantly odd. Even in the most formal of circles, I would have thought a polite expression of interest or sympathy – or both – would have been in order.

"I suppose you heard that I've been in the wars?"

"I did hear something to that effect, yes. Kidnapped, I believe."

"Yes. A horrible experience. Harrowing."

"I can imagine. However, as they say, all's well that ends well. You're free and that, in the long run, is all that really matters. Was there a hefty ransom involved?" he went on, showing a very nice line in red herrings himself.

"No. It wasn't a question of ransom – not money, that is. They were looking for photographs."

"*Photographs*! My goodness! What kind of snapshots must you take to have the abductors of this world baying after you!"

"That's what took me a long time to figure out. Some shots I took at a party where I reckon there were some drug deals being done. I heard later that there was a pretty big time dealer there. If I'd known it before, I'd have left my old Brownie Automatic at home. In fact, I'd have left *myself* at home. The drugs scene is not my scene."

"Nor mine, I assure you… And did they?"

"Sorry?"

"Did they show anything incriminating? The photographs?"

"I don't know. They haven't come back from the lab yet; they should be here any day now. Actually, the thought just occurs to me! I've got a few shots of Catamaran on the end of that reel, a few shots I took the morning of the day he died… I

218

must give them to you when they come, unless, perhaps, you'd rather not be remind..."

"No, no, no! That would be very nice of you. I'd appreciate it very much; perhaps you could call me as soo... when you get them and I could drop by to pick them up. I'd be very interested to see them."

"I'll bet you would, you bastard!" I thought to myself, but all I said was "Right so! As soon as they're back, I'll let you know."

Thanking him again for the use of the phone, the offer of the drink and everything else, I took my leave. He came to the car and I introduced him to Claire. He stood waving after us as we drove down the drive.

"Stop outside the gate and let me out," I said to her as I sat turned, smiling and waving back at the smiling and waving figure of Norris. All smiles. All waves. All bullshit.

"What for?" She sounded as if she knew what for, and only wanted confirmation.

"I want to see what he does now. That was the whole point!"

"I thought the idea was to *prod* him and let Potter take over then."

"That too," I said meaninglessly, and was spared the need for further explanation by the fact that we had reached the gates and Claire had to stop before nosing out onto the road. I opened the door and stepped out. "Come back in thirty minutes but don't stop unless I show myself. If I don't, give me another fifteen minutes or so – then, if I'm still not here, call Potter."

"Frank..."

"Go on now! If he hears us stopped too long, he may smell a rat. Good girl, don't worry," and I closed the door, gently to make no sound. I could hear her disapproval in the way she drove up the road.

CHAPTER 27

I **snaked through** the gate and into the dense shrubbery which bordered the drive. A few minutes later the rhododendrons came to an abrupt end at the edge of a lawn and, from across the lawn, the side of the house looked back at me out of its eight windows, four on each floor. I could see no movement at any of them and only the second from the front on the ground floor was open. I thought that it was the study window but I wasn't sure; I couldn't remember if the window had been open or not when I had made my bogus phonecall to Potter. Towards the back of the house, the lawn had several large trees and I worked my way along until I could cross to the house, using them as cover. Then, bent double, I crept along the narrow path which separated the lawn from the actual building, passing under both rear windows and stopping beneath the open one. As I was about to take a cautious peep over the sill, Norris's voice floated out to me on the still evening air locking me into frozen immobility. I thought he was talking to me.

"Hello?" he said in a questioning tone and I turned, watery-kneed, to face the music. I looked about me when I didn't see his face at the window, still convinced that I had been spotted. "Hello?" he said again and I was within a whisker of saying 'Hello' back when he went on: "At last! I've been trying to get you for the last five minutes... No, nothing's wrong. In fact, quite the opposite, I think. You'd never guess who's just been here... Samson... I swear!... Oh, only to use the phone to ring Potter... No. No idea... I'm sure. He thinks it's about drugs! That's right, drugs... And by the way, he *was* telling the truth about the prints not being back yet... He's actually going to let me have the shots of the horse as soon as he gets them!... No of *course* I didn't mention the negatives!... How could I?... We can cross that bridge when we come to it – maybe the shots are harmless, out of focus or under-exposed or something. Anyway I'll know soon, and we can always work out something about the negatives if needed. I'm hoping that it won't come to that... Yes, won't he just! It'll do no end of good to his broken jaw... I *know* it's not but the way he's been going on about it, you'd think it was smashed in at least ten places. I'm just going to drive out there now to tell him the good news, but I wanted to let you know first... Yes indeed. I feel better this minute than I have at any time since Hynes told me about those blasted photos... O.K... Fine... I agree fully... Yes of course... I'll be in touch." And he hung up without saying goodbye to Tom, Dick or Harry, leaving me not a bit the wiser for having eavesdropped.

I sat there incredulous. I couldn't believe that, from all that, there hadn't been one single clue. Lots of confirmation, but not a sniff of a clue which would help in providing a name. I heard the study door closing, his footsteps in the hall faintly, then the bang of the front door followed by the noise of his car driving off.

I listened intently for a few moments and then pulled myself over the sill and into the study. The key was in the door so I tip-toed across and gently turned it, locking myself in. No point in taking a chance on Mrs Flahive popping in to dust the desk or something.

The most promising prospect of finding something, the grey filing cabinet, was a washout; all the drawers were locked. So were the doors of the heavy mahogany side-board. That left only the desk and, apart from the top left-hand drawer, everything in it was locked too. Somewhat disconsolately I rummaged through the drawer.

Amongst the pencils and paper-clips, the rubber bands and staples, I found an old-fashioned key. It was obvious at a glance that it wouldn't fit the filing cabinet and I didn't even try. Nor did it fit any of the desk drawers or its flap. It did however open the side-board and I hunkered down to take a look.

There were two shelves. From the upper one, cut glass

decanters and glasses winked at me and a large variety of bottles of all shapes and sizes stood shoulder to shoulder behind them. The lower shelf was Norris's pharmacy. In boxes and packets, it contained the usual assortment of liniments and ointments, embrocations and lotions, bandages and lint, wound sprays and cotton wool – nothing at all out of the ordinary. To one side there was a large box of the worming medicine currently considered the best on the market. The discovery of this made Catamaran's worm burden even more mysterious. I took the box out to have a look or a sniff, not quite sure what I was doing, possibly thinking of pocketing a tube and sending it off for analysis, but I immediately lost all interest in worms for, behind the box of worming medicine was another box and *this* box had no business whatsoever being anywhere else other than in the locked Dangerous Drugs Cabinet in a vet's surgery. The box was the unmistakable green polystyrene-moulded half-cube container of Immobilon and its antidote, Revivon.

Immobilon is a powerful general anaesthetic used mainly in equine surgery. When injected intravenously, the animal drops literally on the spot. Other anaesthetic agents will do this too, but the main advantage in using Immobilon is that an equal quantity of Revivon injected intravenously will reverse its actions at once, and the patient stands up almost as quickly as it flopped down. This does away with the usual protracted post-operative recovery period – a period of great danger when lack of co-ordination can cause an animal to lunge and fall about, possibly hurting itself or bursting the stitches the surgeon has just so carefully inserted.

That is the great advantage. However, as everyone knows, every silver lining has a cloud, in this case the fact that Immobilon is absolutely lethal to humans – even a prick from a wet needle is enough to cause death almost before you can get half-way through a decent Act of Contrition. Worse, Revivon, the antidote which is so efficient in the horse, is ineffective in man. There is another antidote for man and neither I nor any colleague I've ever come across would even *think* of using Immobilon without having a plentiful supply of the human antidote on hand, plus an attendant who was able to give intravenous injections and keep on giving them as long as necessary.

I separated the two halves of the box and removed both bottles from their snug polystyrene beds. The Immobilon bottle was not full. I reckoned that the amount missing (about a third) was sufficient to anaesthetize a medium-sized horse. On the other hand, the Revivon bottle was unused, its rubber stopper unpunctured. So whatever had been knocked out had not been woken up again – which defeated the whole purpose of using Immobilon in the first place. Puzzled, I rechecked the contents of the pharmacy – there was nothing of a vaguely surgical nature, not even a suture needle. It seemed odd that Norris should have possessed, and seemingly used, a general anaesthetic when he had no means of doing anything once he had knocked out the horse. Perhaps, I reasoned, the instruments were in one of the locked drawers. And then again, perhaps not.

I'd have given a lot to know *when* the Immobilon had been used. The obvious thing was to suspect it had been given to Catamaran for some unguessable purpose the day he died, but if he had been given it intravenously, he would have gone down at once; intramuscularly would have taken longer but not an awful lot – certainly not long enough for him to squeeze out of his box, climb the manure heap, jump the wall and gallop almost half a mile cross country. Also, Professor Wall would have been sure to have tested for Immobilon residues – it would most likely have been the first thing he'd have checked for. Thoughtfully, I replaced the boxes I had taken out and re-locked the side-board. The Immobilon couldn't have been used on Catamaran; it would have shown up on tests. Maybe it had been used innocently (relatively) on some animal for euthanasia, an animal which had broken a leg or something? That would explain why none of the Revivon was missing. But then, why use only an anaesthetic dose? Why not inject the whole bottle? Or better still, why not use a gun? It would be just as effective, just as humane and far, far safer for the user. Even better again, why not get the *vet* to do it in the first place for Chrissakes? None of it made sense.

It was while I was replacing the key that my eyes were drawn to the state-of-the-art phone on the desk. Suddenly I found myself thinking about his recent conversation – not what he had said but the fact that it was *he* who had made the call. I was sure it was – if it had been the other way round, if he had been called, then I would have heard the phone ringing before he started his helloing, almost giving me heart failure as I lurked beneath his window. Yes. He had made the call. Also, it was the *last* call he had made; he had left straight after. Therefore, if the phone had a recall-button – and it looked as if it must have – then the last number he had called was lodged in its memory awaiting the mere prod of this button to dial it again. Palms sweating with excitement, I lifted the phone and looked. There it was! Bottom left. Recall. I decided to tell whoever answered that I was a Post Office engineer checking faults and ask them for their number but it never came to that. I pressed the button, listened to the whirls and clicks in the bowels of the instrument, heard it ring twice and suddenly there was a very efficient female voice saying : "Good evening. Dr Field's surgery. May I help you?"

"Sorry. Wrong number," I managed to mutter and hung up. Standing by the desk I tried to work out the significance of this bombshell. At least it cleared up one mystery. I now had someone who could give intravenous injections, monitor the stages of anaesthesia, provide surgical instruments and a greater or lesser degree of surgical skills. It also helped to explain the surgical glove dropped by the amateur burglars at the cottage. What didn't make any sense at all was Field being at Bally Ard the morning of the post-mortem and allowing himself to be tied in, however remotely and however plausibly, with Norris. Why had he attended the post-mortem? Had he gone there *specifically* to do so in the first place?

I caught sight of the clock on the mantelpiece. Claire would be coming back at any moment. Remembering to unlock the door, I left as I had come, by the window. When I dodged back out on to the road, some four minutes later, I was just in time to see her tail lights vanishing round the corner. I settled down behind a bush to wait the next fifteen minutes.

While I sat, being investigated by the evening insects, I tried again to fit Field into the picture but, as I didn't yet know what the picture was, it was a task doomed from the beginning, to failure. However, by some lateral routes of thinking, it did get me to wondering about my various dealings with Norris, his horses and his premises.

First, Catamaran. There was obviously something fishy about his accident and death. That was the root of the whole mess, but what exactly it was, was anybody's guess.

Then there was the hunter with the colic. Was that all it appeared to be? Could there have been something dodgy about that too? Hardly. One couldn't really expect a horse to develop a colic to order. No. But one could feed a horse to give him colic – for instance a stomachful of dry bran would swell dangerously when moistened with gastric digestive juices; in fact, a fatal rupturing of the stomach could result from it. There were other ways too, I supposed – one could pour anything into a horse via a stomach-tube. But how could Norris (or Field) have brought on a *transient* colic? By the time I had arrived there, the abdominal functions were back to normal, as were the pulse, heart and respiration rates. In fact, were it not for the sweated up condition of the animal and Norris's say-so, there was nothing to show the animal ever had had a colic...

Even as I thought it, the answer came: there hadn't been any colic! Norris's story had been a complete fabrication, the 'sweat' a bucket of water! Norris would have seen enough colics in his day to be able to make up authentic symptoms, and I had had no reason at the time not to take him at his word. What the hell was going on!

A fat bumble bee lumbered ponderously past, its wings whirring laboriously like it was trying to fly uphill in too high a gear. I peeped round the bush; still no sign of Claire. I hoped she hadn't got cold feet and gone off to Potter – on balance, I thought, probably not. My mind quickly wandered back to Norris and his supposedly colicky hunter. Why? The only answer to that had to be to get me there, to Bally Ard. Why, again? This time the reason took a little more working out. I began to recall various aspects of his behaviour which, at the time, had struck me as odd, but which I had attributed to his upset at the recent loss of Catamaran. He had absolutely insisted that I go into the house for coffee and had then insisted we take it in the kitchen, something which, if I could infer anything from the shocked look on his housekeeper's face, had never happened before. Then he had immediately gone off to make a phonecall leaving me and Mrs Flahive to make small-talk in the kitchen. When he came back, I had been ready to discuss for a while whatever it was he had wanted to talk to me about, but he had almost pushed me out the door in his haste to be rid of me.

Now, sitting in a bush, with full benefit of hindsight, I began to castigate myself for having missed not one but *two* clear pointers which should have alerted me to the possibility that the whole colic business had been a charade. First there was Mrs Flahive's report about how she and Norris had gone about putting prints from other rooms in place of the pictures of Catamaran which, until then, had occupied the walls in the hall. The real significance of this was the timing: this activity had taken place *after* Norris had phoned for me. An experienced owner (which Norris definitely was) would not have left a colicky horse alone for any reason, bar to phone for the vet; certainly not to make some casual makeshift changes in interior decor! Secondly, it was equally out of character for him to decline to visit the horse again with me before I left. Colics are strange things. I've known owners to stay up all night with an apparently recovered horse. Just in case.

At this stage, though I didn't recognise it, I had reached a cross roads in my logic. Unfortunately, I chose the wrong path to follow.

I reasoned, correctly as it turned out, that the reason for getting me to Bally Ard was that the search of the cottage the night before had not turned up the photographs and they wanted to look in the next most likely place, the camera, or its bag. The reason for the elaborate charade with the "colic" was to get me to bring the Land Rover to the privacy of Bally Ard to be searched; they'd have had a tough time doing it anywhere else – the only place they would have been *sure* of finding it parked for any length of time would be outside the cottage during the night but that was on the public road and there was a street light directly outside the gate. And finally, the reason that Norris had insisted on having coffee in the kitchen was that it was at the *back* of the house while the Land Rover was parked at the front, where it would have been overlooked by the windows of the usual reception rooms. He also knew that, in the kitchen, I'd have Mrs Flahive to keep me company so I'd be kept occupied while he went through the camera gear.

It fitted another piece into the jig-saw puzzle satisfactorily, but what I really ought to have been wondering was, why, after such a long time, Norris had suddenly decided to take the pictures of Catamaran off the wall in the hall, just an hour or two before he knew I'd be walking through that hall and passing those pictures? That avenue might have led me to some real answers.

When I heard the car approach, I peeped round the bush; it was Claire, so I stepped out onto the road. The relief in her eyes was obvious.

"Well?" she asked as I jumped in.

"Drive on! Head for Potter." On the way I brought her up to date.

"And you've no idea at all how Field was involved?" she asked when I finished.

"None that I can think of," I replied with some exasperation.

"You said you met him once."

"He was at Bally Ard when I arrived at the crack of dawn to help Professor Wall with the autopsy. The excuse was that Norris was feeling lousy – which was entirely plausible at the time!"

"There must have been a very good reason for him to have been there at that particular time. Otherwise he'd never have put himself in danger of coming under suspicion in the event of the whole thing blowing up later. As has happened now."

"Oh there was a good reason alright. I presume to attend the post mortem, though I can't think why."

"What kind of a guy is he anyway?"

"Field? I suppose he's anyone's idea of a typical GP. You know... well-groomed, well-dressed, well-spoken, probably well-heeled and totally lacking in any form of inferiority complex."

"Age?"

"Early to mid-forties. Hard to say, really."

227

"No doubt a pillar of the community."

"No doubt."

"Isn't Potter going to be thrilled with this," she commented drily, reversing into a narrow space outside the police station. "First Norris, now Field... All he needs is for the third one to be the parish priest, and he'll have a hat trick of the local paragons."

"Let's go and give him heartburn," I said opening the door.

But Potter wasn't in and wasn't expected until eight. We said no thanks we wouldn't leave a message; we would call again later.

"So. What now?" Claire asked across the top of the car, unlocking her door. "Don't tell me!" she held up a warning hand. "You want to mosey over to Field's surgery and burglarize the joint."

"How about finding somewhere to eat." I ignored her sarcasm. In spite of the fruitful harvest, she still did not approve of my visits to Bally Ard.

"A much sounder idea. I haven't eaten since morning." And she smiled sweetly at me, across the roof of the car.

CHAPTER 28

I **approached the** reception desk in the foyer of the Riverbank Hotel and rested my elbows on the mahogany counter that reeked of furniture polish. The good-looking, smartly-dressed receptionist was busy writing in a large, complicated-looking, multi-columned book and I watched with fascination, the speed at which her bangled hand jangled across the page, dipping the pen briefly onto a column here and there, leaving arcane hieroglyphics in its wake. I was reminded of swallows skimming the still sheet of a summer lake, bobbing without checking to scoop insects from the smooth surface, leaving tiny, short-lived troughs on the water, the bow-waves of their beaks. She looked up even as her hand continued across the last few columns.

"May I help you?" Eyes, rimmed with eye-liner like Nefertiti's, showed transient surprise at the battlefield of my face, then sweetened immediately into a professional eagerness to be of service.

"We'd like a meal, please," I smiled, vaguely indicating Claire who was mooching and looking at knick-knacks in a glass case by the door.

"Certainly sir. Grill or dining room?"

"Eh... Grill, I think."

She nodded and made 'go round the corner' motions with her hand. "Just follow the corridor round to the left and you'll find the Grillroom on your right – next door down from the Garden Bar."

"Thank you kindly."

"You're welcome sir," she flashed me a cheery smile. "Enjoy your meal."

229

I collected Claire and we followed the directions to the grill. As we were about to pass through the door, I happened to look up at the name over the frosted glass. "Take a peek!" I caught her by the elbow and pointed up. She backed a step, her eye following the direction of my finger.

"The Catamaran Rooms!" she said with a suspicious smile. "Did you do this deliberately?"

"No, I didn't! I've never been here before!" I protested. Nor had I, but I don't think she believed me – there was a dubious set to her shapely shoulders as I followed her into the dim room.

We slid into the mock-leather seats of a narrow booth by the hessian-clad wall. All about were Catamaran memorabilia. The place was a veritable museum to Knockmore-on-Sea's most famous son – if the term may be applied to a horse. There were photographs on the walls and the support pillars, mostly the finishes of races with Catamaran frozen at the winning post showing varying amounts of daylight between his noble rump and the nose of the nearest also ran. One wall was practically papered with newspaper cuttings, and a glass case in the middle of the room was stuffed with what seemed from where we sat, to be scale models of all his trophies. The cashier's desk near the door was marked by a winning post. A waitress brought menus, gave the table a perfunctory and unnecessary wipe as she squinted sideways at my battered countenance, and retreated.

"It's a wonder she wasn't wearing jockey's silks – or at least jeans, a polo neck, wellies and a riding hat!" Claire joked. "They certainly haven't skimped on cashing in on the famous nag, now have they?"

Any shortcomings in the matter of the waitress's attire were more than compensated for in the layout of the menu. The front cover was a black-and-white photograph of the horse, looking proudly at the camera, as though he knew what it was all about; on the back, there was a potted life history – details of his bloodline, his foalhood, his progress through the sales rings and training rigours, his unbeaten racing career, the races won and the incredible amounts of prizemoney, his retirement to stud, syndication and triumphant return to the place of his birth, Bally Ard. It gave the names of the syndicate members, but the only name I knew was Gilbert Norris's. Inside, the theme continued – overdoing it, I thought. The 'Starters' section was headed, 'Under Starter's Orders'; 'Main Course' had '(Race)' inserted between the two words; what would have been 'Desserts' became 'The Final Furlong'; 'The Home Straight' headed a list of cheeses, and 'The Winner's Enclosure' was where you looked for tea, coffee, etc.

The waitress returned, took our orders and departed again. Claire went back to studying Catamaran's biography and I started to wonder what was behind yet *another* vague sense of disquiet which I had suddenly begun to feel moments before. Vague senses of disquiet and half-heard mental alarm bells were becoming the order of the day.

"Aha!" Claire interrupted my thoughts triumphantly. "Now I see why he was called 'Catamaran'!"

"Why?" I asked, not paying much attention.

"Well, it says here: 'Sire-Ship o' the Line, Dam-Tropical Kayak,' and what do you get when you put two boats together... mmmm...?"

"Eh... A regatta?" I suggested, playing dumb.

"No, idiot! A catamaran!"

"You'd be a horse of a woman if you were fed!" The phrase is a compliment in our part of the world.

The starters arrived, crab claws in garlic butter for me and Queen Scallops for Claire. She fed me a few of the tender tasty shellfish from her fork and I passed her a couple of claws; I also granted her permission to dunk some bread into my garlic butter and ended up having to sacrifice my napkin to mop up the trail of butter-blobs which appeared on the polished deal of the table-top directly beneath the flight path of her saturated bread. The nebulous half-thought still hovered but I knew from previous experience that there was no point in straining at it. Claire finished her starters (and half of mine) and excused herself.

"I want to get an evening paper; I saw some at reception. There ought to be an article I helped to write in it – it was supposed to have been in last Saturday's."

It was while Claire was off getting her paper that the penny finally dropped with a resounding clang. By the time she came back I was trying to put all my thoughts in order. My brain writhed with a tangle of facts, each clamouring importunately to be considered in full before being shunted rudely aside by its attendant implications or by another even more startling one.

"Are you alright, Frank?" she asked, noting my furrowed brow and closed eyes; she paused in the act of sliding into the booth.

"I'm concentrating. Shhh!" I held up an imperious hand, though I didn't mean it to look that way. A lesser woman would have told me where to get off.

Our steaks arrived and I chomped through mine without tasting a bite, all the time filing facts in any order that they'd fit. And boy, did they fit! Eventually, I had gone as far as I could.

"Do you want the story of a lifetime?"

"What is it? 'Genius Comes Down from Mountain and Talks'?"

"No. Better. 'Catamaran Alive and Well'!"

"*Mad* Genius Comes Down from Mountain and Talks Gibberish!"

"Hear me out, O.K.?"

She spread her hands "Sure. Shoot. You have the floor."

"Okay. First fact. I shot a ringer – not Catamaran. You know what a ringer is? A lookalike. A double," I answered my own question as Claire looked confused. Then she turned skeptical.

"How can you tell?"

"The horse I shot had a large untidy forehead whorl and... look at the menu... that whorl's tiny and hardly noticeable." I pointed to the little eddy of hairs.

"You can remember that far back?"

"Can I remember!? That's what I took aim at! I saw it clearly then and I've seen it often in dreams since then... anyway, we can clear it up right here and now – it will show on the photographs. Hang on, I'll just get them from the car. Can I have the keys please."

The difference in the whorls especially in the photo of the head from the front was quite unmistakable. Even their positions were different. The whorl on the horse I shot had been smack dead centre on the forehead whereas Catamaran's whorl (as per menu cover) was slightly eccentric, high and to the right. Q.E.D. Claire whistled.

"Right. Now let's go back to the beginning. For some reason yet to be worked out, Norris, Field and the rest decided to fake Catamaran's death and to make it seem like an accident. To do that successfully they had to find a ringer or at least a very passable likeness and they had to make sure that those who knew Catamaran well enough not to be fooled were out of the way. Basically that meant P. R. Steele, his vet, and Tom Kelly, his live-in groom.

"I presume they knew – maybe six months ago – that Steele would be going abroad for his son's wedding and that there'd be a locum taking over who wouldn't know Catamaran from Adam, eh... his horse from his elbow, as it were," I inserted, inspired, "at least not in the flesh and certainly not well enough to doubt Norris's identification. I was supposed to meet Catamaran's understudy for the first time, lying broken at the bottom of he cliff, and shoot him. That was to be my *only* role in the scheme. However, I ended up with two unscheduled appearances, the first when Steele took me along to Bally Ard the day I arrived, and I met the *real* Catamaran; Norris did his best to prevent me from seeing him and, when he couldn't, had the groom cover him with a horse rug to hide as much of him as possible. The second was when I called in on Monday morning, the same day the horse died, and met the *ringer* in an uninjured condition. On that unforeseeable occasion, the three understudies came together: me, Hynes, and this unfortunate horse who only had a few hours more to live.

"No doubt this was the last thing that Norris would have wanted, but, even if he *had* known that I'd called, I'm sure they'd have gone ahead anyway; they had to get the job done and get rid of the body before Tom Kelly returned, because he knew Catamaran better than anyone."

"They broke into his mother's house themselves and roughed her up, didn't they?" Claire interrupted, jumping the gun slightly.

"Either that or they hired thugs. It couldn't have been a coincidence. Believe me these guys left nothing to chance."

"Are you sure the groom isn't involved? Maybe his mother's break in *was* just something that happened, and, because of it, he had to be unavoidably absent – kind of compassionate leave." Claire was obviously finding it hard to believe that people would rough up a widow living on her own for the sole purpose of making her son come to visit her, for no better reason than as an expedient diversionary tactic.

"Almost one hundred percent, he's innocent. If he *was* involved, he'd have been invaluable at Bally Ard for handling the horses. Catamaran is a real handful for anyone, even Norris. I think if Kelly was involved and his mother's break-in had been a coincidence, sure, he'd have had to go to be with her... but they would have postponed the horse's 'accident' for a week or so. It didn't matter as long as I wasn't getting to know Catamaran in the meantime.

"Finding a substitute for Catamaran would have been the hard part even though bays are the most common colour and clean bays – that is without any white markings – are fairly common amongst bays. They couldn't have hoped for an absolutely identical animal as the whorls always differ. Like fingerprints."

"Are they always on the forehead?"

"Nearly always, but also on other parts of the body – neck, crest, breast, flanks, over the windpipe, backs of the legs – you usually find them there too and they differ in size, shape, number, position; in fact when a horse has no other distinguishing features, the whorls are the main means of identification. There's some talk of them starting to blood-type all thoroughbreds but, as far as I know, it hasn't begun yet. In fact, it can't have – if it had the whole scam would have been impossible, a non-starter.

"So. Assume they managed to find a passable lookalike, they then had to consider whether they ought to gamble on me noticing the whorls (which there's no way that I would) or, more likely, Professor Wall, the pathologist, whom they knew would be called in. They knew that he would have Catamaran's file with him and *that* would have had his passport, a document with all his distinguishing features (in this case, his whorls) marked in; for all they knew, an autopsy might automatically *begin* with a comparison of whorls etc. So they arranged it so that the body whorls would be caked with mud and thus indistinguishable. That left the forehead whorl – a much more noticeable mark. Like people, horses are more easily recognisable by their faces than their bodies. And the forehead whorls in both animals were quite different. Which left them with a ticklish problem.

"The most obvious solution was to have it removed altogether by having the horse shot! I imagine only a vet could legally shoot a horse without the insurance people trying to wriggle out of paying up, so that's where I came in.

"The most tricky part of the affair now began. The horse had to be injured to such an extent that attempting to cure him would be out of the question, but, at the same time, not badly enough that he'd die before the vet got there to shoot him, if you see what I mean. That needed very fine judgement and a fair bit of luck. It was also necessary to ensure that the vet, when he got to the horse, wouldn't have any other means of killing him – such as a lethal injection – and so would have to use the shotgun which, lo and behold, just happened to be lying propped against a rock. That was accomplished by telling me that the horse was *already dead*: there was no *point* in taking any medicines with me. So they achieved their aim brilliantly. One dead horse, forehead whorl punched away with two shotgun shells, body whorls caked with mud. No one would question his identity: the highly respected Norris said it was Catamaran and he should know. Also Catamaran's purple-sprayed muzzle-wound completed the illusion. I presume that, when Catamaran sliced the bit of skin off his muzzle, Field performed a similar operation on the other horse; it wouldn't have been difficult. Jesus! They were so lucky! That nose wound would have been enough on its own to convince anyone! If it wasn't for my untimely and unforeseeable photos they'd have got away with it."

"It all sounds very logical, Frank. Almost too pat. There must be a flaw in it somewhere. Talk me through it."

"I just did!"

"From Norris's side. Pretend you're Norris, Field and the other. How would you do it? I mean actually do it? Do you want dessert?"

"No. I don't think so, thanks."

"I'll have something. Go on. Talk me through it."

"Okay. I'm Norris, right? Well I knew six months ago that my friend, P. R. Steele's son is getting married on such and such a date and that P. R. will be off to America around this time so I begin to plan. Using the material to hand, an undistinguished-looking horse and a doctor who can handle medicines and do bits of surgery, the plan takes the form it does. We find and buy a lookalike horse and store him somewhere. In anticipation, I let the dungstead build up all year so that it almost reaches the top of the yard wall. I buy a pet brown rat and keep him in storage. I arrange from Rent-a-Thug that Mrs Kelly's house will be broken into on such and such a night. Everything's ready on time, Steele goes to America, Tom Kelly goes to Cork and Frank "Gullible" Samson and Pat "Scared-Of-Horses" Hynes duly arrive to take their respective and appointed places. That day I swap Catamaran and the ringer about using some kind of bridge over the trough at the yard gate so that neither hoofprints nor wheel-tracks will show in the mud.

"Next day in the morning I buy or shoot a couple of rabbits. In the afternoon we take the ringer – again across the bridge over the trough – and lead him down to the floor of the quarry. We put the rat into his box, ruck up the straw and put scuffmarks on the concrete floor and snag some mane-hairs on the door frame and that's the box O.K. Catamaran's rat phobia is well-known.

"Now I ride my hunter around the yard, up on to the dungstead and jump him down the other side. He's a good hunter so it's no bother to him. We gallop across the fields to the scrub, and on to the edge of the quarry, at the bottom of which the ringer stands patiently beside the mud hole; he has already had a sedative. I snag a few tail hairs here and there on the bushes, ride back to the yard, across the bridge and stable the hunter. Then I remove the bridge, lock the yard gate, shut the terrier up in the horse box beside the gate, outside the gate, so that he's not off chasing birds or clouds or flies or whatever, when he's needed to discover and kill the rat, and go on down to the quarry. I leave the gun and the rabbits beside a rock. My accomplices are ready. Dr Field has the Immobilon in the syringe and the "instruments" are ready for use. The stage has been set.

"I return to the house and call for the vet (who I know will be out on his afternoon rounds, as usual, across the mountains). I keep calling until the receptionist tells me she's contacted him and that he'll be here in twenty minutes. Then I signal my "surgical team". Field anaesthetizes the horse and we smash a couple of legs with a sledge-hammer. Field cuts between the hind legs with a scalpel and then taps a piece of metal into the wound; we've just broken the piece of metal off the dumper. Then we hammer up and down one side to cause bruising consistent with a fall and, our work completed, we manhandle the horse into the mud pool so that only his head is out. We do that by rolling him over so that the side we've bruised will be the side on which he'll be found lying. We pull him the rest of the way. When we walk out of the pool we leave muddy footprints but it doesn't matter as last one out throws buckets of mud all around both to cover the footprints and to simulate the effect of half a ton of horse falling fifty feet into a mud-hole. Then we remove the sheet of plastic or tarpaulin on which we've performed our "surgery" – to avoid getting blood on the ground – take off our waders or whatever protective clothing we've had on and hide the lot for removal later. Then we leave and I go back to the house to wait for the vet. How's that for a reconstruction?"

"Pretty impressive. Are you sure you're not one of the gang?"

I smiled. "Do you see any flaws in the logic?"

"Flaws no. Wrinkles, one or two."

"Such as...?"

"What would have happened if the horse had died before you got there? What about the forehead whirl then?"

"Whorl, not whirl. An 'o' not an 'i'. I don't know. It probably wouldn't have been the end of the world. Maybe Field was hiding in the bushes and if the horse had died, he'd have then shot it and later claimed that he'd found it while *he* was out shooting and, realising the extent of the injuries, had shot him on humanitarian grounds."

"Would they have got away with that?"

"Possibly, when the extent of the damage was known. Or maybe they'd organise a 'break-in' to where the corpse was kept overnight, decapitate him and claim it was the work of trophy hunters ... I don't know. I'm sure they had all sorts of contingency plans."

"You said it was difficult to find a path through the thicket at the bottom of the cliff? Into where the horse was lying?"

"Yes. I couldn't find the narrow twisting path that Norris had taken when I tried to lead Potter in later. We had to brush and push our way through. Why?"

"Then how did the horse get through? How did they lead him in without getting tail hairs etc. caught on the scrub? Like they faked up on the rim?"

"Jeez! You're *really* thinking! I don't know but there would be ways; use a different path – it was a fairly large thicket; cover him in some kind of blanket like a jousting charger or like a picador's mount. Again I'm sure that they had it all worked out to the last tiny detail."

"Okay. They probably had. What about the anaesthetic you reckon they used? How come the pathologist didn't find traces?"

"That's a harder one. Maybe they used some very fancy human preparation which wouldn't be tested for. But that would be very chancy, wouldn't it? How could they know how the horse would react? How could they know it wouldn't show up on the test? Maybe Dr Field knew of something..."

"Would that be why he attended the autopsy? To see if the professor spotted something amiss?"

"Hardly. If Professor Wall *did* find something suspicious, then it was too late for them to do anything about it anyway, and, by being there, Field would've tied himself into the picture – just to know a few hours early that the game was up. Norris could have attended and done every bit as good – if all they wanted to know was whether or not they had managed to fool the pathologist."

"Then just why was he there? There had to be some very good reason, besides curiosity."

"It certainly wasn't that."

"Did he take part? Help in any way?"

"Nope. Stood by the wall nearly the whole time."

"Did he make suggestions?"

"No."

"Ask questions?"

"No."

"Open his beak at all?"

"Just to note that the horse didn't have a gall bladder. Horses don't."

"So his presence at the autopsy had no effect whatsoever on the course it took."

"None that I can think of."

"So was he there to find out the result?"

"Hardly. There was nothing confidential about it. Norris was told about it immediately afterwards and was sent a copy of the report. As was Potter."

"Well there had to be a *medical* reason! Otherwise, as you said, Norris could've attended – not Field, the doctor. But he didn't try to interfere and he didn't have to be there to get the result, so he must have been there to observe *how* it was done. Can you think of any reason why they'd want to know how exactly the pathologist wielded his knife and saw?"

"No. None at all."

"Then what's left?"

"The samples. A medical man would have been needed to see what samples were taken – well, maybe not 'needed' exactly, but certainly 'desirable'. Check how much of each organ, from what part of the organ, that kind of thing. But again, what good would that do them?"

"Exactly. If the Professor found the drug they used when he got back to his laboratory then it wouldn't have been much use to them being able to say: 'Ah! He got that from the kidney or liver or whatever'. At that point it would be of no consequence, as they'd be in big trouble already. The game would be well and truly up."

There was silence while we tried to figure out Field's role.

239

"Are you sure they used drugs? I mean could they have managed it without?" Claire asked.

"How?"

"Well... the ubiquitous sledge-hammer... A tap on the noggin with that..."

"What if you missed? If you didn't flatten him with the first swipe, he'd go *berserk* and kill all around him! Too chancy. Much too chancy. Also it'd leave a mark on the head, split the skin, crack the skull. No way. Also it wouldn't account for Field's presence at the autopsy. That *has* to tie in with the samples."

We kicked the problem around another bit while we drank coffee, eventually deciding that we weren't going to get anywhere and that we had best dump the whole thing in Potter's lap.

"After all, it *is* supposed to be our few days together, isn't it?" I said.

"True. True. That it is," Claire nodded vaguely, obviously still picking over the puzzle. I patted my pocket.

"I haven't got any money on me. How are you fixed?"

"I've got enough."

"O.K. I'll owe you. Pay the lady, stick that menu up your jumper and let's see if Potter has reported for duty yet."

On our way to the police-station, Claire brought the subject up again. "Would it be possible to treat the samples with something which would remove all traces of drugs?"

"I very much doubt it. In fact, I'd say, definitely no."

"So to summarise: the samples Professor Wall took at Bally Ard almost certainly contained drug residues and, when he examined them in Dublin, they didn't."

"That's about it... Christ! You've got it! Another horse! They switched the samples!"

"That's what I reckon!"

"It wouldn't have to be a thoroughbred, let alone a ringer! It could probably even be a donkey or a mule. A pony anyway! Just the same age and dead for the same length of time as the ringer. So that the tissues would be at the same stage of ageing and decomposition as the ringer's. That's it! You hit the nail on the head! Field came to see what samples were taken and while Professor Wall and I had breakfast with Norris, he rushed off, removed the same samples from the horse they had shot the previous evening, and substituted them for the samples which were in Professor Wall's bag which Norris had asked him to leave in the study. Jesus! They're amazing! Frigging amazing!"

"Well... It fits. Not without the odd question, mind you, but it does fit."

"What questions?" I demanded.

"Suppose the Professor's briefcase had been locked? Suppose he locked it in his car? Suppose he refused to leave it in the study and insisted on having it with him during breakfast? Suppose he refused breakfast altogether and headed straight back to Dublin? If any of those things had happened, their plan was wrecked. And not one of them could be dismissed as a million to one chance. In fact, if you think of it, the briefcase being locked or unlocked would be fifty-fifty either way. No?"

"I suppose so," I admitted grudgingly, but I was by now so convinced that there had been a third horse, an organ donor, that I felt there had to be a way round the potential snags which Claire had pointed out. "Okay," I said, "let's take the easiest one first. I don't think there was any chance that Prof. Wall would have refused breakfast. He'd been driving since about four a.m. and working for the previous hour. So forget that one. Agreed?"

"Agreed. Slim chance."

"Nor would he I think, have been so churlish as to insist that his case – it wasn't a briefcase by the way, more a glorified toolbox – that his case come with us to the dining room. Norris made the point that he'd have found its presence very upsetting – again very plausibly – and he pointed out that the study could be locked. In fact he locked it, if I remember correctly."

My mind was now back in the warming sunlight of that morning. I saw Professor Wall, Dr Field and myself, the three of us, the autopsy finished, rounding the bend in the road from the stable yard and coming into view of the side of the house. Norris immediately came out through the French doors and crossed the lawn towards us. He led the professor

241

and me into the house through the same French doors. Obviously he had been watching, on duty, and equally obviously (now) the whole purpose of this piece of stage management had been to prevent the professor from getting near his car which was parked outside the *front* door where the obvious thing would have been for him to have left his case before going into the house through *that* door. "How about that for an explanation? Acceptable?"

"What a crowd!" Claire shook her head in amused disbelief. "Wow!"

"As for locked cars or cases... I presume one of them was an expert locksmith. After all they managed to pick the lock on the Land Rover the day they stole the film from the camera. When I got to it it was locked – I'd have noticed if it wasn't. I always lock it. Always."

"But didn't Potter say that the people who broke into the cottage were amateurs who couldn't even open a simple door lock?"

"Yes. But he also thought it possible that the reason they smashed the bathroom window might have been that it was the only way in where they couldn't be seen from the road. It was bright when they arrived and there are always people strolling up and down that road. Maybe that's why they kept away from the door. And," I added smugly, "that ought to be that! Any other questions?"

"None," Claire replied. "At least, not for the moment. Give me time."

But during the time it took us to get back to the police station she still hadn't come up with any. Nor had I, though I worried furiously at it, like Patch shaking the limp remains of the sacrificial rat.

CHAPTER 29

*B*ut **Potter** wasn't there. What's more, he wasn't expected back for some hours yet. The duty officer, whom I hadn't met before, told us that all available personnel had been summoned to the east of the county, where a mountain fire was spreading and threatening two villages and a young Norwegian Spruce plantation.

"What time do you think he might be back?"

"I couldn't really say. It depends on how they're getting along with the fire. Do you want to leave a message?"

I thought for a minute. Probably Potter hadn't told anyone about the finger pointing at Norris. Better wait and see himself. "No thanks. It's not that important. I'll call by later."

He looked at me appraisingly. "Is it about the kidnap?"

"Well, yes and no. It's just something I thought of which might be helpful but it can wait. A small point which was bothering the Inspector. It's not important."

"Okay. If you don't think you ought to tell me about it now. I'll tell him that you called."

"Thanks."

"What now then?" Claire asked as she pulled away from the police station.

"I don't know. Maybe we can go back in an hour or two to see if Potter unexpectedly got back early. We can phone anyway."

"He seemed pretty certain that he'd be away for the whole night."

"Let's drive somewhere and go for a walk. I've a feeling we can do better. There are so many bits that must fit somewhere. It's only a matter of finding the right niche."

243

We headed south into the mountains and soon reached the peak overlooking Knockmore.

"This is where I got the message about Catamaran. I sweated bricks all the way to Bally Ard."

We drove on in silence. The more I thought about the plan and my role as gullible catspaw, the angrier I became. In a short time I had worked myself up into a state of severe self-criticism, mercilessly castigating myself for mistakes made, inconsistencies unnoticed. We parked by a gate into a forest which had been planted some twenty years before, climbed a stile made of logs and walked along the untarred road which wound its way through the trees.

"You know, Claire," I mused, "when I think about how often I screwed up, it's embarrassing."

"Sure. In retrospect everything's so clear, so obvious. Of course you didn't screw up! Don't be ridiculous!"

"If only I'd taken his car number instead of trying to shoot a hole in the tyre."

"You were being chased by a lunatic with a rifle for Chrissake!"

"Or the horse... On Saturday evening, he's leaping and bucking about like crazy. On Monday morning he's docile..."

"So? You thought he was *sick*, didn't you? And what about the purple nose? That was the same, wasn't it?"

"Then I find a horse I was told was dead was alive. And I didn't think *that* odd?"

"How *did* you figure that one out? I haven't wanted to ask."

"I suppose I thought that the horse had been in such deep shock that the vital signs were depressed to the point that he didn't breathe for whatever length of time Norris was looking at him or else that Norris was so shocked he didn't notice."

"That's plausible. So where's the problem?"

"What about the rabbits?"

"What about the rabbits!?"

"Norris had me throw them away in the clearing after he'd shot them way down the land. If he didn't want them, why had he bothered to carry them as far as the clearing in the first place? Why hadn't he thrown them away down the land or just left them where he shot them?"

"Oh that's a hard one to answer alright! Indeed why didn't you wonder about rabbits when you'd only a minute before shot one of the most expensive creatures on God's earth? Unforgivable! Inexplicable! Remiss!" I think she was getting genuinely fed up with the litany.

"So here's another one. A real lulu. An experienced vet is called by an experienced owner to see a horse with a colic and finds that since he called, the experienced owner hasn't gone near the horse! Oh no! He's spent the whole time moving photographs off the wall – defestooning the hall and a couple of rooms of photos of Catamaran, the late lamented."

"What are you talking about?"

"Remember I told you about the bogus colic? No? Well that was how they duped me into bringing the Land Rover to Bally Ard to have the films stolen. Victims making housecalls! What next? Norris called and showed me a perfectly normal horse. He said it had had colic until a short while before, described perfectly the symptoms, which he must have seen a hundred times before; he'd chucked a bucket of water over the animal to show the dumb vet how much the poor creature had sweated with pain. Then he lured me into his house, on the pretext of wanting to talk to me, hardly said a word before leaving me in the kitchen with the housekeeper and rushing off, presumably to rob my camera bag of films, before returning to almost march me off in his haste to be rid of me!" I paused to draw an indignant breath. "It was his housekeeper who told me about taking the pictures of Catamaran off the wall."

"I don't quite follow how you think you screwed up on that one."

"Norris would've known how important it is to walk a colicky horse and keep it walking all the time. Only something very important would keep an owner from doing so. Therefore removing Catamaran's pictures must have been very important. Suddenly. Weeks after his death. Why? I never asked myself, did I?"

"Tut. Tut. Why on earth should you have been on the lookout for suspicious circumstances or loose ends? You didn't even *know* at that stage that the horse's death wasn't an accident."

"And what about the worms?"

"Worms? What worms?"

"I checked a dung sample from the horse I thought was Catamaran and it had worm eggs in it."

"You told me about the dung sample but you said it had *sunflower seeds*. You didn't mention worm eggs."

"No. I suppose I didn't."

"Why not?"

"Well you were just a nosey reporter then, weren't you? And I didn't want it getting about. It'd look very bad for Steele."

"Stick together you vets, don't you?"

"No more, I imagine, than members of the NUJ."

"So where did the worm eggs land you?"

"Well, I also checked the hunter that supposedly had colic and he had *no* worms and I twisted so many hypotheses to explain away the discrepancy that my head was spinning. The obvious one was that 'Catamaran' was from a different place which was under a different form of management... but did Samson the Bright see the obvious? No way."

"Is that all?"

"For the moment."

"Good!"

At this point we got back to the car and we drove on, not heading anywhere in particular. Now I was beginning to feel guilty!

"I'm sorry I dumped on you back there but there are times when I feel so dense! The whole thing, the whole fucking plan relied on having an idiot of a vet. A retard. And I hate being made to look a fool."

"Who doesn't? And there's no need to apologise. You didn't dump on me. We just talked it all out. Do you feel less of a twit now?"

"No comment."

"Can you think of any reason why the whole thing was so elaborate?" Claire asked after we had gone another mile in silence.

"That's just what I've been trying to figure out, but I can't. It doesn't seem to make sense. If it was a straight insurance rip-off, they made a bags of it. The timing was totally wrong.

They've lost millions by not waiting a couple of months."

"Maybe their hand was forced. Maybe they had to do it while whatshisname, your employer, was away? After all, they couldn't have organised the date of his son's wedding to suit their own schedule, could they?"

"Hardly. But it still doesn't make sense. If it was just for the insurance, why not actually *kill* Catamaran? He's worth nothing now anyway. He's supposed to be dead so they can't sell him, stand him at stud or anything! They could use him on their own mares exclusively and hope that in a few years time, they'll have Derby and Oaks winners all over the place, but there's no guarantee that his foals will be as good as their father. And they couldn't sell the foals – not for any reasonable price. They could never get a certificate from a good stallion. Shit, even the *best* stallions around now wouldn't carry the prestige of Catamaran or go near his prices! So why do it? They stood to make much more money, legitimately, over the horse's breeding life." I was not, I knew, expressing myself very clearly; it was more like thinking aloud but Claire seemed to follow my drift.

"Could Norris have discovered that Catamaran had some fatal illness or something that would reduce his value enormously or the value of his foals?"

"If that was the case, then it probably would have been *Steele* who discovered it. Also, if that's true, then there'd be even *less* reason to keep him alive. A horse that was dying anyway?"

"Despite the arguments, they must have some way of either selling him or breeding from him. Otherwise they could have spared themselves all the trouble and hassle that's going to descend on them tomorrow morning."

"If they sell him, it'll have to be as a pet, a point-to-pointer or as dogmeat," Claire winced, "and that will nett them from a few hundred to a couple of thousand, max. As for breeding, sure they can breed him – to ponies and draught horses and Grade C hunters. For a couple of pounds a go; just because he *looks* nice. They can't wangle him on to the register. That's run by Wetherby's and Bord na gCapall, and God knows who else, and it's about ten times more carefully guarded than Debrett's or Burke's Peerage."

247

"Does Wetherby's cover the whole world?"

"No. Just Britain and Ireland as far as I know. The Americans have their own. So do the Australians, the continent, the Middle East, Japan, etcetera. I'm not sure about all this, mind you. I'm not very well up on the thoroughbred industry."

"Then what about selling him abroad? To some country where the register is not as tightly run as it is here?"

For the first time a vaguely tenable theory had come up. It didn't by any means breech the impenetrable wall of contradiction that faced us, nor allow any light to pour through. It was no more than a brick of that wall around which the mortar might be slightly suspect. There wasn't anything to actually support the theory. All you could say for it was that it couldn't be rejected out of hand. I mulled it over in silence.

"You know, you might have hit something there, Claire."

"It's a possibility?"

"The best so far. There's no proof, or no way of finding out if it's true or not, but that should all come out tomorrow when Norris and Field start answering questions."

"The lawyers are going to make a fortune out of this one," Claire mused knowingly. "Presuming that he's been insured against abduction, assassination, accidents, sickness, sterility, etc., the syndicate are going to demand payment, but, knowing Insurance companies, they'll try to wriggle out of it by bringing in Interpol, invoking extradition treaties and God only knows what else. If Norris and Field refuse to play along, it could take forever to find Catamaran. He's probably a million miles away by now with a completely new identity."

Suddenly the feeling came over me that I oughtn't to accept *that* conclusion without examining it in detail. I leaned back against the headrest, closed my eyes and began to work at it and after a while a further logical avenue offered itself for exploration. I turned to Claire. "Pretend that you're the one who's going to take Catamaran out of the country. How would you go about it?"

"How do you mean?"

"Just that. You want to shift Catamaran to an unknown destination – the destination isn't important – how would you do it?"

"Fly him out I suppose."

"Okay. Let's consider that. From where?"

"One of the airports; Dublin, Shannon, Cork, Knock, Belfast... Does it matter which airport?"

"No, it doesn't. Security is tight at them all, right? So he couldn't be doped and stuck in a crate and loaded up. The crate would be searched. That's what the Israelis tried to do with that Nigerian exile they'd kidnapped. They doped him and tried to get him out in a crate from one of the smaller airports in England..."

"Stansted. I remember the case well."

"That's right. But they got caught didn't they? And a Nigerian exile is much smaller and easier to hide than Catamaran. Also, with the Nigerian exile, I don't suppose that it mattered too much to anyone, except himself and his loved ones, if he arrived in good shape or not, as he was for the chop at home anyway, but in Catamaran's case, it's imperative that he arrives in top shape."

"One of the smaller airports where security wouldn't be so hot?"

"They only take small planes. Nothing big enough to carry a horse in safety. And the security is just as tight anyway."

"Okay. Then one of the main airports but I'd walk him aboard, pretending he was another horse. Ship him openly. Bluff."

"You'd have to have papers, health certificates, etc."

"I'd have arranged those already. Before swapping him with the ringer, I'd have taken him off to some other place, called in a vet (*not* Steele) and arranged for him to have his papers done. Only I'd have told the vet that it was another horse, make up a name. Then I'd ship him out under the false name. Description would tally perfectly and Bob would be my uncle!"

"You have the makings of a great crook. But leaving aside the fact that the vet you tried to fool would probably want to see the horse's papers – which would have "CATAMARAN" written all over them – there's always a veterinary inspector at points of embarkation to examine an animal before it leaves."

"So? My papers are in order. It's no problem."

"Would you take the chance that the vet mightn't recognise

Catamaran? After all, he's one of the best known personalities in the country and most vets are racing fans and he's been in the public mind a lot lately so there's quite a good chance that the vet might think that the horse bore an uncanny resemblance to the supposedly late Catamaran. And get to wondering about it."

"But you said yourself that Catamaran had no distinguishing features like white legs or stars and things…"

"Ah! There's the catch! He has now! A scar on his muzzle which was widely reported when it happened a few weeks ago. I think that *that* would be the feature most likely to give the game away. Specially when you consider that it still probably has a violet tinge. That spray stuff stains like hell and lasts for ages."

"I see what you mean," Claire said thoughtfully. "How about bribing the vet?"

"I'm sure that vets are as open to bribery as anyone else but that would *really* make him look twice at the animal and in about ten seconds flat, he'd have made the connection, put two and two together and what might start out as a hundred quid backhander could very well become a ten thousand quid backhander or an open invitation to blackmail or an outbreak of honesty, fame-seeking or greed in the form of the expectation of a rich reward from the Insurance company. Too chancy."

"Disguise the horse? Dye a leg or two white?"

"Possibly. I'm not sure how good a job can be done, whether it would be undetectable or not. Assume that that too, is chancy. Any other ideas?"

"Send him out by ship."

"The same arguments apply. Almost."

"Why only 'almost'?"

"Well you could use a small port where security mightn't be quite as tight and you could possibly put him on board in a box or a crate. In fact, you'd have to, or people would wonder what a classy-looking stallion was doing being shipped from a tiny port where such a thing had never happened before. But you couldn't keep him in the box for the whole voyage and then the crew would get to know about it and that would lead to more awkward questions."

"So what would *you* do? I can see by your obnoxiously smug expression that you've got it all worked out." She smiled to show she didn't really mean it.

"Well, in view of the fact that there's nobody looking for Catamaran, unlike Shergar, where the cops were searching under people's *beds* almost, I'd wait it out for a while, until the heat died down and nobody was talking or thinking about Catamaran any more. By which time the wound on his nose would have healed too. *Then* I'd ship him out by air using false or forged documents."

"You think that he's still in the country then?"

"It's quite possible. Maybe even probable."

"You'd worked that out when you asked me how I'd go about it?"

"Yes."

"So what was all the question and answer stuff in aid of?"

"Just to see if you came up with any route that I hadn't thought of."

"It sounded suspiciously like an ego trip to me," she said a bit dubiously.

"I'm sorry if it did. I promise you that it wasn't."

"Okay, I believe you. So now see if you can just as cleverly come up with *where* he is." If there was a barb in it, a morsel of pique, her voice didn't betray it.

"Probably where the other horse was kept before the substitution."

"Agreed. But where was that? Hey? That's the problem, isn't it?"

And a few miles further on, that too came to me in another flash of inspiration, when I had stopped even thinking about it.

CHAPTER 30

*I*t began as a repeat bout of self-recrimination. I really ought to have been alerted to the fact that something strange was going on the moment I discovered the worm eggs. I put a lot of thought into trying to work out possible reasons for that – in fact, I had probably thought of all the possible causes *except* the right one! But the explanation should really have leaped out and hit me smack between the eyes when Norris told me, while I was attending the supposed colic, that he carried out a very strict dosing regime, especially when the efficacy of the dosing had been proven a few hours later when I checked the hunter's sample and found it clear. But no; instead of clarifying matters for me, this glaring inconsistency had mystified me even more.

Thinking of the dung sample automatically led me to thinking about the other discrepancy between it and the sample from the hunter: there had been several complete sunflower seeds in the first, their hard black and white striped husks knocking against the pen I had used as a swizzle stick. In the hunter's sample there hadn't been any. But it hadn't struck me as odd. I suppose my mind was occupied with thoughts of worm eggs and anyway, there could have been many explanations – it might just have been a seedless sample, or the hunter might have been a better digester, or Norris might have given the secret ingredient to Catamaran only... Now it struck me that I'd have to rule out *that* option; the sunflower seeds were *not* Norris's secret ingredient for Catamaran's daily ration as the dung in which they'd been found had not come from Catamaran. It had come from the *ringer* and it seemed highly unlikely that *that* unfortunate animal – being kept for the sole purpose of being shot – would be given anything more than ordinary horse nuts and hay, that his feed would be dickied up with tasty morsels of *any* sort.

But yet, sunflower seeds there had been and, if the horse hadn't been deliberately fed them, he must have picked them up from his environment and he must have picked them up within the previous few days for them to have been still in his gut. Without any expectations of coming up with an answer, I wondered vaguely where there might be sunflower seeds scattered about. A feedstuff compounder? Possibly, but too many people about. A health food shop? Hardly. They are usually in the middle of towns. No; not a health food shop. A pet shop, then? How about a pet shop? They'd have sunflower seeds for people who kept parrots and other psittacines as pets. Psittacines? *Psittacines!!*

The thought had almost passed me by before I recognised its significance... The kitchen at Bally Ard, feathers all over the place, the wild, free-flying psittacines in the wooded oasis in the middle of the bogs miles from anywhere, Norris's good friend...

"*Vernon!*" I exclaimed, almost shouted, startling Claire. "*That's his name!* Vernon! I'll bet you a pound to a penny that that's the third man, the one who kept me prisoner. It's got to be! It all fits like a glove! Turn the car! We're going back! We must go back!"

She wanted no part of it. She kept driving and saying 'no' in different ways; then she pulled over into a lay-by and continued to say 'no' in more different ways. Finally, still protesting, she turned and headed slowly back towards Knockmore, her eyes slitted against the low sun.

"I think you're crazy! Why can't you just leave it all to Potter now? There's no reason to think that the horse won't still be there in the morning. You're probably right in your thinking, Frank, but why take more risks? Wasn't prodding Norris enough for one day?"

"Maybe the horse *won't* be there in the morning. Maybe they'll decide that the whole thing is getting chancy now – me escaping, me calling on Norris, telling him that we know they want photographs... Maybe they feel that it's just a matter of time before we cop on... Maybe they're afraid that the police will get to them from another angle – the red Cortina, finger-prints in the house, witnesses who saw Vernon coming or going from the house; any slight fears could panic them. Suppose Norris just happens to run into Hynes again this evening and Hynes tells him I was asking about the shots of the horse? Maybe this, maybe that, maybe the other. Who knows what could happen?"

"What do you intend to do?"

"Scout around. That's all. I swear," I added when she looked dubiously sideways at me. "If Potter goes to Vernon's place tomorrow, he'll have to do it legally, search warrant and all and, if Catamaran *isn't* there, we'll have given the game away and they'll be able to spirit him away from wherever he is. And that'll put paid to our chances of ever finding him. All I want is to have a quick look. Ten minutes. In and out. Fifteen minutes max."

"Hmmph!" She sounded as if she didn't believe a word of it; yet, she had to concede the logic of finding out if the horse *was* there or not. "Where does Vernon live?"

"I don't know. Someplace out in the mountains or on the bogs. A wooded oasis, miles from anywhere according to Norris's housekeeper, but I can't very well phone her and ask her for the address."

"We can get his address from the telephone directory."

"He doesn't have a phone."

"Now *how* do you know *that*?"

"I heard Norris telling Field that he was going to drive out to tell the third man about my visit to Bally Ard. If the third man had a phone, he wouldn't have had to drive. Great brain, huh?"

"So how do you intend finding out?"

"It should be easy. Any man who keeps all those parrots fly-ing free must be pretty well-known locally. I'm sure that he comes in to town now and then to shop or have a drink or whatever. The shops will be closed by this time so we'll ask in a pub."

We passed by the first four pubs we met after arriving back in Knockmore, on the grounds that they didn't seem like the places where Norris or his friends would stop in for their gin and tonics – referred snobbery which was going to cause big trouble before the night was out. At last we pulled up outside 'The Oyster Bed Lounge Bars', studied it for a moment and decided that it was a much more likely prospect. We had already decided that Claire should do the asking as I was known in the town, almost famous at this stage, and we didn't want people getting to wondering why the vet who had shot Catamaran, who had been kidnapped himself and almost shot as well, and who was supposed to be on leave, should be looking in a pub for the address of Vernon, the parrot man. Claire was to pose as a friend of a fictitious niece of Vernon's who wanted to look him up, as she found herself in the general area.

I watched her cross the road to the bar with its pale neon lights trying to make an impression on the evening light. Five minutes later she was back with detailed instructions on how to get to Clashard, Vernon's isolated domain.

"One guy even offered to come with me to make sure I didn't go astray in the dark," she laughed, sliding in behind the wheel.

"I'll bet he did," I retorted drily.

Claire's directions were good and as we drove west into the sinking sun, she picked off her landmarks one by one. Somewhat less than ten miles from Knockmore she indicated right and announced with satisfaction: "This is it. The second right after the third house beyond the church with the telephone kiosk across from it. Simple." At least she seemed to have shed some of her misgivings about the project.

For the first half-mile or so along this side-road there were houses and small fields surrounded by dry stone-walls but, once we breasted the first rise and began the descent into the first shallow valley, these vanished, and the only signs that man had ever been there were the road and the long rank of poles which marched beside it carrying current to Clashard. On each side, the bog stretched away; on our right it rolled in dark waves to merge with the evening sky while away to the west it lapped against distant mauve mountains which pushed like a fistful of knuckles into the turquoise skyline. The sheer immensity and emptiness of the place soon began to gnaw away at Claire's resolve and I could see her doubts return.

"No heroics, Frank. Okay?"

"No. Of course not."

"Of course not. Of course not. That's what you said before at Bally Ard and you went back and *broke* in!"

"This is just for a quick look-see. I want to see if Catamaran is there and I want to get a look at Vernon. Balaclava or no, I'll know if he's the same guy."

In silence, Claire steered around huge lichen-bearded boulders which looked as if they should have been sucked under aeons ago; we skirted the tiny lily-covered lakes which nestled in every hollow like blobs of liquid sapphire and crossed the many sluggish brown streams which tried vainly to drain the sodden landscape. At last, coming to a private decision, she nodded to herself and muttered: If it were done, when 'tis done, then 'twere well it were done quickly."

"Neat that." I tried to lighten the atmosphere. "One of your own?"

She laughed a short snort.

"Just kidding. Macbeth. Right?" I beamed at her.

"Right."

"Did it at school. I was Macduff. Won in the end too. But it was tough. Wife, kids…"

"All your pretty chickens."

"Those too. Go easy around the next corner. There may be three witches having a barbecue."

But around the next corner we found ourselves looking across the valley at the tops of the conifers of Clashard.

CHAPTER 31

We left the car hidden behind a long turf-reek and walked the last few hundred yards to the top of the rise beyond which lay Clashard. Hunkering down in the sedge, we took stock.

Two long narrow lakes converged, almost meeting just below us. A short river completed the link and the road spanned this on a little concrete bridge, before vanishing into the ubiquitous rhododendrons which flourished in the acid soils of the region. A few tall hoary old conifers poked up through the shrubbery and, in the fading light, bright bursts of plumage flashed between them, parrots finding their roosts for the rapidly approaching night. Clashard occupied the triangle between the lakes, stretching back some quarter of a mile or so; beyond this, the endless bog resumed its suzerainty. The road went no further than Clashard. There was nowhere for it to go.

We couldn't see any buildings, but a pencil-thin column of turf-smoke climbed unwaveringly into the still evening air, marking the position of the house. There was a sudden whoosh, and a flock of doves rushed by over our heads, flying in from the west; I watched them settle some distance beyond the house.

"That'll be where the stables are." I whispered. "There, where those doves landed."

"How do you know?"

"Well at this stage, they're in for the night, and doves wouldn't roost in trees if there were buildings available. If there *are* sheds or outhouses, then that's where they'll be."

"My, my! Who's the regular little woodsman, then?"

We watched for another five minutes but there wasn't a peep from Clashard, neither sight nor sound of activity.

"Perhaps Vernon's not there. Maybe he's already left. Got the wind up and left without even putting out the fire," Claire suggested.

"I doubt it. Norris will have been here with the good news that the cops are looking for drug pushers in Dublin. He may very well *not* be here but I doubt that he's fled in panic. More likely gone off on a mega, celebratory pub crawl. Anyway I'd better go down and check it out."

"I wonder if he has a dog?" Claire whispered.

I hadn't thought of it. I, who spend my entire working life keeping a wary lookout for dogs as I go from farm to farm, hadn't even *thought* of a dog. It was a chastening thought – not the possibility of there being a dog, the fact that it hadn't occurred to me.

"Naw!" I said with re-assuring scorn. "Not with all those valuable birds about!"

"Why not?"

"They might eat the birds! Natural enemies!"

"Then why don't dogs eat sheep? They're even *more* natural enemies."

"That's different."

"Why? Why is it different?"

"Well… sheep are sheep and parrots are parrots…"

"And bullshit is bullshit. I think he *has* got a dog because of cats. Now *cats* eat birds *and* climb trees – they're *really* natural enemies. And dogs discourage cats, they're natural enemies too. So, my enemy's enemy is my friend and therefore he probably has a dog. Or two. Or a whole goddam slavering *pack* of them!"

"So he may. Let him. I'm going in and that's that."

"So am I. And that, too, is that."

"Are you sure? It's kind of stupid. If we both go there's the risk of us both being caught, and there won't be anyone to go for help."

"If you go, I go. There's no point in trying to talk me out of it. If, as you say, it's just a quick look around, then there's no danger. If I'm not there, I'll be beside myself, thinking you're off doing the crazy hero again."

"Okay. Okay. You win. Give me a couple of minutes before you follow. I'll wait just across the bridge. Any sign of danger,

258

you stay where you are. Understood?"

"Of course. Don't worry! One hero is enough in any set-up! At the first sound of the baying of the Rotweillers, I'll be back in the car, doors locked."

I looked at her in horror but she smiled, kissed me quickly and whispered: "Good Luck."

"Good luck to you too."

I gave her the thumbs-up and left, working my way down through the sedge until I met the bridge. Then, half expecting to hear the howls of an outraged Doberman, I dashed across the bridge and slipped into the bushes. The only sounds were the gurgling of the river and the drumming of my heart. A minute later, Claire materialized by my side. Moving like a wraith, she almost bumped into me, and gave a little squeal as I put my hand out to stop her.

"Jesus, Frank! I didn't see you!"

"No, but I saw you. That white dress is a dead giveaway. You'd better stay well into the bushes."

We moved towards the house, our progress muted by the muffling carpet of old leaves, and came upon it sooner than I expected.

It stood on the other side of the road from us, the west side. Silhouetted against the dying dusk-sky and the last, lingering translucence of the lake-waters, we could just about make out its outlines. It was a single-storey cottage in the shape of a T, the cross bar of the T being nearest the gate and the leg stretching out from it, running parallel to the road in the direction of the stables, or where we had decided the stables were.

There were four windows in the crossbar, all in the same wall – the one which faced towards the bridge; all of them were dark. In the leg of the T, there were two windows, with a door at the end. The door was open; from the window nearest it, pale light poured out, splashing a yellow rectangle on the hard-packed gravel of the tiny forecourt, which was little more than a widening of the road.

The room from which the light came was clearly the kitchen – we could see the corner of a crockery-laden dresser and some copper pans hanging on the wall. We watched for some time but there was no sign of any movement inside.

Pushing my lips to Claire's ear, I whispered: "I'm going to sneak across for a peep." I felt her stiffen slightly, and to make sure that my proposed action wouldn't be mis-represented and lumped under the heading of 'heroics', I went on: "It's necessary. He must be about somewhere; he'd never have gone off and left the door open, whatever about the light, so, if he *is* in there, we can move much more freely up at the sheds and finish our business quicker. Also I want to see if he actually *is* my gaoler."

"But you don't know what he looked like, your gaoler."

"Doesn't matter. I'll know him." And I knew that I would.

I pushed silently through the leaf-screen and stood at the edge of the forecourt, just outside the pool of light. There was no one in the part of the kitchen which I could see from where I was, so, first testing the gravel with a cautious toe to see if it crunched underfoot, I tiptoed across to the wall and carefully peeped through the window. Nobody. I retraced my steps, skirted the light, and crept in to the wall again on the other side of the lighted window – between it and the door. And it was at that moment that I heard the footsteps.

I froze, flattening myself against the wall, and slewed my head towards the sound. Though I had prepared myself for sudden discovery and consequently shouldn't have been so rooted, for whole seconds I stood unable to move, unable even to think. On reflection, the thing which had reduced me to such jelly-like impotence was not the fact that someone was coming; it was the measured tread of the approaching steps. I had heard that same tread approach my cell, twice a day for four days, and, each time I'd wondered anxiously if they weren't the harbingers of bad news – there never had been any way of foretelling what new twists my predicament might have taken during his absence.

I shook myself free of the vice-hold of atavistic fear and rapidly considered my dilemma. I was trapped in a patch of dark with my back literally to the wall – he was up the road to my left and the light was spilling out from the kitchen window to my right. If I streaked for the bushes across the driveway, I'd be clearly outlined against the light and, if I moved up the road to get my head below the bright patch, I would run right into him. What made this course so unacceptable was the quite likely prospect that he would have a gun – he had had a spare rifle in the boot of his car at the German's house, even though he had had the overwhelming advantage in that situation; now, with me loose and him feeling insecure, it was quite possible that he'd be travelling alert and armed, even in the precincts of his own home. I did the only thing I could; I slid round the door into the tiny dark porch and waited for him to arrive, intending to nail him with a haymaker of a punch as soon as his figure was outlined in the entrance.

The footsteps advanced inexorably, tramping towards the doorway; when they were almost outside, I bunched my fist and swung back my arm. Then they stopped. For one awful moment I thought that he had seen me and was now standing outside, gun at the ready, preparing to make his move. I screwed my fists tighter and crouched in the darkness, coiling to make a desperate spring at his knees, hoping that his gun would be pointed at the level of my upper body. I was vaguely surprised that he had seen me because there hadn't been a break in his stride or an acceleration of his pace as he approached. Then came the sound of heavy boots being scraped on a metal boot-scraper. I relaxed slightly; I still had the element of surprise and the advantages of weight, height and years. And desperation. I waited.

His boots must have been very muddy because the scraping went on and on, and he was still only on the first one – there hadn't been a pause in the grating noise during which he could have changed feet. I lurked, ready to lash out as soon as he appeared in the door.

I felt reasonably confident that I could overpower the obviously unsuspecting Vernon and probably tie him up and lug him off to Potter and that was fine as far as it went. But what if Catamaran was *not* at Clashard? Then we were as badly off as ever – in fact worse. If Norris or Field began to suspect that all was not well (for example if Vernon failed to arrive at a pre-arranged meeting or some such), then maybe they might destroy the horse, the only irrefutable evidence to lift my theory from the realms of speculation into the area of provable fact.

As the scraping continued outside, I wondered if I mightn't chance going on in through the house and finding a back door. At first, I discounted the possibility of this move because I assumed that the door leading on from the porch opened directly onto the kitchen, and the flood of light which would stream through as soon as I opened it, would immediately give the game away. Then I noticed that the door was completely dark; no slits of light marked its edges and no exclamation mark of bright yellow shone through the keyhole which I could feel with my exploring hand. When Vernon started on his second boot, I gently depressed the handle and eased the door open the faintest of cracks, proceeding with great caution in case the absence of light around the door was due to nothing more than a perfect fit and a blocked keyhole. But no light came through. I pushed it far enough in for me to slip through and, closing it gently behind me, found myself in yet another porch, this one so small that it could have had no other function than as a kind of draught excluder against the wild winter winds which would howl unchecked across the vast empty moors and hurl themselves against the isolated cottage. This time, the door to the kitchen was clearly outlined in light and, as the clang of leather and metal studs on iron continued outside, I went through quickly, into the bright kitchen.

The room was small and full of furniture; a quick glance showed me nowhere I could hide and no back door. The only exit led towards the rooms in the crossbar of the T, and, being careful not to pass between the central ceiling light and the window which looked out on to the forecourt, I hurried through this door and entered a short corridor. There were two doors opening off the corridor, one on either side, opposite each other. The one on the right was to the bathroom. I thought it most unlikely that there would be a door to the outside in a bathroom, so I pressed quickly on down the corridor. I didn't even *open* the door opposite – for one thing, the faint light from the kitchen shining down along the corridor might have been strong enough to cast a telltale glow through the window and, for another, I knew already, from my observation of the house from the bushes, that the door through which I had entered was the only one on that side anyway.

The scraping stopped as I passed into the sitting room, increasing the urgency of my search. There were two windows in there, the two central windows of the crossbar of the T; there were also two doors, one opening to a room on the right, the other to the left. The latter I ignored, knowing it to be doorless, and I gently pushed open the other. It gave on well-oiled hinges, without a squeak. I stood for a moment in the entrance and listened. There was no sound from the kitchen and I had the impression that Vernon had not yet come into the house. The delay made me uneasy. Could he have seen Claire? Had he noticed the white of her dress in the bushes across from the door? Had she moved a fraction and been seen? Or snapped a twig? Or sneezed? I had no intention of hiding away until I knew that Claire was not in immediate danger. Then there was the sound of the kitchen tap running, and, knowing once more where he was, I stepped into the room and closed the door. The time lapse between the end of the boot-scraping and the noise from the kitchen was most likely due to nothing more than the fact that he had been busy removing the heavy boots outside; it also explained why I hadn't been able to hear him crossing the floor to the sink. He was now in his stockinged feet, or had put slippers on. At any rate, his footsteps weren't audible any more. I'd have to be extra careful.

I stood quietly inside the door and listened again; he was still in the kitchen, by the sound of it, preparing his supper. Crockery clinked and cutlery rattled, a fridge door opened and a kettle began to sing, there was the scrape of a chair being moved and the sawing thrusts of a breadknife. I took advantage of his industry and switched on the light.

There was no outside door. The window was small and deepset and its sill was crammed with a collection of house-plants and small ornaments, including an assortment of old, strangely-shaped, coloured bottles; so the window had to be excluded as an exit possibility – even if I had been willing to risk being able to move all the bric-a-brac quietly in the dark, I wouldn't have been able to replace them from the outside, so, when Vernon discovered that they had been moved, he would put two and two together, deduce the fact that we were on to him, and the fate of Catamaran, if he was elsewhere than Clashard, would be sealed.

Beneath the window was a small table on which stood a brass lamp and several magazines and books; beside it, its seat under the table, there was a high-backed chair. Opposite the door, within easy reach of the table, a low bookcase stood against the wall, its contents consisting entirely of volumes concerning parrots – lots of expensive-looking reference books, bound volumes of 'Cage and Aviary', box files with titles such as 'Breeding, 1973-1977', 'Lorakeets', 'Macaws (Hyacinth) and Cockatoos (Sulphur Crested)' written in a spindly hand on gummed labels. Above the bookcase a rack had been fixed to the wall to hold three fishing rods which all looked to be of split cane, and a landing net. Further along that wall there was a tall darkwood cabinet with closed doors. The back wall was free of furniture but was covered by a huge chart which looked like a genealogical table. The fourth wall was occupied by the door to the sitting room, the light switch and a large glass-case of stuffed parrots. There was no way out and nowhere much to hide. I switched out the light and retired to the back wall to think.

Should I rush him as he was eating his supper? Should I wait until he came into this room? Would he come into the room at all? In case he did, shouldn't I stand by the door in order to maximise the advantage of surprise? Would I be better to sit it out and wait until he went to bed before making my escape and beginning the search? If I did that, and he stayed up for hours, what about Claire? Would she wait, not knowing what was going on in the house? If not, what action would she be likely to take? Go for help? Try to come in search of me?... The questions were endless. It was the same as when I had been working out the permutations and combinations of the likely effects of my actions when I was dreaming up the 'GI Truss', trying to do the impossible, trying to cover everything.

A toilet flushed, sparking off a Pavlovian desire in me to have a pee. Perhaps I *ought* to tackle him – get it over with, citizen's arrest. Surely he'd never have a meeting arranged with Norris and Field for *this* hour of the night? The chances of them finding out to-night that their accomplice was in the hands of the police would be remote. Catamaran would be safe. Anyhow, he most likely *was* here in Clashard.

The light in the sitting room went on, and a sudden patch of yellow flowed under the door, like water from an overflowing bath, illuminating the room just the faintest bit. There was a click from the other side of the door, followed at once by the voice of a newscaster and soon after, a flickering bluish light flowed under the door too, to mingle with the steadier yellow. Taking advantage of the extra illumination, I began to re-examine the contents of the room with a view to finding a suitable weapon to aid me in my citizen's arrest. There could be no mistake this time, no escape for him. If he managed to elude me or outfox me as he had done before, we'd lose Catamaran, Vernon, Field and Norris and I could only imagine Potter's reaction to that. Worse, we could also end up dead if he managed to elude me long enough to get his hands on a gun. I ruled out the fishing rods, landing net and chair as possible weapons and was trying to decide between the brass table lamp and one of the larger bottles when I noticed a key jutting out of the lock of the tall cabinet. If I had noticed it before, it hadn't registered. Quietly I turned it and swung the door towards me. The door blocked off the faint light which might have shown me the interior, so I explored it with my hand, very carefully and slowly, in case it was full of glassware or other noisy articles. Instead, my cautious fingertips brushed wood, shaped, polished wood, the stock of a shotgun. I felt up and down along it twice to make sure I wasn't dreaming, but no, the cold sleek barrel, the rounded trigger-guard, the warm stock were all real. There were four guns in the cabinet; grasping the last one firmly, I tugged it gently and, with the slightest resistance, it came loose.

Still hardly able to credit my good fortune, I broke it open; it was empty, which wasn't surprising. Cradling the gun in my left arm, I explored along the floor of the cabinet and found nothing, but, beneath the section which housed the guns, I found a drawer which contained boxes of cartridges. I loaded the gun, snapped it closed and put a handful of cartridges into my pocket.

Now Vernon was in the sitting room again; I heard him

265

placing a tray on a table and turn up the volume on the television as the theme music of Miami Vice started up. I hesitated a moment, putting the finishing touches to my plans, but, before I could move, the door opened, the light came blindingly on, and Vernon walked in.

At first he didn't see me. He crossed to the table beneath the window and picked up a magazine. Flicking through the pages, he turned towards the door and, just as I was about to say 'Good evening, Mr Vernon,' or something equally inappropriate – his head jerked up as if his neck was spring-loaded and he stared at me in horror. Eyes and mouth wide open, he tottered back a step or two, the magazine falling from his suddenly nerveless fingers to the floor.

"Good evening, Mr Vernon," I said.

CHAPTER 32

I **thought he** was going to faint, he was gasping and swaying about that much. His face developed a nasty greenish tinge which exaggerated the lividness of the huge bruise on his right jaw. As I waited for him to get over what must have been a nasty turn – at least he *looked* as though it had been a nasty turn – I examined the bruise with more than a touch of pride. I tried to get him to move, but he showed no sign that he had even heard me, let alone had any intention of complying. After another couple of minutes, he seemed to have recovered slightly – at least his breathing had slowed – but he still leaned on the table, drooping against it like something filleted, wearing the expression of one who has suspected all along that it couldn't last. Claire would have likened his demeanour to that of Macbeth, when, from the grey turrets of Dunsinane, he had observed Birnam Wood on the move.

I didn't trust him. Not an inch. My nose still hurt like hell, a salutary reminder of the last time I thought I had him by the short and curlies. Also the history of our brief relationship to date had been one of a battle of wills and illusionary skills. In similar circumstances, when our positions had been reversed, I had resorted to psychological methods to dull his alertness and I wondered now if he wasn't trying to psych me, play me at my own game. I tightened my grip on the gun and repeated: "It's all over, Vernon. Let's go. *Now!*"

When I raised my voice, it seemed to register with him; he stirred, looked blearily at me and said in a broken voice: "Give me a minute please. Just a minute. I don't feel well."

"You've had your minute already. Now, come on! Let's get going. It's getting late." He buried his face in his hands and

267

began to shake his head back and forth, side to side. I watched him like a hawk, still half-suspecting him of acting. "Come on! Let's go!"

Wearily he pushed himself away from the support of the table and tottered towards me. I backed into the sitting room, keeping a wary eye on him and stood out of arm's reach, beckoning him with jerks of the gun to go down the corridor ahead of me. He turned to do as I directed but, as he passed the chair in front of which his supper tray had been set, he sank into it, and seemed to pass out.

"Get *up*!" I commanded sternly, but his head remained lolling back and his eyes stayed closed. "Very well. If you think I'm going to come close enough to you to lift you up... then, think again. Stay as you are. We've both got plenty of time." I backed to the television set and, rather than searching for the on/off button, slid down along the wall and pulled the plug, bringing to a sudden end, a high-speed car-chase along a palm-lined boulevard featuring lots of characters in highly-coloured shirts.

"Catamaran is up at your sheds, isn't he?" I asked, dropping my voice in the sudden quiet. "Isn't he?" I waited. "Answer me. He's here at Clashard, right?"

"Catamaran is dead." The voice was weak but what it said sent a shiver through me. Apart from a natural desire to save the horse, we might need him alive to get convictions. The horse I had shot had gone to the knackers yard as soon as the autopsy was over. There would be no exhumation.

"What happened to him? How did he die?"

"You shot him."

"Hmmph!" I snorted in relief. "If I believed that, I wouldn't be here now, would I? No, Vernon. I shot another horse, a ringer, a dead ringer in fact. There've been lots of dead horses, haven't there? I shot one; you or Norris or Field shot another for his bits and pieces, his samples... but nobody shot Catamaran. No way. Who's going to buy him? You may as well tell me. You'll be telling the whole story to Inspector Potter in a short while anyway."

"I don't know what you're talking about." The voice wasn't any stronger but it was defiant – it was also a bit strangled, courtesy, no doubt, of the *coup de grace* of the GI Truss.

"Oh yes you do! You guys made so many bloomers, it's a wonder it took me until tonight to figure it out." I reeled off a list of their mistakes, the errors and oversights that had led me inexorably forward, step by inevitable step, to where we were now. As the damning list unfolded – the worm eggs, sunflower seeds, the rabbits which ought to have been left where they had (supposedly) been shot – Vernon winced and flinched as if they were real physical blows. "And why steal only the film? Why not take camera and all?" I continued without mercy. I was trying to shake him, to rattle him so much that he'd tell me the whole story but, as I went on, I could see that it was having the opposite effect. He shrank further and further into the chair as the hammer-blows of each fact, each slip up, fell upon his hapless head and, by the time I came to a halt, he was huddled in it, punch-drunk and beaten, not fully aware of what was going on.

"Won't Potter get a nice surprise when he finds out what three of his leading citizens have been getting up to? Conspiracy to defraud; cruelty to animals; breaking and entering; assault on Mrs Kelly in Cork; kidnapping; assault and battery; attempted murder; and I'm sure he can think of ten or twelve more charges to add to those."

He had had enough; he now looked like Methusaleh, crouched in the chair; he seemed to have physically shrunk. I let it be. There was no point in going on. He was destroyed. All that was left for him was to contemplate the horror ahead of him, arrest, humiliation, trial, degradation, imprisonment.

"Let's go and have a look at the horse first," I said in as kindly a tone as I could manage. "I'm sure that it'll count for something if he's being looked after well." Actually, it probably wouldn't matter a damn but Vernon clutched eagerly at the specious straw.

"I fed him just a while ago. He's fine – never better!" He arose from the chair, all anxious to show me just how well he had looked after Catamaran – as if I had some say in the matter. Obviously he regarded me as a judge, jury, hangman and all. As well as nemesis. "Come with me. I'll show you," he said, almost eagerly, setting off towards the kitchen. I still wasn't willing to take any chances, so I kept the gun pressed firmly into the small of his back as we shuffled along the corridor, waiting for him to try something on.

We didn't make it to the kitchen. My heart froze, and I almost pulled the trigger in a reflex jerk when, as we passed the doors to the bathroom and the room opposite, there was a metallic click from each side of me, one from each room, and a voice, laden with menace, growled: "Drop the gun, Samson. *Now!*"

With a sick feeling in the pit of my stomach, I did as I was told and shuddered as a gun was placed at each of my temples.

"Don't move. Not an inch! You so clearly reeled off all the charges against us just now, it seems that blowing your nasty, suspicious, interfering brain out wouldn't make matters a whole lot worse. Where's the girl?" The now not-so-suave voice of Vincent Field, MD, custodian of the health of the good citizens of Knockmore and the surrounding hinterlands.

"What girl?" I stammered from between clamped jaws.

"Look! I'll tell you this just once! Don't give me any more bullshit. Answer the questions quickly and truthfully. I meant what I said about things not being able to get much worse. Now where's the girl who was looking for directions an hour ago in The Oyster Beds? Beautiful, tall, white dress, looking for 'Mr Vernon who keeps parrots'." Field raised his voice to a squeaky falsetto in a vicious caricature of a woman's voice.

"I left her in Knockmore."

"Okay! *That's it*! I *warned* you about bullshit."

I thought that that was the end. I got ready to make a dash for the kitchen where Vernon had gone and was sitting at the table with his head resting on it, oblivious to what was going on fifteen feet away.

"Easy, Vincent! Take it easy for God's sake! What will that accomplish? Steady on." Norris spoke for the first time. "Look here, Samson, you were both seen coming up the road here. Your lady friend was driving – does that prove to you that there's no point in trying to pretend that she's in town? Now tell us where she is and we'll try to wrap all this up in as amicable a way as possible."

"Amicable my arse!" Field muttered threateningly on the other side of me, his voice a savage hiss. "Geez! *Amicable*, he says! Good Christ!"

I said nothing, so Norris went on: "Dr Field saw her – and heard her – in the bar, so you might as well co-operate. We'll find her sooner or later, you know. I'm sure you don't want her hunted down like an animal? Wouldn't it be much better to tell us where she is and then we can all go to her? You'd both be together. You could look after her. Reassure her... Desmond!" he called into the kitchen as Vernon began to rise from the table, "where are you going? Don't go out there, Desmond. Sit down again like a good chap. Just for a moment."

"Who's going to look after the birds, Gilbert? Who will look after the birds?"

"*Fuck* the birds!" Field whispered violently to himself. He seemed to be rapidly losing control.

"Don't worry Desmond. We'll arrange everything. We'll talk about it in a moment. Just wait there where you are."

While all this was going on, I was cursing myself for having been so stupid as to seek out a bar which looked like the kind of place that Norris and his friends would frequent, the watering hole of the bourgeoisie of Knockmore. Unerringly, I had found it. The only problem was that one of his friends was actually *in* the bar at the time – Field. The possibility had never crossed my mind, and it ought to have.

"Well?" Norris turned back to me with a mildness almost as sinister as Field's murderous venom. "Where is she? We haven't got all night, you know."

"Probably already gone for help. She most likely saw you arrive. She was keeping an eye on the gate from the hill out there."

"Well, my boyo," Field took over again with triumphant relish, "if she *is*, she won't get far because she'll be *walking*. You see, we found your car and let the air out of the tyres. If she walks *on* the road, we'll get her; if she walks *off* the road, the bogs will get her. Maybe she's already up to her charming titties in a swallow-hole! Maybe you should tell us where she is before she goes under forever."

"I honestly don't know where she is at this moment," I said, praying that Field's crudely put theory wasn't a reality, feeling that it wasn't, that Claire was too sensible to tackle such hostile, alien territory in the dark.

A thought struck Field. "Hey!" he called. "Vernon! Is Samson's woman in the house? Hey, Vernon! Did you hear what I said? Is she in the house?"

But Vernon's head had gone back down on the table and he was taking no further part in the proceedings.

"She's not in the house," I said quietly.

"Maybe you ought to have a quick look," Norris suggested to Field.

"Okay. Good idea. But watch this bastard. Maybe I ought to search him first. Maybe he's got Vernon's pistol in his pocket."

"Inspector Potter's got it."

"Yeah?"

"Search me if you like."

"Oh I will. Don't you worry, I will. Cover him Gilbert. Well."

"In fact, Potter also has a letter explaining everything to him. He could be on his way now..."

"Come come, Samson. You distinctly told Desmond that Potter would be *surprised* when he found out what three of his leading citizens had been up to. We heard you, didn't we Dr Field?"

"We sure did! We heard it all – every bit. Don't believe him, Gilbert. It's just another one of his stories."

"I meant: surprised when he opens the letter," I tried lamely.

He finished patting up and down my trousers, even feeling in my socks; now he started on the side pockets of my jacket.

"You made good time getting here," he said conversationally, searching through the contents of my left pocket and replacing them one by one.

"Your co-patron's directions were explicit."

"Made it without a stop, I expect?"

"That's right," I answered, only seeing the trap I had walked into after the last word had irretrievably left my mouth.

"Which means that you had left your supposed letter at the police station *before* you came to the bar looking for directions? Mmmm? Am I right?" he insisted when I didn't answer at once.

"Yes." I said it in a small voice, seething at having been caught out so simply.

"Strange. Surely you could have got directions from the police. *Everybody* knows where Clashard is. I assume, according to your cock and bull story, that you want us to believe that you'd only deal with Potter, and that he wasn't at the station? But why didn't you contact him at home? Surely he wouldn't have minded for something as big as this?" His tone was heavy with sarcasm as he finished with my left pocket.

"He wasn't at home. There was a mountain fire somewhere, and he had to go there."

"He's right, Vincent. I heard about it this evening. A big fire." Norris sounded just the tiniest bit worried.

Field continued as if he hadn't even spoken. "Well then, why didn't you ask the garda you left the supposed letter with, how to get here? You could easily have phrased it in such a way that he wouldn't get suspicious – you with your talent for inventing on-the-spot stories."

I was spared the need for answering that by Field's sudden exclamation. "Well, lookee here! What have we got here, then, hey?" He made a low whistle.

I looked down at his hand. In it, he held the wallet of prints they had searched for for so long. It had been in my inside pocket since the restaurant earlier in the evening. My heart sank.

"Jackpot, Gilbert!" He gloated. "We've hit the bloody jackpot!"

His excitement as he drew the glossy prints from the wallet was almost feverish. "Cover him very, very carefully Gilbert," he squeaked. He jammed his gun into his pocket and began to leaf hurriedly through the sheaf of photographs, becoming more and more anxious as he came on one shot after another of the party. Suddenly he stopped and let out a long breath of relief. "They're here! They're here! At long last..." He was bending towards the light from the kitchen, the better to inspect the photographs – there were two light switches by the bathroom door and I could see a bulb hanging from the ceiling of the corridor, but nobody seemed to have thought of switching it on.

"What are they like?" Norris asked impatiently. His attention was riveted on the prints but there was no easing of the pressure of the gun against my temple. I wondered if I should take a chance and run, but decided against it.

"They don't seem to be *too* bad... There's one of the head which might have proved awkward. I'll give them to you in a minute."

Field had dropped the other prints on the floor and was going through the photographs of Catamaran's understudy for the second time, this time more thoroughly, examining each one in detail. Still, they hadn't switched on the light. At this stage, Vernon rose from the table in the kitchen and came down the corridor; he walked straight by us as if we weren't there, and we all moved to one side to let him through.

"We've got the photographs, Desmond," Norris said as he passed, but Vernon walked on in a defeated shuffle, seemingly unaware that he was being spoken to.

"Let him go," Field said ruthlessly, glancing quickly after the stooped figure. "He's washed up anyway." He turned his attention back to the prints and counted them. "...six, seven, eight. Did Hynes say how many shots were taken?"

"No. He just said a 'good few.' I didn't think it prudent to press him, and in any case, he probably wouldn't have known."

"I wonder if there are any missing. Or is this the lot?"

"Are they all there?" Norris turned to me.

"Don't *mind* that bastard!" Field said derisively. "I wouldn't believe the time of day from him."

"Count them." Norris said.

"I just did. Eight."

"No. Count them all. Those ones on the floor too."

Field bent and scooped up the scattered prints, thumbed through them, then looked up with a beatific smile which bordered on the satanic. "Thirty-six! Well, what do you know! Bingo! A full roll. All present and accounted for. It looks like the end of the road for you and your lady, I'm afraid, Samson. Doesn't it though? The photographs for the fire and the bog-hole for you two."

This time, there was no interruption from Norris, no effort to soothe Field's violent intentions.

"You can't expect us to believe that story now, about a letter waiting at the station for Potter! Only a complete idiot would have left a letter and neglected to put the photographs, the *evidence*, in with it. And whatever else you may be, you're not a complete idiot. In fact, you're too damn clever by half, too clever for your own good and too clever to leave walking around. You, Samson, are what I would call... a loose end."

I was scared almost witless. There was no way out. Norris's gun was boring into the side of my head and Field's was coming out of his pocket again. If I tried to tackle one of them, the other would surely get me; if I tried to make a run for the kitchen, they'd both get me. With a curious numb detachment, I hoped that Claire was, by now, well hidden or far away...

"Admit it, Samson; there is no letter." Norris said.

"Of course there isn't!" Field interrupted testily. "Look, Gilbert... if there was, he'd have left the photographs, right? Or at least a few of them! But they're all *here*! As for copies... forget it! It would take a day to have copies made – at *least* a day, if not longer – and if they'd got on to us a day ago, then we'd be in prison by now, wouldn't we? Come on. Let's get this over with. I don't like it any more than you do, but what the hell else can we do? Aye?"

I thought of trying to convince them that Potter really did have copies, that he had already been pointed in Norris's direction, but I knew it would be pointless – they wouldn't have believed me. Field would have had the inevitable answer: Why, if what I said was true, hadn't Potter come to interview Norris? In the end, I'd have to give the only answer that fitted: Because he only had circumstantial evidence. And that, in the end, wouldn't have made the slightest bit of difference to their plans for me.

"Now," I said in a smug voice which I hardly recognised as mine, "count the *negatives*." I don't know how, or from where, the thought came. My subconscious must have vaguely remembered Potter telling the photographer, some hours ago to come prepared, that the negatives were missing. Of course they were. Claire had taken them to Dublin to give to her editor. But that was weeks ago and I had all but forgotten.

Shaking inwardly, I imposed a superior smile on my unwilling features and held it grimly while Field pulled the celluloid strips from the wallet. He looked worried as he started to count.

"Seven. Seven strips."

"That's right," I nodded. "And there are four frames on each strip. No? Seven fours are twenty eight. Twenty eight negatives, thirty six prints. Where are the other eight? The eight negatives of the horse?" That stymied them. There was a sudden aura of doubt in the gloomy corridor. "If I were you I'd check to make sure that the two strips that are missing *are* the ones of Catamaran's stand-in. As you say, you can't trust me... I may be untrustworthy, gentlemen, but, I assure you, I'm not daft! They're with the letter I left for Potter, along with a menu from the Catamaran Rooms at the Riverbank Hotel. The difference is as clear as day. *They're* his evidence. If you don't believe me now, go ahead and shoot me. Add murder to what you've already clocked up."

"Jesus Christ!" Norris breathed, fear in his whisper. The gun at my head relayed the shaking of his hand, and I prayed hard to my newly-discovered Guardian Angel not to let it go off accidentally.

"Shut up, Gilbert!" Field shouted. "Let me think! It's *another* of his tricks!" But his outburst lacked conviction.

Norris heard the hoofbeats a split second before I did. He stiffened and cocked his head. They grew louder and louder until they drew abreast of, then shot by, the cottage. Norris's head turned, following the passage of the horse as if he could actually see him through the wall.

"Catamaran!" he said in disbelieving shock. '*The bogs!*" he cried, and, all else forgotten, legged it for the kitchen.

Field was no less affected. "The horse! The bitch has let out the fucking horse!" His voice was a croak, as if this was the last straw. As he still had his gun pressed hard into my rib-cage, I stood stock still, dreading his next move.

Suddenly the gun was gone. He took a few steps towards the kitchen, remembered me, stopped, and began to turn. I didn't see him complete the turn because I was already in the bathroom pushing the bolt of the door home with clammy, sweaty hands. A cord brushed against my cheek and I pulled it. With a click, the light came on.

CHAPTER 33

During the next few minutes there was chaos outside the door of my bathroom. Field ran from the kitchen to the corridor several times, calling to Norris, when he was in the kitchen, to come back and help recapture me and find Claire and, when he was outside the door, alternately pleading with me to open the door and threatening me with dire consequences if I didn't do so immediately.

"Come out of there at once, Samson!" he ordered, pounding at the door for the third time in half as many minutes.

"You've got to be *joking*!"

It was the first time I had answered him and I only did so to keep him talking. It had suddenly become clear to me that my only way out was going to be the window. At first I had planned to stay in the bathroom hoping that Field would follow the horse, *then* go out through the door, retrieve the gun or get another from the cabinet, and link up somehow with Claire. But in this, I had discounted Vernon as a threat, written him off. Now it dawned on me that the bathroom, far from being the refuge I thought it, could be a deadly trap. If Vernon woke up enough to stand guard in the corridor with a gun, while Field went round the back of the house to the bathroom window with another gun, then I was as good as dead. So I answered Field to keep him there.

"Samson!"

"What?" I took an almost empty shampoo bottle off a shelf over the bath. I would have to break the glass – apart from a narrow, hinged top flap, the window was fixed.

"I *know* you're in there…"

"How did you work that out?" If it wasn't so serious, it

would have been farcical. I uncapped the bottle and held it under the tap to give it more weight.

"So you'd better come out... *right now...*"

"Piss off!" I screwed the cap back on tightly and hefted it in my hand, eyeing the tough opaque glass of the window.

"I'll shoot!" He warned.

"Shoot away," I said, wondering if he was now wielding the shotgun; if he was, his threat could be dangerous.

"Fuck you!" There was a sharp report, a thunk of wood, and a little splintered area appeared in the door at about eye level, but the bullet didn't come through.

"Fuck you too!" I shouted defiantly and threw the bottle as hard as I could at the window.

The heavy glass shattered and fell out, leaving a jagged hole into the night. Pulling sharply on the light-cord, I plunged the room into darkness and rushed to the window.

"Samson! Samson!" Field hammered on the door, panicked as he realised what was happening. "The window! He's getting out the *window!*" I wondered, as I pushed out the remaining shards with a jacket-covered elbow, if he was talking to himself or whether, in fact, Vernon *had* re-entered the fray. As I put my leg over the sill, I heard the pounding of his feet, rushing into the kitchen, heading for the back of the house.

Seconds later and just seconds before Field arrived panting, I gained the sanctuary of the shrubbery and crouched in the pitch black barely daring to breathe. A matter of feet away, Field stood quietly, alert for any telltale sounds of my retreat out in the dark. I stayed as I was, frozen in immobility, trying to still the pounding of my heart. The only sound was Norris forlornly calling: 'Catamaran, Catamaran,' off in the distance.

What seemed like hours later, but in reality, was probably no more than a minute or two, Field's impatience began to simmer. Fanned by the repetitive plaintive cries of Norris out on the bogs to the south, he started shifting uneasily from one foot to the other – I could tell by the crunching of glass fragments; then suddenly, unable to contain his frustration, he roared: "Damn you Norris! Get back up here you stupid bastard! We can get the fucking horse in the morning!"

But Norris's cries went on unabated and Field eventually, muttering fierce oaths, left. Before leaving, he fired two shots wildly into the bathroom and there was a clamour of breaking glass mingled with the whining ricochet of the slugs as they bounced off tiles and enamel.

I waited for a long time after he had gone; there was always the danger that cunning might re-assert itself in his distraught mind, in which case, knowing that I couldn't have gone far in the interval between my escape through the window and his arrival outside it, he might be lurking silently somewhere near-by, waiting the tiniest sound to reveal my whereabouts.

While I waited, in an increasingly uncomfortable crouch, I tried to second-guess Claire. Would she have moved into the bushes up by the stables as soon as she had turned Catamaran loose, or would she have come back down to our original posi-tion opposite the door so that she could watch the results of her diversion? At first, I opted for the first choice – that she was up by the stables. Then I changed my mind. Catamaran had passed the house at a flat-out gallop and it didn't seem likely that he would do that, in the dark, unless there was someone chasing him. Simply released, he'd probably be content to sniff about investigating his surroundings, nibbling the odd bit of grass. Slowly, I stretched my right leg which was getting cramped.

If Claire *was* in hiding across from the door, and if Field had actually gone to fetch Norris back from his futile chase on the moors, then she would have seen him leave, but she still couldn't chance leaving cover to come looking for me because she'd be unaware of Vernon's whereabouts and, hav-ing no way of knowing that he was *hors de combat* – if indeed he was – she'd be forced to stay where she was or risk running into him.

A further, highly unlikely possibility suggested itself. Could she have actually ridden the horse? Been on board as he gal-loped past? The thought filled me with dread. I knew she was no horsewoman and the very *idea* of her trying to handle a highly-strung animal like Catamaran, at a flat-out gallop in pitch dark, strange terrain didn't even bear thinking about. Anyway, why would she have decided to ride him? She could get him to gallop by chasing him and, as she didn't know that her car had four flat tyres, she would never have been trying to ride him to summon help. Unless she had tried the car first...?

No. I fixed the idea firmly in my head that she was still on the premises, hiding in the bushes and probably, by this stage, petrified with fear. Having heard the three shots, she would have to conclude that I might be wounded or dead and that she could now be on her own, sole quarry of a murderous hunt. I wondered how long she'd give me before trying to make her way to the car and another worry cropped up: if she didn't know about the flat tyres, she would try to drive off and, once she started the engine, she'd give away her position and narrow down the field of search. I had to still her fears and warn her away from the car. Ignoring the possibility that Field, Vernon, or both, might be lurking nearby, listening intently for some tiny giveaway sound, I cupped my hands to my lips and shouted: "*I'm alright Claire! Don't go near the car! Stay where you are!*" The sound rang around in the woods in the still night, and, satisfied that she must have heard it, I crashed through the shrubbery out into the open and headed for the front of the house. I had to get as much distance as I could between me and the place where I had made my public announcement and I had to do it as quickly as possible before any hunters arrived. Relying on the darkness to hide me, or at least to make a snap shot difficult, I streaked across the forecourt and into the bushes where we had stopped when we first arrived. Claire wasn't there. At least, I couldn't see the white of her dress; I called her name, but so softly that it would be inaudible outside a range of about six feet. I listened for her answering whisper but none came. However, I did hear Field's voice out on the bog arguing with Norris to leave the horse and to come back to the house and find 'those two'. I couldn't judge how far away they were but it was a distinct comfort to know that they were, for the moment anyway, at a safe distance. I began to make my way towards the sheds.

Suddenly, I saw her. Diagonally across from me, a wraith-like figure, insubstantial, almost diaphanous, materialized from out of the dark wall of bushes; melting through it, it seemed to hover a couple of feet over ground level. The illusion was due to the fact that only the dress could be seen and it obviously contained something live; legless, armless and headless it pulsated in seeming levitation.

"Psssssst," I whispered loud enough to reach the apparition which promptly dematerialized back in through the leaf-wall at great speed.

Breaking cover, I rushed across the intervening space and found my ghost shaking and sobbing just inside the cover of the leaves. I held her tightly in my arms until the shaking subsided and she clung to me as if she was never going to let go.

"It's all over now! There, there, my love. We'll be safe now, I promise. They won't find us and they'll go away soon." Over and over, I whispered words of comfort and at last, she calmed down somewhat, but she didn't loosen her hold on me.

"Oh God, I thought you were dead."

"Shhh. Not so loud. Did you not hear me calling you?"

"I did; but I didn't know for sure if it was you or if they were trying to trick me." Probably, my voice had been muffled by the bushes making it slightly different, like someone trying to imitate it.

"Anyway, you saved my life and there's no argument about that. I was almost a goner. They found the photos in my pocket."

"Who got shot? Vernon?"

"Nobody has been shot. Those shots were just Field chancing his arm. He's gone off the head. Raving. Vernon is too, but in a different way; he seems to have collapsed completely. He's still in the house, as far as I know. You didn't see him come out, did you?"

"No. Just the other two; the two who arrived after you went in."

"We'd better stay quiet. I can't hear them talking on the bogs now."

For the next hour, Claire and I played the mice in a deadly game of cat and mouse amongst the bushes, moving as infrequently as possible and only at the onset of padding, surreptitious footsteps.

Early on, when our first move had brought us into a low dell with a shallow trough of soft mud in its lowest point, I smeared Claire's dress with the oozing, glutinous slime so that now she was as invisible as I was; though she protested at first and shuddered as I applied the black foetid goo front and back, she agreed with the wisdom of it and later, when one of them – we couldn't tell which – passed within a few feet of us, her camouflage was all that saved us from discovery.

Once or twice, at the start of the hide and seek we disturbed roosting parrots but my initial fear that their flapping and squawking would betray our position proved groundless because the alarm spread through the woods, from tree to tree, and soon, the whole place was a hum of vaguely complaining psittacines. It was both a blessing and a curse; it helped mask the inevitable tiny sounds of our movements and whispers but, on the other hand, it also made it harder for us to hear when someone was nearing our position.

As the night ground on relentlessly, the strain became almost unbearable and we held a whispered discussion. We both felt that our luck couldn't hold forever, that our chances of being found were increasing as their search became more and more methodical.

"If they get flashlights we're jiggered," I whispered, wondering why they hadn't.

"If they could have got flashlights, they would have been using them by now," Claire whispered back. Reasonable enough.

"You're right. Still, I think we ought to make a move."

"A move to where?"

"The lake. The one over that way," I pointed to the west.

"Which way?" she asked, missing the point in the dark.

"The one over at the back of the house. It's fairly narrow at this end and we could swim it and then just sit them out, out on the bogs."

We sat in total silence for a few minutes and, only when we were absolutely sure that there was nobody near us, did we begin our slow move towards the lake. Feeling our way carefully in the dark, we had covered only a short distance when all at once there was the sound of a car approaching. For one heady instant, I thought it might be Potter, then I knew that it couldn't be. He had no way in the world of tying in Vernon with Norris, apart from as a friend, no reason to suspect him of complicity in the crime. He didn't even know what the crime *was* and the two facts which had enabled me to make my belated deductions were unknown to him – the worms and the sunflower seeds. And anyhow, only a vet or a parasitologist could have worked out the worms angle.

We crouched low as the car approached, turned in the forecourt and stopped; the engine was left running, but, over its low hum, we could hear voices. It was hard at first to distinguish whose voices they were or what they said but there was no mistaking the urgency of their tones. Then we could plainly hear Field impatiently calling Vernon.

Moving much more quickly now, we edged forward towards the light, anxious to see what was happening. The lights grew brighter as we approached, and, finally, there was just one layer of leaves between us and the open space in front of the house. The car – Field's BMW – faced away from us but the headlights had been left on so we could see, in clear silhouette, everything that happened.

First there was only Field standing beside the car looking about him. It was impossible to tell from his stance what his frame of mind was but I could almost feel the tension and desperation which surrounded him like an aura. Alert as a cat, his gaze roved along the wall of leaves that surrounded the forecourt willing it to tell him where we were. Then suddenly he looked towards the house and moved to open the back door. Immediately, Norris came out leading Vernon by the elbow. Norris was talking to him, his voice so low that we could barely hear it, but it had a pleading, reassuring quality about it as if he was trying to make Vernon believe that everything was going to be alright. Together, they put Vernon into the back seat and his slumped, dejected figure promptly lay down (or fell over) and was lost to our view.

"Watch that Vernon doesn't sneak out of the car again!" I said urgently. "It could be a trick."

But nobody got out. Field, having closed the back door, went and sat behind the wheel; Norris went back into the house. A moment later, the kitchen light went out, Norris re-emerged, locked the door, and, crossing in front of the BMW, got in at the passenger side. That was it. Seconds later they were gone and Claire and I were alone in the darkness of Clashard. I reached for her and hugged her closely to me; breathing great breaths of relief, we stood arms around each other, listening to the fading sound of the receding car. In the quiet of the moor night, we could hear it for a long time, maybe for miles, and, not once did the engine noise falter, not once was its smooth purr of power interrupted. It just got fainter and fainter.

"Well," I said, still whispering from habit, "if anyone has got out again, they've had to jump from the moving car."

When we could hear the sound no more, we moved quickly towards the house. Hesitating long enough to grope for a stone in the herbaceous border, I smashed the window of the room opposite the bathroom, reached in, found the latch and climbed through. I felt my way to the door, into the corridor, and located the light switch by the bathroom door. The shotgun was still lying there. As I headed for the gun cabinet, I checked that it hadn't been unloaded. I chose another gun – a double barrel – loaded it, and put a box of cartridges into my pocket to replace those that Field had confiscated when he searched me.

Quickly, I went to the kitchen. I had seen briefly, on my previous visit, a key board fixed to the wall by the outside door. There were twelve hooks on it, three rows of four, and each, bar one, was occupied by keys in bunches or singly. All except the last one had labelled keyrings. I ran my hand along the rows; Feed Shed, Aviary I, Aviary II, Aviary III, Breeding Shed, Macaw Flight, Loose Box (Loose Box? If the key was here on the keyboard, then how had Claire managed to open the door?), Boat Shed, Garage (I lifted it from its hook), Tool Shed, Pump House, House Door (this one was empty), General. This last hook suspended a large bunch of keys on several interlocking rings that looked as difficult to disentangle as a Chinese puzzle; but the car key stood out clearly as it was the only one with a black plastic finger grip and it was also marked with the Ford logo. I took the whole bunch. There probably was a spare key for the front door as well amongst the bunch but it wasn't worth the time to find it and I went out the way I had come in.

"Any noises?" I asked Claire as I climbed through.

"Not a whisper, but I'm glad you're back all the same." She gave me a possessive hug which I couldn't return, being laden with guns.

"What now?" She asked, taking the smaller of the two shotguns.

"We head for Knockmore and try to get the cops to head them off."

"They'll be hours gone by the time we get there. They've let the air out of our tyres, remember?"

I held up the bunch of keys and rattled them. "We go there by red Cortina."

On the way to the sheds, I asked her how she had got the locked door of the loose box open.

"An iron fence-post. I worked it loose from the ground. It wasn't hard because the ground is as soft as butter. I used it to lever the hasp of the lock off the door jamb. That's why I was so long arranging the distraction. Surely you don't think it took me *that* long to think of letting the nag out?" In the dark, I could sense her smile.

"Claire, you're amazing! I'm not kidding! I was a goner. Another minute and that was it. I owe you one life." Then a thought struck me. "How long, in fact did it take you?"

"To get the door open? Ten minutes? I'm not sure. Why?"

"It can't have been silent work. Lots of noise, was there?"

She didn't answer for a moment, aware of what her answer would have to imply. "Well... yes... I suppose there was."

"And you had no way of knowing if one, both or all three of those cutthroats weren't sneaking up on you, attracted by the noise?"

Again, I could sense her little enigmatic smile. "Well I just had to do something..."

"Does this mean that we're engaged?"

She laughed. "You had the keys of my car in your pocket. I couldn't run!"

I drew her to me and kissed her tenderly on the mouth. "All I can say is thank you."

"You're welcome. It's good for the damsel in distress myth to get turned on its head every so often."

We found the garage, and rather than look for a light switch which would have left us brilliantly illuminated like fish in an aquarium in a dark room, felt our way up along the car. The plastic grip made the key easy to find by touch and I unlocked the door. When I opened it, the interior light came on. The red Cortina.

"I hope she starts now," Claire said.

"She will. If there's one thing that a man who lives six miles from the nearest house, at the end of a road with no traffic, and who has no telephone, will have, it's a reliable starter and battery. Hop in."

The red Cortina started first go. I gave Claire the gun and the box of cartridges. "In case they're waiting for us somewhere down the road and we've got to circle the wagons. You load and I'll fire."

"Do you think they will?"

"No. At least, I hope not."

They weren't, and twenty minutes later we pulled in at the police station in the main street of Knockmore.

"You know, Frank," she said as we walked to the door, "I've just remembered. I meant to give you those negatives today – I had them in my bag all ready to give them to you when I arrived, but when I saw what a mess you were in, they went clean out of my head."

Despite the warmth of the night, I shivered.

CHAPTER 34

Potter and his exhausted, smut-stained contingent arrived back from the fire some twenty minutes after Claire and I had intruded on the napping night-duty officer. He took one long look at us, blinked tiredly as if he wasn't sure that we really were there, and then put two and two together.

"Is that the red Cortina outside?"

I nodded.

"Whose?"

"Desmond Vernon's."

"*Vernon*?!" He gawked at me.

"*The parrot fellow*?!"

"That's the one."

"God Almighty! What's he got to do with all this? Vernon from Clashard out in the bogs?"

"The same man. We've had an eventful time since we last saw you."

"Maybe you'd better come into the office and tell me about it." He led the way and, before closing the door, called: "Could somebody please make some coffee?"

To say he was flabbergasted was an understatement. As the tale came out, bit by bit in chronological sequence, his attitude changed gradually from one of frank scepticism to a kind of punch-drunk, can't-believe-my-ears acceptance. But now it was no longer a matter of hypothesis; now there were facts, solid, irrefutable facts, eye witnesses' reports, a live Catamaran out on the moor, photos, a menu cover, no loose ends. But it was the doctor's involvement which capped it all for him, the last straw.

"Vincent Field! Nawwww... I can't believe it! Christ above,

sure I play golf with him most Sunday mornings! A fourball –
we both play off five!" He shook his head in sad disbelief; obviously it was almost unthinkable that a five handicap man could
possibly be involved in such goings on. I could see the sudden
grim set to Claire's mouth and I knew what she was thinking:
one law for the rich and one for the poor; one for the five
handicappers and one for the pitch and putt merchants. But
she held her peace, obviously making allowances for the
inspector's red-eyed exhaustion. I think that she had also been
impressed at the speed at which the duty officer had sent out
an all-cars alert as soon as we had told him our story, notwithstanding the prominence of the citizens involved.

"What have you done so far, Murray?" Potter asked when
the duty officer brought in the coffee on a stained and rusted
tray.

"Radioed our men in the squad-car and telephoned Galway,
Gort, Castlebar, Claremorris and Loughrea. I gave them Dr
Field's number, the BMW, not the Volvo. That's all so far, sir".

Potter looked at him as if he considered his actions somewhat peremptory and the officer, interpreting the look correctly, continued defensively: "Mrs Field has called three times
already tonight sir. The doctor left home after surgery for a
drink at 'The Beds' but she had to phone there because there
was an urgent call for him, and they told her that he'd already
left. Around nine. She hasn't seen or heard from him since. It
ties in with what they're saying, sir." He indicated us with the
least perceptible inclination of the head. Claire's grim look
returned; I suspect that she was thinking that, without corrob-
orating evidence, he would never have issued the alert, not on
our say-so alone; her new-found respect for the impartiality of
Irish justice took a nosedive back into the basement of her
cynicism.

"I'll have to speak to Thelma Field. Have you told her anything about this business?"

"No sir. She hasn't rung since they," another conspiratorial
nod, "came in". He acted as if he and Potter were speaking a
language that Claire and I didn't understand and were trying
not to let us know that they were talking about us. I didn't
know what the point of it all was.

After the conspiratorial officer had left, Potter phoned his wife and once more, pressed his boundless hospitality on us. Neither of them would hear of us trying to find a hotel and Fernditch was out because my locum, the *locum's* locum, had moved in there in the afternoon. The red Cortina was impounded so we opted to walk the half-mile to the house, while he went round to visit the unfortunate Mrs Field.

When he returned nearly an hour later, Claire and I had both showered and were being fed by the tirelessly hospitable Joan. I had put on the same clothes again but Claire's mud-smeared dress was totally unwearable and, while it churned round in the washing machine, Joan Potter had dug up a T-shirt-cum-nightdress belonged to her daughter and Claire now sat in the clinging, slightly-too-small, jersey garment; it stretched across her breasts and came almost halfway down her long bronzed thighs, and carried a picture of the Pink Panther in repose, eyes closed, nose giving rise to a long waving line of Zs which ascended towards a crescent moon.

"How's Thelma?" Joan asked anxiously as Potter opened the door – she had gone silent as soon as we heard his car pull into the driveway.

"Not too good, I'm afraid."

"Do you think I should go over?"

"No. She'll be alright. I waited until Jim and Doris came. They're going to stay the night."

"Should I ring her?"

"I wouldn't. She knows you're concerned. Leave it till morning."

"Oh God, it's awful. The poor woman."

There followed some sporadic, listless conversation, carried on in short, shocked, and often unfinished, sentences. Claire and I kept silent; there wasn't a lot we could say – we couldn't even *pretend* to be sympathetic, as the fugitives – *especially* Potter's golfing buddy – had, over the last few hours, being doing their damnedest to murder us. Then Potter got his second wind and became professional once more.

We went over the story again and again, fact by minute fact, detail by tiny detail. At last Claire asked to be excused and said goodnight; as she turned to close the door, her eyes locked onto mine for a few fleeting seconds, then she raised her hand briefly, said goodnight and went on out. After that I had trouble concentrating on Potter's questions – her look had spoken to my soul. It had said: 'I want you' and 'I wish we could be alone' and 'my body needs you'. My imagination took over, elbowing out any semblance of attention and Potter, who must have been knackered himself, soon gave up.

"You're tired Frank. We both are. Let's get some sleep." He stretched, and, through a prodigious yawn, suggested that we take it up again in the morning. He stood up, filled himself a glass of water from the tap and, carrying it carefully, crossed to the door. "Goodnight," he said, going out.

"Goodnight," I replied and headed for the sitting room where I was to make do as best I could on the sofa. Soon I was sinking towards a deep, deep sleep and, like the Pink Panther I dreamt of, sending ZZZs towards the ceiling. Sometime later my dream was interrupted. To force the analogy, my ZZZs became XXXs.

There was the gossamer touch of floating thistledown on my cheeks and lips and I moved my head away; but it came again at once, this time whispering softly. "Frank? Frank, are you asleep?"

I awoke slowly and unsurely, half-unwilling to respond to a dream about whispering, lip-brushing seedlings, wanting to get back to my dreams of the Pink Panther and the first thing I saw, lit softly by a street light somewhere outside the window, was the Pink Panther, in the flesh – or rather, the other way round; the flesh was in the Pink Panther. My eyes waveringly followed the wavy line of Zs up to the crescent moon and beyond passing the graceful line of the neck, the small determined chin, the gently smiling lips, the delicately sculpted nose and stopped when they met the smiling eyes of Claire.

"Are you awake?" she whispered softly, leaning down to touch me with another thistledown kiss.

"I am now. What's wrong? Can't you sleep?"

She smiled again. "Oh, I can sleep alright; the trick was to stay awake. I wanted to say goodnight to you properly, not..." she raised a hand in a repetition of the wave she'd given me earlier.

"That was the most erotic wave I've ever seen," I smiled, now fully awake, reaching out to put my arm round her and pulling her gently towards me. "So. Say goodnight in your proper way."

She came down to me, her hair falling on my cheeks, her mouth finding mine in a long passionate kiss. Suddenly, she pulled her head back a few inches and looked laughingly into my eyes.

"How's that?"

"That's it? A proper goodnight? It's great!"

"You didn't let me finish. I was going to say: How's that – for starters?"

"Oh very significant. Very meaningful. Does it mean you're proposing to me?"

Claire clasped a hand to her mouth to prevent a sudden giggle from leaking out into the silence of the sleeping house. "I didn't know it was a leap year," she said softly.

"See if you can find a pen, some paper, and a calculator, and we'll divide by four. Perhaps it is."

"Shh! You'll waken the house. I was thinking of a more silent type of proper goodnight."

"Right now, the only danger I see," I nibbled her earlobe, "is that, with all our talk, we might wake the Pink Panther. Do you not think," I whispered slowly, rubbing her cheek, "that it might be a wise move to put him on that chair over there by the door and let him continue his sleep while we... continue our conversation? Mmmmm?"

She looked down at me, smiling surmise in her lovely eyes.

"If he does wake up, he'll make an awful racket... De-dum, de-dah, de dah..." I hummed a few bars of the theme music.

She didn't reply; her eyes never left mine as she stood, walked to the chair and, with one smooth, breath-taking move, pulled the T-shirt over her head and dropped it. Heart pounding, mouth dry, I held out my hand towards her and, with the grace of a real panther, she came to me and lay by my side. As I was about to kiss her, she put a finger to my lips.

"Do you think we should, Frank? What about the Potters?"

"You picked a fine time for second thoughts! I'm sure

they'd be all for it but, if you like, I'll go up, knock them up, and ask them for their votes."

"Stop teasing!"

"Seriously, I'm sure they'd be all in favour – they're only human, after all. And did you ever wonder why they never managed to get their Paso Doble to championship standard?"

Before she could ask me about that one, I brought my mouth gently down on hers.

CHAPTER 35

Next morning, I set about helping Potter to compile his evidence. The obvious thing was to try to put a name to the horse I had shot, and find its previous owner; once he had that, Potter could trace the route by which the hapless animal had arrived at the bottom of a quarry in the west of County Galway, so badly battered that there was nothing else for it but to destroy him. As soon as offices were open I rang Bord na gCapall, The Irish Horse Board. One of my best friends at Veterinary School was now its Breeding Manager. "

Declan Forbes, please," I told the girl who answered.

"Whom shall I say is calling?"

"Frank Samson."

"Hold the line please," she sang. "I'll see if he's available".

"Thank you."

I waited and hoped that he was. He had an encyclopaedic knowledge of, and a consuming interest in all things equine. During our college days, while the rest of us, if put upon, would perform a song or two, do impressions of various staff-members, or re-enact in outrageous pantomime, famous or infamous incidents in the lives of our classmates, Declan's party-piece was to grab an empty Guinness bottle by the neck, hold it like a microphone, and, closing his eyes, begin, in a perfect impression of the voice of Peter O'Sullevan: "Good afternoon ladies and gentlemen and welcome to Presbury Park..." For the next twenty minutes he would do a full commentary on one of the Arkle/Millhouse Hennesey Gold Cups with hardly a pause for breath. In his Peter O'Sullevan voice he would break to announce that "we're going over to our man in the paddock for latest news of the betting" and then give all the betting changes in the voice of whoever the man in the paddock was. He would trot out all the data on all the horses (not just the two principals), their breeding, their owners, trainers, jockeys, form, handicaps. During the race itself, we were kept abreast of the position of all the horses; fallers were announced with the appropriate brief rise in tone, and, a few seconds later, another break in the commentary to announce that horse and rider (both by name again) were up and alright; when the field was going out of sight we would "go over to our country camera and Nigel" (Something or Other Double-Barrelled), with the appropriate voice change. The climactic last furlong could glue a whole pubful of people to their seats and would have the veins standing out on Declan's head and neck as Arkle and Millhouse fought it out, toiling their sweat-flecked way to the winning-post.

"Hey, Hair!" Declan came on the line. "How's it going?"

"Great, Dec. How's it going yourself?" 'Hair' had been my nickname at college. Samson. Hair. Hardly very original or ingenious.

"So-so. The usual. I've been wanting to have a chat with you – the man who shot Catamaran."

"You make me sound like Marshall Pat Garret."

"Who?"

"Marshall Pat Garret, the man who shot Billy the Kid."

"Fair dues to you. I'd hate to have been faced with it."

"You'd have done the same thing without blinking. You should have seen the poor bastard. It was the easiest decision ever. No choice."

"I heard. I was talking to Stephen Wall the other day." With a smile, I noted that Declan, now that he was a member of the establishment, so to speak, was on first name terms with the greats of our profession; to most general practitioners, apart from those who had actually graduated with him, he would always be Professor Wall.

"Dec. I need a favour with no questions asked. Can you help?"

"Well, unless you've changed, you're not going to ask me for anything that'll cost me my job. Shoot. What can I do for you?"

294

"Do you have a list of all the throughbred stallions in the country on your computer?"

"Sure. Every single one. Why?"

"What d'you mean "why"? You promised! No questions. What I need is a list of the stallions nearest to Catamaran in age, height and markings. Taking those three criteria in combination, that is."

I could feel the pregnant silence at the other end as Declan seethed to put two and two together but he stoutly confined himself to: "Catamaran had no markings."

"Who are you telling?" I laughed, a mirthless one. "What I mean is, stallions that are clean bays like him *and* are much the same height *and* much the same age."

"That's no problem, Frank. But I'm beginning to regret agreeing to no questions. It all sounds very mysterious."

"I'll tell you about it as soon as I can. And it is mysterious, believe me. Or at least, it was. How long should the check take? It's very important."

"Give me your number there. I'll phone you back in less than ten minutes."

He phoned in less than five.

"Hair?"

"Yes?"

"I don't know if it's good news or bad, but there aren't any in the category you want. I went two inches either side of his height, a year either side of his age and the only clean bay thoroughbred stallion in that bracket was Catamaran himself."

This took me aback somewhat; in fact, it stumped me. "Are you *sure*? Not even *one*?"

"Absolutely sure Frank. In case there was one that had died or been sold abroad or whatever, I went back over the past two years and – nothing. Zilch. If there was one, I'd have him for sure. I've got every thoroughbred stallion in the country on here, from Catamaran down to the most useless, from the most recently registered – say, going back three weeks – to the stars of yesteryear, the geriatrics who are now in retirement out at grass. Every one."

"What about stallions from abroad? Imported ones?"

"If they're throughbreds, they're in our computer. Whether

they arrived in Ireland by stork, plane or boat, it makes no difference – we'll have them on record." He waited for my next question and, when it didn't seem forthcoming, presently asked: "Does that help you at all, Hair? With whatever problem you've got?" he added, nudging. I could tell that he was itching to question me.

"It thickens the plot, Dec., but thanks all the same. I'll be on to you as soon as I can and I'll explain all. Right now, it's more or less sub judice – that is, provided I'm not barking up a wrong tree altogether. I must say that your news makes some more thinking necessary. How's Jo?"

"She's great – getting bigger and better every day."

"The baby's expected in November, right?"

"Early December. The fourth."

"Give her my love."

"Will do. No sign of you giving us the big day out yet? No prospective Mrs Hair in the wings? The world isn't heading for a population explosion of little Bristles?"

"You'd never know," I laughed. "Give me time. Tell me, are you still doing the Cheltenham Gold Cup thing?"

I could hear him smiling. "Only when I'm asked to."

"That's a relief!" There was a time when he would do it any time anywhere; he had once done it, sotto voce – but not very – during a particularly boring anatomy lecture on the course of the fifth cranial nerve or some such. "Listen, I've got to go. Talk to you soon and thanks again." Absentmindedly, I replaced the receiver.

Declan's news was a setback. Obviously more groundwork was called for, some fundamental reconsideration. Provided I wasn't totally off the mark. I decided to go for a walk, get some fresh air, clear the head.

I walked up a narrow side-road near Potter's house, up towards a hill encrusted in the gold of flowering gorse bushes. Bonzo, Potter's geriatric, retired police-dog, scraped arthritically along beside me. Deaf as a post, he had seen me go out the gate, and, struggling dutifully to his feet, had lumbered after me, pink tongue lolling happily. Now, he was leading me by a length and a half as we went up the hill. Useless ears erect from habit, nose sweeping the ground ahead like a mine-detector, he scraped along, his nails scuffing over the rough surface of the road. As we topped the rise, I reckoned if anywhere was going to banish mental cobwebs, then this was the spot.

In contrast to the unusually dry and warm weather of the previous few weeks, the morning was bracing. During the night there had been some rain, and the countryside had a clean, fresh-washed look about it. Along with the rain had come the first autumnal breeze, and this was still playing about the hill-top, dropping the temperature, singing in the telephone wires and causing an agitated rattling in the yellowing leaves of the young sycamores by the road. The sun was as bright as ever but here wasn't anything like the same heat from it and, low in the clear-washed sky, groups of small clouds bustled by at speed, dragging their dark shadows along the ground. When one of them passed over me, I shivered, and, hunching down into my anorak, squeezed my arms tighter against my sides.

Catamaran. I wondered whether he had been rounded up yet by the team which, the previous night, Potter had ordered to stand by for departure at first light. Catamaran would be alright. Then what about the other horse? The one who wouldn't be alright? Catamaran's understudy, the one which, according to Bord na gCapall's supposedly infallible computer, didn't exist. But he *did* exist, or at least *had* until I put paid to him. I had shot him, Professor Wall had autopsied him and Gilbert Norris had cried crocodile tears over his broken corpse. He had existed alright. No doubt there.

So how could Declan's computer have said that there wasn't a ringer for Catamaran? I had seen both horses and they were sufficiently alike to pass my not-inexperienced eye. I'd certainly have noticed any big discrepancy in either height or, notwithstanding Norris's blanket, colour. I would also have spotted any age difference (outside a year or so) as I had seen the ringer's teeth on two occasions – once when I put the bit in his mouth on Monday morning and, later that day, when he lay dying and slack-lipped at the foot of the cliff. I toyed briefly with the notion that the ringer might have been located and purchased abroad and then smuggled into Ireland but that would have involved a task of Herculean magnitude and I abandoned the idea, at least for the moment.

Perhaps the ringer had been got off the register by reporting him dead? But Declan had gone back two years and hadn't been able to find a match for Catamaran. Could the plan have been more than two years in the hatching? Unlikely. I put that suggestion on the back burner too, with the proviso that I would ask Declan if he could cross reference stallions by their owners' names. If the ringer *had*, by some chance, been reported dead more than two years ago, then it probably had actually been owned by one of the three conspirators. If it hadn't, they would have needed the collusion of its owner. Too complicated.

I dismissed outright a thought that the ringer might never have been on the register at all. Colts, if they are to be kept for breeding have to pass a very strict inspection by a panel of experts. If they don't pass, they must then, by law, be castrated. To think that the ringer might as a yearling have been kept entire and not presented for inspection was to presume that the plan was years old, hatched before Catamaran ever set foot on a racecourse!

I was being funnelled back to the inescapable conclusion that the ringer had to be an Irish horse. That was 99% sure. If that was so, then, because no ringer existed on computer, the ringer had to have been altered in some way to *make* him a ringer. That was another inescapable logical conclusion. Wryly I thought that I was beginning to think like Paul Markham spoke and for the umpteenth time wondered what the hell an iconoclast was. I'd have to look it up. I'd have to be able to *spell* it first. I shook my head. *How* could he have been altered?

I sat down on a large rock, shielded from the chilling wind by an even larger one. Bonzo watched me for a moment to make sure that I was settling – at least for a few minutes – and, having decided that I was, and that therefore, both his lying down and getting up again would be worth the hassle, he positioned himself over a comfortable spot, rotated creakily a couple of times, then collapsed like a stringless puppet, and promptly fell asleep. I furrowed my brow and got back to thinking.

The three criteria I had specified were age, height and colour. Of these, the first two were unalterable and anyway, Declan had allowed a very wide margin of variation for them. The ringer had to have matched age-wise and height-wise. Therefore I was left with colour. The ringer could not have been a clean bay. He had to have had some white on him somewhere, a patch which they had managed to hide. So far so good. QED.

So where would the white patch or patches be? The face or the legs, they were the only places I had ever seen white patches on a bay horse. QED again.

So how would they hide them? Dye? Would they chance dyeing a leg that was due to be immersed in water? If it washed off or changed colour weren't they done for? Dyeing a white patch on the face would be even more chancy – matching the colours exactly would be a tall order, failing to do so, a disaster... In the end I was almost ready to concede that with their customary thoroughness, they had indeed managed to make such a dye.

Almost as an afterthought I considered the only other colour one might find on a bay horse, flesh marks – pink areas of unpigmented skin on the muzzle. I reckoned that dyeing these would be out of the question as, every time the horse drank, he would wash off a little more of the dye. In no time the pink would be back through. The only way to remove flesh marks would be by surgery and even then... *surgery*!

Suddenly it was there! Plain as could be. The ringer had had a flesh mark which Field removed under local anaesthesia. He then repeated the operation on Catamaran, removing a similar area of skin! There was no need to have the wounds identical or even nearly so – I was not supposed to see Catamaran and neither Steele nor the groom would ever see the ringer. Nobody would ever be comparing the wounds! Convinced I was right, I jumped up, nudged Bonzo with my toe and we jogged briskly back down the hill to the house. I rang Declan again.

"Listen," I rushed, not giving him time to speak. "One more favour, a big one. Can you run that through again, the same parameters, only this time, allow a fleshmark. Is that possible?"

"Sure it is. But can it wait? I'm just on my way into a meeting of the Breeding Committee. Oh hell," he said, hearing my disappointment, "let them wait. It'll only take three minutes. You at the same number?"

"Yeah."

"Stand by for take off."

He rang before I had finished the coffee that Joan Potter had brought me. I nearly spilled it as I grabbed for the instrument. "Yes?"

"Hair?"

"Yes. Any luck?"

"Five."

"Five!" I hadn't expected that many – a feast or a famine.

"Five. Do you want them all?"

"Yes. No! Let me think. Wait a minute. Just the ones with the flesh mark confined to the upper lip."

There was a moment's semi-silence as he whispered his way down the list. "Two," he announced. "'Passarato' and a horse called 'Second Fiddle'. Never heard of him. Have you?"

"No," I answered, thinking that I had probably met him though – lying broken and dying in a quarry. It certainly couldn't have been Passarato – after Catamaran he was the second most famous stud horse in the country. "Who owns Second Fiddle?"

"Wait'll I see... Michael Halligan in Waterford owned him at last inspection but there's a COO on the file dated April 12th..."

"A what?"

"COO. Change of ownership. C for change, O for of, O for..."

"I thought you had a meeting! Stop messin' and get on with it!"

"Okay okay. A COO to a Desmond Vernon, Clashard, Knockmore-on-Sea, County Galway. Which, coincidentally just happens to be where Bally Ard is too!... What the hell is going on Frank?"

"Can't you guess?"

"I *am* guessing, but I don't believe it!"

"Believe it. I can't say more on the phone."

"Jesus Christ!" He breathed.

"Give my regards to the Breeding Committee," I said and

hung up.

Before going into the kitchen to join Joan Potter for the eggs and bacon which I could smell and hear sizzling, I phoned Bally Ard and asked a tearful Mrs Flahive if she could arrange for her son to go to Clashard to look after the birds. She had heard the rumours and found Norris absent when she went to Bally Ard in the morning, but she still couldn't believe it was true. I couldn't give her much help. I couldn't confirm the rumours and I couldn't say that they weren't true, which in effect, was confirmation in itself. Potter had warned me not to tell anyone anything – a man was innocent until proven guilty. Leaving Mrs Flahive as I had found her, I went to the kitchen.

Potter arrived a few moments later. He was driving Claire's car and brought in the overnight bag which he had found in the boot.

"Isn't she up yet?" He looked at the ceiling.

"The poor girl's had an awful night of it," Joan said defensively. "Out on the bogs, being chased around in the dark, and it must have been three o'clock this morning when she got to sleep!"

"You could add an hour on to that," said Potter, not looking at anyone in particular.

"Did they get Catamaran?" I changed the subject.

"No. There's still no sign of him, but it's big country up there."

"How about the fugitives?"

"Not yet. But there's a nationwide alert out for them."

"How's Thelma?" Joan asked.

"I didn't have time to call over. Maybe you'd drop by for a couple of minutes later on?"

Suddenly they were shaking their heads again, and going on with the I-can't-believe-it routine, making clicking noises with their tongues.

"The horse I shot was called Second Fiddle," I announced. "Aptly enough wouldn't you say?"

"How did you find that out?"

I told him. "He was bought in Waterford. By Vernon. Last April."

301

"Well Holy God! Would you believe it?" Potter swallowed a thoughtful mouthful of strong tea and, with his tongue, worked a wad of bread loose from between his gum and his cheek. "That seems to be that then, doesn't it? The missing link. Now all we need to know is what in the name of God they intended to do with Catamaran, a horse that's supposed to be dead. Ah well," he reached for another slice of bread, "no doubt that'll all have to wait until we catch them..."

After breakfast I took the bag up to Claire. She was still fast asleep, her rich brown hair cascading wildly over the pillow.

"Hey! Wake up Sleeping Beauty!" I whispered, bending to kiss her.

"What time is it?" she asked slowly, opening her eyes.

"Half ten."

She stretched sinuously, arching her neck, rotating her head and extending her arms to the limit behind her. The Pink Panther rippled and twisted as she moved.

"Go easy," I warned. "You'll wake the Pink Panther."

She stopped in mid-stretch and fixed me with a mock-cynical eye. "It's time for even the Pink Panther to be awake, so you can banish any considerate thoughts you may be entertaining about leaving him to rest undisturbed on a handy chair."

"I wouldn't dream of suggesting such a thing! I agree with you. It *is* high time for all panthers, pink or otherwise, to be awake. But this one's still asleep dammit! Suppose I were to stroke him gently under the chin for a few minutes...?"

"Frank!" she growled warningly.

"Just to wake him," I protested.

"We're going to have to put you on a course of Down Boy tablets!"

"Oh no! Not the tablets! *Please*, not the tablets! I was just kidding! Honest!" I kissed her again and straightened up. "Here's your case. Potter collected it and your car. The car's outside." I walked to the door. "Joan says there's lots of hot water if you want to soak in a bath rather than take a quick shower. See you down there."

I closed the door and went down the stairs thinking that Claire was getting more beautiful by the minute, and wondering when she was going to stop.

302

CHAPTER 36

"**S**o Field removed the telltale fleshmark from Second Fiddle's muzzle, a simple matter of stripping off the pink skin under mild sedation and local anaesthesia, and then duplicated the wound on the muzzle of Catamaran. It only had to be a reasonable approximation of the dimensions of the wound because neither horse was supposed to be seen by both vets; Steele was to treat Catamaran and never see Second Fiddle, and I was only supposed to see Second Fiddle and accept that he was, in fact, Catamaran. The fleshmark turned out to be a boon to them – there'd been so much made of the flesh-wound and the fact that it was sprayed purple. It was almost like a trade mark."

"Wow!" Claire said, digging her spoon into the cereal bowl which had long since given up snapping, crackling or, for that matter, popping. Since she had come downstairs, we had gone over the whole thing again, trying to figure out the last part – where Catamaran was bound for.

Joan Potter was more often out of the kitchen than not, as the telephone rang incessantly. The news was seeping along the grapevine and the press and media were in full cry, demanding information. Her conversations were brief and didn't go beyond variations on: "I'm sorry, he's not here."... "I don't really know." ... "No comment."... "Good day."

Once she came back and said: "That was your paper, Claire."

"Did you tell them I was here?"

"Not as such. Not right here. I said I knew you were about somewhere because they asked me. They asked me if it was true that you'd been in a shootout."

303

"What did you say?"

"No comment."

Claire laughed. "That'll shake them. But I'll have to phone in a story soon; if I got scooped on this, I'll never be forgiven. Never."

Five or six phonecalls later, it was my turn. "It's for you, Frank."

"For me? Declan Forbes, no doubt. He's the only one who's got this number." But it wasn't Declan. It was Lord Roscahill, one of the syndicate members.

He explained that, as the member of the syndicate nearest the scene of the... eh... the scene of the... incident, that is, as it were, eh... the other members had asked him to take over the rounding-up of Catamaran.

"Not really on, Samson. Eighty-three next June, you know."

"Oh, I see. Then it would be difficult," I answered, wondering whether to add 'Your Lordship' or 'M'Lud' or what the proper format was. I didn't get the chance to make a choice.

"I'd like you... Samson... if you would... to take over the business. I gather the police haven't yet succeeded in doing so?"

"Not unless they've done so in the last hour or so..."

"Well, with Norris... ah... ah... ah... absent," I couldn't tell whether he had a stutter or was just searching for a nice word for 'on the run', "...eh... he is likely to be absent for the ...f... f... foreseeable future" (stutter alright) "would you think...?"

"That's really not for me to say." It was the nearest thing I could think of which meant 'No comment' and didn't sound too curt.

"Of course. Sub you... you... you... judice and all that. Very proper. Put it this way, Samson. As his vet, with res... responsibility for his welfare, do you consider that it is in Ca... Ca... Catamaran's interests that I take over looking after him?"

"Yes I do." I was thinking that even an eighty-three year old peer knew that there was more than one way to skin a cat.

"Good. Then, will you do it? Supervise the row... row... rounding up? I might add that money is no object; for you or all the help you may need to... to... t... to hire and I shall send you my hell... hell... hell... ...icopter at once."

I thought for a second. With a helicopter and all the help I wanted, it shouldn't be an enormously difficult task. I had been planning on going off with Claire for a few days – we both needed the rest – but she was going to be busy writing her story and filing it, so this day was going to be a write-off anyway. Then there was the satisfaction of finishing off what I had started, and even the chance to realise a long-standing ambition – flying in a helicopter. Finally, there was the mention of money. The memory of letters from and meetings with my bank manager flooded back.

"I'd be delighted," I said.

"Good man! I must say that it will be a great comfort to know that, when he is rounded up, Catamaran will be under the soup... soup... soup... supervision of the best vet in the country!"

That was going a bit far, I thought. "Well, I'd hardly say..."

"Did you not raise him from the dead, Samson? Aye?"

"Point taken," I laughed.

"The hell... hell... helicopter will be there in about an ow... ow... ow... ...hour. Cooke, the pilot, will give you all the information you need to contact me as soon as you've been suck... suck... suck... successful. Thank you again, Samson. For all you've done. Be... Be... Be... Believe me, you won't find the members ungrateful or unappreciative. Goodbye and Good Luck."

"Thank you." I hung up and must confess to a small knot of avaricious wonder in my belly. I hadn't thought about rewards before, but now that the subject had come up, I couldn't help wondering what a group of eight multi-millionaires might consider a fitting way to prove that they weren't being ungrateful or unappreciative.

I went back to the kitchen and told Claire and Joan Potter that I was staying on to organise the round-up.

A few minutes later, Claire managed to get hold of Potter and got his permission to call in her story. She vanished back up to the spare room and was clacking away at the keys of Joan's portable Olivetti when I went to say goodbye before heading off on a borrowed bicycle to join the helicopter which had clattered in over the town, circled a few times, and finally set down on the football pitch of the local school.

CHAPTER 37

*T*he pilot introduced himself as Kevin Cooke as we lifted off into a blustery sky, watched by the entire staff and student body of the school, plus a sizeable section of the town's population. Seated wide-eyed in the plastic bubble, trying to hide my excitement, I watched the upturned faces below get ever smaller. The flimsy machine swayed alarmingly as it went straight up – more or less straight up – and I hoped I wasn't going to be sick. The queasy vertigo didn't pass until we picked up speed and began to move horizontally.

"Where to?" Kevin asked, turning to me. I noted his suppressed smile; presumably, he found my ill-concealed discomfort a laughing matter.

Deciding to forego speech for the moment, I pointed over my shoulder, and my discomfort became outright fear as he banked the machine in a tight turn. This placed him about three feet higher than me, and left me hanging in what suddenly seemed a very flimsy harness, the only thing preventing me from crashing through the fragile perspex and hurtling to the ground, spinning unnaturally zillions of feet below. I didn't dare grab anything to steady myself; in the narrow confines of the bubble, everything looked to have a vital purpose – with my luck, I'd surely grab the ejector-seat button (for the pilot's seat no doubt), the brakes, or the self-destruct knob. By the time I had convinced myself that it was most unlikely that a helicopter would have any such devices, we had straightened out onto a relatively even keel and were clattering towards the bogs and Clashard.

"First time up?" Kevin grinned.

I paused a moment before answering, as if I wasn't quite sure – nonchalant like. "Yes."

It didn't work. "Don't worry. Most people get a bit woozy the first time. You expect it to be like your regular jetliner to Majorca or Malta or wherever, but it's not. Not a bit, really."

"No it's not," I agreed wholeheartedly. "Have you been doing it for long?"

"Five years steady, earning my crust – mainly in the gulf and the North Sea. On and off for a couple of years before that. How far is this place?"

"Not long now – I think."

"But we *are* heading in the right direction?"

"We should see it as soon as we get over that hill. I'm pretty much a stranger in these parts myself, but, if it's not over this hill, it will definitely be beyond the next one. We can't miss it – it's the only thing out on the bogs for miles and miles." I was beginning to enjoy myself, grinning in marvelling delight as he pulled her up to clear an approaching hill.

For once, my sense of direction hadn't let me down, and, as we clattered over the summit and the far slope dropped precipitously away beneath us, we could see Clashard a few miles off to our left. Dark and abrupt on the immensity of the pale sedge-brown bogs, it was as obvious as a lump of coal on a fawn carpet.

We searched our way up to it, doing long zig-zags at about a hundred feet. Then we hovered over Clashard itself in case Catamaran, never having experienced real freedom before, might have returned to the security of man-made structures. We were trying to decide whether to land or not, when a uniformed garda came out onto the bridge and waved to us. It was a friendly wave, as opposed to a beckoning wave, so we waved back and continued our search out over the bogs to the west.

It took us an hour to locate him, and, by that time, I was beginning to worry. The terrain below was treacherous – hollows and tussocks, indistinguishable beneath a heather covering, soft quagmires lurking beneath deceptively green, grassy surfaces – the moor could be a dangerous place, even for the ponies which spent the whole summer roaming at will over it; for a total stranger, like Catamaran, it was fraught with all sorts of traps. I began to have visions of him, once day broke, and he could see that he was free, laying his ears back and taking off in a joyful gallop, assuming that ground was ground, just like the Curragh or Epsom or Longchamps, or his paddock, or all the training grounds and practice gallops he had ever been on – firm, level, pothole-free, almost manicured.

We found Catamaran in a narrow gully. He had located a herd of semi-wild Connemara ponies – all mares and foals as far as I could make out from the air. My fears had been groundless; not only had he not been injured, he was actually at work, and the unknown owner of a scrawny and creaking white pony mare was getting for free, what a mere forty highly-privileged owners had paid hundreds of thousands for in the just finished stud season.

"Whoooo-eeeee!" Kevin shouted. "Would you look at that! Nookie in the mountains!"

"Pull over to one side, out of range," I said, laughing. "We don't want to scare the mare at this delicate stage. If she suddenly took to her heels now…"

"Ouch!" Kevin made a face of exaggerated agony and the helicopter slid away from the bunch.

We landed on a reasonably firm patch some half mile away, and made our way back on foot. I carried a rope, which Kevin had in the chopper, fashioning it into a crude halter as I walked. I knew I was being overly sanguine but equally, I would have felt a right twit if I *had* managed to get a hand on his forelock and then had nothing to slip over his head. Catamaran, back on the ground now and dubiously sniffing a gorse bush, jerked up his head as soon as we broke the skyline, and, with a sharp snicker of alarm, immediately led his new-found family at a brisk canter out onto the open bog, and away to the north. We didn't even *try* to follow.

Clattering back to Knockmore to pick up some help, we passed over a man unhurriedly leading a grey pony across the bogs.

"I'll bet you a fiver, Frank, that that's a mare that your man below has in tow. And another fiver that she's on heat. Look. He's headed straight for where we landed. We pinpointed Catamaran for him."

"I hadn't thought of it, but I won't take you up on the bet." I gave a mirthful snort, shaking my head in disbelief.

"Galwaymen! Cute whores every one of them. They'd mind mice at a crossroads!" Kevin said.

"So it would seem."

"And the cute whores in the west are cuter whores than the cute whores in the east..."

"Where are you from yourself?"

"Galway!" he replied and bellowed with laughter.

Though I didn't know it, and wouldn't have believed it if you had told me, the flight back to Knockmore marked the end of the success-phase of the search for Catamaran – at least for several days. Mea culpa. I accept responsibility – but only for the first day's fiasco. I underestimated Catamaran's enjoyment of his freedom and his determination to hold on to it, and I didn't bring enough help with me to deprive him of it. After several short-lived efforts to drive him towards Clashard, the only place within miles where he could be cornered, we gave up. Each time, he would co-operate for a while, walking with his herd within the loose frame of the stretched-out human cordon; then, with a contemptuous toss of his lordly head, he would lead his family at a smart unstoppable trot through a gap and head back north to the point from which we had just carefully driven them.

But the next day was different. I had taken on another six helpers, which should have been more than enough. The ponymen, now numbering five, lent a hand. I ought to have known better; it was too much to expect them to be whole-hearted in their efforts at rounding up the famous sire before he had finished covering their mares.

The first drive ended in shambles when, as we neared Clashard, one of the pony-owning fifth columnists dropped on one knee to tie a shoelace while his accomplice immediately in front rushed forward to 'tell Jim something,' as he later (with almost credible shamefacedness) explained. It was enough for Catamaran; he had been looking around him worriedly for the past ten minutes, but now, seeing the welcome gap, he swerved suddenly towards it, the herd flowing after him, and thundered through. My apoplectic indignation was borne with innocent sheepishness.

Two hours later we were back to where we had been – within four hundred yards of the road and the bridge into Clashard. This time I watched the ponymen like a hawk, shouting warnings if I thought that there was any sabotage afoot. Some of the serious helpers were equally vigilant, but only those who didn't have friends or relatives amongst the ponymen. They had also become quite grumpy because, as the day wore on, clouds of midges rose from the heather and sedge and their torments were almost unbearable. Besides, they were on a fixed rate of twenty quid a man to round up the horse and, the sooner it was over and done with the better.

Scarcely daring to breathe, I watched Catamaran place a testing hoof on the rough surface of the road, not forty yards short of the bridge. He stopped and the unquestioning herd stopped with him. So did we. He looked about him, at the now almost solid wall of silent, watching men surrounding him on three sides. The road to the right was blocked, the way to the bog across the road was blocked and, behind him, half a dozen men cut off any retreat. Reluctantly, he turned towards the bridge, the only way open to him, and led the way across into the rhododendron-clad grounds of Clashard. We piled through the gates after him. Accelerating slightly, he moved up past the house towards the stables. It was only at this point that I felt I could relax; even if he went on past the stables, he would soon come to the back fence of Clashard and there we would corner him, halter him, lead him back to the safety of his stable and lock him in. Then I could leave Potter in charge, phone Lord Roscahill and take off with Claire for our longed-for break together. She had gone back to Dublin the night before and, as I followed the horses up towards the sheds, my mind was already thinking of pulling up outside her flat, not even caring if Paul Markham's Porsche was outside this time, running up the stairs two at a time, maybe even three, folding her in my arms...

Something was wrong. I heard one of the serious helpers moaning 'Oh shit!' and jerked my attention back in time to see Catamaran, at the head of the herd, streaking through a cut-out section of the back fence of Clashard, heading exuberantly, once more, for the wilderness. I sagged listlessly against a hairy granite boulder and watched with smouldering fury as the herd surged across the bogs. Catamaran, keeping his pace to what was an all-out gallop for the ponies and foals, only slackened off when he had led them free of the confining embrace of the diverging lakes.

Wearily I headed for the helicopter with two of the more honest helpers, leaving the saboteurs to their celebrations. The chopper could only carry four, three plus Kevin, and he'd be busy for the next hour or so ferrying in the posse. If I had my way, I'd have let most of them walk in the hope that the midges would eat them alive.

"What now?" Kevin asked as we took off.

"Tomorrow. It'll have to be tomorrow. We'd hardly get them rounded up before nightfall... Did you see where they stopped *this* time?! Farther away than ever! Right up beside the forestry! Anyway," I added grimly, "is there any point with that bunch of no-good bastards?"

After we landed, I went straight to the police station and stormed into Potter's office, emerging fifteen minutes later, somewhat mollified. Potter had promised to send out three gardai with Kevin, first trip in the morning, to supervise the drive. From a public phonebox, I called Lord Roscahill's number to report yet another failure and was lucky enough, yet again, to escape the embarrassment of having to tell him face to face; he was out, like yesterday, and his secretary promised to pass on the message.

While Kevin was away to collect the second-last load, Tom Kelly walked into the hotel bar, where I was having a calming beer. He had come as soon as he heard that Catamaran was alive and he was as fussy as an old hen about the plight of his beloved charge. His pale face went almost white when I told him that Catamaran had been covering nearly every pony mare in Connemara over the last two days. Even his brilliant red hair seemed to pale.

"I tell you, he'll come to me!" he insisted.

"Don't be too sure," I warned. "He's changed a lot since you saw him, Tom. He's been locked up in Clashard for a long, long time and now he's gone native and become a family man. Any experience he's had with men in the last few days won't have done anything to make him trust us."

"I tell you, he'll come to me!" he repeated dogmatically.

Consequently, when Kevin arrived back to the football field, Tom and I were waiting for him to go out for one last try. Tom had bought a blue plastic basin and a half-stone of oats.

"Blue is his favourite colour," he explained.

Kevin scratched his ear. "Bejasus now. Can you beat that?" he said quietly to himself.

Without actually touching the soft ground, Kevin left us at a point a little distant from the horses.

The ponymen were back on duty, each carefully watching to see that his mare was covered. Now there were only three; we had flown over two as we made our approach. They waved up at us as we passed over, cheekily and cheerfully, then they continued their way towards the road. Kevin, sensing the enraged disapproval of the red-headed groom, refrained from comment though I could tell that he was bursting to make some remark. I knew that he was on the side of the ponymen – he had helped as much as he could with the attempted round-ups but he found it hard to see any harm in Catamaran siring a crop of Connemara Pony Half-Bred foals. So, for that matter, did I and if it hadn't been for the constant danger posed by the treacherous unfamiliar terrain, I'd have been laughing openly too.

Under the close scrutiny of the knot of men who sat a little distance off, the groom and I approached the herd. Sending fierce scowls in the direction of the ponymen, Tom began his soft overtures to Catamaran. I stood well back. Talking soothingly and constantly, he edged towards the wary horse, inch by inch. Catamaran must have recognised him because he didn't take off at once; neither, on the other hand, did he come trotting up all full of welcomes. The blue plastic basin was also a great draw – having eaten nothing but dry sedge grass and woody heather for the past few days, the Pavlovian responses awakened by it were probably the main reason why he didn't run off. Nearer and nearer Tom went, never once ceasing his soothing murmuring. Neck fully extended, Catamaran sniffed at the basin in the outstretched hand. Gradually, Tom pulled the basin back. Catamaran's neck stretched until it could stretch no further and then, with only the slightest hesitation, he stepped forward a pace, coming almost within reach of Tom's free hand. The hand began to move, very very slowly, towards the horse and I found myself holding my breath. Just as pale, freckled hand and velvet, violet-tinged muzzle were about to meet, a low-sized black and white sheepdog darted past me and ran straight at the mares and foals. The commotion was instant – they scattered out of the path of the streaking animal and took to their heels, followed at once by Catamaran. He caught up to the main bunch in a few strides and, pushing through the field, as he had so often done on the track, he led them away towards the forestry a mile away.

In cold fury, Tom berated the ponymen, and I've never before heard such abusive and insulting language used in the second person plural. Two of the ponymen were profusely apologetic, the third said: "Moss! Come to heel, Moss! Yer a bad dog, Moss! Sit!" But his heart didn't seem to be in the scolding.

For his part, Moss sat, as ordered, and looked confused.

CHAPTER 38

*T*he next day there was no sign of Catamaran. I would have been in a right state except that the ponies had also vanished. So, even more tellingly, had their owners, and it wasn't hard to figure that the ponymen had taken them into the forestry so that they could carry on the business of enriching the bloodlines of Connemara ponies for generations to come, without interruption. We made several flights during the day, including sweeps over the forestry, a young plantation which stretched for miles in a straight line along the foot of the mountains. It wasn't until the last run, just before dusk, that we found them. The herd was back to its original size and the ponymen had left.

"What do you think, Frank?" Kevin asked, circling the busily grazing horses; they had had nothing to eat in the forestry – nothing grows under densely stocked conifers.

"Hardly much point in trying to get him now, I'd say. It'll be dark in another half-hour. Would you agree, Tom?"

"I suppose, after all he's been through already, another night out isn't going to make things any worse," Tom replied grudgingly. He still hadn't got over his outrage at the sabotage of his near miss, or the blasphemy of Catamaran being used on pony mares. "At least those ignorant bastards have gone," he added savagely. "I hope all their mares miscarry!" There was no consoling Tom.

"Head for home, Kevin. In the morning I'll get Potter to round up a crowd – a decent crowd this time – and we'll make sure we get it right."

Flying over Clashard, Kevin surreptitiously nudged my knee and, with a tiny nod, directed my attention towards the road. I craned my neck as he obligingly banked the helicopter and, in a moment, I saw it – a decrepit blue Land Rover with horsebox on tow, moving towards Clashard. Another pony-owner. Kevin grinned at me but neither of us had the heart to tell Tom.

As soon as we landed, I phoned Lord Roscahill's number and, once again, was in luck. I had just missed him but the secretary would pass on the message. As usual. The man never seemed to be at home. Then I went in search of Potter.

"No luck, Frank?"

"No luck. But at least he's back out on the bogs, in the open, and the local Breeder's Association seems to have called it a day – the usual lads anyway. There'll probably be a fleet of them queuing up again by morning; the first of them was on his way up the road as we came in."

"Old blue Land Rover? Grey horsebox?"

"That's the one. Have you been talking to Kevin?"

He shook his head. "That's Nick O'Beirne. He went through town an hour ago. In fact, he stopped to ask me if Catamaran was still loose."

"Christ!" I said, amazed. "Are you absolutely sure you can't stop these guys from bringing their mares?"

"How can I? The bogs are commonage. There's no trespass. For centuries all the townlands around have grazed their stock on them during the summer. The fact that Catamaran is out there doesn't alter that! In fact, if I was to look into it, *he's* probably trespassing because there's some old law which says that unless a farmer exercises his rights to the commonage by grazing it at least every third year, his right lapses by default. Needless to say, Bally Ard never uses the bogs, not with their type of livestock. And anyway, Norris is only a ninth owner, so the rights wouldn't extend to the other eight as they don't live in the area. It's Catamaran who's breaking the law!"

"So go out and arrest him," I grinned.

Potter grinned back.

"Seriously though, Peter, what if one of these local smart lads caught him and held him for ransom? It could happen y'know."

"I know. But first, they'd have to catch him, wouldn't they? And if you and your helicopter and your army of helpers and Tom Kelly aren't able to…" He shrugged, then went on: "But

315

if anyone has a chance of doing it on the sly, it'll be Nick O'Beirne. That fellow would have six different thoughts thought while you and I were struggling with one simple one. Six complicated ones too."

"Well then, what if he...?"

"Look Frank. If he catches your horse, he'll have him outside the door of the station here an hour later. I'd stake my life on that. He's as honest as they come."

"If he's so clever, how come it took him until now, three days later, to bring his mare?"

"The same thought struck me and I asked him."

"And...?"

"He said his mare wasn't rightly on season until today. He said that today is the second last day. Would that be right?"

"Indeed it is. That's when mares ovulate – the second last day of heat."

Potter promised to 'see what he could do' about getting together an honest team to help with the round-up the following morning. He would send three gardai out with Kevin at dawn, to prevent any more vanishing into the forestry, and that was about all he could do.

"By the way," I asked, turning in the door on my way out, "any news of Norris and the others?"

"Not really. I heard they phoned Norris's solicitor in Dublin, but he's refused to make any comment other than that he doesn't know where they are. Of course, I'm more or less out of it now. For the big time stuff, the powers that be have taken over."

"That's not really fair, is it?"

"Fair or not, I'm just as pleased. I know the three of them well –especially Vincent Field. I used to play a fourball with him every Sunday morning."

"I know. You told me. You both play off five."

I went back to the hotel, showered, changed, lay on the bed for ten minutes and went down to join Kevin and Tom for dinner.

That night, I almost got into trouble again. Trouble of a different kind.

Kevin had gone off on a date. It was beyond me how he had even managed to *meet* someone, let alone arrange a date, as he had been in the air or on the bogs every minute between sunrise and sunset since he had arrived in Knockmore. But, after dinner, he borrowed the Land Rover and left, whistling and reeking of aftershave.

Tom had gone out to Bally Ard to do some packing. He had arranged for a lift and decided to stay the night in his old quarters. I promised I'd collect him at five, while Kevin was ferrying the first load, the law, out to the bog.

"Be up!" I warned as he left.

"I'm always up by four-thirty," he replied, and I got the impression that he was implying that anyone who wasn't was a lazy slacker.

That left me on my own. I bought an evening paper in the foyer and went through to the bar to have a pint and a go at the crossword before heading for bed. I was half-way through the pint and about one twentieth of the way through the crossword when I became aware of a figure standing beside the table and looked up. 'Up' wasn't very far.

She was about five foot nothing, blond curls all over – just this side of an Afro, pretty face with a coquettish expression which didn't seem to be put on, and a voluptuous figure which, though I obviously had to leave a thorough study of it to a later surreptitious examination, was packed into a mauve silk blouse and turquoise dungarees. She was smiling widely at me. I smiled back.

"Having trouble then?" The accent was pure Coronation Street.

"Sorry?"

"Having trouble with crossword?"

"Not really. I've only started and I haven't been concentrating very hard."

"Let's have a look then." And she pulled out a chair and sat. "Now then." She settled herself and pulled the quartered paper over to half way between us. Wordlessly she put out her hand for the pen and I relinquished it. "Let's see." She began to read the few words I had already filled in, checking them against the clues and giving each one the thumbs up as she found it correct. While she was doing this, I was carrying out my surreptitious inspection – she could have been the one who had given Dolly Parton her body-building lessons.

"Twelve across is 'Hispanic'. Clue reads: 'His great fear is that he will be living under the French,' eight letters, blank blank S, blank A, blank blank blank. Hispanic. Alright?"

"Alright. Write it down." But she already had, and was moving on.

"That gives us 'A' as second letter of seven down," she continued in her broad Northern accent. I half-expected her to say 'Ee ba goom,' which was as silly of me as it would have been of her to be waiting for me to say 'Begorrahs and Bejabers'.

"Oooo! Saucy, this one! Seven down, nine letters, second letter 'A': 'Make the Italian take off her clothes before she washes them'. Well I never!" she said in mock horror. "Is this an *Irish* newspaper?!"

"Yes."

"Pretty red-blooded lot you, aren't you? Going by crosswords! There must be lots of fire in the Celtic veins!" She smiled at me teasingly, but I just gave a kind of simpering shrug and studied the paper. I could feel her looking at my bent head and I glanced up at her. She had only been waiting for the eye contact. "Aye?" Both her look and her smile were quizzical.

"So it has been rumoured," I grinned back at her. All the while I was uncomfortably aware of dainty, feminine, scalloped lace burgeoning softly against mauve silk, the fabrics moving against each other almost audibly as her bosom rose and fell with her breathing.

'Oh ho,' I thought to myself. 'Do I really want this to go the way it seems to be going?' The answer was an emphatic yes, followed at once by an equally emphatic elbow in the guts from my premature conscience – very premature; one would have expected any decent conscience to have waited until *after* its owner had transgressed. The conscience was in for a hiding if things carried on as they had started. I was smiling at her – it wasn't a leer, but there was a certain amount of suggestion in it, enough not to be ambiguous – and she was smiling at me, knowing where it was leading and not moving away from

318

it. The next sentences would probably go something like this: She (holding her gaze but putting a little bit of defiance or challenge into it): "Well is it just a rumour or is it true?" (Smile plus possible slight arching of the eyebrows). Me (gaze becoming harder, smile moving a notch or two leerwards) "Well there's only one way to find out, isn't there?" (Smile becoming almost cheeky grin, eyes dropping for quick, appreciative tour of body and returning to her eyes with even more defiance, more challenge)...

"Laundress," she said.

"What?" I said (suggestion vanishing from smile, meaningful look breaking up in confusion). Why was she telling me she was a laundress?

"Laundress. 'The' in Italian is 'La' and 'take off clothes' is 'undress' and put them together and you get 'Laundress' who washes them! Simple!"

"Write it down," I said, wondering if Claire didn't have a doppelganger lurking about somewhere.

I bought her a lager and me a pint and then two more and we finished the crossword. She did most of the solving, as I was, in equal parts, being distracted by the obvious perfection of her figure and with wondering what I'd have done if the conversation had gone as it had seemed to be going. Could I have betrayed Claire? So soon!? Wasn't that exactly how she had been hurt before? She deserved better than the 'what she doesn't know won't hurt her' school of thought. No way! No way would I have let her down. I soon got the opportunity to find out.

"So," I said, coming back with two more drinks and feeling all virtuous, "how long are you going to be around?" General stuff. Safe.

"I'm not really sure. I ought to be here while Monday. Here's to two fabulous black eyes," she said, smiling cosily across the rim of her lifted glass.

Automatically, I raised my pint in response. "Do you mean to tell me that you don't know when your holiday ends?"

"Holiday? This isn't holiday! I'm a working lass."

"Really? For some reason, I thought that you were on holiday. What do you work at?"

319

"Reporter."

"Oh." I hadn't meant it to show, but it must have. The ego took a sudden nosedive. All along I had been coasting along on the assumption that this very attractive woman had approached me because of my good looks and stayed because of my charm and wit and, though I had more or less decided not to do anything about it – because of Claire – I was definitely enjoying the ego trip. Now it turned out to be nothing more than a variation on the theme of paying for two salad sandwiches and a bowl of tepid, watery oxtail soup. She noticed.

"Hey! What's wrong with being reporter?" she asked, glass halfway to cupid's bow lips.

"Nothing's wrong with being reporter," I smiled, copying her accent and dropping the article. Some of my best friends are reporters. As they say." I should have added: 'Including the loved one,' but I didn't.

"I get it!" she smiled speculatively at me, raising her eyebrows. "I know! You think I've been chatting you up just to get some sort of story by sneaky route." She smiled again, this time broadly enough to produce two gorgeous dimples. "That's it, isn't it?"

"No. Nothing like that. Were you chatting me up?" I smiled again to cover the discomfort of being found out.

"Probably was, at that. I really have a thing about men who get involved in all these hair-raising adventures. Rugged types, you know."

"Pshawww!" I snorted in amusement. "If only you knew!"

"No 'Pshaww' about it. Shiners are dead giveaway."

"How do you know I didn't get these from walking into a door? Or from being beaten up by a little old lady for looking a second time at her handbag?"

"The story's out. I know it all already. So you see, I don't *have* to chat you up to find out what happened. I'm here to cover whatever happens *next*, and all chatting up in the world won't tell me that before it happens, now, will it?" The dimples returned.

"No, I suppose not." I laughed and my ego, having taken a compulsory count of eight, bounced back up off the canvas, fighting fit.

320

"You know, if you'd been alive last century, I'll bet you'd have been off discovering source of Nile or climbing Alps or summat like that. Born adventurer..."

"I'm afraid to go into Galway on my own!"

"Don't believe you!" She laughed. "I'll bet there's not much that you are afraid of." Suddenly the timbre of her voice got softer. Her eyes softened too. "If I told you that I was afraid to walk back to my hotel on my own, that there were some strange-looking characters following me around" – she smiled to show that she was just making it up – "I'm sure you wouldn't abandon me to my fate. You'd be there with me, scattering the pervs to left and right, hacking a path to safety for the damsel in distress. A real Sir Galahad..."

I looked at her sideways in a manner which asked her to pull the other one and smiled. "You've got me all wrong!" I laughed. "And I'll bet you always thought you were a great judge of character!" I nodded towards her nearly empty glass. "Would you like another one of these?"

"I'd love a nice coffee," she said, "but they don't serve coffee in this bar. Cheap joint!" She laughed. "Do they even give you a kettle and makings in your room?"

"No."

"I knew it! Cheap joint!" She repeated and then paused for a moment. "Well they do in my hotel. If you want to walk me along there to keep me safe and protect me... I could make us some coffee. Or tea. Or... whatever.." She smiled again and drained her glass.

"Well..." My ego, at this stage, had gained weight and, aided and abetted by imagination and hormones, was about to deliver the KO punch to my reeling resolve. I was now merely toying with it.

"Are you always so shy and reticent?"

She looked at me with exaggerated licentiousness and growled: "Only when there's no 'Z' in the month."

I laughed. The shattered vestiges of my resolve gave one last heave and it must have showed fleetingly in my face.

"What happened fire in veins of Celts?" She mocked gently, invitingly, caressingly. "I always thought that I'd inherited my fiery blood from my grandfather. He was Irish..."

"Really? What part?" (Last minute effort by my resolve to change the subject and steer me away from the brink of capitulation).

"Clare," she said unknowingly. "A place called Fanore in Clare."

The irony of it! Of all the thiry-two counties of Ireland, her grandfather had to pick County Clare to emigrate from!

"Actually, my fiancée's name is Claire," I said, promoting our romance slightly to an engagement.

"Oh!" the curly-headed reporter said, recognising at once that I wouldn't have mentioned it had I not wanted to back off. "Obviously, I didn't get full story, did I? I didn't realise that you were committed, not available." She smiled again. "I'm sorry," she said apologetically.

"So am I," I answered regretfully and very truthfully.

We continued our conversation in much less suggestive and personal vein for a while. I told her as much as I could think of about the Catamaran affair but, as she had already said, she knew it all before and she really *was* just waiting to see what the outcome would be. After a while two reporters who knew her came across to join us and I excused myself on the grounds that I had a four o'clock start in the morning, and left.

I took a short walk to clear my head before heading for bed and, on my way back through the foyer, I slowed my pace passing the door to the bar. The curly head saw me and she waved. I waved back and, worm that I am, spent a while picking through a postcard rack by the receptionist's desk, the idea being, I presume, that she might come out, spot me there and start her 'fire-in-the-veins' routine all over again. Then, having virtuously fought her off the first time, I could argue with my conscience (afterwards) that I had never suspected that she would start at it again, that I had been cleverly, unforseeably, wickedly seduced, that I was blameless, that I was innocent, that I had, to all intents and purposes, been raped. Anyway, she didn't come out, and, after five minutes of waiting, I entered the lift and virtuously pushed the button with 3 on it.

I lay on the bed and held a book in front of me but I wasn't reading; I was dreaming of dainty scalloped lace pushing out against mauve silk, but soon, without any trouble at all, I had eliminated the mauve silk.

Three times, I almost went back down to the bar and three times the Guardian Angel gave me the red light. What eventually decided me against doing so was the realisation that I didn't even know her name; and though I argued that a rose by any name at all would smell as sweet, it did seem to make the whole thing a bit animal. So I stayed put. Mr Goody Two-Shoes.

Claire phoned just before I dropped off, and, when she asked what was wrong, I said there was nothing wrong. Then she said that there was, she could tell, so I said that I was tired and slightly worried about getting Catamaran off the bog tomorrow. Then she said that she loved me and I replied that I loved her too and she asked me how much and I said this much. Then we hung up and Frank Samson, worm, slept fitfully (as befitted a worm) until the alarm-clock attacked his ears at 4.02 a.m.

CHAPTER 39

Bleary-eyed, I drove out to Bally Ard shortly after 4.30, hoping to catch Kelly still in bed, but he was up, and looked as though he had been for hours.

"How come you get up so early – even when there's no work to be done?"

"You get used to it when you've horses to feed and muck out and ride out. I like to get up at about sunrise," he said with what seemed to me to be more than a slight touch of sanctimoniousness, but maybe I was being over sensitive. "Anyway, you know the old saying: 'The early bird catches the worm'."

"That's all very well if you happen to be partial to worms," I said drily, turning into the first streets of the still slumbering Knockmore. "Look. The empty milk-bottles are still out! If it's before the milkman, it's too early."

"I'd've thought that you'd be an early bird too, mind you," he observed.

"Early enough. Between seven and half past, unless there's an urgent call; and in spring, as often as not, there is – calvings, lambings, prolapses, milk-fevers, tetanies... the lot. Anyway, it's often ten or eleven at night when I finish. Enough is enough." I remembered a friend of mine at college who had gone into practice on his own as soon as he had graduated; he had gone all out to make a name for himself, and a living. From five until eight every morning he did the routine small animal operations which had been admitted the day before, the spays, castrations, tumour removals etc.; then he worked a full day on the road, finishing about six thirty; from seven to nine, he held his clinic and after that he did his books. Then, he did his nut. After two years, he cracked up and had to take six months rest. He had done more work in those two years than I would do in four, but I was still going strong whereas he had burned out faster than a motor-biker's cigarette. You're better off pacing yourself.

We sat in the concrete shelter in the schoolyard. The morning was blustery and still held the chill of night. The sky behind the school was alive with light changes, but the sun had not yet climbed above the building, and we sat in cold shadow. I huddled down into my anorak and, after listening a while for the sound of the approaching helicopter, began to drift off into an uncomfortable doze.

"We better get him today," Tom said, "before the rain comes. The bogs will get soft inside a day."

I stirred and eyed the sky. Apart from a few small wisps of cloud, it was clear. "You think it's going to rain? The sky seems clear enough."

"It's not the sky, it's the dust. When you see it behaving like that – running around in little circles all over the place, it means it's going to rain. When the dust acts excited, the rain is on the way." He pronounced this with a kind of superior finality.

Vaguely I wondered about it – I had never heard that dust behavioural peculiarities could be used as a forecast for rain. Indeed I had never even heard that dust could 'behave'. Half asleep again, I wondered if Ted was an animist or animatist or whatever you call those people who believe that there are deities in all objects, animals, rocks, plants, water, earth, fire – and dust too, presumably. I wondered if there was a goddess of dust and, if so, what she was like, and if she ever wore mauve silk blouses... I awoke with a start and fixedly scrutinised a little eddy of dust which was acting excited, rushing hither and thither, twisting rapidly, rushing off somewhere else... and I wondered if the dust deity might not be a goddess at all, but a *god*, and if so if his name was Eddy...

The noise of the helicopter was just becoming audible when I came up with the answer to the dust business. In the west of Ireland, where the annual rainfall is about eighty inches, dry spells long enough for the soil to become dust are not very common, so, if you *do* have dust you're already overdue for rain; and when the dust is being blown about, it means that there's wind and when there's wind, especially from the west, that means that the chances are that it's pushing clouds, bloated with the evaporation of the Atlantic Gulf Stream, closer and closer to the coast, clouds, that, when their bellies rip open on the peaks of the mountains along the coast, will disgorge themselves over everything.

Feeling smug and scientific and of deductive mind, I led Kelly out to where the helicopter was rocking gently to its touchdown; running doubled up under the rotors, we climbed in.

"Do you guys get up for a few hours every day, whether it's fine or not," Kevin laughed in greeting as he sent the machine straight up.

"You were a long time on the first run," I remarked as we headed for the hill before Clashard.

"I was. I did a quick look round after I dropped off the fuzz... because Catamaran wasn't with the horses."

"What!" I exclaimed, icy-footed spiders running over my skin.

"Christ above man, what do you mean?" Tom shouted above the noise.

"He wasn't there. Just the horses on their own. The ponies."

"What about ponymen?" I asked anxiously.

"None, though that Land Rover we saw going up the road last night is still there, half-hidden in the shrubs near the gate. But there's no sign of the owner, a guy called Nick O'Beirne, one of the cops said. His mare is with the others alright – the same cop says he knows the mare because she keeps beating *his* mare at the shows every year – but there's no sign of your man at all."

"Are there any other mares besides Nick O'Beirne's? Any new ones?"

"I don't think so." He thought for a moment. "Maybe another guy came with a mare and managed to take Catamaran off into the forestry, alone with his mare, and they'll be back out in an hour or two."

I knew that that wouldn't be so and so did Tom.

"No," he said. "The other horses would have followed because Catamaran is their leader now. They'd go where he went. If they could," he added darkly.

"And if that's the way it was," I reasoned, "then O'Beirne has gone with this other man and he'd surely have taken his own mare along too, wouldn't he?"

"I suppose so," Kevin admitted. "Specially as he was first in the queue and all."

The three gardai were standing together a little way away from the ponies, long shadows attached to their feet. As we passed over the herd, I counted the ponies; there was only one extra – a grey mare; she was well-muscled and beautifully groomed and stood out amongst the shaggy mountainy animals almost as starkly as Catamaran had. She seemed a bit lost in the wilderness.

We touched down just long enough to let Tom off, in case Catamaran should suddenly show up, and immediately took off to search the bogs.

"A brown horse on a brown bog," I said. "That mightn't be too easy."

"I'll spot him," Kevin replied confidently. "It takes a while to get used to seeing things from this height, but I won't miss him."

"I'm glad to hear that. I think we should just fly around the ponies in a widening circle. If he is lying injured somewhere, the herd probably won't have moved far away from him. In fact, I'd have expected them to stay right with him – even if he was... dead. For a day or two anyway, they'd stay around."

"You think he might be dead?"

"No. As I said, the herd would stay with him. And that's what worries me. I think he's no longer here. I think he's gone."

"*Gone*?! Jesus! Gone where?" He glanced quickly at me.

I shrugged and continued to peer out my side.

"I was just wondering," Kevin said after we had been circling for a few minutes and were now more than a half-mile from the herd. "Maybe he went off on his own for a rest. After all the screwing he's been doing over the last few days, and all the bad grub he's been eating, maybe he's just tired out and taken a day off?"

"I doubt it. If he was tired, and he probably is by now, he'd just hang about with the other horses and give up screwing

327

until he felt up to it again. There's nobody forcing him."

We flew on in silence, searching the bogs below, losing hope as the circle widened. We were now well out of sight of the horses, even from the air.

"There! Below!" Kevin said suddenly as we passed over a tiny, gorse-covered hillock.

"Where? Is it Catamaran?" I asked urgently, craning my neck to see out his side.

"No. It's a pair of shoes."

"Horseshoes?"

"No. Men's shoes... There, you can just see them sticking out from under the furze... D'you see them?" He pivoted the helicopter around on its nose so that my side faced the hillock, and held it hovering. At last I saw them – two black boots, heels together pointing up; either they'd been propped up like that or somebody was still wearing them.

"I see them. Whoever's wearing them is lying under that bush. Can you land here?"

"Not right here because of the slope, but over there looks okay. Do you reckon it's the Land Rover guy, whatshisname?"

"Nick O'Beirne. Could be. Probably is."

"He wasn't moving, Frank. And he wasn't trying to hide from us either or he'd have pulled his feet in after him. Unless," he added grimly, "he thinks he's an ostrich." He landed, a bit bumpily.

"We better get over there as quickly as possible," I said, opening the door with one hand and grabbing the emergency bag I had kept in the helicopter since the round-up started, with the other.

Taking an ankle each, we gently pulled the dead weight out from under the low bush, stepping back and hauling carefully until the long, thin body was lying in the open. I dropped to my knees. The pulse was weak and thready and the respiratory rate slow. He had lost a lot of blood from a wound on his temple, almost identical to the wound I had received from the golf club. It had blackened and congealed all down the side of his face and neck, sticking his hair down. By contrast, the other side of his face was chalky white, cold and clammy to the touch. I took my stethoscope from the bag, opened his shirt and listened; the heartbeat was not strong but it was steady. As the human animal was pretty much a stranger to me in terms of physiology, I wasn't quite sure about his heart sounds, but they sounded a bit ropy to me.

"He needs a doctor pretty quickly," I said, jamming the stethoscope into my pocket, "we'd better carry him to the chopper."

It was hard going – the ground was rough and dotted with prickly gorse bushes, often without enough space between them to allow us to walk two abreast with the unconscious figure supported between us, and it was a good ten minutes before we managed to cover the short distance and manoeuvre the long loose limbs and torso into the back.

"It'll have to be Galway," Kevin said.

"That's right! I completely forgot. Knockmore's answer to Albert Schweitzer is on the run. How long will it take?"

"Thirty minutes. I'll radio ahead so they'll be set up for us. Anyway, even if the local GP was here, it'd probably be the same thing – he'd just send us on to Galway – so this way, we're saving time. Hang on there."

The chopper roared into the sky, engine protesting. At the sound, Nick O'Beirne's eyes fluttered open momentarily, then closed again.

Tom Kelly and the three gardaí were halfway along to where we had landed. As we shot at full speed over them, all the time gaining height, they stood still, looking up, and I could plainly see their panting chests and the mystified expressions on their faces. Having seen us land, they had obviously thought we had located the horse. Kevin waved down at them, then reached under his seat and pulled out a walkie-talkie set.

"Come in, come in," he said in a professional monotone.

"Where are you going?" the half-angry question came up to us.

"We've found Nick O'Beirne. He's badly injured and we're taking him to hospital in Galway. No sign of the horse. You guys stay on here and I'll be back as soon as I can. Good luck." Without waiting for further questions, he switched off the set and put it back under the seat. He turned at once to the regular radio, switched to the emergency frequency and advised them of the problem. They said to leave it with them, asked him his present position and what time he expected to be at the hospital, and signed off.

"Can't keep those boys talking too long," he remarked as we entered a long valley between two mountain ranges. "Just as well we got on to them when we did. Reception would be lousy in here. How's the patient?"

"The same. Holding his own. I think."

There was an ambulance waiting beside the landing pad as Kevin almost slammed the helicopter down. Within seconds Nick O'Beirne was being whisked the few hundred yards to the door with CASUALTY in large red letters over it.

"What do you want to do now?" Kevin asked as we stood by the helicopter looking across at the ambulance being unloaded.

"Have a cup of coffee?"

"I was hoping you'd say something like that." He grinned quickly, locked the helicopter and stretched luxuriously in the bright morning air.

In the hospital, I bought two cups of lousy coffee from a machine that didn't look as if it would entertain any complaints, and two soggy cheese sandwiches wrapped in clammy cling-film which reminded me of Nick O'Beirne's cheek, from a lady inside a tiny cubby-hole booth; she didn't look as if she'd accept any complaints either.

Twenty minutes later, Kevin went off to return to the search. Now it had become Potter's business again – Catamaran had probably been stolen and a citizen had been almost murdered by the persons who stole him. I opted to stay at the hospital in case Nick O'Beirne came to and could tell me anything. On my own, with time to think, I got depressed. I had spent days trying to capture the horse and failed. I was doing the job with the full co-operation of the owners and the police and I... correction... I was *supposed* to be doing the job, was *trying* to do the job, and I had failed. Then some fly-by-night rustler comes along during the dead of night and walks off with the horse.

No wonder I felt lousy.

CHAPTER 40

I **followed the** trolley with the still inert form on it, from the examination cubicle in Casualty, along a corridor where everyone's shoes squeaked, and into the service lift which was supposed to be for hospital personnel only. The orderlies looked at me as I squeezed in, but made no objections.

"How is he?" I asked, after the door had sighed closed and we had begun our ascent. The face had been cleaned and the head bandaged, and he looked as if, though still in the general vicinity, he had moved a step or two away from death's door.

"Are you a relative?"

"Not really. Just a very close friend," I lied. "Closer than a relative."

"What happened anyway?"

"I'm not quite sure. Do you think he'll come round soon?"

"Where did it happen? The accident or whatever?"

"Out on the bogs in Connemara. What did the doctors say?"

"He certainly walked into no door out on the bogs," he smirked.

"That's for sure," replied the one at the back of the lift, with a knowing grin; it was the first time he had said anything. In that fashion, my questions being parried, we arrived at the fourth floor, and squelched along the polished corridor, which, not being subjected to the wear of constant traffic, like in Casualty, actually sucked at my rubber-soled runners like the bogs on which I had lost Catamaran and found Nick O'Beirne. At the door leading to the Intensive Care Unit, I was firmly turned back – not even the orderlies could enter; they rang, waited, stated their business over an intercom, and handed over the trolley to two others who made a brief appearance in

331

the doorway, capped, gowned and masked. I retreated to a window alcove across the corridor, and settled down to await news of the patient.

I must have been a couple of hours there. I managed to buy a paper from a man with a trolley, who didn't seem to believe me when I told him I was a patient awaiting admission to ICU, and kept insisting that he was only allowed to sell newspapers to patients, as I handed him a pound and told him to keep the change. At one stage, a nurse came out and came over to me, but she obviously had done the same course in How To Give No Information as the first two orderlies, and, when she left, I was none the wiser about what was happening in the inner sanctum of ICU.

"You're the man who arrived with the patient in the helicopter?"

"Yes. How is he?"

"Could I have his full name and address please," she asked, totally ignoring my question and poising her pen over the clipboard she carried.

"I think he's Nick O'Beirne. How's he doing?"

"You *think*!? You mean you don't *know*?" She raised her pen away from the form.

"I never saw him before in my life. I just found him like that and brought him here. Is he coming round?"

"Then why are you waiting? If he's a complete stranger?"

"I need to talk to him as soon as possible. Do you think he'll be able to talk soon?"

"Are you with the police?"

"Sort of. As a consultant." I thought the word 'consultant' might work well in a hospital, open a few doors. "So when can I see him?"

"Then you can't tell me anything about," she looked down at her form, "next of kin, marital status, number of children if any, telephone – home and business, occupation, employer's name and address, home address, wife's maiden name, age, social security number, health insurance and if so, number of policy, family doctor, religion, name of religious pastor, or annual income?" She looked up hopefully. "Or previous medical history?" she added.

"No. I'm afraid not. Not one of them. Look, can you tell me if he's showing signs of regaining consciousness? Please... It's important." And I gave her my most winning smile.

"I don't know what I'm going to do about this." She looked disapprovingly at the offending form for a moment, then brightened. "I suppose we could treat him as an unidentified traffic accident victim – for the moment. I'll have to ask sister." Then she turned and vanished back in through the door, leaving me with my most winning smile still stuck foolishly on my face. I went back to the paper.

I had almost finished the crossword and was trying to figure out the solution to 'Yes, in France and Germany, the board may be of medium importance', in five letters, when I became aware of positive, proprietorial footsteps approaching along the corridor; looked up to see a man in a brown suit walking briskly, followed by two others in white coats. Without a pause, they passed into the ICU. When they came out I was waiting for them, almost blocking the door.

"Excuse me. Have you just been to see the patient with the head-wound who was brought in by helicopter earlier this morning?"

"May I enquire why you ask?"

"I found him and brought him in."

"But I gather that you don't even know who he is."

"That's true. I'm almost sure he's Nick O'Beirne and it's very important that I talk to him as soon as possible. It's police business and it's confidential." I had decided not to mention Catamaran because, by this stage, the whole country knew about Norris, Field and Vernon being involved, and, in his nearest hospital, I wasn't sure how many friends Dr Field might have amongst the staff, or to what extent they might be unwilling to assist in his capture. So I said it was confidential to avoid questions.

"Are you a garda?"

"I'm acting undercover. Believe me, if it wasn't so important that we find out as quickly as we can who attacked this man, or if we had any other way of doing so, I wouldn't have been sitting here for the last few hours."

"Do you have any identification?"

333

"No. I'm sorry. As I said, I'm undercover."

"It's all pretty irregular," he said. One of the young doctors behind him nodded sagely in agreement.

"Look," I said, sensing a chance. "If what I said isn't true and if I meant him any harm, I'd hardly have rushed him here in the first instance."

"I wasn't suggesting that you might be trying to *harm* him," he said sharply. He thought a bit more. "I don't know...," he mused to himself dubiously, weighing it up; the sycophant in the white coat behind him shook his head in sympathy with the great man's dilemma. Obviously, he wasn't just a yes-man – he could be a no-man, too, when the occasion arose. Adaptable chap.

"Well at least, it's good to know that he has improved," I said.

"How do you know that he has?" The consultant asked sharply. The toady looked affronted and raised a nasty eyebrow at me.

"Basic police-training deduction. If he hadn't, you'd just have told me that he couldn't talk with anyone, no matter *how* important it was. You'd have told me it was out of the question and sent me packing, no?"

That seemed to sway him. "Give him ten more minutes to get himself orientated and then you can talk briefly with him. Will they take long? Your questions?"

"No. I shouldn't think so. A few minutes, five at most."

"Very well then. As long as you don't overtax him. The sister will be on hand to keep an eye on you. I'll have her informed that you're to be admitted for a short visit." He turned to instruct one of his retinue, but the door was already swinging closed behind the toady.

"Thank you," I said humbly; consultant neurosurgeons like the favours they dispense to be properly appreciated.

I went back to the window-seat and wondered what sort of questions to ask Nick O'Beirne and what sort of answers I'd get and if it might lead me back on to the trail of Catamaran and if it didn't would Lord Roscahill and his syndicate decide not to show their gratitude in a fitting manner after all and how my bank manager was... In the middle of all the conjecture, I solved my remaining crossword clue. I wrote 'OUIJA' in the space for five down, left the paper on the window-ledge for someone else, went across to the door, and knocked.

In an anteroom, I donned cap and mask, and had a disposable paper gown wrapped around me. I pulled on a pair of plastic shoe and leg covers and went on into the quiet of ICU. The silence was cathedral-like, the only sounds being the bleeps and pips of electronic monitoring instruments, televising the vital ebbs and flows of the inmates, and an odd moan or hacking cough from one of the cubicles. Nick O'Beirne was in cubicle seven. He looked up as the door opened, his eyes every bit as aware and alert as my own.

"Hello there," I muffled through the mask. "How are you feeling?"

"Fine now, thanks. Bit of a headache, but otherwise O.K."

"I'm Frank Samson."

"The new vet, eh?"

"The *temporary* new vet. We haven't met, have we?"

"No; the cattle have been healthy for the last few months, touch wood. But I got a card from the office on Tuesday to say you'd be coming to do the TB and Brucellosis test next week."

"We can always put it off to another day. We're both a bit battered."

"Not unless you want to. If you're game, I'm on." He paused. "I believe I owe you my life. The sister here tells me you found me out on the bog above Clashard and brought me here by helicopter. Just my luck. I've always wanted a go in a helicopter and when I get it, I have to be asleep for the whole trip! Thanks anyway. Times may not be great, but I'd prefer to be alive."

"I'm afraid I'd have tripped over you and not seen you; you can thank the pilot – it was his sharp sight that saw your boots sticking out from the furze bushes. However you managed to get there. Are you up to talking about it? Would you mind if I asked you a few questions?"

He gave a sharp laugh. "As long as they're not damnfool questions about my next of kin and religion and all that, fire away. I've just spent ten minutes answering the most unbelievable rubbishy questions for that little nurse out there."

Suddenly, I felt much less guilty about my intended interrogation – if his medical attendants could browbeat him in the interests of bureaucracy, I thought that, in the far more noble interests of justice... I decided to extend the range of it and pursue any leads that looked likely. "What happened anyway, do you remember?"

"Oh, I remember alright. I presume you won't approve, but I took my mare up to the bog when I heard that Catamaran was loose. I'd have gone up earlier but she wasn't rightly on; I was hoping every day that you lads wouldn't capture him before she was covered."

"Was she covered?"

"I think so, but not until after dark. Anyway, I decided to wait the night in the Jeep, to make *sure* that she got covered the next morning. I thought I might manage to catch the horse too. I was going to hold the mare while he served her and then throw a lasso on him while he was still on her if you see what I mean."

"After he'd finished, no doubt," I grinned and then realised he could mistake the sentence for disapproval, as my grin was covered by the mask. However he caught it from my eyes and my tone, grinned back and said: "Of course!" I wondered why I hadn't thought of that; it was the one way to make sure that Catamaran would stay in one place.

"So," he went on, "I left the mare with the others, had the bit of grub I brought with me in case I'd have to spend the night, and went to sleep in the back of the Jeep. She was backed well into the bushes, into the Rosadiddilums, as I used to call them when I was a kid, just in case there was anybody trying to drive into Clashard at night – I didn't want to block the road. Anyway, at about three or a little after, I woke up because I could hear an engine coming up the road. Then I saw lights go by and this Toyota Hi-Ace pulled up at the gate, just a little beyond where I was. I opened the window and I could hear all these voices talking in a foreign language."

"Could you tell what language?"

"No. It wasn't French or German or Italian or Spanish – I don't speak any of them, but you know the way you can recognise them? I don't think I ever heard this language before. It sounded a bit rough to me. Anyway, there was a lot of door-closing and yap, like someone giving instructions, and then they set off out onto the bogs. I could see torches and very powerful lights which were probably car headlights being worked off a hand-held battery, the same as they use for lamping foxes and rabbits at night. Well, I was thinking that a bunch of foreigners on the bogs in the middle of the night were probably up to no good, so I decided to see what they were doing.

"It was nearly black dark – there's only a tiny moon these nights – but I couldn't use the torch because they'd see it. I could just about make out the number plate on the van because, lucky enough, the moon, small and all as it was, was shining on the back of the van. The number should be in my jacket pocket. Give the nurse a shout there and she might know where my clothes are. Did I have my jacket on when you brought me in?"

"Yes," I replied, rising and pushing the bell beside his bed.

"Then, unless they searched me, it should be there still. I couldn't see anything else in the van except a pack of cigarettes on the dashboard. It was a gold-coloured box with a strange brand name on it. Very foreign looking. I never saw the likes of it before."

"How come you were able to see the cigarette box and the writing if the moon was shining on the back of the van? Did the roof not shade the dashboard completely?"

"Oh it did alright, but I angled the wing-mirror to reflect the moonlight along the dashboard just to see if there was anything that might give me some idea of who they were."

"Smart move," I said with genuine respect, remembering Peter Potter's statement about Nick O'Beirne being able to think six thoughts while another man would be struggling with one; he had come up with a very acceptable plan for catching Catamaran single-handedly and he had improvised the most meagre resources to check the possibility of finding some way of identifying the mysterious visitors, from the contents of their locked dark van. He had also taken the van's number. Of course he had! Only a complete fool would have missed that one, I thought wryly.

"Anyhow, all I could make out were these cigarettes. Sorry

337

nurse," he broke off as the door opened, "but could you possibly try to find my jacket for me; I need something out of it."

"You're not allowed to smoke in here!" she said sternly, having obviously heard the word 'cigarettes'.

"Well now, I *know* that! I don't smoke anyhow. It's a bit of paper I need." When she had gone off, he continued: "Anyway, where was I?"

"Cigarettes."

"Oh yes. Well, there was no more to be learned from the van so I followed them out onto the bog, travelling slowly in the dark. Those bogs can be dangerous in the day, never mind the night, but they aren't too bad right now because of the long dry spell. I suppose it must have taken me a half an hour to get as near to them as I was intending to go and, by this time, they were all together and there was fierce commotion. At first there were lights all over the place like Will O' the Wisps but, by the time I got there, they'd come more or less together and the horses were in the middle. I lay down behind a rock to see what was going on, though I had a fair idea by then. They tightened in the circle of light until the horses were pushed together in a close knot in the middle. I could see your stallion in the bunch looking all worried and confused but he was blinded by the lights and kept turning around in circles. Suddenly, one of them threw a rope over his head, then another, and another, and I'm not sure if there wasn't a fourth. He went mad, lepping and bucking and squealing like a pig and started pulling like hell. Unfortunately, he pulled them down towards me and I was in two minds what to do. If I moved, I most likely wouldn't find more cover in the dark and they might spot me in the open and, if I stayed, they might be on top of me in a moment and it would be too late to move. When they were about a hundred yards off to the west, they managed to calm down Catamaran and I thought I was safe, but, however it happened, didn't one of the buggers just happen to shine a light straight on me! It must have been pointing towards me when he switched it on, because before that, any time a beam seemed to be swinging in my direction, I was damn quick to get my head out of sight. They saw me and there was an immediate hullabaloo. I ran, but I fell three times in as many yards.

Next minute there was a load of them on top of me and that's as much as I can remember."

"That's a lot. That number-plate should do it. You've been a great help and I hope your mare has a fine foal."

"Oh, she will. If she holds, she will. The breeding is in her – from her side anyway." We both laughed. "You've been through the wars yourself, I hear…"

"You can say that again! It hasn't been the easiest couple of weeks for the good guys, has it?" By the time the nurse came back with his jacket, I had told him the whole story.

I phoned Potter with as much as I had got from Nick O'Beirne. When I gave him the registration number, I had an uneasy feeling that he'd be thinking to himself how all this trouble could have been averted if I had managed to do the same for Vernon's red Cortina, but, if the thought did occur to him, he gave no sign of it. He asked me to stay put until he rang me back, in case there was anything else he needed to know from Nick; I said where would I go anyhow, gave him the number and hung up.

I waited by the phone for a long time. It was a pay phone in the corridor and nightied or pyjama-ed patients kept shuffling up to it, putting their few bob in the slot and talking for ages to their loved ones as if it might be the last time ever, which, on reflection, in view of the location and their circumstances, was not beyond the bounds of possibility. At last, worrying that Potter might have been trying to get through all the time and getting nothing but the engaged signal, I took my place in the queue and, when my turn came, faked a long conversation about Uncle Jimmy's rupture, the complications arising therefrom, and his fifty-fifty chance of pulling through – all of which had the people behind me enthralled. It kept the patients' patience from wearing thin and probably did no end of good therapeutically, as none of them could have had *half* the troubles which Uncle Jimmy had, and were, as a result, probably bucked up greatly. In the meantime, of course, I kept my finger on the little buttons and, when the phone suddenly rang while I was explaining about his *third* haemorrhage, several of them looked puzzled, but said nothing. I suppose they didn't want to cause any more annoyance to a man whose Uncle Jimmy was already going through hell on earth.

When Potter answered, I covered the mouthpiece. "Excuse me please; won't be long but this part is private." With sheepish, guilty looks, they dispersed and became absorbed in looking at holy pictures etc.

"Frank? Frank? Are you there?"

"Here. What news?"

"Oh, I thought we'd been cut off. First the reg. It belongs to a self drive firm operating from Shannon. They rented it yesterday to a group from the Eribuh Islands which landed an hour or two before, on a private Lear Jet. The pilot is Danish. He's been back and forth to the plane a few times so he doesn't seem to be with them. I asked Shannon to have him call me when he shows up next. They've no address for him."

"The Eribuhs? Aren't they in the Indian Ocean somewhere?"

"That's correct. I've looked it up. Seventeen islands spread over a few hundred square miles, all but two inhabited. They seem to have been ruled, at one stage or another, by all the European empire nations and by the Arabs – mainly to dislodge pirates who used to infest the area. The islands were dirt poor until two years after independence. In 1949, a small earthquake dislodged a slice off a mountain and uncovered the richest seam of diamonds in the world. Then offshore oil deposits, which were originally thought to be small and unworkable, turned out to be vast and easily recoverable with developing technology. There's half a million locals but two million foreigners work in the oil fields. Water is their main problem; they keep digging artesian wells but all they ever come up with is oil, and there's more grass on my front lawn than there is in the whole blessed country. The ruler is a king and the government consists of all his sons, that's thirteen or fourteen – I couldn't swear – each of whom is minister for something or other. Apart from the ruling family there are lots of very wealthy men, minor nobles and the like, or cousins of the rulers."

"My my! Who's been doing his homework? Now. Who owns the plane?"

"I don't know. It's registered to a Cayman Islands company,

340

but who the ultimate owner of that company is will take a while to trace. Unless, of course, the pilot knows. That's the main thing I want to ask him. I also want to ask him if he knows anything about the reason for the trip. The clerk in the car-hire firm thought that there was something about a trout fishing trip, believe it or not!"

I laughed. "I can see how trout fishing would be a big thing in The Eribuhs. Just drop a worm on a thousand foot line down an artesian well and haul 'em in."

"The other thing is that Norris and his mates have turned themselves in in Dublin. Without Prejudice, if you please."

"Without prejudice, my ass! Anything from them?"

"No. And I wouldn't bank on it, either. They're surrounded by an army of hot-shot lawyers and God knows how long it'll be before we even get to *talk* to them."

"Catamaran might be gone by then. To The Eribuhs, I presume."

"I know. We'll have to keep after him independently of them."

"Is this jet big enough to take a horse?"

"Don't know, but I'll check. I've put an impediment of departure on it, so, even if they do get him aboard, they won't be allowed to take off. The pilot asked for the plane to be fuelled and, by the amount he ordered, he must be almost empty. So Shannon tells me anyway. But the plane hasn't been fuelled yet and I've told them not to, so he can't take off at all, with or without permission. He's grounded. No juice."

"Good. Is there anything else you want me to ask Nick?"

"I don't think so. How is he, by the way?"

"He'll live. He seems pretty O.K. to me."

"Tell him I was asking for him and keep in touch. How're you going to get back to Knockmore?"

"Bus it, I suppose. There's one at one-thirty. See you then."

"Right so."

When I hung up, there was a scramble for the phone, those without crutches having a distinct advantage.

I went down to the ground floor and bought a cup of tepid, weak tea; it wasn't quite as bad as the coffee. I sat in a corner and tried to get my deductive facilities going again; they had

341

lain dormant for the last few days while I dealt with the totally non-abstract business of trying to round up Catamaran.

It didn't require Holmesian deduction to work out that the man who was going to buy Catamaran was from The Eribuhs and that he was vastly wealthy. But, from what Potter had said, most of the citizens of those islands fell into that category, having, as it were, to beat a hasty retreat for the high ground nearly every time they stuck a spade into the soil. Now it became a matter of narrowing down the field. I took another sip of tea and grimaced.

What would a wealthy businessman do with a priceless stallion who was also hot? Sell him on? If so, he would have to have a client lined up already, as Catamaran wasn't the sort of proposition that anyone would get involved in on spec, in the hope of making a quick profit. He could just as easily remain on someone's hands. I decided that it was pretty immaterial whether there was a middleman or not; in the end, there had to be a Mr Big who was fully aware of what was going on and may even have orchestrated the whole affair and there was no reason *not* to assume that that person was an Eribuhean billionaire.

Next step. What did he want him for? The only thing I could think of that you could possibly use a horse for were, as a pet; to ride for pleasure; to look at; to plough with; to pull loads with; to race; to breed from; or to eat. The only one of these that made sense was the last but one. At a pinch, Catamaran might have been intended for racing but it was hardly likely, as he was getting on and had been too long out of training. So I was left with breeding. And that meant that the wealthy Eribuhean was already into horses in a big way – it was unthinkable that a casual dabbler would get involved in such a heavy outlay for breeding on indifferent mares. That was my limiting factor – a wealthy Eribuhean who was also involved in thoroughbreds in a major way - and the right man to ask about that was Declan Forbes. Checking the change in my pocket, I made for the phone again.

CHAPTER 41

*T*he public phone on the ground floor didn't smell as much of ether, carbolic or hospital, but it didn't work as well either – somebody had unscrewed the mouthpiece and broken it putting it back. When I got through to Bord na gCapall, I could hear the professional voice of the switchboard operator at the other end but she could hardly hear me, and I had to repeat the name several times before she got it. I ended up shouting, Declan Forbes! Declan Forbes! so loud that all conversation in the waiting area ceased and people began to settle back to listen. When Declan came on I shouted at him to call me back on the number on the fourth floor which, luckily, I remembered, consisting as it did of five sevens and a three. I remembered looking at it and wishing I was playing poker. As I slammed the phone down and raced for the lift, the people waiting had a cheated look about them.

It must have been meal time or doctors' rounds because there was nobody at the phone when I arrived. In a few moments it rang.

"Declan?"

"Hiya, Hair. That's a much better line."

"Different phone. Listen..."

"Have you rounded up Catamaran yet?"

"No, and that's why I'm calling."

"What's the problem?"

"Catamaran. I didn't manage to round him up but *somebody* did – last night. He's gone, Dec."

"*Gone*!? Gone where?"

"I don't know. Gone off the bog. When we went out at first light this morning, he wasn't there..."

343

"Holy Hell, Frank! How could you lose him?"

"I did. Listen... Can you tell me if there are many Eribuheans involved in the bloodstock industry, I mean in a biggish way."

"Many what?"

"Eribuheans. People from The Eribuh Islands."

"The people of The Eribuhs are called Tiarmi, Frank."

"Tiarmi? What's Tiarmi got to do with Eribuh?"

"I don't know. What has 'Dutch' got to do with Holland or the Netherlands?"

"I get the point. Personally, I've never been able to understand why, if the people of Poland are called Poles, the people of Holland can't be called Holes," – Declan awarded the old schoolboy conundrum a dutiful guffaw – "but, to get back to my original question, are there many *Tiarmi* in breeding in a big way?"

"A few. Why do you ask?"

"Tell you later. Who are they, do you know?"

"Well, as I said, there are a few, but only one who's involved in a *really* big way."

"Who's that?"

"Prince Alaramos. Known to his friends as Al. He's their Minister for Sport and Recreation. His father is the king. He's a member of the syndicate. The prince, not the father."

"The Catamaran syndicate?"

"Yes."

"I don't remember any name like that on the list of members," I said, thinking back to the menu.

"Actually, the share is held in the name of Spanish Park Stud but it's the same thing. He owns *it* – along with a dozen or so others here and there around the world. Would you like to tell me what exactly is going on?"

"I'm not quite sure myself," I replied, at first hedging but then deciding to tell him as much as I knew, or thought I knew. I told him Nick's story and about Potter's investigations into the number of the rented minibus and let him do the deducing himself. After I had finished, there was a long silence from the other end.

"You know," he said at last, in a forced casual tone, "it's

344

strange that you should ask about Prince Alaramos today of all days..."

"Why?"

"Because I've just had a phonecall from the boss, our chairman. The prince is flying in this afternoon to go racing at the Curragh. I have to go down there and join him, to cater for his every little need. I always get that job when there's an important breeder in town and it's screwed up my schedule."

"His visit is unexpected then?"

"Most. All the big names arrive for the classics – I get distracted running from one to the other on Derby day or for the Oaks – but today is just a Mickey Mouse meet – only a couple of thousand for the feature race."

"Maybe he's coming over to buy?..."

"You're not the only one to think that! Word is out already that he's on his way, and half the owners with anything at all to sell are going round with a look on their faces of mercenary bordering on avarice. But I very much doubt it."

"Why?"

"He rarely, if ever, does his own buying. He's a good judge of a horse but he nearly always gets middlemen to act for him. Buyers know that he'll get what he wants, so, if they know that it's for him, the price quadruples. Filthy rich he may be, but stupid he's not."

Prince Alaramos began to look more and more like Mr Big every moment.

"What does your duty to the prince involve?"

"Just being with him. I join his party at the course, stay with him till the end and then we usually have dinner afterwards. He's a genial host. I know him pretty well at this stage; we're on first name terms – he calls me Declan and I call him Your Highness."

"Heh! Well, anyway, if you're thinking what I'm thinking, then maybe you could pay extra attention to your duty today and stick to your man like a poultice – you know, go to the loo with him and all that kind of stuff."

"Well... within reason."

"If anything's going to happen today, it's going to happen at the Curragh because I imagine that HRH will want to be directing the traffic personally – he'd hardly have come over otherwise. Wouldn't you think that Spanish Park would be a quieter place?"

"Jimmy Farnley manages Spanish Park and he's as straight as a die. Maybe that's why."

"Maybe that's it."

"What are you going to do, Hair?"

"I haven't really thought that far ahead. Probably go to the races – take the afternoon off, like! So I may see you there."

"Okay." There was a pause. "D'you know, I've just thought of something this minute. Last year, or early this year – I'm not sure which and it doesn't matter anyway – the word was about that the prince was trying to buy out four of the other share-holders…"

"Which four?"

"Any four. It didn't matter. What he wanted was a controlling interest in Catamaran, which would have given him the voting power to decide where he'd stand at stud. I presume that he would have whisked him off to his stud in The Eribuhs – he's got this enormous, incredible, controlled-environment stud there; I've been in it and it's the size of ten airplane hangars, all air-conditioned. Outside, the temperatures are up to nine million in the shade but inside, it's a morning's Mayfly dapping on Lough Corrib. Anyway, true or false, the story went that he offered the first four who'd sell to him a fantastic price, the idea being to cause a panic, because, if he succeeded, the other four shares would have fallen drastically."

"Why?"

"Because the horse's value would fall!"

"Why again? I don't understand this business."

"First of all, because sending a mare to The Eribuhs would be a long, expensive and dangerous journey; secondly, keeping a mare there would be very expensive because of all that controlled-environment stuff; thirdly, his brother, Prince Something-or-other is the Minister for Agriculture who has the power to allow or refuse animals entry into The Eribuhs. Also, I'd say that the cost of insuring him would have gone up a lot."

"Why should he want him in The Eribuhs so badly? This bad, like?"

"To breed to his own mares. He's got a lot of very useful mares there right now, as good a bunch as there is in one place together anywhere in the world."

"Why not bring his mares to Ireland and save all the hassle? He must have lots of room at Spanish Park."

"It's not that easy. Each owner is allowed to send only two mares to Catamaran and even *they* have to be vetted by the other members, to see that they're of sufficiently good breeding and pedigree to warrant the nomination. The other nominations come from other breeders. If Alaramos got the controlling interest, he could change that rule – I heard that he wanted five mares per member at the outset but, as he was the only one with five mares actually good enough for Catamaran, the others turned it down. My guess is that, at the moment, he could have up to twenty mares good enough, and maybe he has more. In the past three or four years, he's gone into breeding in a huge way, all computerised etcetera."

"That all fits in nicely with what we've been thinking, Dec. Listen, I'd better start arranging to get to the Curragh, so I'll see you there... Needless to say, you don't know me from Adam."

"Of course. See you later."

"By the way, did you happen to hear how many members were willing to sell to him?"

"One contact told me two and another said three, but then it all died down. The syndicate was scared but, apart from those two, or three, they stuck together. When he couldn't get the majority he needed, the Prince withdrew his offer."

"Did you hear who they were?"

"I heard first that it was Norris and Cuthbertson, the brewery man, but my second contact said it was Norris, Samuelson and Georgie Karyanikis. So take your pick."

"At least both lists had Norris."

"I'd say that that's correct. He's not in the same league as the others in any way. He sold all his mares and, I believe, mortgaged Bally Ard to the hilt. And I still don't know how that got him enough to buy in. I mean you're talking *millions*."

"Perhaps it didn't. That's probably where Field and Vernon come in – as extra backers."

"I never heard of either of them before but you may be right. They'd have to keep it quiet because the syndicate frowned on mini-syndicates as members. Too complicated and can lead to trouble at voting time etc."

"I can see that. How it could. Okay, see you later." I hung up, feeling that it had to be right. It all fitted.

There was no doubt now in my mind that the prince from The Eribuhs was the man behind it all. As I went off in search of more change to phone Potter, I tried to work out the sequence of events that had led up to the whole elaborate charade.

I started by assuming that Norris was feeling the financial strain of his investment and, when the prince's offer to buy at an inflated price came up, he had to jump at it. When it fell through, he must have been disappointed, to put it mildly. He could, of course, have offered to sell his share at face value but that wasn't the same as getting the much bigger price which he had first been offered. Perhaps it might even have been a loss-maker because, with interest rates etc...

Having almost tasted the big money and then having seen it whisked away, must have whetted his appetite to get out from under his debts. At that stage, he would have begun to dream of some way to get the deal back on course and what he had come up with had been almost foolproof. It would also have been more lucrative. Much more.

If Alaramos had been willing to buy out four shares at an inflated price, then all Norris had to do was offer him *all* of Catamaran at a *fraction* of that – say for the price of two shares or three. As Alaramos wasn't troubled by the problems of how to get the horse onto the register in his own country, and was being offered total ownership for less than he had been willing to pay originally for a mere majority share, the offer would be extremely attractive to him. There would be an added bonus insofar as Norris could add the share of the insurance pay-out to what he got from Alaramos, while Alaramos could deduct his share of the insurance from the amount he had to pay. Only the insurance company lost and they would have laid off so much to various underwriters anyway, that, in the long run, it would be hard to find anyone who would actually go hungry because of the scam. It was so neat, it ought to have come off.

I phoned Potter and told him what I had come up with – he had stopped even vaguely resenting getting all his information from me. He agreed that the Curragh was the place to watch but, at the same time, he wanted to keep a close eye on Spanish Park Stud and he was going to get onto the Tipperary gardai as soon as we hung up, warning them to keep a low profile, in case word reached the prince that the police were unusually active around Spanish Park. If Alaramos acted in the belief that he was, like Caesar's wife, above suspicion, then he might just be that bit less careful and watchful. Once warned, he might be able to take what Potter called 'Appropriate Evasive Action to Avoid Apprehension or Detection'. He sounded like a character from Winnie the Pooh, and I was left with the impression that there was a form with that title on it to be filled out in block capitals using black ink only, in triplicate. He promised to pick me up at the hospital in time to get us to the Curragh. Kevin was still out searching, but he would call him in straight away.

Shortly after one-thirty, I heard the rotors of the approaching helicopter and went to the asphalt square on which we had landed that morning. The square had a large white 'H' in a white circle in the centre and I meant to ask Kevin whether it was H for Hospital or H for Helicopter, but I forgot.

CHAPTER 42

By three o'clock we were circling above the race-course. Potter wanted to do a quick looksee to see if we could spot a horse box 'parked in a suspicious manner' – whatever that would have looked like. The Curragh is the centre of Ireland's bloodstock industry, and today was a racing day, so horse boxes were in plentiful supply but whether any of them they was parked in a suspicious manner or not, not even Potter could say.

"This is hopeless," he conceded after a few minutes and Kevin and I silently agreed.

There were four other helicopters in the helipark, and space for three times as many again. Looking about me as Kevin gently rocked our machine to the ground, I noticed that all of them were of a different design to ours, and no two were the same. I had never realised that there were so many models available; to me, it had always seemed that there were big helicopters and small helicopters and that was that.

As we walked towards the entrance gates, the public address system began to call out information concerning the next race and we shuffled along in the queue which I hadn't expected to be so big. Declan had dismissed the meeting as being 'Mickey Mouse' and I wondered, not being a racing man myself, what the attendance would be like at a big meet. I paid my few bob and passed through the turnstile. I felt an odd rush of adrenaline; a gladiator entering the Circus Maximus, not knowing what I was to be pitted against.

Inside, we held a rapid war council, standing in the rushing stream of punters, flowing singlemindedly past us, towards the bookies' stands or the queues at the tote windows. On the

350

track, the horses were already being loaded into the starting gates.

I was the only one who knew Declan, so *my* role was clear. I would find a position from which I could see the stands, and locate the prince's party. Kevin and Potter would look around, mingling with the crowd, nosing about the stable areas to see if they could locate any of the Tiarmi. (I had been a little disconcerted to discover that they both knew the people of The Eribuhs were Tiarmi; I pride myself usually on a fair standard of general knowledge and feel I'm pretty hot stuff when it comes to quiz programmes on TV and radio. And, to make matters worse, when I casually asked if either of them knew *why* they were called Tiarmi, they said no, they didn't, but Potter told us with a smile, that he had once heard them being referred to as 'Eribuheans!'. We all laughed, me longest and loudest. Then I gave them a concocted explanation which sounded very erudite; when you know that nobody is in a position to contradict you, you can do things like that. I spent the next ten minutes feeling petty.)

Going on the presumption that the best seats in the stands would be directly in front of the winning post, and that that was where the prince would be, I chose an area some distance away along the rails. It was the area popular with the punters, presumably because that was where the last tussles for position would take place in the final furlong from home. With Kevin's powerful search-party binoculars hanging round my neck, I let myself be pressed against the white single rail by the six-deep crowd.

"They're off!" blared the tannoy, "and first to show is..." There followed a list of names.

The field, bunched close in the first few hundred yards, thundered towards us, drawing only muted shouts of support from the crowd as the horses galloped past – it was too early yet to say what was going on. As they vanished out of sight round a corner, those of us who had been leaning over the rail watching the order of their disappearance, straightened up and began to listen intently to the loudspeaker's commentary and, when it announced that they were coming back into view, we all leaned over again. This time, the excitement was palpable and a swelling roar coursed along the rails, a wave of sound travelling at the same speed as the leading horses, but some thirty yards ahead of them, as if the noise was a surging bow wave created by the hard-pressed horses.

The leaders passed us, foam-flecked mouths emitting hard crunching breaths, hooves rippling on the firm turf, sweat-soaked shoulders responding with a last effort to the urgent strokes of the whip. The roar of the crowd pushed them to greater effort and heads turned as one, to follow the last flying gallop of the contest. But my head turned farther than any other, because, raising the binoculars, I began a steady search of the cheering crowd in the stands.

In the half-empty stand, I quickly located Declan. He was moving backwards and forwards rapidly in his seat, as if he himself was riding; his arms, bent at the elbows, were pumping in and out, giving his imaginary horse his head. The look of sheer excitement on his dark, boyish face said everything. The seats to his right were empty. On his left, an elderly lady in a fur coat and white gloves waved her race card vigorously, eyes bright blue beneath bright blue hair. Next to her was an elderly man whose face I knew but couldn't put a name to – he sat back stiffly chewing a gnarled knuckle, gaze riveted on the finishers. Beside him was a beautiful woman in her thirties, her dark, Mediterranean features animated with the thrill of the finish, sallow hands clasped high in front of her bosom and, beside her, a handsome man of indeterminate age. His skin was darker than the woman's, his features alert and serious. And he was paying no attention whatever to the race. Shocked, I saw that his black eyes were staring straight at me, their gaze coming right down through the prisms of the field glasses to lock mine. Totally disconcerted, I immediately lowered the binoculars and tried to give the impression of being absorbed in the order in which the also-rans passed the post. It was a stupid thing to do. As I obviously hadn't been interested in the winner and the placed horses, turning suddenly to look at the stragglers wasn't going to fool anyone. Cursing myself roundly for panicking, I now realised that I ought to have just passed on from the prince and continued my inspection of the rest of the occupants of the stand. That way, I just might have passed off as a reporter for a social and personal column or even a busybody celebrity watcher. More misjudgements, I regret to say, followed.

The crowd broke away from the rails and headed off towards the bars or the bookies, depending on whether they had lost or won. I hung around for a moment, ostensibly lost in a study of my race card, trying to act nonchalant; I was afraid that, if I left too soon, the prince might think I was bolting. That too, was an error – it would have been far more natural for me to have moved with the crowd. In the next minute, we paid for my mistake when Potter and Kevin joined me, thus identifying themselves to His Highness as friends of mine and therefore, potential enemies of his.

Dejectedly, I told them that I had probably blown their cover and almost certainly had blown mine. Both had the presence of mind not to turn towards the stands, and we leaned our elbows on the rail and stared out over the race course.

"He must have suspected something, but I don't know what or how. Everyone else was glued to the winning post and I was so sure it was safe to have a look! Bugger it anyway!" I said in disgust, "I thought it was the perfect time to check. What the hell do we do now?"

"Which one is he?" Kevin asked.

"Don't look now, but there's a group of them sitting about half-way up the stand, straight in front of the winning post. There's an elderly lady with blue hair with them. The one nearest us is the prince, Declan Forbes is the one at the other end – beside the lady with the blue rinse."

"Probably the best thing now is for us to find somewhere where we can see him but he can't see us, and then just try to tail him when he leaves." Potter's suggestion was about the best we could come up with and, after another few minutes, during which I could almost feel the prince's eyes boring into my back, we decided to leave separately and to look for different exits from the stand.

"Right," said Kevin, who was to go first, "time to go. Time to tail His Royal Highness. I've never had a bit of royal tail before, so it'll be a first," he grinned and winked at us.

I laughed mirthlessly, but nevertheless I was thankful for his

353

ever-exuberant personality. "Good luck," I said.

"Yeah," he grinned back, "you too," and he pushed himself away from the rail. "Wow!" he said as soon as he turned, "would you look at that for a piece of ass! Whooeee!" He knocked at least four syllables out of the word 'ass'.

Automatically, I turned, and my heart sank when I saw Claire advancing across the ticket-strewn ground towards us. Her face lit up when she saw me and I had to force an answering smile; it was too late to signal her to go back and I could only submit to her embrace and kiss, and hope that the prince had turned his attention away from us and missed it all. The less people he could associate with me, the better.

"Hello Inspector," she smiled at Potter, "I'm sure you're not having a day off? Even though you deserve it."

"No. That'll have to come later, when we get this lot sorted out." Potter looked miserable; he, too, realised the implications of the prince being able to connect Claire to us. It would have been very handy to have had her as the tail. It was just rotten luck that we happened to meet up in full view of the stands. Everything was going wrong.

"Claire," I said, "this gentleman here is Kevin, the pilot. Kevin, this piece of ass here is Claire, the lady love. His words, not mine," I explained in answer to Claire's raised eyebrows; Kevin, not in the least put out, bowed gravely and said "*Enchante*."

"Is this a coincidence?" I asked her.

"No. I phoned Knockmore to see if you had any news, and they told me you had gone to the Curragh. So, as it's only half an hour's drive from town, and whatever it was that brought you all here must be newsworthy, I thought I could do worse than to come along and hang about for a while. So tell." She looked from me to Potter. "What's happening?"

While Claire was talking, I tried to survey the stand, without it being noticeable that I was doing so. Facing the winning post, I put maximum right hand lock on my eyeballs and turned my head gradually until I could just about see the stand in my outer peripheral vision. I had to close my left eye because all *it* could see was the bluish mound of my still-swollen nose. They were still in their seats, but the prince was no longer looking at me; he was engaged in conversation with the dark beauty on his right. As I turned my eyes back to normal position, I noticed his head just beginning to turn in our direction again.

Potter was explaining the latest developments to Claire while Kevin stared at her in open admiration. I was busy trying to think of a way to contact Declan to see if he knew how the prince had come to spot me. Once Claire knew what was going on, she insisted on joining in, and she said she'd look through the crowd for Tiarmi on her way to find an exit from the stand which she could cover. She, Potter and Kevin left together. A few moments later, I left, looking for a phone.

The girl who answered the phone knew Declan. As Breeding Manager of Bord na gCapall, he was a well-known figure throughout the industry, and she told me that he had been in the office earlier to arrange for refreshments to be served during the meet to an important person who was at the races. She didn't specify who it was but she made it sound mysterious. She asked me to hold on while she had him paged over the public address system, and warned me to give him a few minutes to get to a phone before giving up. "I'm pretty sure he's still here," she assured me.

"Thank you."

I waited and listened to the announcement being called out a few times over the air. At last, panting slightly, Declan came on the line and said 'Hello' in a tone which suggested that he was half-afraid of who might be at the other end. It was understandable. I had given him some heavy news just four hours before and he still didn't know all the facts. I presume that he was worried that his caller might be someone of whom he knew nothing and was wondering how to play it.

"Declan? Relax. It's only me."

"Christ, Hair, he's on to you! I thought you said he didn't know you from Adam! He pointed you out to me and to Jack Murphy and asked us if we knew who you were or if we'd ever seen you about the place. I said that I didn't know who you were. But how did he know?!"

"I think he was just guessing that someone might be on his trail, but he can't know who I am. He must be worried right this minute about anyone at all who seems to show an interest in him. Unfortunately, I picked the finish of the last race to study him through the binoculars, thinking that he'd be caught up in the excitement, like everyone else, but wasn't he looking straight back at me! Like a fool, I acted flustered and guilty, so he knows that my interest in him is strong enough to keep me from watching the end of the race and, if he's a bit nervy, he'll put two and two together. How does he seem to you, Dec? Normal? Jumpy?"

"Definitely not his usual affable self. He's got something on his mind and he hasn't taken any interest in the races. He's looking about him since we got here, wary – almost jumpy. Yes, definitely nervy," he concluded.

"Any idea about what brought him over for such a small race meeting?"

"No. Not a clue. But it's a real flying visit alright because he's already apologised for the fact that he won't be able to host the usual dinner at Chez Pierre tonight. He's got to leave immediately after the last race. He said that I should go ahead with the Murphys and eat anyway, and put it all on his account, but I don't really fancy an evening with them so I told him that I had promised Jo I'd be home before eight as we had an important family occasion. He said he hoped I hadn't come to the races on his account and, whereas it was a delight to see me always, I should never come if there was anything else I had to do instead."

"Charming." I said drily. "A regular Prince Charming, isn't he?"

"Oh, he's all that."

"Did he say where he was going after the races?"

"No, but earlier, when we were in the bar, his lady friend opened her bag to get cigarettes, and I just happened to see what looked like tickets – travel tickets. I could see R-O-S-S-L on one, so I presume that the tickets are for the Rosslare ferry. Those letters were all I could see so I don't know whether it's Rosslare to Fishguard or Rosslare to Le Havre. But it struck me that the most likely reason she'd have them in her bag, *with* her is that they're going straight on there afterwards. Otherwise she'd probably have left them wherever they're staying.

Wouldn't you agree?"

"Most likely. Does the prince have property in France? Does he own a studfarm there?"

"I'm way ahead of you Frank. I know what you're thinking, but it won't help you decide which ferry he's taking. If any. He has *two* farms in France. But he has two in Britain also. So put that in yer pipe and smoke it."

"You're playing a blinder, Dec. Keep it up."

"The things I do for old time's sake! I'd better get back and look after my prince."

"Good man. That's the spirit. Intrepid to the last."

"It's my job, for God's sake!"

The next race was about to begin and, the crowds having gone to the rails again, the rest of the enclosure was almost deserted. I wandered round the back of the stands in search of the others, and found them, one by one, covering exits from the stands. Only Kevin had anything to report.

"He's just gone back up into the stand, Frank. You missed him by a whisker. I tried to follow him when he left but he kept looking behind him and I had to stay too far back, so I lost him. I'm sorry but it couldn't be helped. I saw him going into the VIP's car park but, by the time I thought it was safe to follow, he'd vanished. I came back here to see when he came back."

"How long was he away?"

"About ten minutes altogether."

"He must have left just after Declan went to the phone..."

"It was just after I heard the loudspeaker paging Forbes; I wondered if it was you calling him. Forbes must have gone out by another way because he didn't come down here. I got a good look at him and I'd have known him again."

"Have we enough juice in the helicopter to get us to Rosslare if we have to?"

"Rosslare? Is that where he's headed?"

"Possibly. Is there enough juice?"

"Buckets. What's the next move?"

"We wait, I suppose. Potter says that there are at least another two exits from the stand and that I ought to go and cover one of them. I hope I haven't arsed it all up by letting

357

him know he's being watched. If he changes his plans at this stage, then who knows what he'll do? Rosslare, which we're not even sure about in the first place, will most likely be out. Anyway, I'll go and look for this other exit and hang about. See you."

As I walked along, I worried about the wisdom of us being split up into four un-coordinated units. We had no plans, no organisation, no way of signalling each other if the prince should leave. The ridiculous situation could arise where one of us would see him leave and then be faced with the impossible choice of following him solo, or letting him off while going to tell the others. The first course would leave three of us hanging about waiting for the prince to appear, long after he had gone, while the second would defeat the whole purpose of the exercise — to find out where he went. I thought that a far better plan would be for two of us to wait in the VIP carpark to find out what kind of car he had and the other two to sit outside in the roadway in Claire's car, so that when he did come out of the carpark, he could be followed. There probably wouldn't be more than one exit on to the road so it would be much easier to watch than the many exits from the stands. I stood behind a tractor with Curragh Racecourse written on it, and watched the exit through two panes of dirty glass.

The race was in full flight and the roar of the crowd told me that the horses were in the home straight. I decided to wait on watch until the next race began and then to go in search of Potter to ask him what he thought of the approach of watching the carpark. Officially he was in charge. The race ended and the area behind the stand became crowded again; several people came down from the stand but none of them was the prince or any member of his party.

"Would Dr Francis O'Hare of Cartfield, Illinois please go to the nearest telephone. Repeat, Dr Francis O'Hare of Cartfield, Illinois to the nearest telephone please. Thank you."

I almost didn't spot that the cryptic loudspeaker summons was for me. It had to be Declan; it could hardly have been a coincidence. Hair was my nickname and Cartfield was the name of my parents house — Declan had often spent weekends there when we were at college. Abandoning my post, I headed for the nearest phone, picked it up and said in an exaggerated drawl: "Dactur O'Hayy-ah heey-ah... You gotta call fo' me?" It was pure Texas, but I didn't know what an Illinois accent sounded like. Neither, obviously, did the operator.

"Just hold on a moment sir and I'll put you through."

"Hair?" Declan's voice was urgent and excited.

"Yeh. What's up?"

"He's just bought a horse!"

"What? Where?"

"He wasn't there when I got back from talking to you the last time but he arrived a few minutes later. Just before the last race, Tom O'Malley arrives and sits beside him and they talked all the way through the race. I couldn't hear what they were saying but I've seen enough horses bought and sold to know that that's what was going on. Anyway, O'Malley has just left with a glazed expression, clutching the walls for support; he must have got a mad price."

"Where's he gone?"

"To fetch the horse's papers, I'd say. He lives just down the road from here, three minutes drive."

"Don't tell me Alaramos is going to pull *another* switcheroo! That would be just *too* much!"

"No way! Not this time. The horse he bought is grey, seven year old, and a mare! She's in the stables at the course here. She was to run in one of the later races, the second last, I think. It's the Mickey Mousest of them all, a kind of novelty thing, confined to local Curragh horses. You get all kinds of things running in it every year though this one's not a bad mare really."

"Is she good enough for him to want her for her own sake, for breeding?"

"No way," he replied with scorn, aghast at the very idea. "I can't understand it. As I said, he nearly always lets others do the buying."

"Except this time, huh? This must be a *real* emergency. I suppose Tom O'Malley couldn't be involved?"

"I doubt it very much."

"What's he like anyway?"

"I don't know, Hair, if you are at all familiar with that

359

quaint old phrase: 'Unmitigated Bollocks'?"

I laughed. "So can you think of any reason why the prince should want *this* particular animal?"

"No. It seems crazy. She's a nothing. Granted, last time out she won, but that was another Mickey Mouse affair. In France."

"He sent a horse all the way to *France* to run in a Mickey Mouse race?"

"He had space in the box. He was sending over two good horses for two good races, so he sent the mare as well. He knew she'd win and that would at least cover the cost of the diesel. Just as well he did; the other two weren't even placed."

"Hang on, Dec." I said, beginning to see some light. "Back up a bit there. When was this race in France?"

"Last week. Why?"

"So her papers for entry into France are still in date, right?"

"Yes. I thought of that but you can't send a bay stallion out on the papers of a grey mare."

"I know, but she's a good excuse for putting a horsebox aboard a ferry bound for France, isn't she?"

"So? What good will it do him to send the mare back to France? How is that going to get Catamaran out?"

"Just supposing, Dec that there was a hidden compartment in the box, like a false bottom in a suitcase..." I trailed off, letting him think for a moment.

"I see what you mean! But hang on. Why bother with the mare? There's no law against sending an empty horsebox over by ferry; they could be going across to collect horses! If there was a secret compartment, they could put Catamaran in there and send the box out as empty."

"But suppose," I persisted, "*after* they'd declared it empty, horse noises began to come from inside the box? That'd land them in a right pickle, wouldn't it? Having the mare in there would get over that problem nicely."

"Jesus! You could be right at that! But why not go as empty and give Catamaran a shot of something to make sure that there were no horse noises? No! Don't answer that! That's stupid! He's too valuable to take any chances with and I suppose Alaramos hasn't a tame vet in Ireland who'd give the shot and there's no way he'd chance letting a layman do it. It'd have to be a general anaesthetic."

"Also he'd have to be knocked out at the other side too. He would have recovered fully by the time they reached France and he most likely would be kicking up a fierce racket after being confined in a false-bottomed suitcase for thirty hours or however long it takes."

"Of course! And there's no way that anyone would chance knocking him out again so soon! That's it, Hair. That's it!"

"I think I'll go down to the stables and have a look at this mare. By the way, what was all that about Illinois?"

"An extra red herring. To fool the people. Deep, huh?"

"It worked. It damn near fooled me. Anyway," I said, resuming a Texas drawl, "as we say stateside, 'Have a nice day'."

"You too, Dr O'Hare. And I think you're on the right track. If there are any other developments that you should know about, I'll contact you again in the same way, only this time I'll page a... a... Mr Tim Carmody from Sligo, got that? It's the name of a nephew. It might seem odd if an American doctor was paged twice in such a short time – specially if it happened on each of the two occasions on which I'd excused myself."

"Tim Carmody, right. You're a natural at this cloak and dagger stuff," I said, and broke the connection, anxious to get going to find the prince's latest acquisition.

CHAPTER 43

Kevin was nearest to me, and I stopped by, on my way to the stabling area, to tell him about the grey mare. We agreed that the best policy now seemed to be to follow the mare, and he went off to get Potter and Claire, while I went on to the stables to locate the mare. They were to wait for me outside the stables until I had found her and, if possible, ascertain when and where she was going. Then we would all follow.

As I drew near the stables a feeling that it was all over, bar the shouting, grew within me, but the excitement and the anticipation which should have accompanied it was dented by one worry – Potter.

On the one hand, it was a comfort to have him along – he could call on help if needed and be sure it would come; he could also effect arrests properly, etc. – but on the other, he was in charge of the investigation, and he could call the shots. If, for instance, some of the prince's hirelings turned up at the racecourse, to take the mare away, would Potter decide to put the arm on them and charge them with assault on Nick O'Beirne, or would he be willing to go for broke? Would he let things ride until we found Catamaran, or would he opt for the safer approach? I worried about this as I hurried along through the crowds. At the first sign of trouble, Alaramos would change his plans and Catamaran would be hidden away again; he might even decide to cut his losses by destroying the evidence – getting caught in possession would mean that he'd be warned off the turf everywhere, a consideration which would probably weigh more with HRH, than the loss of millions.

The thought struck me that there would be security at the stables and that I might need a story to gain access. I still had the stethoscope in my pocket, where I had put it after we had found Nick in the bushes. At the hospital, had the neurosurgeon refused to let me see him, I was going to try the direct approach – hang it around my neck and breeze in as if I were on the staff; I had used it as a prop once or twice before to gain access to hospital wards outside visiting hours and, while other intruders were being driven away by heartless matrons, I had strolled in as if I owned the joint. I saw no reason why the ploy shouldn't work equally well here. I stopped to consult my race card and picked the name of a trainer at random.

"Afternoon," I said brightly to the man in the booth who began to stare suspiciously at me when I was still twenty yards away.

He nodded curtly but I could see him looking at the stethoscope.

"Michael Reilly asked me to have a look at 'Honeycomb' before he goes out. Can you tell me which box he's in?"

"What's wrong with Honeycomb?"

"Nothing, I hope. I shouldn't really say anything... but he had a bit of wind trouble, a bit of panting, last week on the gallops and I want to make sure that it's cleared up before he runs." Absentmindedly, I picked up the bell of the stethoscope and wagged it at him.

"Where's Mr Collins today?" The question was more conversational than suspicious.

"Wedding. His sister's getting married."

"His *sister*?! Mr Collins has a sister young enough to be getting married?"

"Widow," I said. Obviously Mr Collins was no spring chicken. I had thought of chancing a daughter or a son but I'd have been stuck if Mr Collins was in his early thirties or if the keeper of the stables knew him well; maybe he had no children; or he had and they were all married; maybe he was a bachelor. As he nodded me in, I was thankful for the forethought I had given the matter. Then I wondered why the hell I had to make such unnecessary pitfalls for myself. Why not just say he was at a wedding. Period. Never mind whose.

"Box 56," he said. "A fair way down, on your left."

"Thanks," I said and passed into the quiet of the stables.

I could have been unlucky. If Honeycomb happened to have been in one of the first few boxes, I might have found it hard to explain why I was wandering off down the passageway looking to left and right. By the time I reached Box 56, I had seen every colour of bay and a few chestnuts, but only one grey, and it was a gelding. I nipped into Box 56, patted Honeycomb on the nose a few times and then came back out. I glanced back towards the minder's cubicle but, against the bright afternoon light streaming through the open doors, I couldn't tell whether he was watching me or not. I walked the rest of the corridor – there were only a few more boxes anyway and most of them were empty. None of the horses was grey. I hurried back to the door.

"How's Honeycomb?" the keeper asked.

"So-so. If I were you," I winked, "I wouldn't put anything on him today. I'd say that that grey mare of O'Malley's is the best bet of the day. She won nicely in France last week you know."

"Hmpph!" he snorted, "You haven't backed her already, have you?"

"No," I answered, puzzled. "Why?"

"Don't. She's been scratched. She's sold. O'Malley came in a while ago and took her off."

"What! Took her away? Just like that?"

"Aye. Just like that." He snapped his fingers.

"Wouldn't you think he'd have let her run at least!"

"Wouldn't you? I'd say he must have got a big price for her. He had a couple of coloured lads with him and I wouldn't be surprised if they were Tiarmi. I hear Prince Alaramos is here today. If *he* bought the mare, then Tom O'Malley got what she was worth times over. I never thought that mare would be in the prince's class."

"Blast it anyway," I said, trying not to appear too interested in the transaction, "I was half-thinking of putting in an offer for her myself. I heard he was willing to sell her and the main reason that I came here today was to see her run."

"She's alright mind you. There's nothing wrong with the mare; she's strong and she's honest, I mean to say, but she's not in the class that the prince deals in. Sangster or O'Brien or

364

Firestone wouldn't cross the road to look at her, but she'd be alright for the small man. No offence."

I smiled. "Sangster and O'Brien and Firestone were small men once too. We've all got to start somewhere."

"True, true. Too true."

"Well, it's the quickest bit of work I ever saw," I said, shaking my head. "When did they take her?"

"About five minutes before you came in. You just missed them."

"Maybe she's still outside. I'd like to have a look at her – to see what I missed. I'm a devil for punishment."

"She's gone. They loaded her straightaway onto the transporter."

"Jesus that was quick!" I snorted. "Ah well... maybe I'll drop by O'Malley's yard when I leave. If the truck is there I might pull up for a look. What kind of truck were they driving?"

"I didn't see it myself. I'm not allowed to leave here until the last horse is gone."

"Of course not. Then... how do you know that she was loaded?"

"O'Malley's lad. He told me when he came back. I don't think that he was too pleased at the way she went. He helped them load her so he'd know. I can ask him, if you like."

"I don't want to..."

"It's no trouble. He's down the passage. Georgie!" he bellowed without warning, "Georgie!"

A blonde head popped out from a box down along the right. "Me? Were you callin' me, Patsy?"

"Yeh. C'mere son. I want you a minute."

We didn't get much from Georgie. The mare, which went under the lofty name of 'Nimble Nimbus', had been loaded onto an ordinary horse transporter which was immediately driven off by the 'coloured chaps'. He hadn't even noticed what colour the truck was because he was that upset at the time. "I still am," he said and sounded it. "I got her ready for this race for months and she'd have won. The boss couldn't even wait an hour!"

"She won her race in France," I pointed out.

"Hmmmph! I wasn't there to see her."

"Maybe you'll see her winning again soon."

"Maybe. But I won't be the one who's looking after her, will I?" Georgie seemed determined to knock maximum mileage out of his gloom. He had an answer for everything – except my roundabout questions about the horsebox.

"Did she go off with other horses?"

"No. She was all alone."

"Was it just a single box then?"

"No. A two-horse box. A good sized one."

Leaving the gate-minder to console the inconsolable young stable boy, I went out and looked about for the others and was slightly exasperated when they weren't there – we needed to get moving at once. As yet, I hadn't much of a clue what to do, other than a general idea that we should head for Rosslare and the ferry. I waited for a few moments and then decided to head for the back of the stands. I was hurrying along when the loud-speaker spoke out, stopping me in my tracks with a shiver.

"Attention please! Attention please! There is an urgent message at the administration room for a Mr Frank Samson of Knockmore-on-Sea. Mr Frank Samson, Knockmore-on-Sea. Urgent message at the Administration Room. Thank you."

Intuitively I knew the message was trouble. Heading quickly towards the Administration Block, on legs that had suddenly become wobbly, I tried to work out the implications. Who would have used my real name and the Knockmore address? Not Declan – we had already arranged our code name, Tim Carmody, Sligo. It couldn't be Potter or Kevin or Claire – they knew where to find me and they knew how important secrecy was. My name had appeared so often in the press in the past few days in connection with Catamaran's re-appearance that it was bound to attract attention. So, if not Declan and not Claire, Potter or Kevin, it had to be the only other person who knew I was at the races, Prince Alaramos, and I had a feeling that I wasn't going to like any messages from him.

As I raced the last fifty yards to the Administration Block, it crossed my mind that he might be trying to lure me into a trap but I reckoned that if he was going to try any rough stuff, he'd pick somewhere less crowded than the Administration Room.

I pushed through the glass doors and made straight for the receptionist. "I'm Frank Samson. You've got an urgent message for me. It was on the public address just now."

"Oh, yes sir," she replied. "Here it is," and she handed me a small manilla envelope. Trembling I opened it. In awkward capitals, it read:

SAMSON.

IF YOU WANT TO SEE YOUR LADY FRIEND AGAIN YOU MUST GO TO CHEZ PIERRE AND WAIT FOR PHONECALL. IF YOU DO SHE WILL NOT BE HARMED. IF YOU DON'T SHE WILL VANISH. FOREVER.

I read it again in disbelief and horror. In one stroke, Alaramos had made me powerless, reduced me to impotence. The kiss I had given Claire had marked her down as quarry, his insurance. An unwitting Judas kiss.

As I stood trying to clear my thoughts, Kevin and Potter burst in through the door. I went to meet them and almost pushed them outside again.

"Alaramos has got Claire," I said bleakly, as soon as we were away from the prying eyes and ears of the staff.

"I know," Potter said. "When Kevin and I went to get her to follow you down to the stables, she wasn't where we'd left her. We waited for a few moments, in case she'd gone to the ladies, and, when she didn't come back, we went to look. She wasn't in the ladies so we asked around. At last we found a man who said he saw a woman of her description going out the gate with three foreigners – dark foreigners. Then we heard the announcement and came over straightaway. Is that the message?" he asked, nodding at the paper in my nerveless fingers. I handed it to him without a word; Kevin read it over his shoulder.

"What's this Chez Pierre?"

"It's the restaurant where Alaramos usually eats after the races. It's probably the only place he knows around here. Look, Peter; either you go up and arrest him right now or I'm going to go and choke the bastard till he tells me where she is."

"He's gone, Frank. He must have left while we were searching for Claire, or else he came out one of the exits we weren't covering – but he's gone. They all are, Forbes included."

"Christ!" I swore. "What the hell do we do now?"

"Do you know where Chez Pierre is?" Potter asked.

"No, though it'd be easy to find out if we wanted to. But I'm not going to sit in some fucking restaurant while all this…"

"Do you have a better idea?" He was going to play it by the book.

"Give me a minute. If we think, we must be able to come up with something better than that!"

"I agree with Frank," Kevin said. "He probably won't even *call* there. He just wants us tied up, out of the way, until he can get away. We've got to do something."

"Listen, Peter," I said, clutching him by the sleeve. "You can use some authority with the local cops, right? They'll co-operate?"

"Well sure, but…"

"Get a local to sit in the restaurant and take any phonecalls for me. I've never spoken to Alaramos or any of them, for that matter, so whoever rings won't know but that he's talking to me. Then maybe you can get them to drive you to Rosslare – even if they do have a headstart, you'll make it in a squad-car in half the time it'll take them in the horse box and they only left about twenty minutes ago. Kevin and I will try to find them from the air and we can keep tabs on them if we do. If they turn off anywhere, we can contact you on the radio, O.K.?"

"That sounds good to me," Kevin said eagerly. "It covers all the angles – the restaurant, the ferry-port, and all parts in between. He's right, you know." Potter seemed dubious.

"Come on Peter," I urged. "It's the best way!"

"O.K." he said at last.

"Right," I said, trying to hide the relief in my voice. "The sooner we get off the ground, the sooner we can pick them up. If you can organise things from here, it might be best. Listen out for a call for Tim Carmody. That's the name Declan was going to page me by if he had any news. He may come up with something yet, but don't wait too long. See you and good luck."

"You too," he said and, very formally, shook hands with us both.

CHAPTER 44

"**We** *had* **to** ditch Potter," I remarked grimly as we zoomed up and circled the course.

"Ditch him? How do you mean, ditch him?"

"Get rid of him. Leave him behind."

"Why do you say that?" Kevin shot me a puzzled glance.

"Work it out. If we happen to catch up with the prince and succeed in getting our hands on the rotten bastard, our one chance of finding Claire might be to make him talk. If Potter was with us, Alaramos could probably claim diplomatic immunity and Potter's hands would be tied. Personally, I don't give a fiddler's fart for diplomatic immunity. However you feel?"

"You must be joking! Do I look, or act, like a diplomat?"

As we straightened up to follow the main road south, towards Rosslare, I wished I could feel as confident as Kevin seemed. There was a lot of road and, on a racing day, a lot of horse boxes on it. Picking the right one wasn't going to be easy.

"I think," Kevin said, reaching for the handset of his radio, "I'd better try to find out the time of the next ferry from Rosslare." He made his call-sign and while we waited for an acknowledgement explained: "If they have a limited time, they'll have to drive straight through and stick to the main road. If it's not until tomorrow, then Christ alone knows where they can hide. Anywhere!"

His call was answered, he asked for his information and, a few moments later, was told that the next ferry was at 7.15 p.m. To Fishguard. The Le Havre ferry was due to sail an hour later. So we (and they) most likely had an extra hour.

"7.15 or 8.15. If they want to make either of those, then they don't have a lot of time to play around with." He looked

369

at his watch. "Not even three hours to make the Fishguard ferry – they're cutting it fine already."

We decided that the best chance we had of identifying the truck was to pass over a few suspects and land well ahead of them; then I would get off, make my way to the road, and check the drivers as they went by; if there were no likely-looking prospects amongst the bunch, we would speed on ahead, overtake the next few, and repeat the process. The plan was not perfect by any means – for instance, we were assuming that the Tiarmi driver and his mate hadn't been replaced by an *Irish* driver but we had to narrow down the field somehow; otherwise, it would have been unmanageable.

"What makes you think," Kevin asked, reasonably enough, "that we'll find the prince if we find the truck? He's hardly riding with them. After all, the truck left some time before he did."

"It's a chance, but it's the only thing I can think of. I reckon, though, that if we *do* get the truck, we'll find Catamaran inside and *then* we'll be in a position to bargain. We'd have what he wanted and he has what we want. So we could trade. That's another reason why it's best that Potter isn't here. You wouldn't know what he'd feel about me playing fast and loose with other peoples' property, to do a deal for Claire. Like in a kidnapping – even when people are prepared to pay up their *own* money for a ransom, the cops don't like it. You can imagine how he'd view me being willing to hand over a horse that wasn't mine in the first place!"

We passed over the first likely suspect. Kevin sent the chopper over to one side so that we were paralleling the road, about three hundred yards away from it. Through the field-glasses, I checked that it wasn't a delivery lorry or furniture removals truck. It wasn't.

"Want to land up ahead?" he asked.

"Go on a few miles. See if there are any more in this stretch. Then the one landing can do them all."

We came across two more. Speeding up, we rushed ahead and landed in a field of stubble about a mile ahead of the leading lorry. I raced to the road and was just in time to check the occupants as it went past. The driver was a florid-faced Irishman, slightly balding; his companion was a young lad so like him that he had to be his son. I turned and shook my head so Kevin would know. I drew blanks with the other two also and rushed back to the chopper.

"No luck. Let's go." I was panting.

We identified the three trucks we had already checked and raced on. In the next ten miles we passed over five. We both had a feeling about the third one and watched it for a while before moving on. It seemed to be in more of a hurry than the others, changing out of the slow lane often to pass other heavy vehicles which were going only slightly slower than itself.

This time, because of the feeling we had, Kevin set her down in a field which was hidden from the road by a thick hedge and, with a definite sense of rising tension, I leaped out and hared to the gate.

The first one passed, driven by a blonde man accompanied by a blonde woman and two blonde children drinking Coca Cola from tins; a couple of minutes later, the next one laboured along, being driven in too high a gear, by an old man in a battered hat; he was on his own. It left the smell of cattle hanging on the air behind it, and the smell was still there when the third one began to bear down. It had made up a lot of road on the first two and I could hear the urgent whine of its toiling engine when it was still a good quarter of a mile away. This was the one; I just knew it was. I could *feel* it.

The heavy-leafed whitehorn hedge swayed and whipped about in the slipstream, as the lorry thundered past, and the gate was still rocking as I vaulted it. The three men in the cab had been dark-skinned with jet-black eyes and hair; the truck itself was left-hand drive and had French number plates. We were up and away before I got the door closed.

"That's it, the one just gone by! Green cab and varnished wood body. We've got them!"

We picked it up within a matter of minutes, and, having made sure we had got the right one, went up to a hundred feet and matched our pace to theirs.

"Now what?" Kevin asked, looking down at the miniature traffic below. "How are we going to stop him before he gets to Rosslare and Potter gets his hands on him?"

"Maybe he'll stop for a coffee or a piss or something."

"Maybe he won't."

"He's probably well on time. I assume that he's going for the French ferry because of the French number plates plus the fact that the mare's papers are all in order for France. That gives him an extra hour. He doesn't have to be there until 8.15. So maybe he will stop."

For the next ten minutes we followed the truck as it wound its way through the rich green countryside, and all the time we racked our brains for some way to stop it without having to involve the police. We thought of scattering nails on the road, hiring or 'borrowing' a truck or tractor to block the road with, and other equally impractical schemes.

The stream of traffic below passed out of our sight into a tree-lined section of the road some three-quarters of a mile long. From our height, it seemed that the traffic had plunged underground, as the green of the trees and of the surrounding land were nearly the same, and the distance, aided, no doubt by my unaccustomed viewing angle, obliterated the individuality of single leaves or branches of leaves making the foliage look solid – the same effect as you get from viewing clouds from above.

"What about paint?" I suggested, clutching at straws. "If we bought paint, would you be able to fly directly in front of the truck and keep her there long enough for me to chuck it out the window onto his windscreen?"

Kevin snorted mirthlessly, as much of an answer as the crazy idea deserved. "You've been watching too much television," he said.

Maintaining the same speed, we arrived at the end of the wooded section where the traffic became visible once more; there we hovered, waiting for our quarry to re-appear. It didn't.

"What the hell is going on, now?" I said worriedly. I developed an immediate tightness in the throat, a certainty that the showdown was going to be here and very soon.

"Surely they can't have spotted us!" Kevin said.

"I don't think so," I replied, and began to worry afresh. If Claire was in the lorry, and they knew they were being followed, they wouldn't want to be caught with their hostage, and, if they were now stopped... they might be getting rid of her... A sickly fear crawled through me, spreading out from my heart.

"Let me off, here. Put me down. I'm going in. I want to see why they've stopped..." I clenched a handful of the elbow of Kevin's jacket and, with near-panic in my voice and grip, forced him to descend.

"Alright Frank. I'll let you out... but only because it's the best thing to do. Now, calm down. You're no good to Claire or anyone if you get into a flap..."

"*Jesus Christ*! Land, will you! They could be..."

He seemed to be setting the machine down deliberately slowly; I clamped my lips in impatience and watched the ground drifting gently up to meet me. "I don't think Claire is in the truck at all..."

"Why not?" I asked eagerly, hoping he had a good reason, something more concrete than a desire to calm me down.

"Well, the truck left long before Claire... got captured and they wouldn't have been able to transfer her from one vehicle to another, on the main road. Not with all that traffic..."

"Five minutes in a side road," I countered aggressively. "Three minutes!..."

"But they wouldn't *want* her in the truck!" Kevin argued, making it up as he went along. "They must have had a car to get her away in the first place, so why transfer her? Unless they want her to go to France too, she'll have to be transferred back out of the truck again. And that doesn't make sense... She can be as good a hostage in Ireland as she can in France, with only a fraction of the danger of being found out. Believe me, she's *not* in the horse-box."

It made sense. Thankfully. Kevin had strung together a logical argument which went a long way towards easing my fear. I snorted at my stupid panic. "You're right. Just as well one of us is thinking clearly. Anyway, I'll get off and see that they don't come out this end and you'll... what? Go up and see if they've turned back or turned off onto another road?"

"That's what I was figuring anyway. I'll do a big circle at a few hundred feet up; they can't have got very far if they *have* changed route and I'll spot them, no trouble. I'll finish the circle above you and you signal me if they haven't come out. Then I'll go back, land at the other end and we'll both make our way along the road and meet in the middle."

"That's the best. As I said, just as well one of us is keeping calm. By the way, if the truck *is* parked, I won't approach it in case they recognise me; I'll hunker down in the woods a few yards short of it on the opposite side of the road, O.K.?"

"O.K. I'll meet you there and we can decide on what's next then."

I slammed the door and ran aside, as the helicopter zoomed up at speed. A short while later he came back, dropped to tree-top height and hovered questioningly until I shook my head; then he pointed towards the other end and made walking movements with two down-pointing fingers. I nodded and he left.

CHAPTER 45

*A*s soon as I stepped out into the road, I could see that there was no lorry pulled over to the side; there was nothing to be seen but moving traffic. I waited impatiently, anxiously scanning the shaded sides of the road for an opening where they might have turned off and hidden. The logic of Kevin's reasoning had begun to wear thin, and an ember of panic was starting to smoulder inside me again.

I saw Kevin enter from the other end, then set off, increasing my pace to a jog, to meet him. I passed no openings where the truck could have turned off – a thick hedge lined the road on either side all the way. Kevin, however had better luck.

"There's a gate back there, or an opening where a gate used to be; it leads on to a kind of forestry track. That's where they must have turned off – there's no other place."

We decided to force a way through the hedge at the point where we had met; it was some hundred and fifty yards beyond the gate but it seemed wisest to go in there. The gate might be under observation.

There was very little breeze, and the undergrowth of briars and whitethorns rustled and crackled as we sneaked through. The big trees were all old beeches, chestnuts and oaks, and their foliage was way above us; any rustling they did in the higher breezes, was too far up to cover the sounds of our passage as we crept stealthily forward, alert for the tiniest warnings of danger.

Then we heard it. Muffled but unmistakable, off to our left, a horse neighed. It was difficult to judge distance, but assuming that the horse was in the horsebox, it was likely quite close – the box and the undergrowth would dampen the sound a lot.

375

Swallowing hard, I picked up a solid club of fallen timber and turned in the direction from which the sound had come. I glanced at Kevin, and was amazed to see a gun in his hand. It wasn't a large gun as guns go, but it made the gun I had taken from Vernon look like something out of a Christmas stocking. Later he told me that he always had it in the cockpit under his seat in case of being hi-jacked. This provided me with the stuff of nightmares for weeks, an armed pilot and an equally armed hi-jacker blazing away at each other in the cramped confines of that tiny perspex bubble, hundreds of feet up in the sky.

The neigh came again, only this time, it sounded close by and it came from straight ahead. A few steps further on, we came to the edge of a clearing; at the far side, parked tight against the greenery, was the truck.

We stopped when only a thin screen of briars separated us from the clearing and, scarcely breathing, studied the scene. Almost at once, we saw two of the Tiarmi; they both had their backs to us and were crouched in patches of scrubby undergrowth, intently observing the woods. They were both watching the other side of the clearing, which puzzled me. I presumed they had seen or heard the helicopter landing at that side of the woods and, reasonably enough, were expecting us to approach from there.

"Do you see them?" I checked with Kevin in a barely audible whisper.

He nodded slowly without shifting his eyes from the clearing. Then he nudged me. "Weren't there three?"

I nodded. "We can't move till we find where the other one is. I hope he's not on this side," I said and we both peered around nervously.

In the cab of the truck, a radio-telephone suddenly sprang into noisy life and was immediately answered by the third man. Though the words were totally foreign to me, there was a depth of deference in his tone, almost reverence, which made it clear that the one on the other end was Alaramos himself. I'd have given a lot to know what they were saying.

"Which one will you take?" Now that we'd located the missing man, Kevin was all on for immediate action.

I nodded towards the one on the left. "But hang on until we

see what they do after this message. If they leave, we might be better off following them. They can't wait too long if they intend to catch that ferry."

Kevin nodded but kept tapping the butt of his gun into the palm of his left hand with some impatience. He was a man of forthright action. The conversation continued. It was all incoming. The only conversation coming from our man in the cab consisted of two repeated phrases, one of which must have meant 'Yes, Majesty' and the other, 'No, Majesty' in Tiarmi or Tiarmese or whatever the language was called. Probably, I thought incongruously, it was called Eribuhean.

The two lurking in the shrubbery never moved. Not once. They gave no sign that they were even aware that the radio telephone was alive with instructions, advice, orders or whatever, or showed any annoyance that its loud crackling could be heard all over the place, and would be a dead giveaway of their position. I could almost see them physically straining to listen for sounds of approach and to see through the shifting green wall of foliage which chopped off their view twenty feet in front of them. You had to admire their calm in such surroundings – in their own country, their visibility would only be limited by a horizon shimmering ephemerally in the heat-haze, or by barren ranges of yellow-grey mountains.

The conversation went on. Kevin's tapping of the gun-butt became more frequent.

"I think we should take them now while we have the chance. While the radio covers any noise we might make. We'll leave the guy in the cab until the transmission ends..."

"I think we should wait. Give it another minute at least..."

Kevin shook his head in disagreement but waited the minute. It was literally a minute; sixty impatient seconds, no more.

"C'mon," he said.

"Hang on," I said.

"Claire might be locked in that truck," he said.

"Well fuck you," I said, hardly able to believe his duplicity and deviousness; straightening from our crouched positions, we pushed through into the clearing.

Once in the open, we ran at them. My man turned just as I

got to him, his fear-widened eyes racing from my face up along my arm to the raised club, but he had neither time to cry out or to move before I brought it down on his skull with a force that sickened me. It *flattened* him. He pitched sideways out of the bushes into the open, rolled over once and lay still. I hoped to God that I hadn't killed him; I had no idea how hard one should hit a person on the head with a wooden club in order to cause unconsciousness but not death or permanent brain damage. No doubt, as with any other anaesthetic agent, there's a certain dosage range which is ineffective, then a slightly higher (and much narrower) dosage range within which optimum results are achieved; finally, there is the overdose or lethal dose... this was what was going through my mind as I searched his pockets.

Kevin seemed troubled by no such scruples, as he went through his victim's clothes. As I had begun my down-swing, I heard, off to my right, a very brief squeak of fear and surprise, ruthlessly stamped out before it could become even half a shout, by the unforgettable dull thunk of gun-butt on skull. Now I saw Kevin stand up and move quickly to the back of the lorry, turning the gun again so that the business end was pointing forward. I found a pen-knife in the back pocket of my victim's trousers and threw it into the undergrowth. As I stood up to join Kevin, I noticed, in the bushes where my man had been lurking, a cudgel propped in readiness against a small rock. It was almost identical to the one I had used on him. I didn't feel quite so bad.

The ramp was secured by wing-bolts, which in turn were secured by padlocks. We could do nothing without the keys and neither of the men we had knocked out, had had keys on him. Probably they were in the cab. Incredibly the radio/telephone conversation was still going on, but it sounded as if it was coming to an end.

"I wish to God they'd shut up!" I said impatiently and glanced around the corner towards the cab. Immediately the man in the cab began to shout in alarm, brown eyes staring in fear at me in the wing mirror.

"Oh shit!" I swore in self-reproach. Inwardly, I felt sick. This wasn't going to make things safer for Claire.

The man in the cab kept gabbling excitedly and he had an attentive audience. The prince's set had obviously been turned from broadcast to receive.

"Let's get him quick and get the keys!" I shouted and we both rushed to the cab and yanked the door open.

"*Out! Out! Out!*" Kevin screamed at the terrified man, calling him with violent imperious waves of his gun.

The man went silent, dropped the radio handset, gulped painfully and slid across towards the door.

"*C'mon! C'mon!*" Kevin continued impatiently, grabbing him roughly by the arm and hauling him out of the cab so quickly that he almost fell. Somewhere – and not very long ago either – some of Kevin's ancestors must have been stormtroopers. The man was in a shock of terror. I presume that he thought we had already killed his missing comrades.

I left him to Kevin, reached into the cab, caught the radio handset, which was swinging forlornly on its black coiled cable, and pressed the Transmit button.

"Listen closely." I spoke slowly and carefully. "This is Frank Samson speaking." I released the button and waited. Nothing happened. Just silence. I pressed the button again. "I know you've got Miss O'Sullivan, but I've got Catamaran, and I'm willing to trade. If you bring her here, unharmed, I promise you I won't leave this spot for two hours after you leave, nor contact anyone. Two hours. Just bring her here. You and your men and your animals can leave. What do you say?" I released 'Transmit' again. Nothing. "Over," I said hopefully, – he might have been a stickler for radio-telephone protocol. The set remained as dead as ever.

"Answer me, damn you!" I was feeling desperate, getting more scared with every second of silence from the radio.

"Hey, Frank," Kevin called. "Search this guy. Leave the radio turned on. He'll be back on, don't worry. Just as soon as he realises that we have him by the royal short and curlies. C'mon! Give me a hand here!"

Either the man understood some English or he had seen lots of American TV shows. At my approach, he turned to face the truck and spreadeagled himself against it. I ran my hands over him but found no metallically hard bulges. I stepped back and he began to turn round again but, before he could, Kevin hit him behind the ear with the gun, and he fell forward in an unconscious heap on the shadow-stippled ground beside his truck.

While I got the keys from the ignition, Kevin did a quick round of the other two. "They're still flat out," he said matter-of-factly, coming to join me at the rear of the truck and reaching back to stuff the gun, barrel first, down into the back of his shirt collar.

"Jesus! Is that not dangerous?" I asked, as he flicked his longish hair out to make sure it covered the gun-butt.

"No more so than sticking it in the waist-band of your trousers. If it happens to go off on its own in either place, you're humped anyway, so what's the difference? And here, in the collar, it's less likely to be found in a quick search, and it's also reasonably easy to get at unnoticed when you've got your hands in the air or on top of your head. You didn't search him," he pointed at the latest victim, "in that area, I noticed."

"No. I didn't."

"You see? You searched his belt well though."

"Do you think I ought to check his collar?"

"I already did." He grinned at me.

I wondered where he had learned things like that. Or why. Then I wondered what I was doing wondering about such things when Claire was in danger. Maybe she was in the truck after all. Maybe the reason that the prince hadn't come back on to me was that he realised that, as soon as we opened the truck, we'd find Claire and that therefore no deal was needed... We'd have all the aces.

Kevin opened the first padlock, choosing the correct key almost at once, from amongst the large bunch. The second one was proving awkward and he was working through the half dozen which were small enough to fit a padlock when he dropped the bunch; he had to start all over again as he didn't know which ones he had eliminated. Inside there were horse noises and once, I thought I heard a movement lighter and more gentle than a horse could make but I wasn't sure. Anxiously, impatiently, I waited.

CHAPTER 46

"**P**ut up your hands and turn around slowly!" The stern voice from behind froze us both instantly. Slowly, as ordered, we complied. I felt numbed inside, desolate.

"Very clever, gentlemen," Prince Alaramos said. "Very, very clever. You, Mr Samson have been far too clever all along. Much too clever for your own good. Everything was going along fine until you stuck your nose in and fucked it all up!" The crude word sounded strange from a foreigner and even more strange from a prince. For some reason, I always thought that princes and the like were different from the rest of us.

He laughed lightly, as if it didn't matter one way or another, and waved the gun at us. It was the exact same as Kevin's as far as I could make out.

"I thought I knew who you were when I saw you at the races. I had seen a photograph of you in the papers – a fuzzy image I admit, but enough of a likeness. However, when I asked our mutual friend, the good Mr Forbes, if he knew who you were, he said he didn't. That left two possibilities: either you weren't Frank Samson and he honestly didn't know you, or you were and he was *pretending* not to know you. If the latter was the case, then the crisis was even more serious than I realised. It meant that Forbes knew I was behind the scheme... why else would he lie about you? So it became of paramount importance for me to check if you really *were* you, if you get my meaning.

"So." He drew a long breath, as if he was already bored with telling the story. "I went for a walk – that was when this gentleman here," he nodded towards Kevin, "followed me. I had a quick look into the helicopter park and saw Roscahill's machine there. How could I miss it with a great coat of arms on the side?" He laughed. "Such *vanity*! My goodness... Well, as everyone who has been keeping up with the Catamaran saga knows, Lord Roscahill has placed his helicopter at your disposal, so its presence here made it more than a fair probability that you were who I thought you were. Once that had been accepted, I had to check one more thing – could it be possible that two veterinarians of approximately the same age, in a small country like Ireland, wouldn't know each other? As far as I am aware, there's only one veterinary school here, right, Mr Samson?"

In spite of myself, I nodded confirmation.

"So, from my car phone, I telephoned my vet – you probably know him, Patrick Lynch?" – I nodded again; Patsy Lynch was one of the best-known vets in the country – "and told him I was thinking of offering you a job in my country, and could he please look you up in his register and tell me when you had graduated. When he did, I asked him casually if you mightn't be about the same vintage as Forbes, and he looked that up too, and told me that you had been classmates! That, Mr Samson, was when I knew that the game was more or less up, and that I needed some extra bargaining power. So I took it. Her. And very beautiful she is too. I commend you on your taste, and am vaguely envious. A hundred years ago, I would have carried her off and made her one of my many, many wives, but, regrettably, times change..."

"Where is she? What have you done with her?" I growled with as much menace as our relative positions would allow.

"I'll ask the questions. I'm the one with the gun. Suffice it to say that your charming lady friend is safe, and will be, as long as my plans go forward. Put it this way," he said with a sudden smile of self-satisfaction at his flash of wit, "you don't interfere with my breeding programme and I shan't interfere with yours."

"You're a credit to royalty," I said with withering scorn but he ignored me totally, and went on.

"When I saw you standing by the roadside back there, I could hardly believe my eyes. The same hundred years ago, I would probably have thought that you were a Djinn of

Nemesis or something, and have had you put to the sword for being in two places at the one time. But of course, the helicopter explained all."

"You were in the *lorry?*" My curiosity made me ask. I hadn't seen him.

"Of course not!" he scoffed, outraged at the suggestion, "I was in the Mercedes in *front* of the lorry. When I saw you, I knew what you were up to, saw the helicopter following us, came ahead to find somewhere where we could stop, so that you would be *forced* to land and we could talk. And here we are! I've got a full house: you, the pilot, his machine, your lady friend, Catamaran and an alternative route, which I don't want you second-guessing." He looked about at the recumbent figures of his subjects. "We didn't expect you to come upon us so quickly. I miscalculated insofar as I thought you would approach with extreme caution. There again, these poor wretches," he nodded at the still forms of his subjects, exonerating them, "are completely out of their depth. To them, this spinney must seem like the Amazon rain forest. They'd have been every bit as much at home on the pistes at St Moritz. You haven't killed any of them, have you?"

"No. I hope not."

"Good." It didn't seem to worry him too much either way. "Now let's go and get Pitru to open this contraption and fit you both inside. This way, please."

"Where's Claire!" I demanded.

The prince shook his head slowly, and made tut-tutting noises of disapproval. Then he wagged the gun. "All in good time, Mr Samson. All in good time."

"If anything happens to her..."

"Yes, yes, so you said. Now move."

He herded us past the truck and on along a path between the trees. Fifty yards later we came into a smaller clearing, not a lot bigger than the silver Mercedes which was parked in it. I shook my head in self-disgust – the use of the radio had suggested *distance*, and what a fatal assumption that turned out to be.

There was a young Tiarmi standing uncertainly by the driver's door. He saw me and Kevin arrive before he saw the prince behind us and his face showed momentary panic.

"Pitru," the prince said in a commanding tone and followed up with a long spiel of instructions. Then he addressed us. "Pitru will now search you both, so if you please... against the car... arms spread... legs apart... right. Pitru!"

Kevin held his head way back as if he was looking into the sky, making sure that his hair came down as far as possible to cover the gun-butt; at the same time, he would create a slight hollow between head and spine which would accommodate the handle. I watched, out of the corner of my eye, as Pitru searched him thoroughly, carrying out the prince's commands and barked directions, to the letter. Twice, he searched Kevin's lower legs, the second time, actually pulling up the trouser-legs so that the prince could see for himself that there was nothing there. Suddenly his hands were on me; the gun had gone unnoticed.

I was given an even more thorough going over – HRH had obviously decided that I was the one to watch. When Pitru had done, to his master's satisfaction, we were allowed to turn, but warned to keep our hands up where they could be seen. We put them into the air.

While Prince Alaramos gave more instructions to his young servant, I stole a surreptitious glance at Kevin and just about caught the tiny nod of his head. He was going to use the gun.

I tried to concentrate on what the prince was saying, hoping to recognise, amongst the strange guttural sounds, a word or phrase that might give some idea of what was in store for us; once, I thought I heard him say something like 'hailey coppoti' and I reckoned that this might mean 'helicopter'. However, I reflected, glancing at Kevin again, who, by this stage, had low-ered his hands onto the top of his head without challenge, it might just as easily have meant 'dig two shallow graves'.

Turning his head towards Pitru, but keeping his eyes on us, Alaramos began another series of instructions which I pre-sumed, by the frequent use of the words 'horse box' and the repeated mention of Karali, Huasa and Uwani, concerned the revival of his fallen troops.

Suddenly, in the middle of the prince's instructions, Kevin said very quickly: "When I count to three, run."

I heard him because I was standing beside him. The prince

heard him too, but not what he said. Suspending his instructions, he looked at us.

"What was that?"

"I just said," Kevin said, "that this is a real bum."

I nodded in confirmation.

"Just keep quiet," said the prince. "No talking. Understood?" We both nodded dutifully.

He continued to look suspiciously at us for a moment or two, then resumed his instructions to Pitru.

I stole another glance at Kevin. The butt of the gun was already in his hand but he was making no effort to pull it clear of his collar. I could see his index finger searching for the trigger-guard, clearing the hair away so that it wouldn't catch. Not looking forward in the slightest to my role as running decoy, I steeled myself for the beginning of Kevin's countdown, pushing myself away from the Mercedes, against which I'd been leaning.

Alaramos finished his orders and, with a bow, Pitru left, running for the clearing where his felled compatriots lay. We all listened, and, in a moment, heard him calling urgently, 'Karali! Karali!' I hoped that Kevin was going to do whatever he intended to do quickly, before Pitru returned or managed to arouse his comrades. Off in the other clearing, Pitru was now shouting: 'Hiii! Uwani!' and I wondered if he had moved on from Karali because he had successfully awoken him or because he had given up hope of doing so.

"Where are all your men, anyway?" Kevin asked the prince. "We know you've at least twelve over here with you and yet, here, you've only got," he took his left hand down from on top of his head, and began to count on his fingers against the thumb, "one,... two,... "

I tensed. This was it! By taking his left hand down, he had drawn the prince's wary gaze down with it, giving his right hand more of a chance to pull the gun unnoticed; it had also distracted the prince's eyes from me, as I tensed in preparation for my fire-drawing dash, and, finally, it had caused the prince to swing his gun exclusively at Kevin, which might just give me an all-important extra millisecond.

"Three...," Kevin said and I was off, streaking for the

bushes. head and neck telescoped in as far as possible, I raced, braced for the impact of a bullet.

There was a shout, a shot, and, as I threw myself into the bushes, a cry of pain. It was only when I heard that cry that I knew that *I* hadn't been shot – I hadn't felt anything but I've read that you don't, not for the first few seconds. Fearing for Kevin, I twisted as I landed, and, looking back through the leaves, anxiously searched for him. From ground-level, I could see no one. I sat up quickly. Kevin, looking ashen, was kneeling beside the prince who now lay, writhing on the ground, clasping a shoulder with a hand through which blood was seeping. I dashed back almost as quickly as I had left. Wordlessly, he handed me the prince's gun.

"Are you alright?" I put a solicitous hand on his shoulder.

He nodded and rose, slightly unsteadily, to his feet. On the ground, the prince, his face twisted with pain, sat moaning.

"You sure?" I asked Kevin. He looked awful.

"Yeah. Fine," he answered. "I'll be okay."

"Then we better get Pitru before he gets away and warns anyone!" It struck me as I shouted "Pitru!" in as near a copy of the prince's voice as I could manage, that Pitru probably would *not* run away, that he would assume that it was one of us that had been shot; after all the prince was the one with the gun. Still, in case my assumptions were wrong (yet again), I wanted to put him out of action. I was acutely aware of the radio telephone in the truck; if Pitru was keeping an open line to the others – the ones who were holding Claire – and saw Kevin and me coming into the clearing, he'd report that it was the *prince* who had been shot. Then, if they assumed he was dead, and had Claire in their clutches, there was no knowing what form their grief, anger or desire for revenge might take. A cold claw squeezed my heart. "*Pitru!*" I shouted imperiously again, as I moved into cover by the side of the track. Kevin stayed by the fallen prince in case he tried to shout a warning or escape, but HRH now seemed to have passed out, and was lying quite still.

I heard Pitru's rapid approach – no doubt he was used to complying instantly with the prince's summons. As he dashed past, I emerged from my hiding place but he was going at such a lick that I actually had to run a few steps after him before I could reach his head with the butt of his master's gun. With a surprised grunt, he lurched into the bushes and lay still, his legs staying on the path. I was getting quite proficient at this. Stepping across his legs, I went back to the clearing.

The prince was just sitting up, the handsome hawk-nosed face distorted by the pain in his shoulder which he still clasped tightly with his left hand. The cracks between the fingers had filled with narrow lines of drying, blackening blood.

I squatted beside him and considered him for a minute, staring unblinkingly into his pain-filled eyes. "Right. This is it. Where is she? You'll tell us sooner or later, and it's best for all if it's sooner. So. Where is she?"

He returned my stare for a short while, boldly, defiantly, royally. In spite of his seeming Westernization, I could see that, in his eyes, I was a commoner and a foreigner, and on those two counts alone, I deserved not the least respect or cooperation. Then he dropped his stare and shot his glance to the right, towards the car.

My heart leaped with joy and hope. "The *car*!" I said excitedly, "Claire's in the car!" I ran to the huge Mercedes and yanked the doors open. But she wasn't there. "The boot! She must be in the boot!" I banged the top of the rear compartment with the flat of my hand and shouted: "Hang on Claire! It's me. Frank!" Like a man possessed, I tried the button but it was locked. Banging on the boot again and calling on her to hang on for just a few seconds longer, I raced to the driver's door, wrenched it open and pulled the keys from the ignition. As I tried the first few, I kept up a steady, reassuring flow of words to her. At last, one fitted snugly; the lock sprang, and the boot popped open. It was empty.

Devastated, I stared. Nothing but the spare wheel, the jack and a picnic basket. That was it. The sum contents. Either Alaramos had deliberately misled me by looking significantly at the car, or I, in my anxiety, had misread the meaning of his look. Maybe it had had *no* meaning. Maybe, when he hadn't been able to outstare me, he had just looked away, maybe the car had just been something to put his eyes on. Still, he hadn't told me I was going off half-cocked, full of false hopes. He had let me go through the whole heart-breaking, vain charade. Fuck him.

A short nasty laugh came from the grass, the laugh of the one who has the last laugh. It went through me. Gently, I closed down the boot and stood with my hands resting on it for a few seconds. Then I turned towards him.

The bleak look in my eyes wiped all traces of laughter, nasty or otherwise, from his face. Nervously he watched me approach and he swallowed loudly as I came to a halt, towering directly above him. I had lost all traces of human feeling at that moment and it must have shown.

"You rotten fucking bastard," I said slowly, with great malice, and I kicked him in the shoulder. He screamed and fell over backwards, rolling about on the ground, humming his repressed groans of agony. I watched him unfeelingly, waiting patiently for him to sit up again.

When he managed to raise himself to a sitting position, his face had a grey sheen to it; sweat bedewed his forehead and ran in streaky rivulets down beside his nose and around his mouth, to drip off his chin. His lips were pulled back, exposing his perfect teeth, clenched; his eyes were screwed tightly closed. When, at last he opened them, he started in alarm, as mine, mere narrowed slits, were but a few inches away. This time he didn't look away.

"If that woman has come to the slightest harm, and I mean the slightest, you're for it, my friend; you can kiss The Eribuhs goodbye. Do you understand?" I didn't raise my voice at all but my tone was the more deadly for its coldness, its complete lack of emotion. He didn't answer my rhetorical question. "Do you understand?" I repeated, just as quietly and menacingly, and punched him lightly on the shoulder. "I'm waiting for an answer..."

"Yes!" he gasped, his features twisting back into pain again. "I understand."

"Good!" I said in business-like tones. "Now let's go and search that horsebox of yours. Secret compartment and all," I added, and took spiteful satisfaction in the way he suddenly looked at me. "You didn't think that we knew about that, did you?"

"No," he answered sullenly, probably afraid that I'd abuse his shoulder again if he didn't answer.

"Get up or I'll drag you by the shoulder."

As he struggled to his feet I began to wonder about my own ferocity and total lack of feeling. I would never have suspected that I was capable of inflicting such pain on man or beast for any reason, no matter how important. Yet, here I was calmly willing to torture this man until I knew where Claire was, indifferent to his pain. Kevin, whom I had almost forgotten in my private worry, had gone silent. Later, he told me that I hadn't seemed to need any help, but I think that his silence was due more to surprise at the change in me, and possibly disapproval.

Having regained his feet, the prince also seemed to have regained some of his composure. "I enjoy Diplomatic Immunity," he announced pompously.

I suppose that the royal families of this world have become royal by displaying qualities – or vices – in greater measure than others. Obviously, the royal family of The Eribuhs was particularly well-endowed with neck. I looked at him in amused disbelief and shook my head.

"We're not diplomats. There isn't a diplomat, apart from yourself that is, for miles and, what's more you'll see no diplomats – or police – until we've finished with you. Now, get going!" I feinted towards the shoulder but didn't bother connecting.

On our way through the passage between the clearings, I made him take one of Pitru's ankles. I took the other and we dragged him along behind us while Kevin brought up the rear without letting his gun waver from the prince.

I was relieved to see the three Tiarmi still in the clearing more or less as we had left them. I was even more relieved to see that the one that I had hit was sitting on a log, swaying precariously and supporting his bent head in his hands. We were well into the clearing before he became aware of us and, as soon as he did, he lurched to his feet, took a few drunken steps in several directions and collapsed again in the middle of the clearing. The other two were crawling about on all fours like newborn animals. I noticed a splash of vomit by the lorry, where the one from the cab had been when we left him, and made a detour to pull Pitru around it. We left Pitru with his fallen comrades.

While Kevin kept the prince under guard – by standing behind him with an arm encircling his neck and the barrel of his gun nestling under his ear – I undid the second padlock and the ramp descended slowly on its hydraulic rods to the ground. When it began its descent, we moved to the sides, out of the firing line – if there was anyone in there to fire. The ramp hit the ground with a soft thump, but the only sound that came from within was the anxious stamping and whinnying of a horse which sees fresh air and green grass and wants to get at both.

"Push the prince into the opening," I called across to Kevin. "You!" I said to him. "Tell them to hold their fire."

"There are no guns," he said.

"Oh yeah? Well you just pop your head round the corner, in case you're wrong and someone in there has a reflex trigger-finger."

With a look of contempt at the craven commoner across from him, the prince stepped onto the ramp. Nothing happened except that the mare became quiet, no doubt expecting that he had come to untie her and let her out.

I closed my eyes for ten seconds to let the pupils dilate so I'd be able to see in the gloom of the interior, then, gun in both hands, arms rigid, like I'd seen on TV, I quickly rounded the back and faced into the horsebox.

There was just a grey mare, Tom O'Malley's no doubt, and a Tiarmi, even younger than Pitru, just a boy. He stood fearfully at the mare's head, gripping her halter for support and stared from me to the wound in the prince's shoulder. If I'd had horns, cloven hooves and a spear-tipped tail, he wouldn't have regarded me with any more abject terror; I had wounded the prince – which was probably the most grievous crime he could imagine. I made a sign for him to come to me but he stood transfixed looking at the prince every few seconds for guidance or explanation.

"Tell him to open the secret compartment," I instructed Alaramos. "I presume he doesn't understand English?"

The prince continued to look disdainfully at me.

"Tell him," I went on, "that I want him to take out this horse, the grey, and then to open the secret compartment."

Alaramos still looked at me, silently. He had the expression of one who doesn't quite know how to put what he wants to say what he wants to, so that it will be understood and appreciated, but he had a stab at it anyway. "I am a prince," he began. "I cannot be seen to take orders from an enemy. The only reason that I and my family have absolute power in my country is because the people will it. In that sense we are a democracy; and the reason that the people will it is because they believe that we are almost divine. You may force me, Samson, by pain or torture to do your bidding but only when I'm on my own. I suppose that every man has his breaking point, but gods don't, and, to him and the others, that's what I am – a god. I'd rather die than order him to do something that you so obviously have commanded me to. I wouldn't even have a choice in the matter. I wouldn't be the first to die for what, no doubt, you would consider footling reasons. Believe me."

I did believe him. There was a strange air of calm about him, the calm of one who can do no more, who is free at last from the agony of choice.

"Fair enough," I said. "You tell me how the secret door works and I'll do it. I've no desire to shatter this poor lad's illusions."

"You are a reasonable man, Mr Samson. Perhaps we may yet make another bargain."

"Forget it!" The line between deity and wheeler dealer seemed to be a fairly narrow one. "How do I open this?"

He told me, keeping the conversation so polite and genteel that it was obvious that he was trying to disguise the fact that he was in an inferior position so that his subject wouldn't get any ideas.

What looked like the front of the box was in fact a false wall, behind which, stretching from side to side, was the secret compartment. Pivoting on the central pillar, which seemed to be just the forward roof support, both halves of the false wall swung back and came to rest along the central dividing wall which kept the usual two horses apart. When I had led down

391

the grey mare, I followed the prince's calm instructions delivered in drawing room tones, pulled various levers, pushed several knobs and swung back the doors. Inside, in the small compartment was Catamaran.

He had been well doped. He hardly lifted his head when the light flooded into his narrow space. The cramped area had been soundproofed with material like egg-cartons. There was an air conditioning unit in the corner near the top and the only other modification was a broad canvas sling which passed under the horse's belly and was connected at its four corners, to steel hooks in the ceiling, with soft ropes. This was to prevent him from falling. However, he supported his weight on his legs, so I unhooked his cradle and led him, wobbling, into the main body of the box. There, I tied him to a ring in the sidewall.

I could hear the hum of a motor which I assumed to be the air conditioning unit. But, with my penchant for lousy assumptions, I thought I had better check with the prince.

"Is that the air-conditioner motor, that hum?"

"Yes."

"I wasn't sure. With our weather, we don't have an awful lot of call for air-conditioners."

I intended locking all the Tiarmi in the secret space, and I didn't want them to suffocate before Potter arrived. As soon as we were up and away, we would radio and tell him where to find Catamaran and the Tiarmi. They oughtn't to be locked up for more than ten or fifteen minutes – as long as it would take him to contact the nearest gardai. The prince was going to come with us. He was going to be the counter hostage; him for Claire; a god for a mere mortal – they'd have to go for it, the bargain of the week.

The young Tiarmi hadn't moved - he stood stiffly, wild-eyed and uncomprehending, by the wall of the box, with all the confusion of one whose world has just been stood on its head. When I took his arm to lead him outside, he resisted in terror, looking frantically, imploringly, at his prince; but the prince ignored him. Bastard, I thought, a nod or a smile of encouragement would have made all the difference to the terrified youngster – but I was thinking like a westerner again. I half-dragged, half-pushed the lad into the sunshine, and felt him go rigid when he saw the others sprawled about in varying stages of semi-consciousness. I smiled reassuringly at him, which made absolutely no difference. He probably thought I was laughing in gleeful anticipation of knocking him out too.

I indicated that I wanted him to help me support the wobbling figures into the horsebox and, in the end, he understood. He even helped a little. When the four had been propped against the real front wall, I began to close the false wall back into position. Just before I closed the second half, I touched the boy on the shoulder and pointed to him to go through. Straightaway his eyes flooded with terror again and he looked as if he wanted to cry but couldn't in front of his prince.

I turned to Catamaran and began to talk conversationally in his ear as if the incident with the boy was forgotten. "Listen prince," I said to Catamaran, "this young lad is scared to death. Now, he can't know that I'm giving you orders because I'm not even *talking* to you and I'm not using an ordering tone. So you've no reason not to make it easy for him. Tell him there'll be somebody along very soon to let him and the others out, and that he'll be back home soon. Explain to him that it's just a very short-term measure. If you don't, he goes in anyway, and, I swear, I'll shoot you in the other shoulder after they're locked in. I'll keep talking to the horse until you say your bit."

A few seconds later, the prince said something very briefly to the boy. It was only one short sentence so he obviously hadn't done any explaining. I'd say he said nothing more comforting or consoling than 'Get into the box', which, whichever way you looked at it, wasn't a lot in the way of comfort. The boy didn't look any less terrified but he bowed immediately, turned and went in. I locked the door behind him.

Then I picked up a bit of rope, patted Catamaran on his doped rump, descended the ramp, and pushed it up again, returning the padlocks to their positions. That done, I placed the bunch of keys behind one of the wheels, and covered it with a few handfuls of grass. They'd be there for Potter's men to find.

CHAPTER 47

"**N**ow then," I said pleasantly, coming up to the prince, "do we continue in this reasonable fashion or do we get back to the bloodbath? It's up to you."

"I'm sure that we can come to some arrangement that will be mutually agreeable." He was almost smiling.

I shook my head. I was almost smiling too. "You haven't understood. What I mean is, are you going to tell me where Claire is now or do I have to beat it out of you? There aren't any of your subjects looking on now, so you don't have to be godlike any more. Where is she?"

"If I were to tell you that, then there would be nothing to stop you from getting her back and turning the stallion over to the authorities. I'm not used to negotiating in a situation where I might end up with nothing."

"Look. Get this straight. If you leave this country a free man, it'll be due to your Diplomatic Immunity, not because you do some kind of deal with us. There *is* no deal. The horse stays where he is and Claire comes with us. After that, you do your own bargaining with the authorities. Personally, I'd like to put a bullet in you and claim it was an accident. So here's the deal – the *only* deal: Tell us where she is and you don't get any further abuse."

"What about the horse?" he asked calmly, providing further proof of the incredible neck which had made his family royal. But the half-smile had gone.

"Forget the damned horse!" I shouted irritably. "The horse doesn't enter into it. It's the woman – only the woman! And you. So, stop hedging! Where is she?"

"I can make you both rich men. All you've got to do is

leave for half an hour. Pretend you never found us. By tomorrow evening, you have my word that your lady friend will be released unhurt and that you both will be the richer by whatever reasonable sum you may care to mention."

"Do you want to listen to this?" I asked Kevin. "Do you want to do a deal with him?"

"No way! He's not going to be reasonable, Frank. You may as well give him the works." He turned to the prince. "You're a fool!"

"You heard him. The same goes for me. No deals. Now, for the last time, where is she?"

The prince regarded me placidly, almost smiling again, as if he firmly believed that every man could be bought and that we were just going through the motions to up the price a bit. As far as he was concerned, the bargaining, far from being over, was proceeding along standard lines.

"You just don't learn, do you?" I said and thumped him on the shoulder, hard. "That's your trouble. You don't listen."

There was a brief look of incredulity before his face screwed up in pain again, then he sank to the ground and sat, rocking back and fro, biting his knuckle. "Listen to me," I said insistently, "listen a minute. Do you see that piece of wood? That club? Do you see it? Eh? *Look at it*." I caught his jaw and turned his head towards the stout cudgel, propped against a rock by one of his fallen troops, in preparation for Kevin or me, no doubt. "Are you looking?" There was a tiny up and down movement of the head. "Right. Now I can easily pick that up and use it on your shoulder – that is, if you want to go the hard way about it. And I will. Believe me. Then, if you *still* want to act awkward, I'm going to shoot your balls off."

Kevin's head jerked round. The prince went rigid. "Don't think for an instant that I won't. I'm a vet remember? I castrate hundreds of animals every year. No taboos in it for me. And you, my friend, as long as you endanger that woman's life, are just another animal. No taboos. Just like this!" I pointed the gun towards his groin, lowered it so that the muzzle almost touched the ground in the angle between his legs, and pulled the trigger.

He jolted as if ten thousand volts had passed through him,

his eyes wide in terror. Kevin, too, jerked. "Christ, Frank!... You didn't..." he breathed.

"Not this time," I said, grinning wickedly at the grey-faced prince. "Next time it'll be for real. Ten minutes with the cudgel and then we'll be back at this stage again. Or you can prevent the whole business. Just tell us now: Where is she?"

He coughed nervously and swallowed a few times.

"Frank," Kevin said, "I'll have no part in any castrating. If it comes to that, you're on your own. I'll leave beforehand." He winked at me over the prince's shoulder.

"Of course. It's up to you. No one's forcing you. I'd understand – for something like that anyhow."

"She's at the house of my cousin near Newbridge," the prince said, convinced.

I sat back on my haunches and looked at him. "Good," I said. "Good. At last. Can you find it from the air?"

"I think so."

"You'd better. Where are the rest of your men?"

"At the house."

"All of them?"

"Yes. All of them."

"How many?"

"Six."

"Armed?"

Silence.

"Armed?" I repeated in a threatening voice.

"Not all. Three of them. I think."

"You *think*? Don't you know?"

"No. Not for sure."

"What kind of weapons?"

"Rifles. Hunting rifles."

This wasn't good news.

"And the woman?"

"I told you. She's at the house."

"Not her. The woman who was with you at the Curragh."

"She's there too."

"So everybody's at your cousin's house?"

"That's correct."

"Right then. Let's go. But by God, if you're lying..."

On the way we radioed Potter and told him where to find Catamaran and the Tiarmi. When he asked about the prince, Kevin simply told him that His Majesty wasn't with them but that we expected to be able to deliver him soon.

"Newbridge below," Kevin announced a short while later. He tapped the prince on the knee. "It's up to you from here. North, south, east or west?"

"Whichever road leads to Naas..."

"That'll be it over there." Kevin pointed at a thread wending through the rich countryside. The winking lights rushing along were cars reflecting the descending sun. "How far from Newbridge?"

"I'm not sure."

"Approx. One mile? Three? Ten?"

"Three miles would be the maximum. The house is on the left as one travels towards Naas."

"Then we should be there in no time. Keep a good look out."

I was in the back, behind the prince. I had the gun vaguely pointed at him though it wasn't necessary, as I had tied his hands together in front, securing them there by tying the long ends together behind his back – a variation on the GI Truss.

I was worried: it was all very well knowing where Claire was but, how were we going to get her away? Kevin and I were outnumbered and out-gunned and could quite easily be outflanked as well, as the unfamiliar grounds we were about to land in would be well known to the enemy.

At first I could think of nothing more brilliant than marching up to the door, the prince between us, a gun in each of his earholes, and demanding Claire, but this plan would almost inevitably develop into a stalemate – at some stage, the handover would have to take place and, once the prince was out of the firing line, what then?... It was even possible that a couple of them might be crack shots, and, with hunting rifles, telescopic sights, and the like, we might be picked off as we stood beside the prince, notwithstanding the guns in his earholes... Another problem was the language. There was nothing to stop them from plotting and scheming openly, and there was no way that we'd know what was going on...

The prince said suddenly: "There it is, down there. That house behind the trees."

We all looked. I raised the binoculars to my eyes. The house was a decent-sized country house of the last century, square, solid and two-storeyed, not unlike Bally Ard. A long driveway curved round the dense stand of trees which obscured the house from the road and the gate. There was no sign of occupants, no smoke from the chimneys, no windows or doors open, no cars parked in front.

"Are you sure this is it? It looks empty."

"Of *course* I'm sure," he snapped. The old hauteur was coming back.

Kevin kept the helicopter a long way away so that we wouldn't seem too much like snoopers – they were bound to be a bit hypersensitive about such matters. We flew by twice, at a safe distance, but all I could see were the windows reflecting the sun. There was no way of telling if we were being observed. During the second pass, I came up with a plan which, though not foolproof, was a distinct improvement on the first effort.

"Can you do a large circle, like we're leaving, then approach the house, keeping out of sight for as long as possible?" I asked.

Kevin studied the area before answering. "I think so. If we come in at the north west corner of the house, those trees will block the view. Why?"

"I want you to put me down just inside the gate. Behind the woods. Come in as quickly as you can."

"What then?"

"Take off again immediately."

"What are you going to do?"

"Go up to the house and ask them for Claire."

"Just like that?" Kevin asked in a Tommy Cooper voice.

"Just like that!" I echoed.

"And you think that they'll hand her over?"

"Never!" said the prince. "Never without my saying so. I shall have to go with you."

"No. You'll go with Kevin."

"Where to?" Kevin asked.

"Just fly about for five minutes. Then come and hover in

398

front of the house. When you get there, I'll go in, and, if I'm not out in ten minutes, *with* Claire, radio the nearest cops. They won't harm me, I hope, because you'll have the prince in the sky, and they *certainly* won't harm you because the prince might be killed in the resulting crash, so..."

"Bob's my auntie," Kevin concluded. "What makes you think of these sneaky ways of doing things?"

"A long history of personal cowardice. Here's an embellishment," I said, "which ought to add a little spice to it." And I threw, over the prince's head and neck, a noose I had fashioned from the remaining piece of rope. "I've tied the other end to the frame of the seat, so, if he falls out..." The prince recoiled but I tightened the noose with a jerk and whispered malevolently in his ear: "Watch it!" He went quite still.

The noose would serve as very persuasive window-dressing should it be needed during my negotiations at the house; it would also dissuade HRH from making a jump for it, if he started feeling god-like again when Kevin was hovering low in front of the house. In fact, I hadn't tied the other end to the seat at all; that's how accidents happen and all I needed to negate the euphoria of rescuing Claire and Catamaran was to be responsible for the simultaneous public hanging of Prince Alaramos of The Eribuhs, from a helicopter, above his cousin's lawn, before an armed audience of his own subjects.

Coming in fast, Kevin dropped the machine onto the driveway ten yards inside the closed and locked gates.

I slid open the door and squeezed past the petrified figure of the prince. The coarse noose of horse-smelling rope had quietened him into a state of near catatonia. "Leave the door open and, when you approach the house, make sure that HRH here is well displayed. Good luck."

"Yeah. You too." Kevin gave me a thumbs up, and climbed.

I squared my shoulders and started up along the driveway, arms by my sides, palms open to show I was unarmed. I assumed that no one was going to shoot me on sight; however, the nearer I came to the blank but somehow hostile windows, the more I began to worry that I might be thinking like a westerner again.

I was observed all the way, and, from the point at which the drive opened out to become the large parking space in front of the house, I began to locate them, standing deep in rooms, well in the shadows. I saw movement at a window to the left of the door; then, there was a flash appearance at the window *above* the door, but, whoever made it had vanished before I could focus; I caught another glimpse in the next upstairs window to the right, and I reckoned that the same person might have made both – the interval was about right. I had located two, possibly three. As I mounted the first of the three steps to the hall door, a lace curtain in the window immediately to the right, twitched. I looked, and was momentarily shaken to see a pair of expressionless, muddy-brown eyes regarding me coldly, clinically. In spite of a crawling sensation at the back of my neck, I felt a certain amount of relief – at least they weren't going to shoot me on sight.

The three knocks on the polished brass knocker resounded hollowly through the house. I waited, but nothing happened. I raised my hand again but before I could grasp the knocker, the door opened. Only then did I notice the spy-hole hidden neatly in the centre of a carved oak-leaf cluster. The dark beauty who had been Alaramos's companion at the races regarded me coldly.

"Hello," I said, suddenly at a loss for words – I hadn't thought what I was going to say when the door opened.

"What do you want?" Her English was slightly accented.

"Do you know who I am?"

"I think so. I think I do."

"Then you know what I want."

"No."

"You must."

"Tell me."

"I want the woman who is here in the house. Miss O'Sullivan."

"Who said that there is a woman in this house? Who told you there was a woman here?"

"Prince Alaramos."

At the mention of the prince's name, two of his subjects stepped out, one from either side of the door and stood behind her. Each had a rifle but neither was pointing it at me. The one on her left held his facing down, in the crook of his arm like a wild-fowler returning home; the other held his across his chest, a wary soldier on patrol. They regarded me with the same lack of expression as the one who had been looking out the window, and then began to search, with anxious eyes, the grounds behind me, as if they expected to see their prince somewhere out there.

"The prince phoned me at Chez Pierre, told me I should come here for Miss O'Sullivan and said I was to tell you that he had caught the boat." I hadn't rehearsed the bluff, hadn't even thought of it. It just came out and it seemed like being worth a try. She looked at her watch, did some quick calculations and decided not to believe me.

"I do not believe you," she said looking at me defiantly; worry had crept into her dark eyes, nothing much, but it was there, like a tiny flaw in glass.

I shrugged. "How else would I have known where to come?"
She figured that one out too. "Where is the prince?"

"I told you. At the boat. I don't know which boat. That's all he told me. He said: 'Tell...' – I'm sorry, I can't remember your name – 'tell the lady at the house that I'm at the boat and that she should hand the girl over to you.' Me, that is. He said you were to hand her over to me."

She shook her head and managed a slow grimace of disbelief. "Where is he, Mr Samson? Why did he not telephone me instead of you? Or phone me too?"

"O.K. You win. He didn't telephone me and..."

"Where is he?" she demanded.

"He'll be along in a few minutes. That's the truth. He'll want you to give me Miss O'Sullivan so why not bring her here now?"

"I think we'd better wait until he gets here. That is if he is coming. Would you please come inside?"

"No thank you. If you don't mind, I'd rather wait here until he arrives. Which shouldn't be long now." I strained my ears for the sound of rotors, but there was none.

Two more of the Tiarmi drifted casually into view and joined the others behind the dark-eyed woman. Their faces were as inscrutable as statues.

"Are you the princess?" I asked, to break the awkward silence that had developed. Another man came down the stairs, gun at the ready, but he lowered it when he saw there was no confrontation. That made five. One more to go.

"No."

"Oh." Her features were southern European, Italian, I thought, though her accent didn't sound Italian.

"Are you Tiarmi?"

"No." She answered automatically. The worried look was becoming more obvious now, and she too, began to probe the grounds behind me, searching for the prince. She turned and said something to the men. I presume that she told them what was happening because there was an agitated outburst and the confusion of everyone trying to talk at the same time.

"You seem to speak Tiarmi very well," I said, anxious to keep talking and keep the men from getting ideas that I had finished negotiating.

"That is Maltese."

"Oh, you're from Malta! I was there once on holiday. A place called Birzebbugia. Seven years ago, maybe eight."

I saw the sixth man peep through a door, then shuffle across to join the others. All present and accounted for. Where the hell was Kevin! There was still no sound of the helicopter. I continued the ludicrous cocktail-party small-talk.

"Do the Tiarmi understand Maltese then?"

"My language and theirs are both based on Arabic. We can understand each other." She answered my facile questions automatically. There was obvious unease now in her beautiful eyes. In fact, I thought she was going to cry. Then I heard it, the pulsing thump of rotors.

"Ah! This will be the prince now," I said, and, a moment later, coming low, the helicopter edged slowly around the copse, and drifted towards the house, rocking and swaying gently, flattening grass and flowers in its downdraft.

"That is not our helicopter!" She looked at me accusingly. She hadn't yet seen the prince as the sun was directly behind the helicopter and all we could see was a featureless silhouette. She had to raise her voice and lean towards me. She held both hands stiffly along her thighs to stop her skirt from blowing upwards in the draft.

"No. That is my helicopter. But His Highness is in it." I shouted back. I claimed the helicopter hoping it might give me more authority, a bit of status.

Again she turned and spoke to the men and they all crowded forward to stare. Seeing them shielding their eyes, Kevin realised the problem and moved over to the left, angling the helicopter so that the prince was clearly visible. Immediately, an excited babbling broke out.

"Why does he not land?" she demanded, tearing her gaze away from the hovering machine; it was like a monstrous, evil dragon-fly.

"He will, I assure you, just as soon as I walk out through this door with Miss O'Sullivan."

"Who is that man with him, the man who is flying the helicopter?"

"He is the brother of the lady in the house. He is one of her six brothers. They all dote on her, as she is their only sister." Piling it on.

She looked at me again, maybe trying to judge if I was spinning her another line, though at this stage it didn't really matter. The position for her was about as tight as it could be. "I wasn't happy about leaving him with the prince because he's quite violent but I think I've convinced him not to hurt him any more than he has already – as long as his sister is released and hasn't been harmed."

"The prince has been injured?!"

"Yes, I'm afraid so. He was shot in the shoulder before I could stop it. He was lucky. Kevin, the brother, was aiming for his heart."

"Madonna!" she breathed in horror.

"Here," I said unslinging the binoculars that were still hanging round my neck, "see for yourself. As I said, I wasn't at all happy about leaving the two of them together, but what could I do? I'm not able to fly the helicopter myself."

Clamping the hem of her dress between her knees, she pointed the binoculars at the helicopter and did minor adjustments with the focus.

"It's his right shoulder," I offered helpfully. "Can you see it?"

She lowered the glasses in a daze after briefly surveying the aerial tableau. "There is a rope round His Highness's neck!..."

"*What!*" I grabbed the binoculars and focussed quickly. Slowly, I lowered them. "He *promised* me he wouldn't! Jesus! If the prince should faint again or if the helicopter lurched over suddenly... Damn him for a crazy impetuous fool! The bloody idiot! What does he think will become of his sister if anything happens? We'd better get her out here, where he can see her, as quickly as possible. Before he does something *really* drastic."

"He wouldn't!" she said aghast.

I shrugged. "I don't like the way he's deliberately left the prince's door open." I pushed responsibility squarely back on to her shoulders.

She dropped her gaze and thought for a moment, then looked up at the helicopter again, and made up her mind.

"Follow me." She turned abruptly and elbowed her way through the mesmerised throng, handing the binoculars to one of them as she went.

I made to follow her but was stopped by a hand on my elbow, and looked into the troubled eyes of the man who had held the rifle across his barrel chest. There was more anxiety than hostility in his eyes – he pointed towards the helicopter and asked a question, the meaning of which he made clear through sign language; he held his fist to the side of his Adam's apple, gave it two sharp jerks and raised his eyebrows. I nodded, repeated the action, adding – to be *sure* that he got the message – a stuck out tongue, twisted eyes and a gagging sound. Then I shrugged to show that it wasn't definite. There was the hiss of indrawn breath and I pulled my sleeve from his unresisting grasp and hurried to catch up with the woman who had turned at the bottom of the staircase and was beckoning impatiently to me.

"He told me that he would wait five minutes after I had gone into the house. Five minutes, but no more." I told her.

"And after that?"

"Who knows?" I shrugged and, with a worried frown, continued: "The plan was that he'd fly to Newbridge and call the police.. but now, I don't know. The open door... the noose. I hope to God he's not... He's crazy enough for it. To be quite honest, I'm as worried as you are."

"Madonna!" She breathed again in horror and streaked up the remaining steps.

We rushed along a corridor until we came to a door. "She's in here. She's not hurt but she … tried to escape so she may be… sleeping," she explained, fishing into her cleavage and hauling up a gold chain with a stainless steel key hanging on it. She turned the key and eased the door open a crack. I could catch a faint whiff of chloroform. "I assure you that she is not hurt though she may look… eh… untidy," she whispered, suddenly becoming all solicitous, anxious to give no further trouble. She obviously considered me to be the one and only person who might have some chance of diverting the lunatic brother from his murderous plan.

"Shhh!" she whispered. "Go gently," and she began to ease the door inwards. Beyond, the room was in total darkness.

Tiptoeing a step or two in, she reached for the light switch and suddenly, in a blur, a pair of hands clamped on to her extended arm and yanked with such force that she flew out of sight into the dark and crashed with a thud somewhere unseen inside. In the same instant Claire shot from the room, bent double; with hardly a break in stride, she head-butted me solidly in the solar plexus, and continued at a gallop along the corridor, straightening up as she went.

"Claire!" I croaked, staggering back, half-winded. "Claire! It's me! Frank!"

She hesitated, then stopped and turned. Her puzzlement lasted just a second. "Hurry! Run! We'll make it!" she urged, stretching a hand back towards me like a last-leg relay runner getting ready to accept the baton, beginning to move forward again.

"We *have* made it!" I said, rubbing my belly. "It's all over. Really!" I added as she continued to regard me with confusion. Her puzzlement became absolute when her gaoler came limping rapidly from the room and made straight for me.

"Hurry please! Hurry!" She reached for my elbow and started to tug at it. "Come on! Hurry!"

I shrugged off her hand and studied Claire. Her captor had got it right – she did look untidy. "Are you alright?" I asked.

405

"What the hell is going on Frank?" she demanded, bewildered.

"Are you hurt? Did they hurt you? Are you alright?" I repeated.

"I will be when someone explains it all to me." She looked from me to the dark-eyed lady and back to me again. "So tell me."

"Later. There isn't time. Kevin is hovering about twenty feet above the lawn out in front, with a hangman's noose around His Highness's neck and a foot in the small of his back, ready to hang him if you and I aren't out of here in the next couple of minutes."

"I must ask you to hurry! At once!" Our reluctant hostess went behind us and began to shepherd us towards the stairs.

"We need a car," I turned to her. "I don't want the helicopter to land until we're well away from here, and we're not walking!"

"There isn't a car."

"Oh yes there is," Claire said. "I heard one earlier. It pulled up under my window. I couldn't see out because of the locked shutters, but I definitely heard one. There's a car alright."

"No there isn't."

"Oh yes there is."

"Oh no there isn't."

I interrupted the pantomime routine. "We don't go another inch until you produce a car. Not an inch." I leaned against the wall. Claire joined me. I could feel her trembling.

The woman was now in an agony of worry.

"But, he may kill the prince!" she implored.

"Not our problem," I said. "I mean it. No car, no deal. We stay put. Phone for a taxi if you have to, but get a car."

She looked at me appraisingly; then her lovely mouth set in a grim line. "Come with me. I shall order the car to be brought round."

"Aha! You see!" Claire crowed triumphantly.

As we descended the stairs, the woman began to call rapid instructions, but the throb of the rotors drowned her words, and it wasn't until she was amongst them that she managed to make herself heard.

I held Claire back on the stairs and counted heads. Six. Full house. No tricks.

One of the men went out the door at the run and the others turned back to stare helplessly at their prince. We descended the remaining steps and joined the back of the group. Time seemed to have been suspended; the helicopter was in exactly the same position, the prince was still sitting rigidly in the open doorway and, in the door of the house, his loyal subjects were gazing unblinkingly in rapt horror.

I gave Kevin the thumbs up and he answered with a wiggle which sent a horrified gasp through the group. Suddenly I wanted to be outside. If anything went wrong... Looking at their adoring faces, I just wanted to be outside.

"Excuse me," I nudged the woman. "Let us through. He has to be able to see us. All the time. I want to make sure he knows his sister is safe."

"He has seen her," she replied, but moved to the side anyway.

I pushed through the Tiarmi and led Claire out on to the forecourt. The helicopter pivoted rapidly, bringing Kevin's side to face the house. He was grinning hugely as he pointed excitedly towards the corner of the house, before swivelling back to his original position. In a moment, the classic radiator of a Rolls Royce nosed its way round and condescendingly halted in front of us. I moved towards the driver's side but the young driver glared at me and sat doggedly at the wheel, looking towards the house for further instructions. I thought that this was neither the time nor the place to start something so I left it to the woman to sort him out. She made beckoning motions but he stared sullenly back at her, brow furrowed, looking puzzled, *pretending* not to understand her. Exasperated, she turned and spoke with one of the older men who promptly came across, opened the door, and ordered the young rebel out.

"Now go and open the gate," I said to the older man, making appropriate signs.

He looked at me and nodded slowly.

"And come straight back here when you've opened it." I couldn't think of good enough signs for this part, so I steered him across to the house and told the woman what I wanted.

"I want the gates closed again," she objected. "The gates are always kept closed. Always. He will stay at the gates and lock them after you."

I shook my head. "No. He opens the gates and comes back here. I want to be able to count all six of the men, and you, standing here at the door, before I drive off out of sight. I also want them to hand me their guns now."

She looked long and hard at me, then, with obvious distaste, gave the order. There were only three rifles – had the prince not given me the same figure, I would have thought they were holding out. I cradled the guns in one arm. "Is this all?" I asked, deciding to give her a hard time anyway.

"Yes," she answered, tight-lipped.

"No more?"

"No more."

"Yeah. Like there was no car."

She said nothing.

"You better remember that the prince is still hanging up there in the air. No funny business. All of you stay here, in full view of the pilot, until we've been gone five minutes. Now, send him to open the gates and tell him to come straight back."

I went back to the Rolls, opened the boot, and threw the guns inside. Then I went and stood by the driver's door until the gate opener rounded the corner again. Claire was already at the passenger door.

"Ready to go?" I asked her.

She nodded. "Ready. I'll keep an eye on them, you just mind the road."

"Okay, then. Let's get the hell out of here."

I looked up and gave Kevin a wave; I could almost hear his delighted laugh in reply – it was the sort of situation which would appeal to his sense of humour, escape by hi-jacked Rolls Royce.

As I let out the clutch I glanced at the group in the door-way. Not one of them looked in our direction, not even briefly; their attention was focussed on their prince, and we passed unnoticed out of their sight and out of their lives.

Despite the total preoccupation of the Tiarmi with the aerial drama, I was on tenterhooks all the way down the long curving drive; I didn't know what I was expecting to happen, indeed what *could* happen at this stage – I just didn't believe we'd have a free run. Claire was riding shotgun, alert and wary – nothing was going to sneak up on us unnoticed by her; still, I watched the receding house until we rounded the first bend and it slid off the edge of the mirror, then worriedly probed the copse for dark, running, armed figures. I thought we'd had it when I first came in sight of the gates – they looked closed, and, for a few skipped heartbeats, I was sure we had driven straight into a trap. But it was just a trick of the angle, and, moments later, I steered the great car between them and braked, contemplating the road ahead.

"Right or left?"

"Do you know where we are?" Claire asked, still looking behind her. "I haven't a clue – I was blindfolded."

"Somewhere outside Newbridge. About three or four miles. But I'm not sure which direction."

She gave a nervous giggle. "How about getting as far away from here as possible first, and *then* deciding?"

"You're right." I swung to the right.

A few almost silent miles on, we were still wary as cats – Claire continuing to mind our back, me dividing my attentions as best I could between rear-mirror, side-mirrors, the road, and the occupants of oncoming cars. It wasn't until a convoy of three squad cars passed us, heading at full speed towards Alaramos's cousin's house, sirens pulsing and wailing, crammed to the gunwales with gardai, that we relaxed.

Claire flopped back in her seat and expelled a long relieved sigh. "Obviously, Kevin got through to Potter."

"Yep." I breathed deeply and whistled. " Jesus! What a *day*!"

"That, Frank," she said, after a moment's consideration, "must enter the annals as one of the great understatements of our age. Of *any* age."

"Still," I said, ignoring her, "barring a puncture, we're home and dried."

"Practical to the last." She smiled at me. Indulgently. Lovingly.

"Well by God! There's no justice." I pretended to be hurt. "Here we are, after one of the greatest rescues in history, and you're complaining about my conversation! And me ferrying you along in the luxury of a bloody great Rolls Royce!"

"Oh I'm impressed alright, very, very impressed. But I would have preferred a blue one. Powder blue."

"I know, but the powder blue one was at the panel beaters. Still, you have to admit it's a class act. Do you think Paul Markham would ever have rescued you in a Rolls Royce?"

She thought. "Very probably. Only, I'm sure it would have been his own. That is, as long as the time of the rescue didn't happen to clash with a board meeting or an AGM."

I laughed. "You're probably right." I slapped the steering wheel. "I've never even been *in* one of these mothers, have you?"

"No. Although this time last year, I was having the devil's own job keeping out of one."

"How come?"

Hotly pursued by a very persistent sugar-daddy-o. He used to send his Rolls around every day with the most outlandish gifts. It could have been the same car, the same colour and all."

"Maybe it is! Wouldn't that be some coincidence? Maybe he was Prince Alaramos's cousin."

"Not unless the prince's cousin's name is Fergus O'Lafferty, five feet nothing, very pale skin, lots of freckles, thinning salt and pepper hair...?"

"By God now, you never know!" I said. "Did he have a strong Eribuhean accent and a load of oil wells, diamond mines and racehorses?"

"No. A strong Meath accent, a couple of pubs in Navan and Trim, a farm or two somewhere in between, and a construction firm on the side."

"That might be only a cover for tax purposes. Was he a man of regal mien, an obvious blue-blood?"

"No. He was an unashamed, grasping, political grassroot."

"Did he shower you with gold, spices, sandalwood and

whatsit from Samarkand?"

"No. I was introduced to him at a party, spoke with him for about three minutes, and the very next day, began to get presents of the most *outrageously* tarty underwear... you wouldn't believe!"

I looked at her, really seriously now. "Do you still have it?"

And we both burst out laughing.

Coming into Newbridge, I saw a telephone box and pulled over. I thought I ought to make Lord Roscahill's secretary's day for him – the poor man had had enough bad news from me.

I heard the number ring, the receiver being picked up and the coins drop. "Hello?" I said

"Heh... heh... heh... " came the reply, and I thought that the secretary had been reduced to maniacal cackling, until the voice continued, trying again. "Heh... heh... lo?"

The man himself.

Everything was turning up good today.

EPILOGUE

*I*t's been almost a year now since my first trip to Knockmore. I've been back several times since for various reasons, most notably for a sumptuous meal in The Catamaran Rooms, during the course of which Kevin and I were presented with extremely large matching cheques by the Insurance Company. Afterwards, Lord Roscahill, in a private ceremony, away from the blitz of the flashbulbs, matched the Insurance cheque with "a small toe... toe... toe... ken of the members' appreciation" plus a very handsome bronze of Catamaran. They only cast four, one each for Kevin and Potter and one each for Claire and me. Then they smashed the mould. As Claire and I live together most of the time now, we use ours as bookends. He also gave me to understand that Potter had benefited financially and, less circumspectly, told me that "Cuckoo... Cuckoo... Cuckoo Cooke had a rather hef... hef... hef... ty pay packet this month." The upshot of that night's goings on left me a very comfortably off citizen. Crime pays some people. In fact nobody seems to have come off too badly. Except Vernon. He's dead.

Norris and Field were released on bail and are still at large awaiting trial. Norris is back in Bally Ard though he doesn't have Catamaran there anymore. He's now running a riding school and does pony-trekking too. He seems to be doing fairly well from what I hear. Obviously, we haven't met. I've seen him but... no... we haven't met.

Field is back as strong as ever, the local GP, as if nothing had ever happened. I met a fellow the other day who's cousin is on the Medical Council and his story is that the Council's hands are tied in respect of disciplinary action against Field.

The Council can't pre-empt the court's decision and any action by them will have to await the outcome of the court case.

Which may never happen. The strong word has it that the trial will never take place because, if it does, Prince Alaramos, and through him his government (family), will be sucked into the whole seamy mess; at the moment, this would not suit the Irish Government which, since the Catamaran affair, has developed an incredibly close rapport with the distant, exotic islands of Eribuh, a rapport which, a mere year ago, not even the most sagacious foreign policy pundit could even have guessed at.

In fact, at one point during the year, it looked as though the prince and his whole family were going to be exiled. Or worse. There was a full scale revolution in The Eribuh Islands – complete with foreign mercenaries – and for a week or two it was touch and go. In the end the revolution was put down and the hero, according to the press, was none other than Prince Alaramos himself! His bravery, courage and leadership were reported as being exemplary. Obviously he was doing the old god bit again; he was damn good at it. He refused to be flown off the islands after he was injured in battle – shot in the shoulder! It didn't say which shoulder.

One of the results of the unsuccessful uprising was that the country changed its name: it is now officially The Kingdom of Eribuh, or KE for short. With, one presumes, emphasis on the K. There's nothing like driving home the point.

Despite the hiccup of a revolution, the special relationship between the Irish government and Alaramos's father has continued to blossom and this new-found closeness has had its concrete expression in the setting up of an Equine Genetic Research Centre in Kildare (funded by KE), the endowment of a Chair of Thoroughbred Performance Physiology at the Veterinary College (again funded by KE), and I am informed, an incredibly favourable oil deal; but I wouldn't know about that. It's not my field.

HRH Alaramos (war hero) is still a member of the syndicate (why not?) and still graces the racetracks of the world – unlike that lowlife type who once tried to show Catamaran a rat and who was warned off for life. Proper order too.

I often wonder what happened to Pitru, the one who didn't find Kevin's gun. Probably he ended up as one of the unsung hero/victims of the revolution. Due to his volunteering for incredibly dangerous missions.

Desmond Vernon died in captivity. Actually he died in hospital but somehow I always think of him as being 'in captivity'. Like a bird or an animal taken into an alien environment. He fascinated me. Some people say that that's just because he was my gaoler – I've also read that theory in books. But there's more to it than that, much more. What made him do it? From all I've been able to find out about the man, all he wanted from life was the peace of Clashard and the company of his beloved parrots. He was well off, had no material possessions to speak of, nor seemingly any desire for them. He got on well with his few relatives, on the rare occasions on which they met. A confirmed bachelor, he had already made a will in favour of his only relatives of the next generation, two nephews and a niece, his only sister's children. His whole life seemed ordered, designed to provide the least possible distraction from his chosen lifestyle. Then this. Why?

Norris I could understand. He got in over his head financially, maybe just by letting his heart rule his head. It transpired that, as a foal, Catamaran had always been regarded as Norris's wife's foal. His much loved wife had died shortly before Catamaran had started to race so she never knew that her foal had turned out to be a world beater. When he came up for syndication, Norris just had to be in. For her sake. He couldn't afford it but he had to be in.

Field was purely a materialist. He saw the chance of moving in some heavy, heavy company and he was in like a shot. He had everything, all the trappings of success – The Fine House, The Beautiful Wife, The Two Point Three Children, The Cars, The Holidays, The Paintings, The Respect... He even had The Five Handicap! What more could he want? Answer: a lot. A lot more. Anytime, anyplace, anyhow.

But Vernon? My guess is that Vernon got involved out of friendship for Norris. When Norris asked him for a loan and when Vernon saw how much it meant to him, I don't think he'd have refused him. Not from what I've learned about the man since. For the same reason, when he saw how serious Norris's predicament had become, he would have found it almost impossible to refuse to help. So he went along with buying Second Fiddle in his name and storing him until he was required for his brief, painful and terminal role. Then he agreed to store Catamaran while the heat was dying down. At this point, he was beyond being able to back out. He couldn't decline further involvement on the grounds that he had already done enough. So when Norris explained to him that he had to be my gaoler, as he was the only one of the three that I hadn't met, he agreed – very reluctantly I imagine. Paradoxically, he seems to have been a man of great honour, shy but intensely loyal to the few friends he did have. He and Norris had been friends since they had gone off together on the old steam trains from Galway to their first day at boarding school.

Anyway, poor old Vernon never recovered from the trauma of the whole thing. He had lost the will to live and, last Tuesday week, had refused to go on. Physically, they could find nothing wrong with him. He was an incredibly healthy specimen for a man of his age. (As they say). I hope he has found peace in the next world.

Declan and Jo Forbes became parents, dead on schedule, on the fourth of December when Jo, without the slightest effort, gave birth to my god-daughter, Annie.

Potter and Kevin keep in contact and we meet every so often. They seem to have remained the same as ever.

Claire is now a full-blown reporter and a star on her paper. She's had offers to present current affairs shows on TV but so far hasn't seemed tempted to change media. She tells me she loves me madly all the time and sounds as if she means it. What's more, she acts as if she means it, so that can't be bad.

As for myself... I seem to be much the same as Potter and Kevin, the same before and after. Pretty boring, huh? With my sudden rise to riches, I did what all pools winners do – swore I'd never work again. Within a week I had changed my mind. I knew I'd miss the cut and thrust of general practice, the good feeling of being able to help our so-called dumb chums. For the first time I knew that it was a vocation, not just a profession or a job. I was very very happy the morning I discovered that, a frosty morning when my breath vaporised in front of me, the grass was stiff and blue-tinged and a little stream gurgled along between the delicate glass shelves of thin ice which clung tenaciously to is banks. So I'll probably keep at the locum business for another while yet. It's going well and I enjoy moving around the country. Also it gives me a better chance of picking the right area when and if I do settle down. The big drawback is that it means being away from Claire a lot which doesn't suit either of us.

I've thought of making Vernon's heirs an offer for Clashard. I've driven out there a few times and the peace of the place draws me. I can feel what he felt. As I said, I feel a curious affinity with the man. I've also got very interested in parrots and other psittacines. Then I think that the ridiculous situation could arise where I might get sick and need a doctor and the only one in the area is Field and he could have a perfect opportunity to finish off what he tried to do in Clashard ten months ago! Claire says that the only thing sick about me is my sense of humour.

When I try to define how I feel about Claire, it's difficult to put into words. I love her, to be sure, but it goes beyond that. The best way I can put it is by explaining that, while everyone I've ever met who wants to talk about the whole thing refers to it as the 'Catamaran Caper' or the 'Bally Ard Ballyhoo' or the 'Alaramos Adventure'... maybe not in those exact words but you know what I mean... I myself can't think of it in those terms at all.

Even though I was part of the whole thing from beginning to end; even though I almost got myself killed several times; even though I've recorded the whole thing as it happened; even though all these things, I can still only think of it as something that was going on in the background at the time when I first met Claire.